ALSO BY PAUL MALMONT

Jack London in Paradise

The Chinatown Death Cloud Peril

THE ASTOUNDING, THE AMAZING, AND THE UNKNOWN

PAUL MALMONT

SIMON & SCHUSTER
NEW YORK   LONDON   TORONTO   SYDNEY

Simon & Schuster
1230 Avenue of the Americas
New York, NY 10020

First Simon & Schuster hardcover edition July 2011

SIMON & SCHUSTER and colophon are registered trademarks of Simon & Schuster, Inc.

For information about special discounts for bulk purchases, please contact Simon & Schuster Special Sales at 1-866-506-1949 or business@simonandschuster.com.

The Simon & Schuster Speakers Bureau can bring authors to your live event. For more information or to book an event, contact the Simon & Schuster Speakers Bureau at 1-866-248-3049 or visit our website at www.simonspeakers.com.

Designed by Renata Di Biase

Manufactured in the United States of America

10 9 8 7 6 5 4 3 2 1

Library of Congress Cataloging-in-Publication Data
Malmont, Paul.
  The astounding, the amazing, and the unknown / Paul Malmont.
      p. cm.
  1. Asimov, Isaac, 1920–1992—Fiction. 2. Heinlein, Robert A. (Robert Anson), 1907–1988—Fiction. 3. Hubbard, L. Ron (La Fayette Ron), 1911–1986—Fiction. 4. World War, 1939–1945—United States—Fiction. 5. Weapons systems—United States—History—20th century—Fiction. 6. Authors, American—20th century—Fiction. I. Title.

PS3613.A457A88 2011
813'.6—dc22   2010047432

ISBN 978-1-4391-6894-3

For the gang from Avenue C:
Anton Salaks, Richard Siegmeister,
and Sam Hutchins.

Modern civilization is based upon Man's ability to receive knowledge, sentiments, ideas (whether from his contemporaries or from the wisdom of the ages); the "World of Tomorrow" will largely be shaped by his ability, as well as his desire, to communicate the best of his knowledge, his thoughts, his aspirations to his fellow men and to posterity.

—OPENING PARAGRAPH FROM THE
OFFICIAL 1939 WORLD'S FAIR GUIDE BOOK

And I believe
These are the days of lasers in the jungle,
Lasers in the jungle somewhere,
Staccato signals of constant information,
A loose affiliation of millionaires
And billionaires and baby,
These are the days of miracle and wonder,
This is the long distance call,
The way the camera follows us in slo-mo
The way we look to us all, o-yeah,
The way we look to a distant constellation
That's dying in a corner of the sky,
These are the days of miracle and wonder
And don't cry baby, don't cry

—PAUL SIMON, "THE BOY IN THE BUBBLE"

THE **ASTOUNDING,**
THE **AMAZING,** AND
THE **UNKNOWN**

A SINGULARITY

THE DAY BROKE hot for early June. By midday, when the young man returned to the New Yorker Hotel on Eighth Avenue, the heat was so powerful it seemed to physically pound off the sidewalk into his head. He hurried into the somewhat cooler lobby, stripping off his coat as he rotated through the revolving door. His fingers clawed at the necktie knot, the fabric already so damp with sweat it wouldn't untie.

"Hello, Dick."

He must have missed the chubby man with the oily hair sitting in the overstuffed chair on his first pass through the lobby. Or else the man had oozed into the chair while he had been outside. Either way, in typical fashion, he looked as if he had been there forever and that it might take a lot of effort to get him out of the chair. "Hot like New Mexico, yes?" The accent was thick, Eastern European, and unforgettable.

"Worse, Eddie," he replied, grunting as he finally hooked the tip of his finger into the knot and, by careful wiggling, managed to create a pathway that allowed him to loosen the noose around his neck. "Manhattan's soggier."

Eddie's head nod conceded the point. "Still, the heat seems apropos for our mission. One last secret mission. When did you get in?"

"A couple of days ago." Dick dropped into the partner chair, sinking into its cool leather as the elevator doors parted to reveal even more long-lost friends: Dave, Johnny, Julian, their healthy desert tans bleached gray by the dark warrens of academia they had returned to, and their eyes lacking the gleam of the mission.

"Is the Buddha coming?" Dick asked Johnny who, of all of them, would know.

The shrug in response was noncommittal. "Is the wind blowing in from the west? Are the planets in alignment? Have we all paid our obeisance?"

"Is there a reporter within a hundred yards?" Dave asked, finishing his query with a vast yawn.

"Jeez, Dave," Julian said. "Did you sleep the whole morning away? We went down to the Statue of Liberty and had lunch at the Waldorf."

"Hot out there," Dave responded with a still-sleepy shrug.

"You never were one to submit to the rigors of a military life," Eddie said, with a little more sarcasm than Dick thought necessary, but then again, maybe it was just his accent. Dick could never know for sure.

"I went to the Stork Club last night," Dick said, changing the subject. "I saw Hedy Lamarr there. You know what she told me?"

"Wait," Dave said, awake at last. "You spoke with Hedy Lamarr?"

"We had a drink. So? You want to know what she told me, or what?"

"Was she beautiful?" Johnny asked eagerly. "You know?" His hands cut a wavy path through the air.

"For God's sake," Other Johnny, who had just rotated through the revolving door along with a few other familiar faces (though not the Buddha), said. "Dick's a married man."

The silence surrounded them all as if the thick New York air had suddenly poured through the doors and swirled around them. While most of the men had turned to examine the marble inlays on the floor, or the deco lamps, Julian cleared his throat and gave Other Johnny a nudge and a murmur, "Jesus, Johnny."

Dick hated moments like this. He had built a staunch dam to hold off the black pain, thick enough that he couldn't hear its lapping waves, could almost forget. But for all the construction and heavy materials, simple turbulence always caused the dark waters to spill over the top. He felt that the others were aware that he was now soaked and chilled—worse, he could tell that they were afraid that they had been splashed. It was now his mess to clean up. He had to make the others feel good even though he felt awful.

"That's okay." He smiled, trying his best to be reassuring—to let them know the sadness that had touched his life wouldn't touch theirs.

"God, I'm so sorry, Dick. It's just that seeing everyone here again, I forgot about what happened . . . with Evelyn."

"Really, Johnny. It's fine. Don't worry about it."

"Go on, Dick," Julian said. "What could some actress have possibly said to you to so captivate your intellect?"

He took a deep breath, forcing the darkness back behind the dam. "She's an inventor."

"Of what?" Eddie sneered. "Lipstick?"

"Hold on to your hats, fellas. The Ziegfeld girl has patented a method of getting radio signals to hop frequencies across the spectrum so that no one can intercept them or block them except the receiver, which is in such perfect sync that an airplane can control a torpedo in the water below."

The men surrounding him, and there were even more now than there were a few moments ago, grew silent. There was a lot of powerful gray matter in the room, and each molecule was pondering whether such a thing was possible. "How'd she do that?" Julian asked at last, in a subdued voice which indicated that much of his brain was still churning over the information.

"Her co-inventor is a composer who's done a lot of work getting player pianos to, well, play in perfect unison. They've applied the same technique to their invention."

"Wasn't Jimmy Stewart in *Ziegfeld Girl*? The best movies always have Jimmy Stewart in them, don't they? In fact, Dick, you should keep that in mind when you tell your stories. Always try to work in Jimmy Stewart." The faces that had been watching Dick with such attention now swiveled away from him in a smooth motion which reminded him of iron filings being drawn toward a strong magnet suddenly placed in proximity. "Anyway, gentlemen, appears our bus is here." The Buddha had arrived.

The group—Dick estimated about thirty—followed the tall, thin man, as they always did. He led them across the lobby, and as Dick waited for all the others to file through the door, Julian slid up to him.

"You know who died here?"

"Jimmy Stewart?"

Julian shook his head. "Nikola Tesla."

"Really?" A thought occurred to Dick just as the door spun around to accept Julian. "I've got a Tesla story for you."

"So, Dick," Eddie quipped, behind him. "How does Hedy Lamarr plan on putting a player piano in a torpedo?"

The privately chartered bus was sleek, draped in brilliant aluminum like the hull of a brand-new airliner. More men he recognized but hadn't seen in several years milled around its door. Coats were off and the white shirts were stained yellow with sweat. Smart as they were, it hadn't occurred to them to enter the lobby to escape, so they had reddened and withered in the city heat.

Dick climbed aboard behind Isidor, listening to the old man's knees crack and pop with each step, waiting for him to teeter backwards. But Isidor's momentum carried him forward at the last moment, with a last-minute assist from the driver. Dick could see Julian and Eddie had been forced into the back of the bus by the crush of men, and he swung himself into a window seat. He didn't know the man who sat next to him, a lot of people had been involved, especially toward the end. He didn't feel like introducing himself. The stranger pulled his hat down over his face and was soon snoring lightly.

The fully packed bus pulled away from the curb, cigarette and pipe smoke pouring from its windows, and made a left on 34th. He quietly drummed the tips of his fingers against the cool cloth of the seat in front of him, tapping out an exotic Polynesian rhythm he'd never actually heard with his own ears yet had always seemed attuned to. The sun appeared to balance on top of the antenna mast of the Empire State Building as the bus swung another left onto Sixth. The syncopation of his left hand felt a millisecond off, sluggish. He examined the back of his finger as if he'd never seen it before. He had thought that his own dark New Mexico tan would never fade, but it had, and with it, the last physical proof that he had once worn a wedding ring, had once been married. That almost imperceptible weight which had encircled his finger was throwing him off. She had died a little over a year ago. He had only just stopped wearing the ring.

He reached into his pocket and pulled out a pulp magazine; its purchase had been the reason he had left the comfort of the hotel in the first place. He unrolled it, appreciating the crackle of the cover, the already slightly musty smell. The paper was so cheap that it hadn't even been able to absorb the sweat seeping through the fabric right against his skin. As the bus rolled past Radio City Music Hall and the lofty RCA Building which rose above, he ran a hand over it to smooth it. The painting showed a man in a trench coat escaping from a volcano with what appeared to be a Bible tucked under his arm, while a ghostly figure shadowed him. The other pulp that had vied for his money was the latest issue of *Amazing*, and its cover had presented an exceptionally attractive female astronaut battling some kind of robot. But the issue of *Astounding* that he had ultimately purchased promoted the first installment of a novel by L. Ron Hubbard called *The End Is Not Yet*. He'd never read Hubbard before. But after the story he'd recently heard, he wanted to know more.

"Really, Dick?" The Buddha hovered over him, his long, curved pipe clenched between his teeth, his eyes radiant. He had been moving back through the bus, pausing to speak with each passenger. It was Dick's turn. "Is this where a young boddhisattva such as yourself seeks enlightenment?"

"Our future is in pulps like these. In fact, I daresay that if it weren't for the pulps, we might not have won the war."

"Please!"

"I'm serious. Some of the best ideas are found in science fiction."

"And the worst, as well. Monsters from Mars," the Buddha said, with a smirk that threatened to slide from sarcastic to sardonic—he hated to lose an argument more than anything.

"Space travel," Dick shot back.

"Free energy." The smirk was hardening fast.

"Doomsday weapons," Dick said, with finality. The Buddha's mouth twitched ever so slightly and the smirk was gone. Then the Buddha was too, moving on down the bus to hold other conversations, basking in and bestowing his glory.

The charter made its way over the Queensboro Bridge and headed along 25 toward Long Island. Dick dove into his magazine, looking up periodically to take note as the view changed from cityscape to acres upon acres of vast suburban construction projects, overwhelming in their endless sameness, until they gave way at last to rustic farmland, awaiting its time to be sold, developed, paved over, populated. To take its place in the future.

As a sign for the Shoreham exit whizzed past, Julian spoke up from the rear, his voice carrying easily as most of the men were dozing lightly. "Who's up for paying a visit to Wardenclyffe?" This elicited several chuckles from the more alert passengers. But before the itinerary change could be discussed or discounted, the wail of rapidly approaching sirens roused even the deepest of the slumberers. Behind the bus four police-ridden motorcycles had appeared, followed by two shiny Chevy Stylemasters, lights awhirl. The bus slowed down to let the vehicles pass. A pair of the bikes and one of the sedans shot quickly along the left side of the bus while the others moved into a position directly behind.

"They've flanked us," Dick said to the stranger next to him. Adrenaline surged through him, and a quick glance around showed that none of the others was taking this lightly. So much of their time together had been spent in secrecy, living with the fear of espionage, kidnapping, sabotage, treason, or betrayal. This felt like the hammer drop they had all expected—a climax he had given up waiting for, yet somehow, still wanted. He guessed he'd always wanted to see what might happen. What the enemy might do. How he might react.

The driver attempted to slow down but the motorcycle cop in front of him indicated by his wave that he should maintain his speed and simply follow. For the most part, the men sat silently, helplessly watching events unfold. Even the Buddha remained passive. Dick overheard Other Johnny conspiring to put up a fight, but knew the scrawny man barely had the strength or stamina to punch a timecard, let alone a cop—if these were cops and not some enemy in disguise. Still, he strained to listen to Johnny, and Other Johnny, struggling to generate a plan, though he couldn't be sure if it was one of escape or resistance.

Soon the escort forced the bus to follow them as they turned from the highway down a country lane. Picking up speed, they barreled through a small town, the Post Office sign read GREENPORT, running the red lights. The police led the bus into the parking lot behind a long, one-story building and drew the convoy to a halt so that the bus door was positioned only a few short steps from the dark entrance. The driver pulled the lever to open the door, permitting one of the cops to enter. He was young, but old enough to have been in the war; his impassive expression was impossible to read.

"Hey, now." Willis had been riding behind the driver and he now stood to confront the officer. "You can't do this. What's the big idea?"

"Into the building, gentlemen," the cop replied, in a tone that indicated that nothing was up for either question or discussion. The other policemen had formed a gauntlet on either side of the path leading from the bus to the building. Willis looked at the Buddha, who shrugged and nodded. The men began to file off and into the building, past the impassive cops, still as the New Mexico cacti had been.

Even before Dick's turn to rise came, he could hear the sound—a rushing as of heavy winds or surf. He knew he was near the beach, but he didn't think he was close enough to hear it. As he climbed down the steps, it became obvious that the noise emanated from inside the building. He took a deep breath and followed his seat mate in. It wasn't quite as dark inside as it had seemed from the bus.

Someone clutched his hand and was shaking it before he realized that he knew the man who was greeting him.

"Duncan? What the hell are you doing here?" In the rush of all the familiar faces in the hotel lobby, it wasn't until he saw the man's face here that he realized he hadn't been on the bus.

"Hello, Dick! Go on in!" Duncan was grinning from ear to ear, pleased as hell with himself. Before answering Dick's question he had already grabbed the hand of the man behind him to greet him. Dick was hustled along through another door where the source of the loud noise was revealed.

The banquet hall was large and filled with a great number of people, men in uniform as well as women in their church finest and other men dressed as for a day at the bank. They were all on their feet, stamping, cheering, and whistling as the bus passengers filed in to the front of the

great room. The ovation showed no sign of ceasing throughout the entire time it took for the men to finish entering the hall. In fact, when the
doors closed behind Julian and Eddie, the roar grew even louder. Beneath
its onslaught, the Buddha stood like a lighthouse in a storm, letting the
approbation break over him before its spray landed on the others, smiling contentedly as he puffed on his pipe.

A man stepped forward, clapping harder and louder than all the others.
He wore a seersucker suit (it was Long Island in the summer, after all)
and had the healthy glow of one recently off the golf course. The wave of
a hand quickly silenced the room. Then, with the same hand, he gestured
toward the group of befuddled men. "These," he said, "are the men who
saved my life!"

Cheers broke out again, and evolved in three lusty cries of hip-hip-
hooray.

The man in the seersucker suit approached the Buddha and the room
grew quiet. "My name is John White and today I'm the president of
the local Chamber of Commerce. But four years ago, I was a Marine at
Okinawa—part of the Steel Hurricane. And once we took that hellhole,
we knew it was only a matter of time before we used it as a stepping
stone to Japan. I would have died in that invasion. I was lucky too many
times. Thousands of me and my brothers, good American boys, would
have been killed trying to beat down the Japanese. Then, these men—
they ended the war with a one-two punch! Hiroshima! Nagasaki!" He
paused for applause, which lasted a while.

"When I heard they were coming out to Shelter Island for some sort
of brainiac conference, I decided that this was a once-in-a-lifetime opportunity for me. I called a buddy at General Electric, and he called a buddy
at AT&T, and he got in touch with his buddy Duncan MacInnes at the
New York Academy of Sciences, who was organizing the whole thing,
and he helped me plan this little shanghai."

He held out his hand to the Buddha. "On behalf of all those American
lives you saved, I just wanted to say, thank you, Dr. Oppenheimer." The
room began to shake again with cheers and stomps. White had to holler
to be heard over the din as he finished. "Thanks to all of you fellas from
the Manhattan Project!"

Beautiful young women in sparkling short dresses with a faint military echo and high white boots now emerged from the crowd to lead Dick and his friends to open seats at the tables around the room.

"Great," Julian whispered in his ear. "We've got to make small talk."

"Just pretend you've taken some peyote again," Dick replied.

"I don't have to pretend," Julian said, as he guided Dick to a stand behind the chair next to his at a table otherwise occupied by Greenport's high society. "I think I'm having a flashback." The girls of the color guard, having seated everyone, disappeared to the farthest corners of the ballroom. Dick turned around, trying to see where everyone had ended up.

"Hi, there," the plump man across the table said. "I'm Francis Lucia. You can call me Frank. Either of you *paisans* Enrico Fermi?"

"He couldn't come," Dick said.

"Oh." Their table host seemed disappointed. "This is Julian Schwinger," he continued.

"That doesn't sound at all Italian."

"Not even a little," Julian agreed.

"How about Professor Einstein?" the woman who was apparently Mrs. Lucia asked eagerly. "I've always wanted to meet him."

"He wasn't part of the Project." Julian shrugged. "But Dick here has worked with him."

"Hi, I'm . . ." Dick began to introduce himself, but there was a commotion caused by the Buddha being given a seat right behind his. Cries of "Speech! Speech!" shook the rafters of the hall. Now it was the Buddha's turn to hold up a hand and silence a roomful of people at once. He alone remained standing as everyone else took to their seats.

"Thank you all so much for the honor you do us this evening by welcoming us into your community and so generously sharing the fruits of your prosperity with us," he began in a voice that commanded attention. "May you all live to enjoy this new golden age that is now upon us." He paused as if he hadn't considered the meaning of the words before. He repeated them again in a voice so low that only Dick, sitting directly before him, could hear them. "A Golden Age.

"A time when all wishes are granted, when possibilities are boundless, and there are no limits on what the imagination can accomplish. It's been my experience that a Golden Age has usually ended just prior to my arrival. That I missed it. It happened without me. Not this time. All of us together, not just those of us who toiled at Los Alamos, but those who fought their way across Europe or the Pacific, or waited here at home and kept the home fires burning—we have all passed from the end of one era and into the dawn of a new age.

"So let us choose to discover the wonders of this age before it passes, just as we celebrate the glories of past eras. But let's choose not to dwell there in the past for too long, or the future may pass us all by. The sun sets on an era and dawn rises on a new age. Thank you."

Dick felt certain that few in the room had understood the Buddha, but what was obvious was that all felt that they had. Soon after, the ovation faded away, and what then occurred was a riot of roasted meats and fish, pastas of various shapes and sauces, the produce of the region's best farms, and copious amounts of cold bottled beer.

Sometime after nine, the physicists were released from the banquet hall and reboarded the bus. The heat of the day had given way to a breeze-fed ocean cool. Even before the bus pulled away from the parking lot, half its occupants were asleep. Dick was too full to sleep and knew that if he tried to read, it might make him ill, so he tried to make out the sights and shapes in the darkness. Soon they arrived at the edge of water, and Dick watched as the ferry emerged from the mist. After the short voyage, the bus finally delivered its cargo to the front door of the Phillip's Inn, a converted Dutch barn which was to be the site of the conference on the state of physics theory.

Still feeling bloated after checking in and unpacking his small bag, Dick was debating whether or not to turn in or take a walk around the grounds when there was a knock at his door.

"Come on down for a drink," Julian said from the other side.

In the small parlor, the innkeeper poured them each a glass of scotch and they headed outside to a long pier that jutted out into Long Island Sound. It creaked beneath their weight. Dick smelled the pipe smoke before he caught sight of the glowing embers, hovering six feet above the deck.

"Hello, fellas," the Buddha said from the end of the dock.

"Hi, Bob," Julian replied. "It's Julian and Dick. We didn't realize you were out here. We'll leave you to your thoughts."

"Oh, that's all right," the Buddha said. "It's great to see both of you again. We can have a chat this evening before everything breaks down to its subatomic state."

"Great," Dick said. He sat upon the dock and removed his shoes and socks, then rolled up his pants, letting his feet dangle into the cool water. It wasn't long before Julian and the Buddha had joined him.

Julian took a long sip of his drink and then said, "Dick, didn't you say you had a Tesla story?"

"Ugh," he grunted. "If I started that story now, we'd be here all night long."

"I'm wide awake," Julian said.

"So am I," said the Buddha. "It'll be just like New Mexico again, staying up all night listening to your stories."

Dick sighed. "I don't know, Bob. It's about the pulps and I know how you feel about those."

"So change my mind," was the response. "Come on, Feynman. Show us why you've come to be called the Great Explainer."

He swirled the water with his feet, feeling the pressure of millions of molecules flow against his skin. "The first thing you have to understand about this story is that it's mostly true. But the second thing I have to remind you is that we're scientists. And no one should understand more than us that the science of this age tells us that a tale, like time, and even the truth, is relative to the observed. And the observer.

"Believe what you want. This is the story I heard the other night at the White Horse Tavern. When I'm done, you tell me where the science ends and the science fiction begins."

ISSUE 1

THE FREE WILL OF ATOMS

EPISODE 1

THERE WAS NOTHING elegant about *Unterseeboot 213*, but it was powerful, far-ranging, and grimly lethal. At a length of 220 feet, with a displacement of 769 tons, the ship could travel at up to 18 knots when surfaced and nearly 8 below the waves. Its five torpedo tubes were complemented by fifteen mine-launchers, allowing it to deliver death in ways that struck fear into the hearts of Allied sailors patrolling the North Atlantic. One of five in its class, it was the pride of the German fleet, with dozens of kills to burnish its legend.

After days of lurking off the Connecticut coast with the rest of the wolf pack, waiting for the right combination of fog, tides, and clouds, the U-boat finally slid silently past the lighthouse at Montauk Point into Long Island Sound on battery power. Soon after surfacing, the captain sent word to Müllmann that his mission was about to begin.

He was ready for the knock on his cabin door. Eagerly, he made his way through the narrow corridors, ignoring the whispers of the smelly sailors. Ungracefully, he clambered up the ladder to the deck of the ship, emerging into a cold, pounding rain. The U-boat cut slowly but steadily through a moonless black so thick it was hard to tell where the sky ended and the water began. A crewman swept an arc light back and forth through the fog every few moments, dousing it in between the short bursts.

"We are here, Herr Müllmann," the light operator said with a smirk, before being silenced by a glare from the captain.

It occurred to Müllmann that he had never taken the time to learn this man's name, even though he had been aboard the ship for weeks. Müllmann kept to himself.

Müllmann—garbage man. It wasn't his name. But it was the name all had come to know him by.

"Are you certain it's here?" the captain asked without looking at him. There was a tired, wary edge to his voice. He had commanded his ship and men bravely in bringing them this close to the shore of America, but the daring excursion had taken its toll on his nerves.

"It's out there," he replied. "Dead ahead."

"You're sure? There's no Haimoni Island on my charts."

Müllmann sighed. "It was removed from maps by the U.S. Army. But they couldn't remove the island."

"And there's a weapon on this island? A death gas that turns men into monsters?"

Müllmann wrapped his hands around the chain railing, which dripped with salt water and condensation. "I was born in Germany and lived there for fifteen years before my father moved us to New York. Before the call of the Reich summoned me back to the Fatherland, before I met my wife and had a son there, I worked as a garbage man in Brooklyn. Can you imagine that? A proud Aryan son disposing of the refuse of the mongrel races that crowded into the tenements of Brooklyn? But it taught me to be strong inside. To choke back my disgust. To blend in. I knew a better destiny lay ahead. So I studied. Learned. And watched.

"Six years ago, my opportunity to serve the Reich presented itself. The disposal company I worked for was summoned, just before dawn, to send a truck and two of its best men to the piers at Brooklyn. My partner was a Negro and a mute. I was the educated man who kept his mouth shut, hardly spoke with anyone—more mute than the dummy. So we were called in. There had been an accident on board a ship that had docked there, an old tramp steamer called the *Star of Baltimore*. A black ship, old and ugly, the survivor of more seas and ports than this vessel will ever see.

"When we arrived, its decks were crawling with men from the United States Army. Such mayhem had occurred that it was difficult to piece together the series of events. There were dead Chinamen. Lots of them.

Some of them had perished in some kind of gun battle; others had been killed in more horrible ways. There were men who were frozen in terrible poses as if they had died instantly after a moment of pure agony. Then there were others who had been less fortunate to live a little longer, as the skin melted from their bodies and their minds were torn apart. These creatures the soldiers were putting out of their misery. We could hear the gunshots from deep in the bowels of the ship. First there would be shouting. Then . . ." He shrugged.

"That's not what we were there to take care of, though. The bodies were loaded onto Army trucks. We were to cart away pallets of worthless Chinese money that other soldiers brought up from the ship's hold. At first I was afraid to touch it, fearing that it was tainted with whatever disease had consumed the ship's crew. But then one of the soldiers explained to me that the calamity had been caused by the release of a gas from one of the large, rusty container drums that other soldiers were gingerly bringing down the gangplank. Several had come open, but the others were well sealed. Then I was told to shut up and go about my work. So I went about my work. But I watched and I listened. And what I heard was the call of my destiny.

"I overheard an officer mention that this was the fault of a man named Colonel Towers—and that he had met his grisly end at the hands of some monsters in the hold of his ship. This was said as his covered corpse was brought down and thrown indiscriminately with the Chinamen in the back of a truck. Later in the morning, another officer muttered that the gas had been stored safely for years on Haimoni Island and Towers should have left it there. That it was the most dangerous weapon ever created by man. And it had to be locked away again."

"*Wunderwaffe?*" the first mate asked, before being silenced with a hiss from the captain.

He nodded. "It seemed as if the work that morning would never end. We weren't allowed on the ship. All we could do was throw the paper into our truck when soldiers brought it down to us. Eventually, though, the soldiers placed the last bodies on some trucks, the last of the canisters on others, the last of the funny money in ours. Another crew went aboard and undocked the ship, taking it out of the slip and up the river.

Before long, all traces of the day's efforts were gone. We took our refuse to our incinerator, where it was turned into smoke.

"I could have gone home, then. God knows I was tired enough that I should have. Instead, I found myself in the chart room of the Public Library. I went there every day after work for weeks until I found it. The island. It existed."

The rain abruptly stopped. The captain took the opportunity to quickly light a cigarette for him, cupping the flame from the wind and observation. His fingers were trembling so much he could barely hold it. But the smoke, when it finally entered his lungs, was relaxing.

"I kept my knowledge to myself. What was I to do with it? By the time I had returned to Germany I had nearly forgotten about the incident. But soon after the United States entered the war, I was summoned to meet a general in Berlin. He told me of an opportunity to help my country. 'Operation Pastorius.' Others who had spent time in America, as I had, were being recruited to return as saboteurs. Would I do the same? Would I do my duty?

"It was then that I saw my chance to seize my destiny and I knew my return had been the correct decision. I told him I had more to offer. I told him about that morning on the *Star of Baltimore* and of Haimoni Island. He was intrigued, to say the least. So while the other saboteurs were sent to America last year, I was held back for my own mission."

"Good thing, that," the captain said. *U-213* had run aground on the shores of Amagansett in front of dozens of witnesses after delivering the saboteurs and had nearly been destroyed. The inept team that had put ashore had all been rounded up within months and accomplished nothing but achieving notoriety.

"True," he nodded, shivering.

Before he could say another word, the lookout manning the searchlight called out in a low but excited voice: "Captain! Land."

Illuminated by the cone of light, a rocky cliff rose abruptly over the U-boat. Müllmann flipped the cigarette into the water. "There's a deep-water pier on the north side," he told the captain, who uttered a few orders and readied for docking as the crew below sprang to action. Müllmann's chest filled with wildly unexpected joy. The sensation of vindication, of heroic accomplishment, of destiny finally fulfilled, was something to savor forever.

Silently, like a shark circling its prey, the U-boat circled the dead island. It reeked of emptiness. Dead fish and bird corpses were splattered against the boulders while foam-tipped black waves clawed at them, trying to snatch them into their inky depths. His heart leaped at the appearance of the old wooden pier he had studied in detail and only hoped to see again. The docking was the model of German efficiency—swift, precise, and quiet. Within an hour of raising Haimoni Island, a dream he had pursued for these last six years, he took the first steps onto its slippery rocks.

The captain, and an expeditionary team of a half-dozen seamen and officers, awaited his command. At last, he was in charge. He understood the new respect in their eyes, that they realized they were in the presence of a hero to the Reich. He smiled, knowing that his destiny was about to be fulfilled. "Follow me," he ordered, and they fell in line behind him as he headed toward the rocky path he now knew for certain awaited.

Though it was winter the black, barren trees appeared permanently leafless, grasping, striving toward a spring that would never come. And yet they were alive, swaying in the wind as they only would if the sap still flowed, however weakly. The climb over the jagged, wet stones was difficult for the men behind him, but he sprang forward and onward, setting the pace.

"What are we looking for?" he heard the first mate ask the captain.

"That!" he exclaimed. Below the ridge was a steel door, covered in rust, set into a wall of rock. The words U.S. ARMY and a warning to trespassers were still visible through the corrosion. Müllmann let his emotions run away with him at that point and half-slid, half-ran down the stone ramp that led to the door. The sailors were close behind him. He slammed into the door and let his hands soak in its coldness, the smell of rust fill his nostrils. It was real. Solid. He ran his hands over it until he found a latch. It refused to yield—he took that as a good sign. Locked was good. Locked meant *Verboten*. It indicated intent.

One of the sailors stepped forward with a huge wrench usually reserved for adjusting the U-boat's great machinery. It took several men applying leverage pressure on the end, but eventually the snap of metal rang out like a gloomy, minor-chord chime, and the door swung open. He pushed his way past the men and into the darkness. "A torch," he cried. "Bring me some light!"

He reached his hands out before him, feeling for the canisters. But everywhere his hands only met cool stone wall. And when the lights finally cut into the room, he already knew what he would see.

Emptiness.

The great concrete bunker may once have held those canisters of gas. For all anyone could tell now, it may have held as much gold as Fort Knox. But now, it was abandoned. Cleaned out. Only scrapes on the floor gave an indication that something once had been dragged through the room. He heard one of the sailors snicker. Then they were all laughing at *him*. Only the captain remained silent, his clenched jaws throbbing with anger. The old rage that had filled so many of his youthful days flooded through him. America had betrayed him again.

"*Wunderwaffe!*" The first mate spat the word at him and then burst into bitter laughter. Soon others took up the word, mocking him. "*Wunderwaffe!*"

He shut the door behind him and stood beside it for some time, until he turned and followed the crew back to the U-boat. As quiet as they had been on the way to the bunker, they were now boisterous to the point the captain had to calm them several times. It was relief on their part, that there was nothing mysterious, or deadly, waiting for them at the end of the journey. Now all they had to do was evade the U.S. Navy and escape the sound. But running silent was what they were bred for. They could harass Müllmann all they desired and he could hear their taunts, like the calling of the gulls. By the time he reached the dock, the rain had picked up and preparations for disembarkation were well under way. Only the captain waited on the pier. He handed Müllmann a lit cigarette.

"I can't go home," he said, his voice full of emptiness. "I'll be executed for my failure." He noticed the gun in the captain's hand. "I guess you're prepared for that."

The captain shrugged. "I don't particularly want to shoot you. We've already wasted enough money on you. Why spend even a bullet? You've said this place was your destiny? Perhaps you were right, at least about that, after all."

Müllmann lost track of how long he stood there on the dark shore. Long after the sound of the motor had been swallowed by the mist he could hear, or thought he could at least, the taunt. Even when day broke, the sun seemed barely able to pierce the fog that shrouded the island. By midmorning he could see the north shore of Long Island. A mile, he thought. Maybe two.

The tide was still going out and would carry him east and south, toward land. The water would be cold, but with any luck he wouldn't be in it too long. He had always been a strong swimmer, proud of his ability to be the first one in the East River, come springtime, and the last one out in the fall. There was plenty of driftwood caught in the rocks, and rope from lobster pots. A raft was out of the question, but lashing himself to something that floated was within the realm of possibility. At least this horrible island wouldn't be his graveyard. He'd rather take his chances in the water.

There was still light in the sky when he felt sand beneath his body. He didn't know if he had just washed up, or whether his numb body had lain there for hours. Colors swirled above him, clouds, birds, faces. Was he in Germany? Brooklyn? Valhalla? No way of knowing. Was someone shaking him or was it just the surf rocking him? Maybe a shark was eating at him? He tried to speak, to ask for help.

"*Wunderwaffe.*" What had he said? He asked where he was. "*Wunderwaffe?*" Why weren't his ears hearing what his mind was telling his tongue to say? "*Wunderwaffe?*"

"Martha!"

Relief flowed through him, almost as good as warmth. There was someone near. He would not die alone. He clutched at the hand that was upon his shoulder and breathed his gratitude. "*Wunderwaffe.*"

"Martha! Call the police," the voice cried out again. "Another kraut's washed up on the beach!"

He closed his eyes and surrendered to his exhaustion. "*Wunderwaffe.*"

EPISODE 2

THE FUTURE BEGINS in the imagination. He knew that.

He had seen the future as clearly as he had seen the small white jellyfish trapped in the gray-green surf when he had walked along the beach that long-ago morning. They struggled against the endless churn, trying to reach the safety of the deeper waters. They had no sense of future or past. Only a dim awareness of a present that to them would seem eternal. He had appreciated it then and he could appreciate it now.

The cold sea breeze that tousled his hair as he sat on the bench in the park carried with it the scent of that particular day. The zephyr had first risen from the warm sands on the distant shores of Africa, on the other side of the ocean long months ago, losing its heat as it traveled toward America. The faint taste of salt it left on his lips resurrected memories far more distant than the journey of the wind; a gift of the past in the present.

He could remember the vibration of the wooden lever he had held in his hand, thrumming with potential and coiled promise. And when he threw it, the future would happen.

That future now in the past. When everything had gone wrong.

His hands were so cold, it hurt to squeeze his fingers shut. He looked at them, so old, mottled with liver spots and veins that looked like the old wires one would find in the walls of a house, wound around aged sticks which were all his bones were now anyway. There was no lever under his palm. It had taken a lot of strength to grip and throw it. He couldn't have done it now.

The only similarity between that day and this one, the gift the wind reminded him of, was that he knew for certain again that he could see the future. But the futures were very different. That day long ago, not far from the beach, he could imagine the success and acclaim and rewards that lay ahead, how he would spend the rest of his life. Today, he knew that there was little future left to spend, little else to imagine. Like those jellyfish, there was only awareness of tumbling endlessly over regrets and mistakes. Only now, this frigid day, this hard bench in the emptiness of Bryant Park, a bag of crumbs to feed the pigeons.

And the two strange men who had been following him for days. The Russians. The spies.

They were both above average height. One of them was very thin. It made him smile to think how his mother would have felt drawn to him. The other man had an atavistic appearance, as if his ancestors, upon hearing of the science of evolution, had shrugged and decided it held no appeal for them. In spite of the creature's rough appearance, he was the one reading *The New York Times*, while his comrade sipped coffee and watched the ladies in their heavy overcoats dash past on their way to the shelter of the library.

He missed the thunder and drama of the elevated track, torn down four years ago now in the name of progress. Science. Technology. Industry. Now men burrowed like worms under the city, burying the trains where no one could see them, as if things like that should be hidden away instead of celebrated.

He knew they were Russian. The skinny one had bumped into him one morning in the lobby of the hotel and said, "*Dasvidanya*," with a smirk and a tip of the fedora. At least, he was pretty sure he'd heard the greeting in Russian. He spoke many languages but hadn't heard many of them in a long time. Sometimes his own thoughts wandered through a variety of tongues.

Russian for sure, though. It had probably been a bad idea to write so many letters to his old supporters in that government. But he had no friends left in this country, no more sponsors or backers. And he needed friends more than ever. Now that he'd found the Catalan Vault still existed.

So cold. The wind whistled through the park, shaking the few remaining strings of Christmas lights the maintenance crews had yet to bring down. His bag of crumbs was empty but the pigeons still swirled eagerly around his feet, pecking hopefully. He wiped the tears from his watering eyes.

He had rediscovered it quite by accident. Just a small article in the back pages of *The New York Times* he had stumbled across right before Christmas. It would have had no meaning for anyone but him. When he read about the flooding in the basements of a number of Greenwich

Village homes, he found himself laughing with joy. He alone knew the source of the waters. And if the waters still flowed, then the Catalan Vault still stood.

Like Moses, forbidden to enter the Promised Land, he was denied entrance. He could only stand on the sidewalk and fret. Someday, someone would unlock its secrets, but he wouldn't be there to see. He wondered about the transgressions that kept him from reaching his destination. These thoughts occupied his mind more and more each day, until they became a cacophony of failures and regrets. He had stumbled over his own great pride; the fall complete and utterly final. There was no way in for him.

He slipped his cold, aching right hand into his pocket, wrapping his fingers around a slim piece of metal which, in spite of the chill in the air, seemed warm to his touch. This object no longer belonged to him. It was time to pass it off to someone who would carry on his work. That was its future. And it didn't include him.

Rising, his unsteady legs carried him toward Sixth Avenue. One hand held his collar up against the cruel wind, the other continued to clutch the object in his pocket. For years he had carried it; he would not let it slip away now, at the end. He made the right turn on 40th and walked the long blocks to Eighth Avenue, sensing the two spies following him, even as they remained far behind. He quickened his pace to appear as an old man trying to get out of the cold. In fact, he was hurrying because he had only a little time to accomplish what needed to be done before the spies found out. This had been his routine for weeks now, as he'd put his plan together. First, the park to feed the pigeons. Then the scurry back to his hotel, where the boy would be waiting for him.

The lobby was warm and he felt his blood feebly rush to his cheeks. At the front desk he asked for and received a neat sheet of stationery and an envelope. He wrote a quick note, then after one last fond look, placed the metal object inside the envelope, neatly folded up in the paper. The boy was sitting on his usual bench, and as he approached the youth, the two spies entered the lobby as if interested in booking a room.

"I'd like for you to deliver this to my good friend, Mr. Samuel

Clemens," he told the boy in a clear voice, loud enough for the spies to hear, and handed over the envelope.

"Huh?" the lad said. This was neither the expected, nor appropriate, response.

He grew confused and repeated himself. The boy's eyebrows knit together in concern. It was only when he said the words a third time that he realized he'd been speaking in his original Serbian. With an effort, he cleared his mind, recalled his English, and said again, "I'd like for you to deliver this to my good friend, Mr. Samuel Clemens. The address is on the envelope."

"Pardon me, sir, for sayin' so. But ain't he dead?"

"Of course not," he responded, as he always did. "Perhaps you know him better as Mark Twain?"

"Oh, him!" the boy exclaimed, as he always did.

"Please see that he gets it."

"Yes, sir," the boy said with a shrug, no longer expecting even the penny tip that used to be pressed into his hand. As fast as a spark jumping a circuit, the boy dashed through the lobby and out the door. The spies didn't even bother to follow him anymore. They had spent days pursuing the boy down to a building on West Tenth Street and back as he attempted to deliver a package from a doddering old fool to a dead man. At last they had given up. Especially once they had intercepted a few of the letters only to find them rambling musings, gossip from long-ago dinner parties. It had been fun to write those letters to his old friend, reminding him how much he missed the man. But as a plan, it had worked with engineered precision.

Satisfied, though saddened at how easily he had parted with his legacy, he stood by himself in the lobby. For long moments he took in the magazine racks, the top row devoted to tales of tomorrow, slathered with images of rocket ships and strange war machines and ladies in peril of their lives and their clothes. Silly. He rode the elevator to his floor, ready for a nap. Tomorrow he would send another note with the boy, instructions for using what he had sent today. He hoped it wouldn't be so cold tomorrow. His bones still ached.

Stretched out on his bed, he found himself stuck in the past, thinking about the future again. The lever in his hand, the power it would unleash, the dreams it would make real. There was no difference between the imagination and reality, save for the effort to build the bridge between the two. He was sure of that. Faces swirled before his eyes: his mother, Westinghouse, Edison, Clemens. Old friends. And enemies.

The ringing phone brought him back to the present. Such an alien sound, he'd had so few calls these days. He passed his hand through his hair, smoothing it, as if somehow his appearance might be appreciated over the wires. "Hello?"

"I have a call for you," the switchboard operator said.

"I'll take it, please."

There was a short pause as wires were plugged into sockets. Then a voice he hadn't heard in many years, but recognized right away, whispered in his ear. "Nikola Tesla?"

His hand shook as he held the receiver to his ear. "Yes."

"Do you remember the sound of my voice?"

"Yes."

He heard a sound, like gears grinding, high-pitched, through the phone. For a moment, he saw himself standing on the beach again, watching the jellyfish in the surf, turning to look at the great edifice he had constructed rising high in the distance—his instrument for creating the future. A future he now had hope for again.

The future begins in the imagination. He knew that. Now he realized that its birth required a death.

EPISODE 3

ANOTHER THING ISAAC hated about this city, he decided as he looked out the window onto Walnut Street, was the provincial belief the natives held that it was the center of the universe just because independence had been declared there generations before. As a native New Yorker he knew as an absolute that the true pivot point of reality lay two hundred miles to the northeast. He could almost abide the stupidity of the military personnel he worked amongst; most of them weren't from the city and cared for it as much as or even less than he did. But it was the smugness of the mag stand vendor, the butcher, the businessman on the train, the common everyday folk going about their business as if the current war in Europe now didn't matter as much as a war one hundred and thirty years old. A war, by the way, that hadn't even come near Philadelphia. He sighed and took another sip of the coffee that Gertrude had brewed for him before returning to their bed for a few more hours of sleep. It was so bad it almost took his mind off his distaste for this alien city. But he appreciated that his bride had tried.

He put the mug down. Someone at the wedding had said that he had two years during which he could still consider her his bride, then after that Gertrude became his wife. Isaac still had a year to go and he intended to use it. His father had a wife. He had a bride, and he liked the sound of that. As a doctorate candidate, soon to be a professor, he would never be able to provide his with a life of excitement, but with the supplemental income from his mag stories he would at least be able to make her happy. Once the war was over and everything returned to normal, he hoped. Because his bride sure wasn't happy here and now. He was pretty sure that her problem was Philadelphia.

Adventure. John Campbell had actually positioned it as a choice. Join the team of big brains at that Naval Research Station. Put that Columbia chemistry pedigree to good use. Use the power of imagination to stop the Nazis and save the world. Or, just wait to be drafted and be another dog-face in the trenches. In the mud. In the cold. Get shot at. So that was the decision—go to Philadelphia and have an adventure and save the world, or go to war. After all, kid, you're only twenty-one years old.

Isaac sighed, then choked down another gulp of coffee. What he really wanted to do was to stay home, finish his degree, teach, and write. But that wasn't in the cards. It certainly wasn't Campbell's notion of adventure that had sold him. Adventure belonged safely on the page.

He looked at the kitchen table that had come with the small furnished apartment they had rented in Wingate Hall. A thin sheaf of papers propped up its one short leg to keep the table steady. At least the Navy provided all the free paper he could ever use. The Smith Corona typewriter he had bought with the sale of his first story, "Marooned Off

Vesta," to *Amazing Stories.* The free page pinned against its platen by the rollers held three lonely words on a line, perched like birds on a telephone wire, awaiting companionship: *The robot felt*

Felt what?

He had written those words late last night, or maybe early this morning, he wasn't sure. The inspiration had hit him hard, thrown him out of bed. Staggering through the dark kitchen, he'd found the typewriter and started. Before he'd made any more progress than the three words, Gertie had shuffled in and insisted he come back to bed. Isaac wanted to get back to it this morning, but he'd overslept. She was right, he had needed his sleep. But now in the harsh light of day the words just sat there. Lonely. Waiting. Worse, without the words that finished the sentence, there was nothing special about them. What did a robot feel?

All his life Isaac had thought himself special. As a kid in Brooklyn he had felt elevated above the other children because he had been born elsewhere, Russia, and had made the trip across Europe and the Atlantic alone at five years old, a feat none of his Brooklyn fellows could comprehend, let alone have accomplished. His parents had delivered him unto the promised land of America where he had to grow up to be . . . somebody.

On the tree-lined streets of Park Slope he had stood out by virtue of the shop his father, Judah, owned. Candy. He sold candy. Sweets were the one indulgence everyone, no matter how poor, could somehow always afford, his father told him one Sunday afternoon as they worked in the store together. While other fathers went to work in the *schmatta* factories in Manhattan, Judah remained master of his own kingdom, beholden to no one. There was never a panic for Judah to catch the train in time for sundown, no Irish foreman to mock him or keep him late, no boss to complain about the loss of profit on Saturday (though as Isaac's family had strayed from the faith over the years, Saturday business hours became common). Judah made his way proudly down Sixth Avenue, unbowed like so many exhausted others.

At school Isaac had outpaced his class by leaps and bounds, further convincing his family that he was meant for something great. Then he became the youngest chemistry student in the history of Columbia

University, graduating at the age of nineteen and then heading on to get his master's. Chemistry was a sop to his father, who wanted him to become a doctor. But Isaac hated the sight of blood, and though he wasn't sure where chemistry would lead him, he knew for certain it would not be to the operating room.

Even his friends were special, talented, and he missed them terribly. Donald, Damon, and the others back home in New York. Especially Freddie. Only in their company did he feel something close to intellectual equality. He wondered how they were doing. Had any of them come together recently to discuss their latest writing projects, agonize over the slow progress of the culture toward the future, plan a convention, or critique the latest issues of *Amazing Stories* or *Fantastic Adventures* or *Astounding Science Fiction* or *Super Science Stories* or *Unknown*? Maybe not. And not just because Isaac was gone. The Futurians had existed before he joined the club and they had continued without him. But they were busy. Donald was struggling to find work as an ed, having had two mags shot out from under him. Damon was trying to sell stories. And he'd just heard through the grapevine that Freddie had enlisted, but phone calls went unanswered and letters were returned to sender.

Isaac put down the coffee cup, amazed that he had been able to finish it. He ought to write. He could squeeze out a few sentences before he left. His fingers twitched, eagerly. Telling stories was all he had ever really wanted to do.

It had always been easy for him to imagine the future, to travel through deep space, to see other worlds, face the challenges a man would face in alien environments. But ever since he got married, he found he had to struggle to find time to write. The stories were still forming in his mind's eye, images of planets floating alone in space, of ships drifting past the rings of distant worlds. But Gertie didn't seem to understand how much it mattered to him and got frustrated with him when he sat down to do it. It wasn't his job and it wasn't school, she'd point out. What was it exactly, a hobby? A second job, he'd point out. But since it didn't guarantee payment by the hour, she either didn't trust it or respect it. And her lack of confidence in it made him question his—he wanted to prove to her how important it was. How it might someday be more important than his doctorate.

With a twinge of guilt, he turned his back on the typewriter, opened the door, and took the elevator down to the lobby. The spring light of early morning tinted the buildings on the block white-gold. The men of the neighborhood, in suits, overalls, or dungarees, swept past the revolving door of his building heading toward their work in the downtown area. Isaac donned his hat and merged into the stream. There was a man hustling past him on the right trying to read a newspaper as he navigated the sidewalk. His face was hard and pinched. Isaac stepped out of his way only to be shoulder-checked by another man passing on his left.

"Watch it, pal," the man snarled, as Isaac stumbled out of his way. The accent was as thick and ignorant as Philadelphia.

Isaac muttered an apology but the man had moved on down the block while other new men were circling past Isaac and making little sounds of exasperation at the befuddled human obstacle obstructing their way. Someone knocked the hat from his head. The hat, a gift from his father, rolled toward the door of the dry cleaner. Isaac dashed to its rescue, snatching it up before someone could step on it. He brushed a few maple seed pods from it, feeling small and angry.

Isaac slapped the hat back on his head, then put his hands on his belt, feeling for the devices attached to either side of his hips. His thumbs pressed the buttons, feeling the pleasure of the clicks. The vibration thrummed through his body and he felt himself grow lighter as the antigravity field enveloped him. He launched himself into the sky, grinning as the sidewalk fell away from him. Missing the tree branches by inches, he rocketed up and up. Above the tall apartment buildings he could see Town Hall, just a few blocks away. Higher now, in the distance there was the simple spire of Independence Hall. Beyond that, the harbor, choked with the gray flotsam of the Navy. Hovering higher than all the buildings around, he laughed at the people far below, knowing that though they could hear him, none of them would think past their confusion to look up for the source of the sounds of glee. He turned toward the Navy Yard, ready to bound through the sky toward work, or better yet, Brooklyn.

Another body checked against his shoulder, bumping his mind back to reality. The sidewalk came into focus and his hands fell from his belt. Of course, there were no antigrav packs attached to it, no sky-way to use to escape the drudgery of his walk, or the train ride. But boy, an antigrav belt sure would have come in handy this morning.

Isaac bit his lip, realizing that he had forgotten to say goodbye to Gertie. He could go back. He could walk up the steps, take his hat off, and sit down at the typewriter. Maybe later he could crawl into bed again with Gertrude and take a nap. They could spend the day together. She could bring him lunch at the typewriter as he banged out his robot story. He might even be able to talk her into trying to have sex. But the thought of moving against the tide, of standing out, made him shake his head with resignation and he began walking again toward work, looking sharply around him, finding the rhythm of the other robots, becoming one of them, eventually tromping down the steps to the Broad Street Line.

A thought suddenly occurred to him as he exited the train on the south end of Broad Street, and if he hadn't been so focused on keeping one foot stepping in front of the other he might have stopped short again. Maybe Gertie had a point. Did it matter if he didn't write again? He kept walking, past the Port of Call Inn, one of the rough taverns just off the base that lightened the loads of sailors each week. This was the one his friends preferred, though he'd never set foot inside. Isaac didn't particularly like to drink.

Would anyone care if he quit writing? The front gate of the Navy Yard was in sight. Would anyone even notice? Although his destination was now ahead he couldn't quite focus on it, the guard post kept swimming out of his vision. What could his little imaginings even matter in a world where an entire planet had gone to war with itself?

He stumbled through the gate, flashing his ID badge to the same guard who each day failed to recognize him. Even the youngest soldier seemed years older than Isaac felt. The casual swagger of the military man spoke of a physical confidence he himself had never felt. Whereas on Walnut Street he had blended in amongst the faceless masses, here he stood out because of his civilian suit, and it made him feel uncomfortable.

Sailors, Marines, and officers representing all the armed forces moved swiftly along the sidewalks and he felt each one of them took a special moment to give him a snide glance, as if to ask why this young man was not doing his duty. He wanted to explain that he too had a mission, a part to play in this war, that he was using his intellect, his greatest weapon, to help them all.

The Navy Yard had once been an actual island with only a small bridge connecting it to the city. Garbage had slowly filled in the small creek that separated the land and eventually the city just covered it with dirt and paved it over. But the locals still referred to it as League Island. Past the guardhouse, to the left the wide boulevard where Isaac now walked gave way to the parade grounds, where Marine platoons drilled and exercised constantly. He felt his armpits go damp at the thought of basic training—the fate that awaited him if Campbell's group didn't produce.

Across the street, the real estate had been devoted to a row of stately Victorian mansions, buildings that would not appear out of place in Philadelphia's finest neighborhoods, home to the officers. Rising behind those, looming over the houses like a gray wall of metal, were the battleships, destroyers, and aircraft carriers, all bristling with cannons and armaments; the floating weapons that concerned all who toiled here, black smoke roiling out of the stacks even as they rested at port, never stopping.

He turned left on Delaware Street, which ran along the bank of the river, and began the long walk toward the barracks, and his job. Out here, far from the rest of the work of the yard, the Navy had squeezed out a lab for them from a low warehouse. It literally fronted the river; only a few feet separated the building's wall from the waterline, which afforded them a nice view. But it also meant that when they opened the windows on warm days, the overwhelming stench of trash and oil drifted in and stayed. Across the street from the warehouse were several small barracks units, white buildings of no distinguishing character. Three of these were vacant, while the fourth had recently been occupied by a petty officer and his crew awaiting the arrival of a brand-new ship they would then spend the summer outfitting. Bob had once explained that while the ships Isaac had seen being launched in newsreels to great fanfare could float, they were far from finished. They required wiring, instrumentation, furniture, paint, and all sorts of outfitting before they could begin service. That's what men like the petty officer and his crew would do when their ship arrived. In the meantime, they drank a lot, threw their bottles at the lab, darted cigarette butts at Isaac's ankles when he'd leave in the evenings, and complained about the noise caused by the lab's special generators.

Isaac paused outside their barracks. The provisioning department had dropped off a delivery for the shipless crew across the street. Perched on top of several wooden boxes was a case of orange Nehi. The sight made him lick his lips. He loved orange Nehi, and for some reason, it was hard to get in Philadelphia. He had put in a request for some, but now these sailors had nicked it. Recalling the humiliation of being laughed at while dodging their flicked cigarettes, a feeling of righteousness rose within him. Before he really processed what he'd done, he'd quietly lifted the case of orange Nehi and hurried it into the lab.

The twist of a key admitted Isaac into the long research facility. He flipped on the lights. As usual, he was the first one in. The other men he worked with liked to go out after work, hoist a few beers, try to get some sex. So they would always drag themselves in late, complaining of the noise, the stink from the river, the overhead lights, and, ultimately, the intractability of the local women. Isaac never went out with them. Gertrude liked him to come home, and so he did. The guys always made jokes about how jealous they were that he was getting to go home and have sex that was guaranteed and free. He always smiled and nodded.

The lab was divided into sections that would only be apparent to another scientist. The unaware eye would see masses of tubes, coils, and tools. But Isaac could easily see that one station was devoted to exploring radio frequencies and magnetic fields, another was for metallurgic research, and a further station for mechanical engineering. He slid the case under his table, which was covered with the Erlenmeyer flasks, Bunsen burners, scales, a centrifuge, and the vast array of chemicals that applied to his specialty. He loved the selection of chemicals most of all. Even at

Columbia he never had access to the great variety of powders and liquids at his disposal here in Philadelphia. Experimenting with things he had only read about as he worked toward his doctorate was one of the few pleasures of this job. If only the government wasn't so insistent that he turn those pleasures into results.

His eyes fell upon the chalkboard at the other end of the room. Bob had scribbled some epigraphic sentences meant to guide them all, and months later, the words were still there:

CAN WE MAKE IT FLY HIGHER OR FASTER OR BY ITSELF?
CAN WE MAKE IT VANISH?
CAN WE BLOW IT UP BETTER?
CAN WE CONFUSE OUR ENEMIES?

Some joker, maybe even Bob himself, had scribbled NO next to every question.

Isaac looked at the other stations. Each one, like his, had great resources at their disposal. But not one of the mighty intellects that John Campbell had assembled in Philadelphia had come close to developing antigravity devices or invisibility cloaks or radio-controlled rockets, or anything else that they had been mandated to invent.

The opening of the door startled him. No one ever came in this early. An officer Isaac didn't recognize entered cautiously and looked around. He was tall and looked a little older than Isaac, though to Isaac everyone did. He had a great shock of thick black hair and heavy glasses through which he gazed at Isaac.

"Hello," the stranger said, a question and a statement.

"Hello," Isaac replied, almost, but not quite, ready to spill the beans about the orange Nehi.

The man peered around, seemingly surprised at the amount of inactivity, then cleared his throat. "I'm looking for Bob? Bob Heinlein?"

"He's out of town," Isaac told him, beginning to suspect that the man's appearance may not have anything to do with his theft.

"Oh." The man lowered a heavy satchel from his shoulder and began to approach Isaac, though he looked surprised as he reached the center of the room. Desks had been moved to create an open area upon which intricately designed model ships were positioned as if frozen in the middle of battle. Bullen and Williamson were masters of miniature warfare games and spent hours leading other members of the team in epic conflicts. "Looks like somebody's recreating the battle of Guadalcanal." He got down on one knee to take a closer look. "That's the *Washington*. And that's the *South Dakota*. Nice models. They make these here?"

Isaac nodded. "Brinley makes them."

The man rose and offered his hand. Isaac looked nervously at the appendage for a moment, unsure what diseases the stranger had carried in with him. He took a leap of faith and held out his own hand for the ritual.

"I'm Sprague de Camp. Lieutenant," the stranger said. "And John Campbell sent me down here to join Bob Heinlein's team."

"Hey!" Isaac felt a wave of relief and excitement. "I've heard of you. You write for *Unknown*! I've read your stories. I'm Isaac Asimov. I write for *Amazing*. And sometimes *Astounding*. Not *Unknown*, though. Yet. It's gonna be great to have another pulp writer around here. Bob's the greatest, but he's running things so he's all over the place. Hey! You want a Nehi?"

"Grape?"

"Orange."

"My favorite."

Isaac brought out two bottles and quickly popped off the caps. He handed one to the new man, who took it gratefully.

"I can tell from your Brooklyn accent that you're a fellow New Yorker," Sprague said, wiping his lips. His own accent told Isaac immediately that the man had probably never left the Upper West Side. "What are you doing here for Campbell's Kamikaze Group, Isaac?"

"Is that what he's calling it?"

"That's what I'm calling it. He told me I'm supposed to help you all figure out a way to keep Jap kamikazes from crashing into our ships. He promised me death rays that blast planes out of the sky and force fields that protect the ships. And that's just the tip of the iceberg."

"Sounds like our mission." Isaac nodded.

"What are you working on?"

"I'm inventing a paint that can deflect radar from ships and sonar from U-boats."

"Wonderful. How's it work?"

"Well, it doesn't exactly, yet. Right now whenever the paint hits the salt water it turns into a rubbery compound that won't disperse on the surface. But I'm getting closer. At least it doesn't eat through the ship metal anymore. What are they going to have you do?"

Sprague de Camp grinned at Isaac Asimov. "I," he announced grandly, as if there were others in the room besides Isaac, who felt himself warming to the man's expansiveness, "am here to control the weather."

EPISODE 4

"THERE'S NO WAY in hell to keep these FANS happy!"

Even as those words echoed down the corridor of the fifth floor of the Street & Smith offices, the entire building began battening down its hatches. First the typists in the steno pool who spent their days turning the chicken scratches on notebooks into legible manuscripts would quietly shut the door to their large room. Then the secretaries of the other eds whose offices lined the corridor along the way to the elevator banks would shut theirs in an attempt to shield their bosses. This was the signal for anyone still on the floor to hustle the word along to any other innocent souls they might find. Soon, type boys riding the elevators quit ribbing one another; publishers, managers, and executives on the sixth floor seemed to tread more lightly across the creaky boards. Even the great presses below the street seemed to run a little more efficiently, as if extra oil had suddenly been applied to their gears and drive shafts; and the teamsters, waiting to take their cargo of the latest pulps to newsstands across the nation, stopped shouting at each other and turned their idling trucks off. For, even though John W. Campbell was an avowed atheist, when the most powerful ed at Street & Smith lost his temper, he put the fear of God into others.

The word ASTOUNDING had been carefully stenciled on the pane of glass set in the door which led into his office, upon his arrival five years ago, and the word UNKNOWN had been added soon after. It was, Campbell insisted, more than just an acknowledgment of the mags that he published, it was a warning to all who entered that they had better impress him, or suffer grave consequences. The years of relentless clouds of cigarette and pipe smoke had stained the glass a shade of yellowish-brown and constant slamming had loosened it so that now, when he shouted, it actually rattled slightly in its frame.

"Listen to this." He straightened the creases from a folded letter. "'Dear Mr. Campbell. We respect you and what you are trying to do, but we have to ask, why are you trying to ruin science fiction? Bottom line, you need to produce something that folks will enjoy, old fans and new, and so far, we don't see you doing that. The sequels you have put out to the incredible "Collision Orbit" by Will Stewart are just terrible. Is he even writing them any more? Through these stories, your magazine continues to push forward the theory of contraterrene in spite of the laws of thermodynamics, most egregiously, in the recent "Opposites—React!" We feel sorry for Mr. Stewart that you continue to force him to write these tales. It is a waste of his talents. Indeed, we are reminded of the old saying that if God had an editor and He invited the man to see his latest creation, an ocean, the editor would piss in it and then say it was finished.

"'Mr. Campbell, the old fans of *Astounding Science Fiction* are not pleased, and we don't see any new fans shouting any praises. We pray any subsequent episodes offer more than the earlier ones did and return to the direction and promise of the original story—the first and best. Regards, from the ones who pay your salary, the fans who must be adhered to.' Signed: 'Fighters Against Nonsensical Scientification (FANS), Boston, Mass.'

"Why the hell do I bother?" He crumpled up the letter and threw it across the room, where it bounced off one of the many file cabinets before joining other crumpled-up pieces of paper on the floor like so many desert tumbleweeds. "These fellas act like they own this stuff. They don't realize they're only renting it for a few pennies an issue. Do it the same way every time, or else. They have become almost ritualistic about hewing to some canon that they've invented with Verne and Wells above all others, immutable and immovable. This is how cults and religions get started.

"So does that make you science fiction's high priest or prophet?" Bob Heinlein sat on Campbell's ancient leather sofa. With the fingers of his left hand he picked at a flaking piece of cowskin on the sofa arm, exposing the yellow ticking underneath. Campbell's cigarette, jammed into its long black holder, irritated his tuberculosis-scarred lungs and he stifled a cough with his right hand.

"According to the FANS, I'm its Lucifer Morningstar," Campbell grumbled. "The thing that irritates me is that without me, they'd have next to nothing."

"Ugh." Heinlein shuddered. "That'd leave Ray Palmer over at *Amazing* as the Pope of science fiction."

Campbell grew silent and stared out the window, as if he could see all the way to Chicago and into the office of his closest rival. "Not with the writers he has."

"I hear he's been buying some of Isaac's lately."

Campbell threw his hands up. "Look, I can't print everything that kid writes. First, there's way too much of it, and I don't want to get into publishing the Isaac Asimov mag business. Second, it's not all as good as he thinks it is. So if he wants to sell a few of the dogs to Palmer, I don't give a crap. I've still got de Camp, Hubbard, Williamson, also known as the hated Will Stewart. And you, if you'd ever come back and start writing again."

Heinlein shook his head and shrugged at the same time. "I'm retired."

"Who retires from writing? It's hardly work to begin with."

Heinlein suppressed a slight grin that he felt twitching at the corners of his mouth. "I can't run things down in Philadelphia and write for you at the same time."

"Bullshit! You used to write and have a real job at the same time."

"I had a mortgage then, too. But thanks to you, I've paid it off. Besides, this is different. This is war."

"Again, I say to you, sir, bullshit."

"Maybe I'm just out of ideas."

"No. You're the best I've got. It's everyone else who's running out of ideas." Campbell sighed deeply and drew his hand over his face in a gesture of surrender and concern. "I've seen it all. That's the problem. This genre's only about twenty years old and it feels like we're starting to repeat ourselves. Invasions, alien civilizations, rockets, theories. Even you and your generational journeys through space. And I swear to Christ, if I read one more story about death rays . . ." He pounded his fist on his desk, and Heinlein glanced nervously at the pane of glass.

"You're one of those guys who just can't be happy with success," Heinlein said. "FANS aside, most readers love your mags. *Astounding* and *Unknown* are selling like gangbusters. You're selling more and more each month and even killing the heroes. Even *Doc Savage* and *The Shadow* have had to become more like what you put out to just try and keep up. 'Scientific detectives,' that's how they're advertising them now.

"The Army's given you a special office in the Empire State Building *and* your own think tank in Philly to simply come up with science fiction ideas to help win the war. You're top dog! Now quit your bitchin'!"

"Only means there's a pack of hounds right behind, snapping at my heels. I've got the competition on one side—a new and different sci-fi mag hits the newsstands each month picking up all the rejects that I can't print. *Amazing*'s just the tip of that iceberg, let me tell you. Then I've got the FANS who love telling me how much they hate what I do. And finally, there's all of you writers who've got me over a barrel because if I don't pay you top penny per word, you'll be off to another mag."

"Now who's sounding a little like a persecuted martyr?"

Campbell nodded in agreement. "Thing is, I care about the science, I don't care what the FANS say. You know I researched contraterrene physics. In spite of what the laws of thermodynamics may say, there are new laws of quantum dynamics emerging and they're changing everything, from science to science fiction. There is a negative counterpart to protons and neutrons and it could conceivably be used as an energy source someday. That's the story I've had Williamson tell as Will Stewart—and it's the story I wanted you to write. A good story about asteroid CT mining."

As if triggered by a cosmic cue, Heinlein felt a thrumming sensation vibrate through the cushion and up his spine, making the hairs on the back of his neck rise. The great presses in the basement had whirred to life again, churning out mags. What was odd was that a few years ago the presses never stopped so Heinlein never would have even noticed them. Now they ran intermittently. He watched Campbell, who gave no indication that he'd noticed the vibration, though his shoulders seemed to sag reflexively. Heinlein knew that for Campbell the machinery was the gaping maw of a monster that needed to be fed continuously.

He scooped a manila envelope from his desk and tossed it to Heinlein. "Cleve Cartmill."

"Yeah. I know Cartmill. Comes to some of our get-togethers in L.A. He's good."

"He's all right. Those are notes for a story I want him to write. This is all our research. It's about a super-bomb, and I think the science is solid. But I was wondering if you could have your physicist pal at Berkeley take a look at it to make sure. The same way you had him validate my CT research before you chose not to write the stories?"

"Robert Cornog?" Heinlein scratched his head. "He's kind of gone silent running."

"What do you mean?"

"You know I like to bounce theoretical ideas off him from time to time. See if I can make my fiction as plausible as possible, to please you and the FANS, of course. I sent him a letter last month asking him a few questions about some things we were thinking about in Philadelphia. Instead of a letter from California, I got a postcard from New Mexico. No message, just his signature. Very mysterious. I'll send this along and see if I hear back from him. But I'm sure Cartmill will write you a fine story, John."

"This is what I'm reduced to, Bob. Playing minor leaguers."

"We all gotta do our part. There's a war on, you know."

"Yeah. I heard. Goddamn Hitler's broken the whole damn world. At least I've got you and Asimov tucked safely away."

"I'd be fighting in a second if the Navy would have me back." As if to emphasize his point the cigarette smoke finally irritated Heinlein enough that he burst into a fit of coughing.

Campbell looked on sympathetically. When Heinlein had regained his composure, he asked, "How're things in Philadelphia?"

"Ever spent time there?" Heinlein replied weakly, clearing his throat. "Makes even Providence seem downright cosmopolitan."

"You guys figured out how to protect ships from kamikaze attacks?"

"We've got some good ideas. That new guy you sent us, de Camp, he should be helpful. I hope. I haven't met him yet. He's starting today."

"He's a good writer. Smart guy. Has a degree in aeronautical engineering. When I heard the Navy had snapped him up, I begged to keep him stateside. So do me a favor and come up with some results so I can keep him out of the line of fire and squeeze the occasional story out of him. Otherwise it's more death rays for me."

"I'll do what I can. It's easy to imagine how to make a ship disappear. It's more difficult to make it a reality."

Campbell waved his arm dismissively. "Details. Thinking it is half the battle."

"If you say so. By the way, what do I call him. L?"

"Just call him de Camp. Speaking of guys named L. You heard about our other L?"

Heinlein shifted, a spring from the sofa suddenly poking at his kidneys. "No."

"Court-martial."

Now this was a surprise. Heinlein suddenly forgot about the offending coil. "Hubbard was court-martialed?"

Campbell shrugged. "Not yet. But he's heading for one. Crazy Ron, right? Hubbard spent three days chasing a German sub nobody else saw. He ended up shelling a Mexican resort! Mexico accused us of launching an invasion. The secretary of state had to offer an apology in person. Hubbard's going on trial any day now."

"For Christ's sake!"

"There's a guy who wants to be a hero in the worst possible way. I'm hoping he lands up in the brig. It'll keep him safe and at least I'll get some more stories out of him."

Heinlein rubbed the back of his neck. "He's pretty annoying, but I don't know if I want to see the guy in Leavenworth."

"C'mon, he's a good science fiction writer."

"Really? You think so?"

"Hell, yes. And fast. We used to call him The Flash. Guess now we'll be calling him The Flush."

"I'm sure he'll love that. There's a guy who can dish it out but can't take it."

"Yeah, I won't be calling him that to his face."

"Not a good idea."

"I know why you don't want to write for me anymore."

"Why is that?"

"You're too good for the pulps. You know it and I know. You want to write real books. Hardcovers. Only problem for you is that no one's publishing science fiction in hardcover. Maybe someday. For now it's the occasional anthology or the pulps. And I'm betting you're back in the pulps before you're in a book."

Heinlein shrugged. Campbell's ability to turn anything into a bet was legendary. It was one of his classic motivational techniques. "I'm not writing anything, these days. I promise."

Campbell pulled another envelope from his desk. "Well, this is what you're really here for, isn't it?"

"If that's a check, then it is."

"For the last Robert A. Heinlein story." He sighed. "I could have just mailed it to you."

"I have some research nearby."

"Are you heading right back to Philadelphia today? Want to join Dona and me for dinner? She'd be happy to come in, or we could go to Westchester."

Heinlein stood up and smoothed down his pants. Even though he was more than a decade removed from the Navy, he still felt the need to keep the crease razor sharp. "I can't," he declined. "I've got to get a move on."

"Fair enough." Campbell shrugged and twisted another cigarette into the holder. "When are you going to bring your wife out here? Dona's dying to meet Leslyn."

"Actually, I'm going to meet her today and then we're heading straight down to Philadelphia."

"You got her to leave California?"

Heinlein nodded. "Finally."

"That's wonderful news! We can get the wives together."

Heinlein shifted his weight from one foot to the other. "Sure. It'll be great."

"Looking forward to it."

He opened the door carefully, so as not to shake the glass. The usually busy corridor beyond was quiet and empty. "I'll send this over to Cornog."

Campbell shook his hand. "Appreciate it."

"And you know how I handle the FANS? I use a form letter."

"Really?"

"Sure. I check the ones that apply. For example, one of the lines reads, 'You say that you have enjoyed my stories for years. Why did you wait until you disliked one story before writing to me?' Another one says, 'My agent handles business.' There are several that I can check to refuse to do interviews, sign autographs, or help with school assignments. Then I have one that says, 'In answer to your question: Yes/No/No comment.' And then my favorite one is 'Please do not write to me again.' I have a stack of those printed out on my stationery and they seem to handle the FANS quite well. Of course, you might also do what I have done, which is to give them what they want."

Campbell laughed, then shook his head. "It's some kind of a new age we're in now, isn't it?"

"You can say that again. Sometimes I feel like there are entire episodes of my life between the old days and these that have gone missing."

Leaving the half-empty building, Heinlein caught a cab to 34th Street. He mounted the steps into the great Post Office. Inside, he flipped through his ancient address book until he found Cornog's address. After mailing the packet, he dashed through traffic to cross the street into Pennsylvania Station, bought a ticket, boarded the train, and settled in for the ride. He only realized he'd been dozing when the train to Morristown lurched around a hard turn. Wiping the sleep dampness from the back of his neck, he tried to block out the dream he'd just had that he was in a Jap Zero hurtling unstoppably toward the deck of his old ship, the USS *Lexington*. From the cockpit he had been able to see the faces of his old friends, his shipmates, reacting in horror as he drew down upon them.

He looked around at the few occupants of the half-empty car. Some elderly businessmen in their handmade fedoras. A couple of young men, looking scared in their freshly pressed uniforms, kidded each other a little too aggressively.

A soldier, a boy, sat across the aisle from him, separate from his companions, a more thoughtful expression on his face. His hands were empty and his fingers drummed nervously.

"Where you from, soldier?" he asked.

"Indianapolis, sir."

"First time in New York?"

"Yes, sir. But I only got to spend one night there."

"Heading to Fort Dix?"

"Yes, sir." The soldier's eyes narrowed suspiciously, the heavy eyebrows almost hiding them, the warnings of passing along too much information to the enemy or anyone else having been drummed into his head to the point he was probably already afraid he'd said too much.

The conductor called out the next stop, even as the train began to slow down. Suddenly Heinlein felt very tired and old, and a tiny bolt of electric fear stabbed through him. He stood up and pulled from his satchel the stack of mags he had picked up from the newsstand outside Street & Smith. The latest issues. *Astounding* was at the top of the heap. He handed the pulps to the young soldier.

"What's your name, soldier?"

"Sir? Kurt, sir."

"Well, Kurt, I'm sure you've got some long journey ahead of you." He handed the soldier the mags, enjoying the look of surprise on his face. "Hopefully these'll help pass the time."

"Thanks, mister." He thumbed through the pulps, delighted. "I love this stuff." He tapped the top mag with excitement. "Love *Astounding*."

"So it goes," Heinlein told the young man as the train pulled to a stop, iron wheels shrieking. "From one fan to another, right? Morristown. My stop. You be careful over there."

"I'll try."

As Heinlein moved to the exit he finally overheard the soldier muttering to himself as he concentrated on the mags on his lap.

"So it goes," the young soldier whispered.

At the train station, Heinlein caught a cab, blinking as the driver pointed the car directly into the setting sun.

"Where to?" the driver asked.

"Greystone Park."

"Oh, the lunatic asylum," the man said in a knowing locals-only tone.

"The psychiatric hospital," Heinlein muttered angrily.

"Your fare," the driver replied.

Several miles into the countryside that reminded Heinlein of England he could see the looming stone tower of the massive main building rising over the treetops. The sight filled him with dread. In the twilight the complex was fully lit from within, the glow from each window doing little to push back the oppressive miasma swirling around the park. He paid the driver to wait for him and walked up the long, empty driveway. The great brass door protested on dry hinges as he pulled it open.

He saw her right away, sitting on a bare bench near a column by the front desk. A large suitcase sat beside her. Her face, hidden below the brim of her hat, was pointed downward toward fingers that twisted and turned around and around on themselves. He took several steps toward her and she looked up, perhaps hearing his footsteps, perhaps the grating of the door. Her auburn hair spilled out from under her hat and the curls circled her face. The striking blue eyes were clear and focused, but lined with red as if she had been crying. She said nothing as he walked past her to the front desk, only watched. For several moments he spoke with the clerk, concluding with him signing over the check Campbell had given him in its entirety. That seemed to conclude the business and at last he took a seat beside her on the hard bench. He could only focus for the longest time on the interplay of her long fingers; they reminded him of the endless frolicking of a pair of sea otters he'd seen in captivity in a zoo once. She was wearing her wedding ring.

"Hi, Bob," she whispered at last.

"Hi, Leslyn."

Somewhere deep in the hospital behind them a soul began to wail, encouraging other mournful voices to join its sorrowful chorus. Heinlein watched as her fingers tentatively unfurled from each other and one hand slid roughly across the fabric of the dress he had bought for her long ago back in Santa Cruz for their fifth anniversary; her other hand lay in her lap, still twisting and grasping. His wife's hand crept into his and his fingers slid into hers—a perfect fit—as they always had. The far-away cries died down, leaving only the first voice to howl alone.

"I'm ready to take you home," Heinlein said.

Leslyn nodded. "We can try."

EPISODE 5

WHO ARE THEY to judge me?

They are no one.

Don't they know who I really am?

He lifted himself up from the bed. The golden light of the late Pasadena afternoon forced its way through the gaps in the heavy burgundy drapes.

He cracked his neck, hearing the bones and tendons snap like a loose sail in a heavy wind as they sorted out their proper positions. Sara lay under the sheets by his side, but whether she was sleeping or feigning sleep to avoid speaking with him was hard to tell as she was so still and her face was away from him.

He wanted to write, and he flexed his fingers to warm them up for the job of typing. The joints of the knuckles reacted angrily by spreading hot fire up his arms, and with a sharp inhale through his teeth he jammed his hands under his pits, rocking gently back and forth as if rhythm and pressure could beat back the arthritis.

He was thirty-three years old and breaking down like an old man. No, he had to remind himself, that wasn't true at all. Because his father was the broken-down old man.

He was not breaking down. He would rise above it all.

"Ron?" she murmured, her voice full of sleepy concern. At least he now knew for certain.

Hubbard's fingers stopped hurting. He opened his fists, ready to type if a story would come to him. But there was nothing there.

"Are you okay?" Sara asked. He brushed aside a thick strand of the gorgeous red hair which spilled heavily across the pillow so he could see her face. Her eyes were still closed, hidden behind the thick lashes. It was only an optical illusion, but her pale skin seemed to generate its own soft golden glow, pale shadows falling behind the high cheekbones, the scattering of freckles like small brown grace notes, red lips still full from recent kissing. At nineteen she was more woman than he'd ever been with before.

"Fine," he whispered, so close to her ear that he couldn't resist gently tasting her earlobe with the tip of his tongue, causing her to shudder and cringe with a delightfully sleepy squeal. "I'm fine. I have to get dressed."

"You're leaving?"

"Yeah, I have to drive back down to San Diego. I'm being court-martialed. Can't miss the big finish."

She finally opened her jade green eyes. "They can't do anything to you, baby. They can't touch you."

"The hell they can't. They can ruin me."

"No. I mean they won't."

"How do you know?"

"It's not in your cards. There's chaos and change but freedom as well. I had Jack do a reading. That's what the cards say."

"Do they now?" Hubbard rose and began to look around on the floor for his pants. Whenever Sara went mystical he took it as a cue that he'd overstayed his welcome. Then again, if he went to jail, he might not be seeing her again for a long time. "What else do they tell you? I'll be taking a long sea voyage?"

"As a matter of fact, yes." She sat up, tugging the sheet up to cover her breasts but at the same time revealing the flank of her hip which was always a more tantalizing part of her body for him. "I've also invoked some protection."

"What?"

"I've invoked the guardian Isis to keep you from harm." She indicated a bandage down the inside of her wrist that he hadn't noticed in the dark.

"Oh, baby, what did you do? You cut yourself?"

She nodded.

"Was this Jack's idea?"

Sara shook her head. "I did it myself. I did it for you."

Hubbard took her wrist tenderly in his hands. He could see a slight stain of blood through the gauze. "I wish you wouldn't do this."

"Don't you understand that I wouldn't not? I have to do everything within my power to help you."

"This isn't power, Sara. This is mutilation. Damn! Sometimes I think everyone in this house takes things a little too far. You. Your sister. The rest of the Order. But especially Parsons."

She gently twisted her hand away from his grip and then caressed his cheek. "Come back to bed," she whispered, lowering her eyelids and her voice in a way that made the hairs on the back of his neck rise. With a little effort she pulled him against her breast, the thin silk sheet between them. If only he could nestle there forever.

An explosion from outside rattled the windows. Hubbard shot up. "What the hell!"

"Jack's home," she murmured, releasing him, rolling away from him.

Hubbard rose and went to the window, the thick oriental carpet warm and soft beneath his toes. It probably cost more than his house. He drew aside the drapes. Near the grove of magnolia trees at the border of the estate he could see the wisps of a great gray cloud flowing across the lawn, melting away. The dissipating smoke revealed, like a lighthouse appearing out of the fog, a solitary figure, one hand on his hip, the other shielding his eyes from the sun as he peered skyward. After a long moment the man took two steps to the left and an instant later an arrow loosed from the heavens plunged into the earth where he had been standing only a moment before. Dirt showered the man. Hubbard could see the light glinting off the aluminum body of the rocket burrowed into its new crater, sparks and flames spurting intermittently from its tail.

"Jesus," he whispered. "That was close."

"He's okay," Sara said earnestly, her voice soaked with admiration. "Nothing can touch Jack."

Smoke still swirling around him, the man on the great lawn turned and began walking toward his mansion where Hubbard watched from the window. The tendrils of mist creeping around Jack Parsons's legs reminded Hubbard of another time, years ago now, and a cloud of death he barely escaped from, the memory provoking a stab of fight-or-flight response in him that made his knees buckle. He placed a hand against the windowsill for support.

"What's wrong?"

"Nothing." The adrenaline evaporated from his system though his heart still beat more heavily in his chest. "Jack's not one for leaving his work at the office, is he?"

"Jack believes in a future he can create. He can't do it all at JPL."

"Rockets to the moon."

"Not only that. A new consciousness created through a combination of magick and science that will wipe away the old order. That's why we're all here. Even you."

"Still and all, I think I better hit the road." Hubbard turned away from the window. Finally spying his dress whites crumpled on the floor, he began to get dressed.

She sighed and sat up, the suggestiveness gone from her posture. "You know, Jack's really fine with our arrangement."

"Yeah, well, I don't think I need to be throwing it in his face that I'm putting in time with his woman." He looked around until he found one of his socks hooked atop the mahogany post at the head of the bed. Hubbard went around to her side to snatch it down, then sat by her to put it on.

"The old pairings of one man and one woman are archaic in the face of love," she continued. Hubbard was glad his back was to her so she couldn't see him roll his eyes. "Love under will is the only law."

"How does your sister feel about that?"

"She knows that while she may have married Jack, we can both love him."

Hubbard nodded. "Hmm. So that's why she took off with that Smith fella?"

"Helen could return at any moment and Jack and I would find a place for her. Just as we've found a place for you. Here at the Lodge."

"Christ." Hubbard stretched out his fingers before trying to button his shirt. "Sometimes I wonder what I have gotten myself into."

"You're seeking the answers to universal questions, Ron." She sat up to button his shirt as if sensing his distress. Her movements were slow, thoughtful, playful.

Standing, he buttoned the rest of his shirt. "And I thought I was just looking for a great lay."

Sara settled back down on the bed. "I will protect you. You'll see."

"Look," he said, "why don't you come with me? For a few days."

She laughed. "I don't have to go with you to be with you, Ron. Besides, there's work to do here. I'm sure Jack will tell you of it. He has big plans for you. We both do."

Hubbard slipped quietly out of the room and padded down the long, dark hallway of the old Victorian home. Walter Gibson would love it here, he thought, startled at the same time that the dark cloud which had provoked his earlier memories had dislodged a name he hadn't recalled for quite some time. The great banister was smooth and cool beneath his hand. More wood had gone into paneling this one great hallway than had been used to build all the boats he had ever owned. Jack Parsons had inherited his father's mansion and wealth, and the father was probably spinning in his grave at how it had all been debased. Hubbard paused at the door to the attic which he had to pass to get to the main landing. The golden crucifix hung upside down gave him goose bumps though he considered himself in no way religious. The attic, the things that went on up there, the things he had done, gave him the shudders.

This was all Lou's fault. Lou Goldstone was a pulp illustrator Hubbard had met soon after leaving New York for the warmer shores of Los Angeles. Before the war came and everything went to hell. Those years—1939, 1940—they already glowed as golden in his memory. He had finished his term as president of the Writers Guild and realized he hadn't changed a thing. Pulp writers still grubbed for pennies a word and never saw the bigger picture—that their writing could change the world. Jack Parsons wanted to create the future through magick and science?

Hubbard was already creating it through science fiction. He had fought to have his name on his stories and by the time he left the east coast behind he could simply mail in his stories and know that he would be paid for them, and that they would be published. Still one of the fastest writers around, he could generate four or five stories a month, which left him plenty to live on, even after sending something to his wife and children in Seattle.

The Heinleins had been living in L.A. then. Bob and Les. Bob was something more than an acquaintance and less than a friend. The couple had welcomed Hubbard graciously and introduced him to their small circle—electrons and neutrons of science fiction writers, artists and fans flying around the couple at the atom's nucleus. Bob and Leslyn at the center. Lou had been one particle in that orbit. So had Jack Parsons. It was inevitable that Lou would eventually introduce Hubbard and Parsons; Los Angeles just wasn't that big and the world of science fiction was so very, very small.

Hubbard took a deep breath. His mind was of the powerful sort that could silence fears and weak thoughts (a mind a real man could be proud of) and he pushed away all the tattered strands of his life that were nagging at him. He released the pent-up air from his lungs. Suddenly the great house did not seem quite so filled with gloom and poison as it had. For a moment he even thought of turning back toward Sara and bed. But there were matters for men ahead of him and he couldn't seek refuge in a woman's arms forever.

Invigorated, he trotted down the staircase and turned in the foyer toward the kitchen, hoping to grab a beer or cola from the refrigerator to replenish his liquids as he drove toward San Diego.

Jack was seated at the kitchen table, the Tarot cards laid out before him. These had been given to him directly by Aleister Crowley upon his anointment as the leader of the *Ordo Templi Orientis*—the occult epicenter of California, perhaps America. Hubbard didn't know for sure. He'd never met Crowley; the Brit rarely visited America, and certainly not now during wartime. Though he'd heard enough of him through the other Lodge members. Hubbard could literally feel the muscles in his legs grow heavy and his blood chill as he entered Parsons's presence.

The scent of the rocket explosion, a mixture of cordite and gunpowder, mingled with the clogging miasma from the cone of incense smoking away on the table, gave Hubbard an instant, intense headache. Scientist and sorcerer—that was Jack Parsons in a nutshell.

Parsons looked up at him, eyes like jet black pools of oil set into his face. He flipped another card from his deck onto the table but didn't look down at it, peering straight ahead.

"Hullo, Jack," Hubbard said, employing every ounce of the politically charming voice he used with eds and naval officers to indicate comradeship. His blood was frothing in waves through his head; he hoped he could hear Parsons's response over it. "Didn't know you were here."

"Brother Ron." Parsons nodded at him and then, finally, looked down at the card he had flipped. "How's Sara?"

"She's . . . I don't know . . . Sleeping, I guess. I just dropped by a little while ago." He forced himself to walk to the refrigerator and grab a beer—feeling Parsons's eyes upon him with every step. "Say, that was some launch, huh?"

"I thought you said you didn't know I was here," Parsons said with a sense of disinterest, as if he was merely characterizing a thought.

"Sure, well, I knew you were here, I just didn't know you were *here* here, in the kitchen, I meant. Hey, so how's that new business of yours? The Jet Propulsion Lab? I hear you're on the verge of pulling yourselves down some mighty big government connections."

"I've perfected a jet engine which can help planes take off better. There's interest from the Army. JPL might survive the war." Parsons swept the cards up and shuffled them. "Will you be spending the night?"

"I can't. I have to get back to San Diego. Big things are afoot."

"Right. Your court-martial."

"You heard about that?"

"I hear about everything, Brother Ron."

Hubbard took a swallow of the dark beer. "Yeah, well, it's not going to be pleasant. Though, for the record, I did see the kraut sub."

"Of course you did."

"You don't think I did? I know what I saw."

"I'm not saying you didn't."

"Well, I did. I chased that sonofabitch for three days."

"There are things that reveal themselves only to one who is prepared to see them. Were you receptive, Brother Ron?"

"Receptive? I mean, sure. It was my job to be receptive to seeing things. I don't mean that I was seeing things. I just . . . Goddammit!" He slammed the bottle down on the counter, beer foaming out of the mouth. "There was a goddamned Nazi U-boat! There was."

Parsons shrugged. "I'm sure you'll be vindicated in the end."

Hubbard muttered something that was unintelligible even to himself. More of a grunt of dissatisfaction than actual words.

Parsons pulled the cards together into a pile and shuffled them. "Shall I do a reading for you?"

"Last thing I need is that stuff rattling around in my head," Hubbard said with a wave. He grabbed a dishcloth and sopped up the spilled beer.

"I understand." Parsons squared up the deck of cards. "There's an experience I'd like you to consider, Ron. After your current travails end, of course, as they will."

"Hm?"

"There's a ritual—the greatest ritual—whose time has come at last, I believe. It is called the Babalon Working. Have you heard of it?"

"Why would I have?"

Parsons shrugged at the truth in Hubbard's voice. "It is designed to bring about the creation of a living goddess who will change the future forever."

"Uh-huh."

"It requires very powerful men, and magick of the greatest skill and power. You've participated in our rituals before. I know you're the one to be my second in this."

Hubbard thought again of the attic, of the things he had done there with other people and in front of other people. Fueled by alcohol and the illicit thrill of the darkness, the bodies and the nakedness and the freedom. A secrecy that bound all who entered the attic of the Lodge of the Order of the Temple of the East. He suppressed the shame with a burst of pride that he'd mustered the courage to operate so totally outside the expected conventions of society. "I don't think I'm going to be waving my talisman around anymore, Jack," he said. "I'm just a writer and a sailor and I don't think there's a place for me in your future."

"It would just be yourself and me. And a magician of the second degree. Sister Sara."

"Hell," Hubbard said. "No."

"The Great Beast believes she's a vampire, Brother. An elemental demon in woman's form."

"And do you believe what Crowley believes? She's your wife's sister, for Christ's sake."

"Let me tell you how it will be," Jack said in a soft voice, the one he used at the altar in the attic, the voice that slid out from the dark robe like a cobra mesmerizing its prey. "Let me tell you of the Babalon Working. Let me tell you of the three of us, and the ritual which will last for three nights."

Hubbard closed his eyes and inhaled the fumes so deeply that his brain began to scream. It was what he needed to do in order to open them again, look directly into Parsons's eyes, and say, "No."

Later, in the car, heading away from the house on South Orange Grove, the long road of night driving ahead of him, Hubbard rolled down the window to let the wind sweep his mind clean. I'm finished, there, he thought. Finished with Pasadena. I might even be finished with Los Angeles. I will never see Sara again, that's for sure.

No matter how fast he drove, the wind couldn't seem to dislodge Parsons's last words in response to Hubbard's final refusal. The sorcerer's snake voice curled coiled at the base of his spine, creeping upward, tickling at his cerebellum. Said quietly and without menace or malice, meant to be taken as a simple message, and yet one that inspired great fear in Hubbard even as he drove toward San Diego, for it had no other meaning than what Hubbard had always insisted for himself as a right.

Jack Parsons had looked at the cards and only said: "Do whatever you will. It has already begun."

EPISODE 6

GERTRUDE ASIMOV THOUGHT Mrs. de Camp might be the most beautiful woman she'd seen who wasn't in the pictures.

Both the de Camps, the woman who insisted on being called Catherine and her husband who had introduced himself by saying his name rhymed with "Plague," were as creatures from another world to her—nearly like something that had wandered out of one of Isaac's odd stories. They resembled the society folk she had seen coming out of the Plaza Hotel after tea headed for a saunter in Central Park—confident, sophisticated, and just so remarkably American. Comfortable with each other, they shared winks and secret looks, laughed at one another's silliness, acted almost like a single person. She looked through the door of the unfamiliar kitchen to where Isaac sat in one of the big parlor chairs and wondered if they would ever, could ever, be like that.

"Does it bother you when he does that?" Mrs. de Camp asked her, at the same time refilling her wineglass. As she poured, Gertrude studied her slender fingers, which held both the bottle and the wineglass. They were tipped with nails so exquisitely polished Gertrude knew they could only have been done professionally. She herself had only had one manicure in her life and that had been on her wedding day. She ran her forefinger over her thumbnail, feeling the rough edge she had attacked earlier with her teeth, and tried to imagine what it would be like to have them done up all the time.

"Does what?" Gertrude concentrated on slipping the still-warm cookies off the cooling tray and arranging them artfully on the china platter.

Mrs. de Camp sipped the wine. Gertrude wondered how she kept her lipstick from marking the side of the glass the way hers always did. How did Catherine keep her blond hair so perfect while it continued to flow about her and follow her every move? How did she keep her figure? How did she keep her dress so clean and unwrinkled? How did she do this all with the two-month-old toddler Gertrude had met earlier on his way to being put to bed?

"I noticed that Isaac never seems to use your name when he's talking about you. He just says 'my bride' this and 'my bride' that."

Was she being criticized? Gertrude felt the heat as her face grew flushed. That almond cookie was out of place; she adjusted it. "But I am his bride."

"Of course you are. But when he says it constantly like that, doesn't it make you feel a little like his property?"

"I . . . No. I never noticed it."

"You're his partner, honey," Mrs. de Camp said, passing her the other glass of wine, "not chattel."

Gertrude nodded and took the wine but didn't sip it. Like Isaac she didn't like to drink.

"How long have you been married now?"

"One year in July."

Mrs. de Camp smiled with such warmth that Gertrude suddenly felt she had made a friend for life. "Oh, I didn't realize it was all so new to you. Did you have a long engagement?"

Gertrude shook her head. "Actually, we just met on Valentine's Day. I mean, the Valentine's Day before we got married."

"You met him and got him to marry you in five months!? Tell me what your secret is. We'll bottle it and make a fortune."

"It was his idea, really."

"I love that you think so," Mrs. de Camp said with a sly wink, and now Gertrude blushed for real. She had been a bit of a flirt, if she had to admit it.

"I never expected him to propose . . . so quickly," she replied.

Mrs. de Camp sighed as a fond memory took hold of her. "We had a luxuriously long engagement. One year. Mother thought that was far too short. 'A proper engagement should last approximately two years,' she always told me." She leaned in close and Gertrude could smell the jasmine of Chanel No. 5, a scent she had tried on more than once at the Abraham & Straus fragrance counter in downtown Brooklyn but had never even thought about purchasing. "But between you and me, if we hadn't married when we had, that baby up there would have been *tout le scandale*. Poor little Lyman would have been my little bastard."

The de Camps were rich, Gertrude decided. After all, they had rented part of this huge house in Lansdowne, the ritziest suburb of Philadelphia. And there was no way Mr. de Camp could afford a place like this, as big as this, as nice as this, on a lieutenant commander's salary. It even had a name. Yet here she was in the kitchen of Pennock Mansion. She had never known a house could have a name. But Gertrude had never known rich people before either.

Gertrude heard her husband's voice booming through the house: "There are three obstacles which keep our science fiction from becoming fact."

"More of Isaac's laws," she heard Isaac's boss, Bob Heinlein, the man he idolized, groan with exaggeration.

"I'm a Jew," Isaac retorted, "what can I say? I have an innate genetic proclivity toward laws."

Gertrude smiled. Even though he was at least a dozen years younger than the two men, her husband had no reluctance about voicing his opinions to them, and as loudly as he could, it seemed. She liked his confidence—the way he stood up for himself.

"Germplasm is a discredited theory," Mr. de Camp countered.

"A discredited theory is often only one seeking more and better facts," Isaac proclaimed triumphantly. "Now, as I was saying, there are three laws which seem to be immutable except in the face of our fiction, yet almost everything we write about assumes that somehow even these will be overcome by some civilization, perhaps ours, someday."

"What are they?" Mr. de Camp asked.

"Number one: antigravity and artificial gravity don't exist. But we use them for everything from getting off the launchpad to keeping our characters' feet rooted to their ships while in space. Number two: faster-than-light speed is theoretically impossible, but essential to us. Every story we create that has star rovers or time travelers in it is in violation of this fact."

"And the big number three?" Mr. Heinlein drumrolled on his thighs.

"There is no alien life."

"I call bullshit on that," Mr. de Camp said with a laugh.

"There is not any proof of any alien civilization."

"The Pyramids."

"My people built those. I have inherited the weakened back to show for it."

Gertrude felt a tug on her sleeve and realized that Mrs. de Camp had collected the fresh wineglasses and that she was being directed to follow with the cookies into the parlor. As Mrs. de Camp crossed the foyer, Gertrude quickly turned, poured her wine down the sink, and filled her glass with water. A moment later she had picked up the platter and headed into the parlor.

It was like entering a pool hall. The room was filled with thick, chalky cigarette smoke that made her head ache almost instantly. None of the men was smoking. Gertrude looked into the darkest corner of the room and watched a tiny, birdlike woman in the process of lighting one cigarette from the stub of the one she had just finished. Then the woman, pretty but drawn, stubbed out the old one and took a hearty and contented drag on the new, all the while watching her husband with eyes in which even the whites seemed shockingly dark. Dressed in black, Gertrude couldn't tell whether the woman was trying to be fashionable in the bohemian style or was in mourning. Either way, she found Mrs. Heinlein to be a chilling presence.

Pulp mags were scattered all over the room. The evening had started with a review of de Camp's collection, which he had brought with him from New York. ("Not enough clothes," Catherine had jibed, "but plenty of pulp.") The centerpiece were the seventeen issues of *Weird Tales* featuring Mr. de Camp's hero, someone called Conan, written by a Texan who had killed himself. Mr. de Camp had raved about these stories, though neither Mr. Heinlein nor Isaac had read them.

The *Kraft Music Hall* show was playing on the large walnut RCA radio—the largest console Gertrude had ever seen. Bing Crosby was crooning "That Old Black Magic," a song she loved. Mrs. de Camp twirled in rhythm to the music, then plopped heavily into Mr. de Camp's lap as if it had been built for her. He gave an "oof" of delight. Gertrude wished she could do that to Isaac, but she didn't want to startle him. Instead, she sat herself on the arm of his chair. He didn't even notice her. After a moment she reached down and took his hand into hers. He looked up and gave her a surprised smile followed by an awkward wink.

She thought it was the most reassuring thing she had ever seen and it made her smile.

She looked quickly at the three men; they were all so handsome, with their slick hair and distinguishing mustaches. And Mrs. de Camp was so pretty. Gertrude felt she must really stick out.

Mr. Heinlein slid some of the pulps out of the way and picked up a hardcover book. "*The Incomplete Enchanter* by L. Sprague de Camp and Fletcher Pratt. You've written a real book!'"

"Well, they just repackaged the Harold Shea stories we wrote for *Unknown*—my co-author Fletcher Pratt and I."

"Is it doing well?"

"Well enough. We had an offer to write something new or collect these stories. We decided to do this because Campbell was starting to think the character was his. He even brought in a terrible writer to write a new Shea story. May have killed the line. I don't know if I could do that. I mean, I'd love to write some Conan stories or Cthulu tales, but Howard and Lovecraft are dead. It's hard work to come up with a character that catches on. For example, I'd never touch Lazarus Long."

"But I've only written about him once, in 'Methuselah's Children.'"

"Obviously, though, you're going to write about him again, right? I'd read Lazarus Long stories forever. As long as you write them."

"I hadn't really thought about that." Heinlein turned the book over and over before flipping it open and paging through. "This is very nice."

"You know what I just found out?" Isaac asked Gertrude, but speaking loud enough for the others to know that they were to be part of the conversation. At the same time he reached for a cookie and began to chew on it.

She shook her head.

"Sprague was at the great Science Fiction Convention War of 1939."

"Really?" Gertrude said with genuine surprise, turning to Mr. de Camp. "I've heard so much about it."

"Well, it wasn't quite as exciting for me as it was for Isaac," he replied with a shrug. "Though I did see some papers flying and caught a bit of the disturbance."

As Gertrude turned back to Isaac, she caught, out of the corner of her eye, Mrs. de Camp open her mouth as if to inquire and across the room Mr. Heinlein shot her a warning expression and a quick hand gesture that made her mouth seem to pop shut in an instant.

"It's amazing," Isaac continued, not noticing. "We could have met years ago. If those putzes hadn't stolen our convention from us. You could have joined the Futurians."

Again she saw Mr. Heinlein try to cut off a question from Mrs. de Camp, but this time she wouldn't be stifled. "What's a Futurian?"

"Isaac's gang," Mr. Heinlein responded, emphasizing the mystique of the word "gang."

Isaac shifted and she had to let go of his hand. "Well, I wouldn't say it was a gang, per se. Just a group of like-minded individuals who liked to get together and talk about reading and writing scientific fiction. Or scientifiction as we used to call it, back in the old days."

"Because you're so old now," Gertrude scoffed.

"And you had a gang, too, Bob," Isaac continued over her. "I've heard all about the Mañana Literary Society out there in Hollywood."

"What was that?" Mr. de Camp asked the question this time.

"Well, after spending a little time out there and in the company of a lot of people with big plans but little motivation, I decided that there are only two kinds of people—those that say they're going to start writing tomorrow, and writers. Ergo, the Mañana Literary Society—for people who are going to start writing tomorrow."

Gertrude laughed politely while the others reacted as if this had been delivered by Groucho. She had to revise what she'd thought earlier about Mr. Heinlein. The other two men, including her husband, were handsome indeed, but Mr. Heinlein was, well, he was movie-star handsome. In fact, Gertrude would almost pay to see Mr. Heinlein and Mrs. de Camp in a movie together. She nearly said so but realized she would never be able to phrase it in a way that wouldn't end up mortifying her.

"So, you actually just sit around and talk about these scientific fiction stories?"

"Science fiction," Isaac corrected her.

"Is there really that much to talk about?"

Isaac looked over at Mr. Heinlein, who shrugged. "I guess so."

"Salons," Mrs. de Camp said, with a grand air of dawning realization. "You were holding salons. Like the writers do in Paris."

"Sure," Isaac said eagerly. Gertrude could tell when he used that particular tone that he didn't really know what the exact meaning of what had been said was, but that he would find out everything he could about it. Isaac could act obsessively like that when an idea intrigued him. Worrying it the way her old cat, Frieda, would stalk a mouse under the floorboards of their old house in Canada.

"There is no fan like a scientific fiction fan," Mr. Heinlein said, winking broadly at Mrs. de Camp. "John Campbell will receive dozens of letters because of a story I wrote, and debates will rage on issue after issue over the veracity of my ideas."

"But why?" Mrs. de Camp wanted to know.

"I think it's because we're living on the brink of what is known and what is about to be possible. Tomorrow, someone may split the atom or cure cancer. It's all about to happen. When I was a kid, no one could fly. Now we launch warplanes from carriers. In the next ten years, God willing, we win this war, I think those planes will be taking us to the moon. An incredible future is just waiting for us; about to unfold. Everyone feels it. I think what we do as writers is lay out a conceptual framework for people who want to build that bridge to tomorrow. We show, on paper, what might work and what might not. And more important, what the implications are of different choices we make about what kind of future we may have. I think what we're doing is helping inspire and guide people past the perils and pitfalls to a better day."

"How come you never had a gang?" Mrs. de Camp pinched her husband, who grinned.

"I don't know. I guess I always saw writing as a solitary pursuit."

"Well, here's your gang. You should have a name for this Philadelphia salon," Mrs. de Camp added with a sly grin and wink to Gertrude.

"Hey," Isaac said, taking the bait, "that's a great idea. How about the Philadelphia Poetical Foundation?"

"I don't write poetry," Mr. Heinlein said with a grunt.

"How about the Cosmic Realists?" Mr. de Camp chimed in.

"I know," Isaac shouted. "Campbell's Kamikazes. Since we're trying to take out the kamikaze fighters."

"Doesn't have much to do with writing," Mr. Heinlein said.

"I don't know," Mr. de Camp said, "all writers have a bit of the kamikaze in them, don't they?"

It grew quiet for a moment as if everyone was mulling over whether or not there was one name better than Campbell's Kamikazes or whether they actually needed a name or not. Suddenly, out of the dim part of the room, behind Gertrude, a voice spoke, startling her, for she had forgotten that Mrs. Heinlein was sitting in that corner, belching smoke like the dark chimney of a mysterious factory in a bad part of town.

"You chew with your mouth open," Mrs. Heinlein said, directed at Isaac. "You talk with your mouth open, too."

"Les!" Mr. Heinlein seemed to shoot straight up into a standing position. "Stop it." His tone was commanding, yet pleading. The expression on his face was of pain and familiarity.

"It's disgusting." Mrs. Heinlein shrugged and lit another cigarette.

"Isaac, I apologize." Mr. Heinlein stood up. "My wife hasn't been herself lately."

"I'm fine," Mrs. Heinlein said with a dismissive nod of her head. She met her husband's gaze. "I guess we're leaving."

She stood up.

"It's all right," Isaac insisted. "Really."

"I'm really sorry," came the apology again. Mrs. Heinlein silently mouthed her husband's words.

"Yes, I'm so sorry," Mrs. Heinlein said. "I forget how to act around other married couples sometimes. I forget what's expected. For example, are we the only ones who have an open marriage?"

Mrs. de Camp's hand flew to her mouth, but Gertrude could tell that it was more in shocked bemusement than that she was scandalized. Mr. Heinlein's face grew white except for twin spots of scarlet blazing across his cheekbones.

"I mean, it's open as far as Bob's concerned, but not so much for me if I try to be open with someone we know. Right, Bob?"

"Les! That's enough," he hissed. Mrs. Heinlein's gaze fell to the floor.

She expected him to be rough with her, but as Mr. Heinlein took his wife's arm, Gertrude couldn't help but notice that it was done with such tenderness that she suddenly felt sad for both of them. As he ushered her across the room, she flowed beside him in complete compliance, not looking at anyone else but her husband. As Mr. de Camp rose to lead them out, Mr. Heinlein paused for a moment. He looked at Isaac, gave a nod, and said, "The Kamikaze Group. How's that?"

"Good." Isaac grinned.

"Okay, then. Well, good night." He turned and let himself be shown out. Mrs. Heinlein gave a fluttering wave and a slight smile as if she weren't sure why she was being shuffled out, had forgotten that she was the cause of it.

Gertrude couldn't help but brush a few cookie crumbs off Isaac's shirt. He gave her a look of bemused indulgence. A few moments later she heard the thud of the heavy front door closing.

"Well, she's a charmer, isn't she?" Mrs. de Camp said right away. "I hope she didn't hurt your feelings."

Isaac shrugged. "It really is okay. Sometimes I chew with my mouth open."

"Still," Mrs. de Camp said, "there's no place for bad manners."

Mr. de Camp came back into the room as they heard the Heinleins' car start outside. "Anyone want a drink?"

"I guess we should be going, too," Gertrude replied before Isaac could, as she knew he would accept. Mr. de Camp insisted on calling a taxi for them and the four of them lingered on the front porch of Pennock Mansion while they waited. The spring air was cool, but rich with the promise of warm evenings ahead, filled with the fragrance of a thousand blossoming flowers.

"You know, Sprague," Isaac said at last. "What Bob was saying about helping build the future? I've never really thought about it before like that, but he's absolutely right. It's what we're doing here in Philadelphia. We're going to make the future come true here."

"It could work," Mr. de Camp said with a thoughtful nod. "In 399 BC the emperor Dionysius brought together the greatest artists of Syracuse. He didn't turn to his military advisers, or his tradesmen, he turned to the sculptors and the storytellers, the ones with imagination. He told them he wanted a great new weapon to use in the war that was coming with Carthage. You know what they gave him?"

"What?" Gertrude asked.

"The catapult. One of the greatest weapons ever created."

"How'd that work out for him?" Mrs. de Camp asked.

"Not so well. He never did rout the Carthaginians. But not because the catapult failed him. Because the imagination of those who used it was not the equal of those who created it. It was beyond the grasp of the soldiers of the time."

"Maybe you should call yourselves the Catapult Gang," Mrs. de Camp said as the taxi pulled up.

"Bob picked the Kamikaze Group, so that's what it is," he replied, giving her bottom a little squeeze right there in the open in front of everyone.

"Here's what I think," Isaac said, pausing on his way down the steps to the taxi. "I think we're going to give them their catapult and we're going to show them how to use it. We're going to save the world. I believe that. Especially with Bob at the helm."

Gertrude sat beside him in the cab while Isaac continued going on about the two men. Finally she sighed. "What is it about Mr. Heinlein?" she asked, a little exasperated.

Isaac seemed not to notice her tone of impatience, genuinely pleased to answer the question. "Bob? He's the best writer in all of sci-fi. He's amazing. Haven't you read his stuff? I've left it out for you."

"No. You know I like mysteries."

"Well, he's the best chance we have to be taken seriously. If he breaks out of the pulps, we all can." They rode on for a while. "You know, Campbell's run both Sprague and Bob in *Unknown*. He hasn't published me there yet."

She quietly placed her hand on top of his. "Does that matter?"

"All the best writers are in *Unknown*."

They entered the apartment, which was the largest one she had ever lived in but now felt humble compared to the de Camps' lodgings. Small as it was, Gertrude suddenly felt lost in it, unsure where to turn or what to do. Letting her coat slide to the floor, she walked into the bedroom and stared at her bed. Pretty, but nothing elegant. Then she caught a glimpse of herself in the shabby vanity across the room. She kept her thick dark hair short to keep it from getting too frizzy. Even so, she tried to pull a lock or two from either side to embrace her cheeks. Her lips looked thin even with lipstick. Not a face one would ever see in a movie.

She heard a *click* and a *clack*—a couple desultory pokes at the type-writer on the kitchen table. "Isaac?"

"Yes?" He was coming closer. "Yes?" Now he was just in the hallway behind her, grunting as he scooped to pick up her coat.

Gertrude turned around. "Do you want . . . ?"

"Do . . . you?"

"To . . ."

"If you . . ."

"I . . . Okay." She began to unbutton her blouse. Mrs. de Camp could probably do this with a few delicate flicks of the manicured nails of one hand while the other held a full martini glass. Gertrude's fingers felt stubby and uncoordinated.

"You're . . . sure?"

"Yes. Okay."

"Okay. Do you want me to turn off the lights?"

"Yes. Please."

EPISODE 7

BOB HEINLEIN HEARD the explosion as he crossed the marshy parking lot de Camp had dubbed the Swamp. Even as the klaxons began to ring out, he knew it was from the advanced materials lab and he began to run, the mud and muck sucking at his shoes until he finally reached the edge of the asphalt. He ran for several blocks pushing past sailors until he caught up with a base fire truck, siren screaming, rounding the corner onto Philip Avenue, and swung up onto the backboard as it slowed, hitching a ride. He ignored the outrage of the firemen hanging out the window yelling at him and leapt off finally, his gallop turning into a trot as it pulled up before the building—his building.

A small crowd of gawkers had assembled in front of the lab. Another fire truck was already on the scene, its crew forcibly ejecting his team of scientists and engineers, easily distinguished from the military by the white lab coats they wore, from the building as they protested loudly. Held back behind a line of Military Police, Heinlein could see the tall, absurdly thin frame of Leonard Meisel, his resident math genius, yelling at a stone-faced Marine in tandem with Hartley Bowen, his electronics guy. Near to those two stood Asimov, stocky Mutt to de Camp's lean Jeff, right beside him, watching with bemusement. Behind them he could see Tom Walb, easy to spot because he alone refused to wear a white coat over his expensive tailored duds, conversing with Bernie Zitin and Jake, the Negro engineer he had hired a few months ago. No one looked injured; furthermore Heinlein saw neither smoke nor fire.

He pushed through the throng until he reached one of the MPs. His staff saw him and began yelling for him almost in unison.

"What the hell's going on here, soldier?" Heinlein barked at the young man, his years as a naval commander still able to fill his voice with authoritative menace. The soldier's head snapped around and his eyes fixed warily on Heinlein's. "Sabotage," he said, then added, "sir."

"That's not true, Bob!" Meisel shouted.

"Len! Is everyone all right?"

The mathematician pushed up as far as the MP would tolerate. "Yeah. One of the cool room's compressors blew up. It must have overloaded or something. It wasn't even one of the inside ones."

Heinlein breathed a sigh of relief. None of his people was hurt. Thank Christ. He knew those compressors—great noisy monsters that roared and belched behind the building no matter the temperature of the room where they tested the effects of extreme cold on different types of gear.

"The eggheads are out of control," the first MP said snidely to the one next to him.

"Like hell!" Meisel began to peel off his lab coat. It was a ridiculous sight; the only threat those bony arms slipping from their sleeves posed to the soldier was if a sharp elbow caught him in the eye.

"Len! Settle yourself," Heinlein commanded, and the fight blew out of Meisel in an instant, like wind rushing from a deflating balloon. God love the man, he would have thrown a punch. But a slightly humiliated mathematician was far more useful to the Kamikaze Group than a hospitalized one. "Everyone just calm down!"

Someone he didn't recognize caught his eye and he left Meisel and the MP behind. The woman was sitting on the sidewalk across the street that ran parallel to the materials lab, her head between her hands. Heinlein approached her. "Hey," he asked. "Are you okay?"

"I'm lucky to be alive," she said, and then looked up at him. "Your boys almost blew me up."

Heinlein didn't recognize her. Furthermore, he couldn't remember the last time he'd seen someone as beautiful as she was. Brown hair, astray, swirled around her face and spilled over her shoulders. Her eyes were piercingly green, her skin as pale and smooth as a china doll's. The woman literally made him feel dizzy. He was sure she could tell, even as she continued to talk.

"I had just taken a shortcut behind your building when something exploded." The woman tried to smooth her hair. Heinlein noticed the large tear in her gray WAVES uniform dress a moment before she did, her hands moving to quickly cover the garter circling the thigh his eyes had fallen upon. "Really, Mr. Heinlein?"

"Just making sure you're okay," he tried to regroup, but that one quick sight of her flesh had momentarily unnerved him. "Do I know you?"

"Not yet," she replied. "I'm Virginia Gerstenfeld."

"Gerstenfeld?" Heinlein was confused. "But I'm supposed to get a biochemist named Lieutenant Gerstenfeld."

"You got me," the woman replied, extending a hand. "Pleased to meet you, boss."

"Nuts," he muttered. Offering his hand, he helped her to her feet. She was tall—almost as tall as he was. Her skirt fell open again as she stood. He held on to her hand—long fingers, strong, with no sign of a ring—for a moment longer than he should have.

At last, she slowly withdrew her hand from his and used it to gather the loose fabric of her skirt together. "I don't suppose your lab has much in the way of safety pins?"

"I'm sure we could rig up something. Once they let us back in."

"I think I better head over to the PX. Looks like it'll be a while before that happens."

She turned and began to walk away from him with a purpose that so many of the young career women of the day seemed to have. Her dress was pulled tightly against the curve of her backside and Heinlein felt himself staring helplessly again. The lady stopped and he looked up at the sky as she turned back toward him.

"By the way," she said, "you can call me Ginny."

"I will," he promised.

This time as Ginny strolled away he felt certain that she knew he was watching her. One of the firemen, walking back from checking the compressor, stopped in front of him. "You in charge?"

"Every now and then."

The fireman dropped a bent piece of metal into Heinlein's palm. "Someone slipped a wrench into the fan. Jammed everything up. You should tell your eggheads to be more careful with their tools."

An ugly murmur running through the crowd caught his attention. Tom Yani was being dragged out of the lab in handcuffs by two of the MPs. The group of sailors awaiting the arrival of the ship they were supposed to outfit stood on the steps of their barracks shouting, "Jap! Jap! Jap!" Heinlein recognized their leader, Olson, the chief petty officer, a big, ignorant moose of a man who took particular delight in taunting his staff.

"Goddammit!" Heinlein sprinted back to the front of the lab, catching up with the trio as they hit the sidewalk.

"Mr. Heinlein?" Yani's face was calm, but Heinlein could sense the stress in his voice.

"Easy now, soldier." Heinlein skidded to a halt. "Situation's under control."

"Someone stole our Nehi!" a voice from the mob called.

"This little Nip planted a bomb," the MP snarled at Heinlein.

"Like hell he did. Tom Yani's an architect, a damn good one. And he's doing more to whip the Japanese than you sure as hell have," Heinlein shot back. "A piece of shit compressor out back blew. Sounded a lot worse than it was."

De Camp and Asimov stepped up on either side of the small man. De Camp had met the electrical engineer while taking officer training classes at Dartmouth and had recommended him to Campbell. Yani had arrived in Philadelphia several months before de Camp. Since de Camp's appearance a few weeks ago, the two had gone to work redesigning airplane rudder controls so they would function better in the extreme cold weather conditions of the upper atmosphere. The room that simulated cold weather necessary to conduct their experiments, with climate controlled by one of the now-blown compressors, was their creation. The two men were very close. "He's as innocent as I am," de Camp insisted. "If you take him you take me, too."

"I can handle that," one of the MPs said, dropping Yani's arm.

Heinlein stepped between the two men, blocking the MP. The other scientists and engineers fell in behind de Camp and Asimov, while the soldiers and sailors who had been watching events unfold from across the street now began to surge forward, sensing a fight. Christ, Heinlein thought, how did I wind up on the wrong side of this one? I should be in uniform getting ready to fight, not looking out for a bunch of slide rule pushers. The answer, as it always was, was as close as his next breath. The tuberculosis that had forced him to resign his captain's commission back in '33 had scarred his lungs too badly for the Navy to ever accept him back in any other capacity than the one he was acting in now. Nevertheless, he held up his arms, blocking the MP's way to de Camp. "Ease off, Sergeant," he urged. "Unless you want to have a riot on your hands."

The MP looked around, then dropped his hand, almost unconsciously, to his sidearm. They were quickly being surrounded. Someone shoved Heinlein. He spun swiftly but couldn't see which of the sailors had done it. "Sergeant?" he called out. He was always up for a fight, but the last thing he wanted to do was start trading punches with a boy who was about to put his life on the line for his country.

The MP nodded to his partner and within a second or two they had

removed Yani's handcuffs. They gave him a little push away and Heinlein caught him as he stumbled. "Break it up!" the MP yelled at the
crowd. "Move it or lose it." The members of the mob shuffled uncomfortably. Taking on a bunch of scientists and engineers was one thing;
no one wanted to be on the wrong side of an angry MP. "Get your men
back inside," the sergeant growled, stepping forward and placing himself
between Heinlein and the sailors.

"Thanks." Heinlein gave a nod of his head, and his men, except for de
Camp and Asimov, filed sheepishly but quickly back in. The crowd still
milled about, anxious, unfulfilled, hurling humiliating words at the de-
parting men.

"Attention!" A voice rang out over the heads of the sailors, slicing
through the oaths with clarity and weight. The crowd fell silent and
began to part, clearing a path to the officer disembarking a jeep at its rear.
General Albert "Buddy" Scoles, the chief of base operations, was a large
man, fit and imposing. At the sight of him, Olson and his crew slipped
quietly back inside their barracks, no one wanting to be identified. In
moments, the sidewalk in front of the building was clear of everyone
but Heinlein, the two MPs frozen in their salutes, the jeep's driver, a
passenger in uniform, and Scoles. "Morning, Mr. Heinlein," the officer
said with a disdainful smirk. "Off to another great start, I see." He finally
saluted the poor MPs, who dropped their hands and as quickly as they
could, headed away to other business. Scoles nodded toward the building.
"Anyone hurt?"

"Just their pride," Heinlein replied, slipping the wrench into his
pocket. "And we're gonna need a new compressor."

"I'll see what we can do." Scoles rubbed his chin. "Listen, Heinlein.
The Navy's asked me to bring in a little more oversight of the lab. I'm
not taking anything away from you. But since we're both guests of the
Navy, I expect you to make him welcome, just as I'm going to." Scoles
was tolerant of Heinlein and his team, as much as a military man could
be of civilians under his command. Mutual friends had introduced him
to John Campbell in peacetime, and once war came, he'd taken Campbell's call and supported his suggestion to create a think tank. Scoles
seemed to enjoy his stash of oddballs. Every so often he'd drop by to rub

elbows with the writers, throwing story ideas at them in addition to discussing their outlandish weapon and defense system suggestions. But it was always clear, to Heinlein at least, if not the others, that they served at his pleasure.

"Of course," he replied.

After another moment surveying the scene, Scoles turned to the man sitting in the jeep and jerked a thumb toward Heinlein. "This is him," he said.

"I've read your stories," the stranger drawled in a thick Texan accent, as he unfurled himself from the car like a praying mantis emerging from the cover of leaves after a rain. As big as Scoles, this man was long, with limbs that lifted him up from his seat. He reached for Heinlein's hand and shook it in a grip like a python's. "I love how they all tie together. Like a history of the future."

"Thanks," Heinlein said, freeing his hand. "That's what I'm shooting for."

"Bob's the ringleader of my little freak show here," Scoles said. "He's the one who's going to make a ship disappear."

"Well, we're hoping to make it invisible to radar, at least. If their ships can't detect ours, they won't have time to launch kamikazes before we can take them out," Heinlein replied, still unsure who the new man was. Another hire, perhaps.

"Bob, this is Colonel Tom Slick, an old friend of mine."

The name meant nothing to Heinlein, but de Camp spoke up right away. "Tom Slick? From the Yale Loch Ness Monster Expedition?"

"Yup," was Slick's laconic reply.

De Camp nodded with approval.

"Tom's a big one for monsters and mysteries," Scoles said.

"Find any?"

"Mysteries? Yes. Monsters? Not yet. But I'm always looking."

"Colonel Slick's been with the War Production Board for a while now but the Navy finally got their hooks into him. Naval intelligence, to be exact. About time, too. They've come up against a little problem and he told me about it and I thought you and some of your boys might be able to help out a little bit."

"Anything we can do to help, we're always happy to do," Heinlein said.

"Why don't we go inside," Scoles said. "Unless you've created a monster of your own in there."

"Not that I know," Heinlein replied, ushering them through the door to the lab, above which one of his geniuses had painted, in Athenian lettering, the word ARGOS. "But it's still early."

A few moments later and the five men were sipping coffee in Heinlein's cramped office. Introductions had been made all around, though de Camp and Asimov hung back awkwardly, unsure of what the sudden appearance of these officers could ultimately mean for them.

"Sorry about the mess," Heinlein mumbled, sliding some papers around so everyone could sit. Notebooks filled with pages of schemes for walking tanks, flying aircraft carriers, and ray guns were swept aside. Scoles knocked over a pile of pulps which cascaded like a waterfall to the floor. "Research," Heinlein apologized, scooping up the copies of *Unknown* and *Astounding* as well as some of the crappier mags like *Wonder Stories* and *Startling Stories*.

Slick plucked a recent copy of *Amazing Stories* from Heinlein's new stack. A beautiful woman was being pulled through a hole in time by an alien being controlling a ray beam. Evidently the blonde had been plucked from her bed, for her otherwise nude body was barely draped by a silk pink sheet as she was "Kidnaped Into The Future."

Slick held it up. "Is this one of Campbell's magazines? He spelled 'kidnapped' wrong."

"No, that's Hugo's. I mean Palmer's. Hugo Gernsback was the first sci-fi pulp ed. He started *Amazing*—the first of all the science fiction pulps. It's what we all read growing up. But Ziff-Davis bought it from him and now Ray Palmer runs it. Hugo lost *Amazing* when he lost control."

"Of what?" Slick asked.

"The science fiction fan," Heinlein replied. "The most ravenously addicted creature any drug ever created. Once the fan gets a taste of the junk, his craving for it only grows."

"But the craving also spreads like an infection," de Camp continued.

"One fan spreads it to another and they both spread it to others. Readers become critics, writers, and artists."

"The next thing you know, they're forming clubs and holding conventions," Asimov chimed in. "Always trying to use their addiction to imagine the limits of science and technology."

"And how it affects people," Heinlein finished.

"I'm sold," Slick said, turning to Scoles.

"Was this an audition?" de Camp asked.

"More of a gut check." Slick shrugged off the question. "Mine."

"They're all yours." The general took a seat in the chair behind Heinlein's desk with a bemused look on his face. "For now."

Slick rolled up the mag and batted it against the open palm of his other hand. "A few months ago the Coast Guard arrested a German spy. A small fishing boat sighted a U-boat in Long Island Sound. Sometime later this man washed ashore near the North Fork. We've been able to piece together that the U-boat had docked at a small island and marooned him there. He had tried to swim from this speck of rock called Haimoni Island."

"Jesus Christ," Heinlein whispered, as an iciness flowed up from his bowels to clutch at his heart. A fragment of near-forgotten nightmare rose before his eyes, of terror and decay and living death, fighting for his life on a dank shore surrounded by an ink black sea. He placed his hands on the desk to steady himself. "What'd they find there?" he asked.

"Nothing." Slick shrugged. "An Army storage facility. From what I've been told, it was cleaned out for good about five years ago."

Heinlein pushed back the fear with inward relief. He would have bad dreams tonight, that was for sure, if not for the rest of the week. But at least that little outcropping of hell had been exorcised.

"But we don't think Haimoni Island was the objective."

"Why not?"

"Because of where the man came ashore. Shoreham, Long Island."

"Shoreham?"

"It's a resort town on Long Island," de Camp explained. "So what?"

"Any of you know who Nikola Tesla is?"

"Sure," Asimov said, in a tone that indicated he felt he was being patronized. Heinlein knew nothing irritated Asimov more or brought out his petulant side. "He's the inventor of the entire alternate current power grid. If Edison had had his way, every neighborhood would have its own little power station. But Tesla figured out how to deliver electricity over tremendous distances with little power decay."

"They say that he saw his first invention, the electric motor, appear to him in a single vision," de Camp said with a nod. "They say he's the original mad scientist."

"Was," Slick replied. "He died in New York this past January."

"Oh," de Camp said. "I didn't even know he was sick."

"Apparently, nobody did. He died nearly broke and alone at the age of eighty-six."

"What does he have to do with the spy?" Heinlein asked. "Did the spy kill him or something?"

"No. As far as we know, they never had any contact."

"So what do Tesla and your spy have to do with Shoreham?"

"In 1916, Tesla started construction on a project called Wardenclyffe Tower near Shoreham. It was supposed to be able to provide targeted communication wirelessly to any point around the globe. To land, sea, or air."

"That's impossible," Asimov said.

"J. P. Morgan didn't think so. He was Tesla's financier. Rumor has it that he pulled the plug when he asked Tesla how he was going to put meters on people's houses to bill them for this service and Tesla replied that it was to be free. So the project was never finished. Parts of the facility still stand to this day, and so do the rumors. Enough so that when a Nazi spy washed ashore not two miles from it, I was contacted—being something of an expert in the field of rumors.

"I don't think it's a coincidence. I think he was probably supposed to scout out the facility and see what he could find there, then maybe rendezvous with Tesla himself. If men like you and I hadn't heard about Tesla's death, I'm pretty sure he hadn't either."

"Why do you think the Nazis have an interest in Wardenclyffe?" Heinlein asked. "What are the rumors?"

"In the last year of his life Tesla began writing letters to people in government. Ours. Others. We don't know the extent of his communiqués. We do know he was trying to convince anyone and everyone that he had the knowledge to create a super-weapon. We don't know who he may have contacted. Or who may have tried to contact him. His last letters complained of being followed by spies."

Slick placed his attaché case on the desk. "On the day Tesla died, the FBI raided his apartment and carried off everything they could find, including things he had stored in storage facilities as well. Papers, drawings, notebooks, devices. Brought it all down to a huge warehouse on the West Side of New York." He opened up the brown leather case. "They were still going through it all when the spy washed ashore. It was the first place they brought me to after I was briefed. I have to tell you, there were dozens of G-men, poring through hundreds of pages of work—it covered the whole floor of the warehouse. Knowing what I knew about Shoreham, I went straight for the Wardenclyffe notes. The Feds hadn't even touched them yet."

Slick withdrew a thick leather folio and opened it up. The papers inside were aged and yellow. "Fellas, what I'm about to show you is top secret. Everything you want to know about Wardenclyffe Tower you'll find in here. I'm no engineer so it doesn't make sense to me but it might to you."

"May I?" Heinlein took up the binder. Flipping it open, he found a clipping from an old newspaper, a sketch unaccompanied by any article, of a mushroom-capped tower radiating powerful lightning bolts while the earth beneath the structure cracked open to release hell's flames. "This is Wardenclyffe Tower, I assume. It looks impressive, but how can you be certain that this is what your spy was after?"

"The exposure to the frigid waters was too much for him. He died soon after he was found. But he kept saying one word over and over again before he died. And that one word is what convinced me what he was after. 'Wunderwaffe.'"

Heinlein looked to Asimov, who provided the answer instantly. "Wonder weapon."

Scoles cleared his throat and spoke. "Intelligence reports that Hitler has a number of secret projects in development to create these wonder weapons. We've heard reports of radio-controlled rockets, megatanks. I've even seen a grainy photo of the Junkers Ju-390. Six giant engines, three under each wing. Nearly two hundred feet long. It's called the super-bomber. It's possible that it could make it all the way to New York or Washington, D.C., and then return to Berlin. If it ever gets airborne."

Asimov looked sickly. "The Nazis have a group of . . . us?"

Scoles nodded. "Let's hope my group is better than theirs."

Slick held out his hands upward in a gesture of helplessness. "There have been rumors ever since Wardenclyffe was shut down that Tesla was up to something else there other than trying to create a new form of electronic communications. Something potentially devastating. In these letters he wrote in the last year of his life he claimed to be able to use an invention of his to knock an entire fleet of aircraft from the skies or sink an armada in an instant. I believe that rumor and the Wardenclyffe technology are one and the same. I have to think that the Nazis know at least as much about it as I do. I need you to help me find out what happened at Wardenclyffe. We need to know why the Nazis consider it a *Wunderwaffe*. A wonder weapon."

EPISODE 8

HIS HANDS WERE aching, aching. Everything hurt.

The Commander, a fat old man, sat behind his functional metal desk and shuffled papers. Hubbard sat on a hard chair across the room, resisting the impulse to swivel. Through the window Hubbard could see the great expanse of clear blue Pacific water that lay beyond the docks at the San Diego shipyard. How easy it was to see himself upon those waves, sailing away from all his cares, alone and free.

The Commander finally finished rearranging his desk and held up one slip of paper. He cleared his throat as if what he was about to say had been stuck there and needed to be dislodged. "In the opinion of this court in the matter of Lieutenant Lafayette Ronald Hubbard and the Coronado Islands incident," he read, "the evidence and eyewitness testimonies of his officers and crew, as well as the crew of the various support vessels the Lieutenant called upon, including U.S. vessels and air support, lead us to consider this officer lacking in the essential qualities of judgment, leadership and cooperation. He acts without forethought as to probable results. He is believed to have been sincere in his efforts to make his ship efficient and ready. Not considered qualified for command or promotion at this time." He repeated the last sentence again as if he couldn't believe it. "Not considered qualified for command or promotion at this time."

Damn, his hands were killing him. He squeezed them together as hard as he could, trying to force the pain up and out.

With an exasperated groan, the Commander tossed the paper on the desk, removed his glasses, and rubbed his eyes. "You're to be placed on an indefinite leave until a place can be found for you on a ship large enough where nothing you do matters. And that's going to take a while because word's gotten out about you. No one wants to be put in the position of supervising you. There's a war on, in case you haven't heard, and this Navy's officers have better things to do than make sure you don't shell our own troops or invade another country on your own. Christ almighty, Ron! What the hell is wrong with you?"

"Nothing," Hubbard replied weakly, hating the sound of his own voice.

The Commander stared at him.

"Nothing, sir," he finished.

"This is the most mortifying thing you've ever done," the Commander said at last. "This reflects poorly on me. Everyone here's talking about you and that means that they're talking about me as well. After everything I did to help get you that command." He shook his head. "I guess you'll have time to write those silly little space stories of yours."

"They're not silly," Hubbard muttered.

"I have a suggestion for you. Why don't you return to your home in Seattle and be with your wife and your children? God only knows when was the last time you saw them. Don't look so wounded. I hear the stories about you gallivanting around with other women. What do you think that does to your poor wife?"

"We're separated," Hubbard said.

"What is that? That's bullshit. You marry someone, you have

children with someone, you stay with them. That's your responsibility as an adult. Not mucking about with anyone wearing a skirt that you can get your filthy paws on. You're not a young man anymore, Ron. You're an adult. You should start acting like one. I think you need to make a decision."

"About what?"

"About whether or not you're going to have a real career in the Navy or if you're going to continue to pursue writing your stupid space stories. You can't do both."

"They're not stupid."

"What have your stories ever done to save a life? How many Japanese or Germans have your stories killed? I never understood your desire to make up shit.

"The Navy is a career. A man's career, goddammit!" the Commander continued, slamming his fists on the desk, toppling a jar of pencils. "You're not Edgar Rice Burroughs or Zane Grey. You'll never be able to support yourself like they do, by writing. Don't you think if it was going to happen it would have already? At least they're writing books. All you're doing is getting your frivolous little stories printed in those cheap, tawdry"—he paused as if choking on the word—"pulps."

"They're real magazines."

"They are trash!"

Hubbard took a deep breath to push the pain and anger out, letting the view outside carry him away. He knew the sea would only turn deeper shades of blue the farther out he sailed alone. "Look," he said. "My writing work has nothing to do with my Navy career. I wasn't writing stories when I saw that U-boat."

"There was no U-boat."

"There was so. I saw it!"

"You were the only one!" the Commander thundered. "The only one! Why didn't your XO see it? Hell, not one man aboard *PC-815* saw it and you had them chasing it for days."

"I saw it," he replied weakly. "You have to believe me."

"How can I?"

"You're my father." Hubbard sighed. "You're supposed to." Suddenly he felt like he was seven years old again and responsible for leaving the gate open and letting the horse out.

Commander Harry Hubbard sat back in his chair and folded his thick arms across his chest. "That's your fallback position? My parental obligation to you?"

"It would be a nice surprise."

"How about not being discharged? Or not going to prison? Do you have any idea of the strings I had to pull, as your father, to keep those things from happening? That's what a father can do for his son. Now what are you going to do, as my son, to satisfy your filial obligation?"

"I don't know."

"That's not an answer."

"Dad," a bitter laugh slipped from his chest, "it's all I've got right now."

"You're always the big one for shooting off your mouth. Making up stories. Playing the hero. Now you've got nothing?"

"Look, I'm happy to not be going to jail, if that's what you want me to say. As far as the other things go? I'm a very successful pulp writer. I can crank out a story in a night and make seventy-five bucks from it. I'm good at writing, and I like doing it. Sure, it'd be great if I could do it full time, but I want to fight. I want to help win the war. So if that takes me away from Polly and the kids, and it means I don't write so much these days, then so be it. But don't get me wrong, I'm good at it. Someday, I could even be great at it. But I did see a U-boat, as sure as I'm sittin' here, and I hate the fact that you're sitting here acting all high and mighty as if you just saved my bacon when for all your medals and reputation, you're nothing but a paymaster and haven't set foot on a ship of your own since the last war." His knees groaned as he stood up; he'd been sitting in one position for too long. "And as for what I do with my wife and children, that's my business. I provide for them. My writing provides for them. Because God knows the Navy sure as hell isn't."

"Sit down, Ron," his father commanded.

"I'm thirty-three years old, for Christ's sake!"

"I'm giving you an order as a direct officer!"

"What are you going to do, Dad? Have me hauled away? Throw me in the brig for insubordination?" He looked around the tiny office—at all the papers, and the dark corners, and the open sea forever just out of reach. "God, to think I wanted to be like you. Some Navy career. Stuck in your little room day after day. No life. No adventure. Well, the Navy may not give me a ship of my own again, but I don't care. I'll serve on someone else's ship if they'll let me. Somebody's going to need a warm body, somewhere. And if that gets me out there, out where I can do some good, out where I can help someone, then so help me, that's what I'm going to do. Because one thing's for sure, Commander Hubbard, and that is that I am not going to end up like you."

"So that's what you've always thought about me?" The old man looked tired, whipped.

"No, Dad," Hubbard replied. "I wanted to be just like you until the moment you stopped believing in me. Then I realized, I'm not anything like you and I'm never going to be. Furthermore, I think that's a good thing."

"Ron, wait!" he heard his dad say, but his back was already to him and he was walking out the door and down the hallway and toward the light at the end of the hallway where the ocean waited beyond the dock. He heard his father call out one more time but he'd be damned if he ever looked back.

The heavy door crashed away from him and now he was outside, striking out with purpose across the street. Of course, that truck would have to stop for him. Nothing could touch him. Let the driver blast his horn and scream curses. He was invincible and the waves were driving him on.

Reaching the edge of the pier, he finally had to stop. For long moments he considered whether his momentum would allow him to keep going, to walk across the whitecaps until he began to sink and then to swim as if his strength would never fail him.

What if there had been no sub?

Hubbard swung around as if the words had been spoken out loud. There was no one nearby, even the truck had moved on.

There had been a sub.

The charts had indicated a known magnetic anomaly in that vicinity. Maybe that's why the compass had swung so wildly.

The compass had gone wild because a U-boat had passed beneath the ship's hull.

Had it?

The sonar operator and the hydroscope confirmed contact.

Weren't they new and untested? Wasn't he? Couldn't they have pinged a school of fish, and heard their own engines on the cans?

Those men were well trained.

Had he actually seen anything? An oil slick? A shadow below the surface? A periscope?

This is how a war against an invisible enemy is fought. By intuition. By instincts. By guts.

Don't you want to see her? Be with her? Make love to her, right now?

Who?

Sara?

No.

You can't lie to me.

"Yes," he whispered. God, he wanted to be with her so bad. But he wasn't going back there, wasn't going to go back to that house.

He thought of calling her, of having her meet him in a hotel near the base, but he knew she wouldn't leave the crazy stuff behind. And who's to know that Jack wouldn't decide to come along too? Hubbard began to feel a little woozy and sat down on the seawall, his feet dangling ten feet above the water that lapped against the support beams. Bits of wood and rubber trash bobbed up and down in the little surf. He found himself wondering if those pieces of refuse were caught there forever or if the next time would drag them back out and deposit them against some other barrier to rest.

All he'd wanted was a little adventure and look how it turned out. Another piece of trash trapped on the seawall. This was not how The Flash was supposed to end up.

The Flash.

He grinned; he hadn't called himself by that silly nickname in years. But that's what he had gone by. The Flash. The fastest pulp writer in the West. And East, for that matter.

At least he hadn't been imprisoned. He didn't trust that he could thank the old man for that, so he sent a silent thanks out to the universe. He was on leave. No assignment. No one expected anything from him.

His grin widened. Not a bad spot to be in, when you thought about it. Lots of time on his hands, a few ideas in his notebooks, he could turn out a pretty penny if he sat down and started writing hard with all this free time.

If only his hands didn't hurt so goddamned much.

A book might be the thing. He knew that Heinlein hadn't been able to pull that off yet. None of the others had either. Not Cartmill, not Boucher, not any of Heinlein's little Hollywood club, that group of science fiction sycophants. Maybe that was the thing to do. To be the first of them all to really write one hell of a novel. To see his work in a bookstore, in a library, now wouldn't that be a hell of a thing?

Writing a book, an actual novel, that could take a little time, though. A story was easy. A night or two, a week at the most. A few thousand words. Not the necessary tens of thousands. He'd need some solitude for that. Someplace with no distractions. No booze. No broads. Well, at least no Sara.

He thought about heading home, to Seattle, but Polly had closed the door to him. He knew that he could sweet-talk his way back in, but that would do more harm than good, in the end. It was better to just keep sending her the checks and the kids the gifts.

Hubbard had fond memories of Montana and hadn't been there in ages. Maybe he could hole up in a cabin there for a month or two. After all, a book couldn't take that long to write, and sooner or later the Navy was going to realize he was on the payroll but not doing anything.

It came to him and he smiled all over again.

There was one place where he was always productive, in fact, never more productive. It was as if something in the air, or the water, primed his pumps and kept him going. It was a good place to have money, but a guy could get by there without too much either. He had friends there. People who would be happy to see him.

And if there were going to be broads, at least they wouldn't be the demanding type.

He quickly took stock of his finances and then laughed. He couldn't very well count on getting his back pay from the paymaster now. Fifty yards out, a sea lion drifting by barked at him in response. It was as if the universe had answered his gratitude with a "you're welcome." There was bound to be some check from Campbell waiting for him back at his apartment.

Hubbard rose and brushed his pants off. Then he saluted the old bull, who flipped underwater with a splash and a return of the salute with his back flippers.

The grin wouldn't leave his face. It was high time for a little adventure.

EPISODE 9

ISAAC SHUFFLED THROUGH his share of the papers Heinlein had assigned to him. "God," he groaned to Gertrude, "it's too bad I didn't pick up more Russian from my parents."

"Why?" She came out of the bedroom buttoning up her nightgown.

"Most of these notes Tesla kept about the project appear to be written in Cyrillic. Tesla was a Serb. It's close enough to the little Russian I understand to make me know that I wish I knew more. Judah always warned me someday I'd need to know the mother tongue. But no, I insisted, we're in America now. English is all I'll ever need. Pretty arrogant for a six-year-old. Here's all I can remember. *Hello. Goodbye. We have no grain to sell. The Cossacks are coming.* Not much use now, I'm afraid."

Gertrude looked over his shoulder. "Maybe you could have Judah translate this for you?"

"I'm sure he'd love that. 'Vhat,'" Isaac imitated his father, "'I have a candy store to run. You vant I should go out of business doing your job now?'" He caught her smile as he turned back to the papers.

"Well," she said, "Why don't you get ready for bed?" she asked. "It's already late."

"I've got a long night ahead of me," he replied. "There's got to be something here."

"Afraid to disappoint Mr. Heinlein?"

"No," he insisted. "It's my job."

"Well." She sighed, lifting the copper teakettle they had received as a wedding gift from the stove just as it was on the verge of whistling. She knew that it was a sound he hated. "There's always some reason."

Isaac felt a touch of iciness in her tone. "What do you mean?"

She dipped the tea bag she had saved from an earlier pot into her cup and then poured the hot water in. She put the kettle back down on the stove's still-bright flame. "I don't know, Isaac."

"The stove's still on," he pointed out.

"You're always working on something," she said, ignoring him and adding some honey to the tea.

Fascinated, he watched as the steam began to vent from the kettle's spout.

"If you're not working on stuff for Mr. Heinlein, then you're writing your own stories."

"I've got to make a living," he said. "You have to understand that. If I don't write these things, they don't get written."

"I understand," she said, blowing across the surface of her cup. "But I wish you'd spend some more time here in Philadelphia."

The teakettle began to whistle, slowly at first, then growing louder.

"Could you turn off the burner, please?" he asked.

She took a sip of her tea. "I'm here all alone," she said. "You're at the Navy Yard six days a week, sometimes seven, and when you get home you just sit here at the table all night, making more noise on the typewriter than this teakettle."

"I have a lot of ideas," he said. "Would you please turn that off?" The sound was beginning to pierce his temples. "Well, maybe you can help me with my work," he suggested, though he wasn't sure exactly how. He did his own typing.

"Oh, Isaac," she said, "I'd love to, but I don't even understand it."

"I don't mean the Kamikaze Group stuff," he said. "You can help me with my writing. You know, give me ideas and stuff."

"That's what I meant," she said. "I don't understand your writing. I don't understand any of it. I mean, I read it and everything, but I don't understand why you and your friends are so caught up in it. It's all you ever talk about with them. Spaceships and robots and the future."

"It's not all we talk about."

"It always comes back to that. Even when you're talking about the war. Even when you're talking about us."

"Okay," he said, trying to reassure her over the din of the whistle. "I'll stop doing that. Next time we get together with your friends, you watch. I'll just talk about sports like everybody else."

"I don't know anyone here, Isaac!" she snapped. "That's part of the problem!"

He stood up and walked toward her, turning the dial on the burner off, and removing the offending teakettle from the stove. "Sure you do," he said. "There's Catherine."

Isaac was surprised at how harsh her laugh was in response.

"Mrs. de Camp? She might as well be one of your Martians for as much as I have in common with her. And don't even get me started on Mr. Heinlein's wife. I really do think she might be from outer space. We haven't even gone out together to eat in a restaurant for weeks and weeks."

"It's expensive to eat out," he said.

"I'm not your chef," she shot back.

"Fine. Let's go out tomorrow."

"I don't want to go out tomorrow, Isaac. Aren't you listening to me?"

"I thought I was."

"I'm not talking about going out. I'm saying that you brought me down here to Philadelphia and you've practically abandoned me here. Do you know I didn't speak to one person today? Not a one? The last person I spoke to other than you was the grocer and that was two days ago." She put her hand over her mouth and tears spilled over her eyelashes.

Isaac put a hand on her shoulder. The move felt clumsy and she offered no reaction to its being there, so after a moment, he dropped it back to his side.

"I hate it here," she said.

"I'm sorry."

"I miss my parents. I never hear from my brother now he's in the Army. I don't even know if he's alive."

"Of course he is. You would have heard . . ."

The look of anger she flashed at him caused his mouth to shut instantly as if a survival instinct had kicked in. "Maybe I should just go home."

"You are home."

"Back to New York," she cried. "Maybe I should go stay with my mother for a little while until you're not working so hard."

"But I don't want you to do that," he protested.

"I know you don't," she said. "I'm just a terrible wife. I shouldn't even try."

"You're not," he insisted. Now he felt like crying.

"I am. I can tell. You're always walking around sighing and you're just so miserable all the time."

"But not because of you. I'm just, you know, afraid I'll get drafted and I need to stockpile these stories in case I go away so you have something to sell."

"I'm just a burden to you."

"Gertie! You shouldn't feel that way. You're not at all. I'd be lost without you."

"Without me to take care of you, you mean."

"That's not it at all."

"I'm sorry, Isaac," she said. "I just need a little time. Or something."

She slipped past him. He didn't turn, and an instant later he heard the bedroom door click shut. Isaac ran both hands through his hair, clutching at it, yanking it until his scalp hurt. Then he walked to the door and listened for a moment. The sound of her sobbing made his heart ache and he leaned his head against the cool wood. "Gertrude?" he whispered. "Are you leaving me?" But he hadn't spoken the words loud enough for her to hear. After a few more wordless moments Isaac went back to the little kitchen table and sat down.

The words on the papers, which minutes ago had seemed merely indecipherable, were now complete and absolute mute abstractions, separated from all meaning. Scratches from a code for which his mind held no Rosetta Stone.

"I don't write about Martians," he muttered. "Not yet, anyway." Then he thought to himself, I wonder how Martian couples would argue? He filed it in the back of his head as a notion that needed to bake for a while.

Sometimes he was surprised at how little he knew about Gertie. They'd met on a blind date. Freddie Pohl had set them up, telling him that Doë knew the perfect girl for him. He'd never had much luck with women; he certainly wasn't as dapper as Pohl. He'd been warned not to talk too much that evening and so he hadn't. And that seemed to be exactly the right move, because Gertie had allowed him to kiss her good night, and agreed to a second date.

Isaac found himself thinking about their argument, wondering what he had done to set her off. "How am I supposed to know she's so miserable if she doesn't tell me?" he heard himself say quietly. "I'm not a mind reader." Maybe the Martians were, though. It would make for an incredible argument if the Martian husband always knew what his Martian wife was thinking and feeling and about to say next. His fingers found his pencil, and before he knew it he was scratching down a few ideas on the notepad he always kept nearby.

The Martians would need their own language, of course. Maybe telepaths would communicate in images and emotions instead of language. After all, language was just a construction, an inconvenient means of expression. A shared map of the language of the mind for which two partners hopefully had the key.

Isaac's pencil snapped.

He slid one of Tesla's yellowed pieces of paper back toward him and the letters swam into focus. Then Isaac rose and picked up the telephone, asking the operator to place a call for him.

"Hello?" a woman said at the other end.

"Um, hello, um, Mrs. Heinlein," he stammered. "This is Isaac. Isaac Asimov."

There was a long silence and he was about to repeat himself, when he finally heard her say, "Yes?"

"Hi. I was wondering if I could speak with Bob?"

Another lengthy pause. Isaac heard her exhale and could almost smell the cigarette smoke from across town.

"He's still at the office."

Isaac looked at the clock. It was ten thirteen p.m. "Ah," he replied. "Okay. I'll give him a call there."

Without a goodbye, Leslyn hung up on her end. Isaac tapped the hook a few times to raise the operator, while wondering what a Martian telepath might make of Leslyn Heinlein's mind. It might make him cancel any invasion plans. After giving the number for the base, Isaac waited to be connected through several switchboards until finally he heard Bob's tired voice answer the ringing at his end.

"Bob," he said, excitedly, "it's Isaac."

"Hey, Isaac," Bob replied. He sounded tired. "You making any progress with your cut of the papers? God knows I'm not."

"I think I know why," Isaac said. "There's a problem. Do you know anyone who's good with codes?"

Bob was silent nearly as long as his wife had been to the point Isaac began to wonder whether or not phone pauses were a Heinlein family trait. Finally, he spoke. "Yes," he said. "Come to think of it, I know one of the best code men in the world. Why?"

"Because I think what we've got here is a code disguised to look like Cyrillic. That's why none of the words look like real words to me. Because they're not."

"You sure?"

"Pretty sure."

"Okay," Bob said, a snap in his voice as if he'd been reinvigorated. "We need to move on this. I'll pick you up. How quickly can you be ready to go?"

"Go where?"

"We've got to round up de Camp on the way. I'll swing by and pick him up first. Are you ready to go? I'll pick you up in half an hour." Then Bob hung up.

Isaac collected his share of the papers and put them in the envelope Bob had given him earlier that afternoon. Then he closed the notebook he'd been writing his story notes in, too. Gertie wouldn't be pleased to see their argument was the inspiration for his latest story.

He thought about going into the bedroom and changing, but he couldn't hear a sound through the door and figured she must have fallen asleep. It wouldn't do to wake her. Quickly, he scrawled a note explaining that he had to go away on business. He made sure to write "I love you" at the bottom and underlined "love" three times. Then he went to the closet and threw on his jacket and trotted down the flights of stairs to wait on the stoop outside. Soon enough Bob pulled up in his Chrysler.

It was only later, after they had picked up Sprague who was now slumbering in the backseat, that Isaac, watching the lights whiz past on the New Jersey Turnpike, realized he should have invited Gertie to come to New York with him.

She would have liked that.

EPISODE 10

"MYSTERIES ARE NEVER exciting once they're solved." Walter Gibson lifted his eyes from the Tesla papers he'd spread out on his table. Behind the glasses, his eyes were startlingly blue and piercing. "Are you sure you want me to do this?"

When his friend first opened the door, Heinlein had been taken aback by his appearance. Not only had Gibson's hair turned completely, dashingly, silver in the six years since Heinlein had last seen him, but he seemed smaller, as if the core of his inner being generated an intense gravity field that was pulling his shoulders, neck, and extremities inward. He reminded himself that the writer was nearly fifty. "If you're not too busy," he replied.

"Busy?" Gibson laughed. "I'm on vacation."

"Walter Gibson doesn't take vacations. I thought that might be the only word in the English language you didn't know how to spell." Heinlein noticed the other younger men were awestruck in the presence of the greatest living pulp writer. They snuck furtive glances around

Gibson's Greenwich Village townhouse at his incredible collection of magic paraphernalia and *The Shadow* memorabilia.

"It's a situation of my own making, actually." The writer pried open a fresh pouch of tobacco, rolled it deftly into a cigarette in one hand, and then lit it with a small burst of fire he seemed to pull out of thin air; the scent was uniquely, reassuringly Gibson's. "At the height of *The Shadow*'s popularity it was being published bimonthly." He looked sharply over his glasses at the two young men. "That's two books of forty thousand words apiece a month." De Camp and Asimov nearly gasped in appreciation. "Not including the radio shows, comic strips, and articles about magic," he added, with a mischievous wink to Heinlein. "But then, after the hoax, Orson got the call to go to Hollywood, which is what he really wanted all along."

"Were you there for it?" de Camp eagerly asked.

"The Martian invasion? Of course not. But Orson told me all about it. He said there were three rules for a successful hoax. You need to be able to bluff your way out of hell. You need to have a pretty girl around to distract attention. And you need to have an audience that wants to believe."

Gibson took a sip of coffee. "So the new radio show people didn't want me writing *The Shadow* plays anymore, if you can believe it. When the war hit and the paper shortages started, Street & Smith had to decide which mags to put their precious ink towards, and they had to go by sales. You young fellas won out and *The Shadow* got demoted to once a month. Well, when that happened, Nanovic, my ed—you young fellas know who that is?"

De Camp nodded again. Asimov seemed distracted by something in the corner.

"Well, he said he'd quit before that happened, so they fired old John."

Now Heinlein nearly gasped. He hadn't known about that. Nanovic had been around for so long it was hard to imagine the pulps without him.

"Don't you worry about John," Gibson continued. "He's got a PR job now. Tells me it pays better and he doesn't have to worry about other writers missing deadlines anymore. Thinks it's added twenty years to his life expectancy.

"Anyway, I'd been writing two books a month for so long that when the word came down from on high, Street & Smith had quite a backlog of my stories to run through before they needed any more. That was fine with them since they'd already paid for them. That meant they didn't have to pay me for quite a while. I've been on vacation for two months already, and by my count, there's three more months of stories to go before I get called up out of the bullpen again. Same thing goes for the comic strip. So here I am. A victim of my own success."

"That chicken hasn't moved since we got here," Asimov said, pointing out the bird that sat in the gloom of a corner.

"Is that China Boy?" Heinlein said, delighted.

"In the flesh." Gibson rose. Clucking gently, he crossed the room and picked up the white-feathered object.

"I didn't know chickens had such long life spans," Asimov said.

"They don't!" Gibson tossed the chicken to Asimov like a football. The younger man shrieked and shielded his face, as the bird bounced off his raised forearms with a dull thud, then fell to his lap. "Thing's been dead for years now. Litzka had him stuffed. Still talks to him sometimes. Won't take him on tour anymore, though," he added sadly.

"Is that where she is now?" Heinlein asked, chuckling at Asimov as he timidly poked at the stuffed rooster.

"Yeah, some USO tour with Blackstone and his magic show. Somewhere. Out there." He waved his hand.

Heinlein quickly changed the subject. "How's your boy? Robert, right?"

"He's in school, so he stays with his mother until that's over. I'll see him during the summer. I have a place in Maine that I go up to when it's warmer and he likes to come up there. Hopefully at some point this summer I'll be able to see both Litzka and Robert." He gave an involuntary sigh.

Heinlein, feeling bad at having thoroughly depressed their host, tried again. "The new digs are pretty swell."

"Yeah. I like the energy of the Village. Some great jazz down here after dark. You listen to jazz?"

"Not so much."

"Good stuff. You know, they make it up as they play? First-draft music. Kind of like pulps. Plus it's cheaper."

"The jazz?"

"No. The townhouse."

"Ah."

They were interrupted by a quick shriek. Asimov had swept aside one of the drapes to look out the back window and something he had seen startled him. "The Shadow!" he stammered.

Heinlein walked over to the window and saw his reflection in the glass. Then he took an abrupt step back. Red eyes stared back at him from under the brim of a black slouch hat. Twin .45s were pointed at his chest, and on one of the fingers of the right hand, a huge gemstone glittered. "Christ! It's The Shadow!"

Gibson laughed as happily as a child and joined Heinlein's side. By now it was obvious that the shape wasn't moving. "Not The Shadow," the writer chortled. "Pepper's Ghost."

"What's that?" Asimov asked, stepping up to take a look.

"An optical illusion. Created by a Brit by the name of John Pepper. There's a mirror behind the window that's reflecting a small model of The Shadow back into the room."

Heinlein looked out the other window and could see a small box affixed to the left side of the frame. Inside the box, protected by a glass mirror, was a dummy version of The Shadow.

Gibson continued, "Used to be used as a spiritualism stage act, but I like the static effect here. And I'm the first person to adapt it so it can be done in broad daylight. Looks like he's standing right outside the window, doesn't it?"

"Impressive as hell." Heinlein nodded.

Gibson crossed the room and Heinlein couldn't help but notice that his left foot dragged a bit. "You're limping?" he asked.

"Yeah. Had a car accident a few years ago. Left me banged up."

De Camp looked up from the issue of *The Shadow* he'd been thumbing through. Heinlein couldn't help but smile when he caught the cover title, "The Golden Vulture."

"A bad one?" de Camp asked.

"Pretty bad," Gibson muttered, groaning slightly as he lowered himself into the chair. He spread the papers across the table but stared down as if looking through them. "You know, Bob, I've been following your stories in *Astounding* and *Unknown*. You've turned into one hell of a writer."

Heinlein shrugged. "For the pulps."

Gibson turned to the others and pointed at Heinlein. "You know when I met him he was digging graves? Now look at you. I'm betting the slicks pick you up before too long."

"I don't think *Collier's* is ever going to publish scientific fiction," Heinlein replied with a little laugh, trying to imagine it.

"Have you ever read my stories?" Asimov said eagerly.

"You a writer?" Gibson looked at him sharply.

Asimov seemed to deflate. "We all are."

Gibson shook his head. "If the slicks are going to stay alive they're going to publish what's good and what sells. And that's you, Bob."

"Well, that'll be a great call from my agent someday."

"An agent?" Gibson seemed genuinely surprised. "You actually have an agent?"

Bob felt embarrassed. "Well, yeah, Walter. You need one these days. If you don't have your own mag. There's so many different mags out there, who's got time to submit to them all but an agent?"

"An agent." Gibson shook his head. Then he looked toward Asimov. "Kid, you got an agent, too?"

"Well, yeah," Asimov stammered. "We all do."

"Pulp writers with agents. What is the world coming to?"

"You should have one, Walt. I'd be happy to introduce you to mine."

"Hmph." Gibson lit up another cigarette, then scanned one of the pages. "Let's take a look at your little mystery."

Heinlein gave Asimov a small nod and the kid had a seat across from Gibson. "It's some kind of code using Cyrillic, but I can't figure it out."

"Cyrillic is a wonderful language for coding," Gibson interrupted as if Asimov wasn't speaking, "because there are so many variations of it. It's a combination of Greek and Latin. The great thing about it is that there are thirty-three letters as opposed to our familiar twenty-six.

Now some of those letters are phonetic consolidations, such as 'sh' or the y-ee sound in a word like 'boy.' Since there are versions for a dozen different countries, plus the ancient ones before Czar Peter standardized the Russian alphabet, there are literally dozens of different ways Cyrillic can be used as a code. Forwards and backwards, for example, or using an offset code." He winked at Heinlein. "Unfortunately, I can't read Cyrillic."

"But can you help us figure out which version this . . ."

"Fortunately," Gibson cut Asimov off again, "this isn't Cyrillic. It's not even a code."

"Of course it is," Asimov protested. "These are definitely Cyrillic . . ."

"'Yesterday Commander Peary and I lunched together,'" Gibson read loudly.

Asimov's face turned red.

"'I had the roast beef. Later that night I had indigestion.'" He tossed the paper onto the table and began to laugh so hard he had to wipe the tear from the corner of his eye. "It's not a code. It looks like Cyrillic. Hell, it even looks like coded Cyrillic. But this is simply English written with Cyrillic letters."

"Really?" Heinlein picked up the paper Gibson had just sent sailing his way. The words, which moments before had appeared to be nothing more than gibberish, suddenly swam into focus with new meaning. Even with the use of some strange-looking characters, words emerged. "'Soon,'" he read slowly. "'Cmdr. Peary departs and he carries my hopes along with him.' Unbelievable. Seriously, Isaac?"

"I . . . I'm sorry," the young man said. "I was sure it was a code."

"Walter. I'm sorry it wasn't more of a challenge."

Gibson was scanning some of the other papers, lips moving silently as he translated on the fly. He waved a distracted hand at Heinlein.

Heinlein rose and indicated to his companions that they should do the same. "We should get out of your hair," he said.

Gibson looked up at him. "You didn't tell me whose papers these are. One of your scientific fiction friends, I hope?"

"I'm not at liberty—" Heinlein began, but this time it was Asimov's turn to interrupt.

"Nikola Tesla," he said proudly.

Heinlein shot him a look and Asimov's mouth snapped shut.

"The scientist," Gibson said. "Not a writer at all. A real scientist." He removed his glasses and polished them with deliberate intent, checking them repeatedly until they seemed to satisfy him.

"Yeah." Heinlein nodded. "Why?"

"The words 'directed electron force used as a weapon' just kind of jump out at you," Gibson said, referring to the paper he held. "Makes me wonder what's real and what's, y'know, pulp."

"This is all real, Walter."

"Hmph." Gibson picked up the page again.

"Walter. What did you read?"

Gibson cleared his throat and read. " 'Today's newspaper reports confirm the terrible events which happened yesterday. Until today I have not fully understood the capabilities of the device as a directed electron force used as a weapon. I have to be more careful.' That's where it ends. It's dated July 1, 1908."

"What do you think happened 'yesterday'?" de Camp asked, his voice barely a whisper.

"I don't know. It doesn't say. But here's something interesting."

"What?"

"Lyman Binch."

"What?"

"You know that name, right?"

Heinlein and de Camp nodded. Asimov shrugged.

"His name is right here."

"Interesting."

"Who's Lyman Binch?" Asimov asked, nervous at being left out.

"You've never heard of Lyman Binch?" De Camp was incredulous.

"A writer?" Asimov was hopeful.

"He was Thomas Edison's heir apparent," de Camp explained. "Involved in all aspects of Edison's research. Everyone thought he'd run General Electric one day, but board politics seem to have defeated him, relegated him to research. He used to be in the papers a lot, but nowadays, not so much. Not sure how he's connected to Tesla."

Gibson's fingers were drumming lightly and arrhythmically on the tabletop. Heinlein recognized the action, he did the same thing—Walter was typing out their dialogue and his thoughts, an unconscious reflex. "Apparently he spent his apprenticeship with Tesla."

"Before going to work for Edison? I thought Tesla and Edison were mortal enemies."

"They were. But there's nothing like hiring one of a competitor's employees to learn their secrets."

"General Electric has millions of dollars in contracts with the military. I'm betting Mr. Binch will see us if we get Colonel Slick to arrange it." Heinlein picked up the phone. "I'll call Campbell, he'll find Slick."

"I'll hit the library," de Camp said. "If something terrible happened in June of '08 it ought to be in an old newspaper."

"I'll go with you and see what I can learn about Wardenclyffe," Asimov added.

"As long as it ain't in Cyrillic." Gibson laughed, choking on his own cigarette smoke.

Asimov's jaw clenched.

"Okay," Heinlein said. "Sounds like a plan. The Army's given Campbell an office in the Empire State Building to use for his brain tank. We might as well take advantage of that." He glanced at his watch. "It's a little after ten now. Let's meet up there. Room 6217."

"Is that on the sixty-second floor?" Isaac asked, graying visibly.

"Yeah. Problem with that?"

"I don't like heights."

"Seriously?"

"Yeah, I hate 'em."

"Fine. You can wait in the lobby. And let's hope you never have to fly."

"Oh, I never will." Isaac shook his head.

"So, de Camp, we'll meet you in 6217 at 1700 hours. That's five p.m., Isaac."

"I know!"

Heinlein made his phone calls as Gibson showed the two younger men out. When Gibson reentered the living room he flopped down on the sofa while the older man sat in his familiar chair.

"I have a new idea for a magic trick." Gibson picked up a deck of cards from the side table and began to shuffle them, fanning them out and making them dance from one hand to the other. "You've seen the bit where a magician calls someone up on stage and has him pick a card and then tells him what it is. Oldest trick in the book. I want the magician to pass out all fifty-two cards to people in the audience without looking at them, and then tell each person which card they're holding. That's what I'm trying to figure out now."

Bob cleared his throat. "Sounds amazing."

Gibson floated a card through the air. "What's really on your mind, Bob?"

"I've seen you looking better, Walter."

"You've seen me looking worse, too."

"True. So what are you going to do with yourself the rest of the day?"

"Guess I'll write something."

"A Shadow story no one will pay you for? That doesn't sound like the Walter Gibson I know."

"Maybe I should try my hand at some scientifiction," Gibson replied. "It's all anybody wants. And after all, if you can do it . . ."

Heinlein grinned back at him. "Why don't you come with me?"

The coin vanished again into thin air.

"By the looks of things here you haven't been out in quite a while."

"By the looks of what things?"

"The Chinese take-out boxes in the trash and icebox. The nearly empty bottles of booze on the sidecar. The stack of newspapers by the door. My uncle Joe did the same thing. He didn't leave the house for three years."

"I was out yesterday," Gibson protested.

"To get that new pouch of tobacco you opened. Did you go anywhere else but the smoke shop?"

"Maybe you should stop writing scientifiction and start writing mysteries."

"C'mon, Walt. You're a bit of a shut-in, if I'm not mistaken. It's obvious."

"Well, what do you expect?" Gibson snapped. "It turns out I'm too old to be relevant to the war that everybody else is fighting."

"Come on, then. Come with me and let's go see Mr. Binch about his terrible thing. Let's go solve a mystery."

"I don't know. My leg is killing me."

"I've got Uncle Sam's money in my pocket. We'll take a cab." Heinlein held his hands apart in a pleading gesture.

Gibson stubbed out the cigarette. He groaned as he stood up. "Ah, these old bones." He limped to the umbrella stand, an old elephant foot, and pulled out a wooden cane with a silver handle. "Why not?"

"That must have been some accident."

"It was."

"I hope nobody else was hurt."

Gibson shrugged. "You coming or not?"

Outside on Tenth Street they hailed a cab and Heinlein helped Gibson in. "Empire State Building," he told the driver.

"I thought we were going to the General Electric office?" Gibson said.

"I have to stop by Campbell's war office," Heinlein replied. "He told me to pick up a package there. By then he'll have had Slick set up our meeting with Binch."

"What's the pickup?"

"I don't know."

For the first years after its completion, the great building on 34th Street had had a hard time finding renters. Once war began, the U.S. Army became its primary tenant and now the Empire State Building was crawling with soldiers and Army officers. Heinlein told the driver to wait for them, flashed his badge at the front desk, and soon he and Gibson were on the elevator. He felt the pit of his stomach drop to somewhere around his knees as the car leaped skywards. He'd never been this high in a building before. It was kind of exciting.

"Want to drop by the eighty-sixth floor and say hello to Lester Dent?" Gibson asked with a wink and a smile.

"You mean Doc Savage?"

"Same thing these days, from what I hear."

"Well, one of them's pulp and the other's real."

"Which one was that again?"

"Right. Hate to break it to you, Walt, but the eighty-sixth floor is the Observation Deck. Dent got that wrong."

"Or maybe that's what Doc Savage wants you to think."

The doors swung back to reveal the sixty-second floor. They walked slowly down the long bronze and marble corridor, turning corner after corner until they finally arrived at the door of the room they were looking for. There were no lights on behind the dark frosted glass. Heinlein knocked quietly, but there was no answer. He put his hand on the knob. It twisted easily and the door swung open. "Hello?"

The shades were drawn in the dim office.

"Do you hear that?" Gibson whispered.

"Yeah, what the hell is that?" he whispered back. Then, louder, he said again, "Hello."

"Snoring," Gibson said, and banged his cane against the door.

Heinlein heard something heavy roll across papers and then crash to the floor. "What the hell?" He reached for, and found, the light switch. At the same moment a figure popped up from behind the desk. The man was disheveled and disoriented. Pages from the desk he had been curled upon were stuck in his red hair.

"That's your package?" Gibson asked, incredulously.

Recognition flowed into the face of the man. "Bob? *Walter Gibson?* Well, ain't this some kind of the goddamnedest reunion?"

"Jesus Christ," Heinlein said.

"No," the man replied with a shit-eating grin Heinlein was all too familiar with. "I'm still just plain old Lafayette Ron Hubbard."

ESCAPE FROM THE HOLLOW EARTH

EPISODE 11

"THE MEXICAN GOVERNMENT had their panties in a bunch because an American had sunk a sub in their territorial waters. I only did what they couldn't." Hubbard was concluding his tale to his two old friends as the cab bounced them north on Sixth Avenue. On his lap he held a large accordion folder filled with fanzines and magazines he had taken from the Empire State Building office. Things to read if the trip turned out to be a bust. That Campbell had told him to give it to Heinlein didn't seem so important right now. "So Admiral Halsey sent word directly that I be rewarded with some R&R until the waters calm down, so to speak. I figured, since I was on vacation, to head east and see what's up in New York."

"Really?" Heinlein remarked from the back without turning his face from the window. "Admiral Halsey intervened on your behalf?"

"Of course! After all, I had sunk a Jap sub."

Heinlein turned to Gibson and said, "I must have missed that newsreel."

"Well," Hubbard said, understanding that Heinlein would be jealous of his actions; after all, he had been an officer but could no longer serve. "It was a secret mission."

"Ah," said Heinlein, unblinking as the city moved past him, his jaw set. "You sure it's okay to tell us about it?"

"What are you going to do, write about it? It's my story. I'll tell it the way I want."

"Ah," Heinlein said again. What did he mean by that?

"The Navy wants to play it down so as not to scare the civvies."

"Sure," Gibson readily agreed. Unlike Heinlein, Gibson had actually seen service in the Great War and Hubbard could tell that he really understood what combat was like and could appreciate how the chain of command worked.

Hubbard slid out a stapled sheaf of papers. He held it up so the men in back could see the cover. "Cartmill's new story, 'Deadline.' For the next issue of *Astounding*."

Heinlein plucked it from his fingers. "I'm supposed to review that," he said. "That's not for you."

"So, sue me. I needed something to read. Typical Cartmill, so it's not very good. It's about an alien race that goes to work with a new kind of atomic super-bomb. What's crazy is that the science seems pretty plausible. He even goes into detail about how a super-bomb could be constructed—two cast-iron hemispheres clamped over segments of cadmium alloy with a fuse that shatters the cadmium walls, releasing uranium oxide which runs together in a central cavity. The radium then shoots neurons into this mass and the chain reaction of the U-235 begins. The explosion could blow an island, or hunk of a continent, right off the planet."

"Science fiction," Gibson scoffed.

"I don't know," Hubbard replied defensively. "Campbell says he has it on good authority that the science here is spot on."

"Maybe Campbell shouldn't be publishing it, then. Who knows who could get their hands on something like that?" Heinlein sounded irritated as he folded up the story and slipped it into his jacket.

Hubbard shrugged. Obviously Heinlein was in some kind of mood. "I can't tell you how happy I was to see you fellas today," he tried, changing the subject as they rolled through Times Square.

"How'd you wind up here?" Gibson asked.

"Campbell told me I could use the office in the Empire State Building for as long as I needed since he hardly ever goes there. I thought I'd get some writing done. A novel." He couldn't bring himself to tell them that, unbeknownst to Campbell, he had actually been sleeping there as well. In New York, a free room was a free room and not to be sniffed at.

Now Heinlein looked at him. "Really?" he asked in a tone that revealed little of the surprise Hubbard knew he felt. "A novel? Not a novella or a novelette?"

"Nope," Hubbard said proudly. "A real novel."

"How's that going?"

"Well, I just started."

Heinlein turned to stare back out the window. "Hmm."

Hubbard had to admit that he'd been so happy to see Heinlein and Gibson that he'd bullied them into letting him come along. Perhaps "bullied" was too strong a word; he'd persuaded them to invite him. Now he asked. "Where are we going?"

"It's a secret mission," Heinlein said with a slight smile, as if to himself, as the cab pulled to a stop in front of Radio City Music Hall.

Hubbard followed the two men as they walked up the sidewalk and entered the RCA Building, which, though not as magnificent as the Empire State Building, was perhaps more beautiful. The small lobby was lit by hidden wall sconces which reflected off the brushed aluminum ceiling and illuminated the fine linear design etched into the marble and granite. The atmosphere felt alive and vibrant. "It's like walking through a radio wave," Hubbard marveled.

"General Electric created the Radio Corporation of America to handle its communications business," Heinlein said, "but that put it instantly in conflict with AT&T. Rumor has it that the two companies made a secret pact: RCA would stay out of the telephone business as long as AT&T stayed out of the radio business. In exchange, both companies would share technologies with each other and no one else."

"Like the treaties between the ancient city-states," Gibson said.

Heinlein had the guard at the security center make a phone call. While they waited, Heinlein pointed to the Art Deco mural, made of tiles, set into the wall behind the guard. "There used to be a real work of art there. Diego Rivera painted *Man at the Crossroads* across that wall in celebration of workers and science and the future. But he refused to remove a portrait of Lenin that was a small part of it, so Rockefeller had it covered up, destroyed. But I prefer to think that it's still lurking behind the wall here. A secret future waiting to be revealed."

The security guard received affirmation and soon they were ushered up to the sixteenth floor, where a beautiful blond secretary in a light brown dress welcomed them to the offices of General Electric. "Wow," Hubbard said, as she brought them into an office as big as half his house. "So this is what real money gets you." He drew his hands across the polished table. "This looks like it was carved from one solid piece of wood. Some boardroom."

"Actually, this is just an ordinary conference room," the slender businessman said as he slowly entered the room. "You should see the boardroom. Or for that matter, someday you should see the Rockefeller family offices upstairs on fifty-six." He held out his hand, and as Heinlein shook it, Hubbard counted the liver spots scattered liberally across the tissue-thin skin. "Hi, I'm Lyman Binch."

Heinlein stepped forward, shook the man's hand, and introduced the others. Binch's open and honest face revealed absolutely no recognition of the names—not even Hubbard's. He looked at the three men in their street clothes. "You say you're with the Navy?"

"That's right," Heinlein replied quickly. "We've been sent to ask you a few questions, if you don't mind."

"Well, General Electric is always proud to serve its country," Binch said. "You're lucky you caught me in the city. I'm usually out at the West Orange lab." He indicated they should sit down in the thick leather chairs. Hubbard tossed his binder of mags on the table, where it plopped loudly. Binch eyed it for only a moment but Hubbard still found himself putting a protective hand upon the folder. Finally, the man looked up and said, "What can I do for you, Mr. Heinlein?"

Why did everyone always assume Heinlein was in charge?

"Please, call me Bob. We're just here to ask you a few questions if you don't mind. You used to work with Nikola Tesla."

Binch nodded. "My first job after MIT. I was an electrical engineer with his company for a few years. Then I was recruited by Thomas Edison. Been a company man ever since."

"What do you do?"

"I'm vice president of research."

"There was no love lost between Tesla and Edison."

"That story's been told a dozen times, gentlemen. Edison created one way to power the nation. Tesla invented another. The War of the Currents was an ugly affair, waged mostly through public relations. Ultimately, though, Tesla's method was better, and now most of us get our electricity through his method instead of Edison's direct current."

"Three-phase alternating current at sixty hertz," Hubbard said.

Binch nodded. "Powerful enough to be delivered over great distances and still keep light bulbs from flickering."

"Why did you leave Tesla's company?"

"Well, let's just say that while Edison hired geniuses, Tesla was the genius. And a stable of geniuses may be depended upon, but it is impossible to hedge against the failure of one genius. J. P. Morgan saw that. So did I. Mr. Tesla never recovered from his eventual setbacks.

"If only Edison and Tesla had remained friends. Edison could have warned him to stay away from Morgan. Morgan is the reason this company is called General Electric, and not Edison Electric. He brought in Charlie Coffin to run the company instead of Tom."

He waved a hand expansively to take in the room, and the view of the East River. "However, things worked out fairly well for Tom. It's been a dozen years or so since his death, but I still miss him every day. You know his son is the governor of New Jersey?"

Heinlein nodded as if he knew that. "Would those failures and setbacks of Tesla's include Wardenclyffe?"

Binch blinked a couple of times at Heinlein's question, then gave a little laugh. "That's what you really want to know about? Wardenclyffe? I should have known."

"There are a lot of rumors about it."

Hubbard leaned forward. He'd never before heard the odd word (it sounded Welsh) Heinlein had used, but the discussion promised to be intriguing. He had to wait a little while longer as the blonde returned with a coffee tray and served everyone before withdrawing again.

Binch sighed, as if the act of reaching back into his memory was difficult. "Wardenclyffe might have changed the world, had it worked. Imagine being able to listen to the same radio station anywhere in the world without the need for a broadcast network. Imagine the earth itself as the broadcast medium. That was Tesla's dream. The World Broadcasting System is what he called it. That's what we tried to build at Shoreham.

"The facility itself was a wonder. The main building was designed and built by Stanford White. Do you know his work? Washington Square Arch? The old Madison Square Garden. Half the great mansions of Fifth Avenue. It's no joke to say that New York would not shine half as brightly had it not been for White. Wardenclyffe Tower was his last commission before he was murdered by a husband jealous of White's rumored despoiling of his young actress bride. Tragic." Binch sipped at his coffee. "White was a true gentleman."

He set the china cup down in its delicate saucer. "An iron tower one hundred eighty-seven feet tall rose over the building. It was double the original size Tesla had called for, and part of the reason the project ran out of money. At the top was an inverted half-dome structure, also crafted of iron beams. It looked like a giant gleaming mushroom rising from the farmland. You could see it from the water, too. Have you ever seen what's come to be known as a Tesla coil?"

Hubbard looked to the other men; they hadn't either.

"They've become popular in Hollywood horror movies. You see them used to create the great arcs of electrical lightning effects in the sets of mad scientists. It's actually a type of resonant transformer invented by Nikola. The tower at Wardenclyffe shared some principles with the original coil, but was modified to oscillate electricity into a signal and project it into the earth through rods that went down into a pit that was one hundred twenty feet deep. That signal could then be detected by a device about this big"—he held out his hands in front of him at slightly wider than shoulders' width—"and carried in a case. This case would not have to be in any way connected to the tower, but needed only to be in direct contact with the earth at coordinates directed by Tesla himself. The case was to test for the signal we never got to send.

"From the mushroom cap, a signal could also be sent which was supposed to bounce along the outer layer of the earth's atmosphere where the sun's radiation and the atmosphere make a kind of conductive barrier; what scientists now theorize to be the ionosphere, but Tesla called the ether. Had it worked, Tesla would have broadened the oscillation frequency considerably to allow anyone with such a device to plunge a wire into the ground and receive his signal. Ships at sea would, of course, receive the signal bouncing off the atmosphere."

"That's impossible," Hubbard heard himself snort and clapped an embarrassed hand over his mouth. Heinlein shot him a look that reminded him he was only a guest here.

"Nikola had created so many other miracles. The electromagnetic motor, for example. And he invented radio, though Marconi stole his patents out from under him. Even now that theft is being reviewed by the U.S. Supreme Court. Hopefully, the patents will be returned to Tesla and he will be vindicated. So many miracles he could claim. How were we to know that this one was, in fact, impossible?"

"The cases you were talking about," Gibson said quietly. "Did Admiral Peary have one?"

Binch nodded. "Yes. That was going to be a huge publicity coup. Admiral Peary would receive a message from Tesla while at the North Pole."

"In 1908?"

"Yes."

Gibson nodded at Heinlein, who slid some papers from a folder he was carrying. "What did happen in 1908?" he asked, sliding one page to Binch.

Binch seemed surprised to see the paper. "Where did you get this?"

"Like I said," Heinlein replied, "we're with the Navy. Now, Tesla wrote there that something 'terrible' happened. What was it?"

Binch shook his head. "I don't know."

"What?"

"I don't know. I remember that day. We were to test part of the machine. But when we arrived that morning, Tesla wouldn't let us in. Said things had gone awry. But when I asked, he wouldn't clarify it.

"The next day Tesla said that something had, in fact, happened, but he never told us what it was. He made us swear to cease all testing until he modified the machinery. But we ran out of money before we ever got the chance to try again.

"We had our suspicions. Some felt that perhaps Tesla had been wrong about the magnetic resonance of the earth, and that the signal was delivered, just to the wrong place. Others thought that perhaps the oscillation frequency was off and that Tesla had delivered a blast of pure electrical energy someplace completely random. Others said it was perhaps a combination of both."

"What do you think happened?"

"I think Tesla failed. I don't think it worked."

Hubbard thought for a moment. "What if some of those other fellas you worked with were right? What if the oscillation frequency was off? How powerful would something like that be?"

"Our generators were capable of creating millions of volts in an instant. It would have created an incredibly powerful burst of energy."

"A death ray?"

"Gentlemen," Binch said, laughing. "Nothing happened. Wardenclyffe was a bust. You want to know what happened? Reality happened—1926 happened."

"What do you mean?" Heinlein asked.

"Look, as a scientist, Nikola was more of an engineer. The principles of magnetism and electricity, these were wide-open fields of exploration. Those men, Tesla, Edison, they could run down a hunch and if they got a result they came up with an explanation, the theory, after the fact. Then they'd start flipping more switches. Trying new things. What happened was that in 1926 Schrödinger and Heisenberg and the rest of them described quantum theory. That changed everything.

"Tesla's world was fundamentally Newtonian—equal and opposite reactions, everything mechanically sound. Friction generates heat. But the quantum boys, what they led us to was a universe of smaller and smaller particles, each behaving by their own rules. Tesla thought that electromagnetic energy was the foundation of the universe. Quantum theory showed that electromagnetic energy was only radiation from the interaction of subatomic particles. The findings of 1926 showed why Nikola could never have been successful in 1908. The real reality never changed. Just his."

"He never really recovered, did he?"

Binch shook his head. "No. For a couple of reasons. Financially, no one would ever back him after Wardenclyffe. And the failure ate at him. Nikola was always high-strung and caught up in his own mind. I think the struggles and the failure caused him to unravel. He spent his last days in Bryant Park, feeding pigeons, I've heard. The Army didn't like that too much."

"Did you see or hear from him at all?"

"Just one time. You have to understand that the day I left him to go work for Tom was the day I died as far as he was concerned. But just this past December he called me, or rather, an Army corporal called me. From the lobby of the Empire State Building. For some reason, Tesla had caused a commotion there. He'd asked to speak to Admiral Westinghouse, then to me. And so they found me. The corporal said that the old man was afraid he was being chased by spies and was trying to hide, but that the basement was no place for him. I don't know why, on that day, he thought of my name. But I told the corporal he was a harmless old man and to please release him. That was the end of it as far as I was concerned."

"Any idea whatever became of the Peary case?" Gibson asked.

"Lost to the ages, I suppose."

Hubbard tapped idly on his folder, trying to put all the pieces about Tesla, Wardenclyffe, and Heinlein together. But it made less sense than Cartmill's super-bomb story.

Binch looked at the folder. "Are those more of Tesla's notes there? I'd love to take a look at them."

"Hm? Oh no," Hubbard said, caught unawares. "This is some other secret weapon stuff."

Heinlein interrupted him quickly. "I'm afraid all of his old papers are the property of the U.S. government now."

"If you'd like me to look those over and see if there's anything of interest in there I'd be happy to."

Heinlein packed his papers away. "Thanks. I'll let you know if we need to take you up on it. Is there anyone else from the Wardenclyffe project we could talk to? Any coworkers you can think of?"

"I'll put a list together." Binch stood up as the others did and looked at his watch. "I see it's lunchtime." He turned to the blonde as she entered the room. "Miss Davis, will you escort these men to the Rainbow Room, please."

"Oh, that's okay," Heinlein started to protest, but Binch held up his hand. "Please, you came all the way from Philly. The least I can do is see you get a decent lunch at the top restaurant in the city. It happens to only be an elevator ride away. And the view up there is astonishing."

"Sounds great," Hubbard said, accepting on behalf of the others who obviously could, in his opinion, screw up a free lunch.

"I'll have the list prepared for you by the time you finish."

The Rainbow Room was, as advertised, one of the most elegant spaces Hubbard had seen in ages. After entering through a bar, the restaurant was a circular ring around a great gleaming dance floor which was not currently in use. The swells of the city filled the tables and the aroma of rich food filled Hubbard's nostrils and made his stomach gurgle. "Mm. Beef bourguignon." He was literally licking his chops as they were seated. Unfortunately, the blonde had left them in the care of the maître d' and had slipped away, so he was denied the pleasure of her company.

"What do you think, Bob?" Gibson asked, after they placed a drink order.

"It's a hell of a room."

"I meant about the things Mr. Binch said. Did he fill in any blanks? Did he explain why your spy might be interested in Wardenclyffe?"

"A spy!" Hubbard sputtered.

Heinlein shook his head, as if irritated at Hubbard's exclamation. "I can see why someone might want to poke around and see if there was anything to it. Just like us. What'd you think, Walter?"

Gibson took a sip from the beer he had just received. "Hard to say. The big question to me is, why did Tesla call off the testing, right? Either it didn't work and Tesla knew he had a colossal failure on his hands and went into cover-his-ass mode until he could figure a way out. Or something did happen and it scared him so badly he called off the experiments."

"Do you think something happened?"

Gibson shrugged. "I don't know. It's clear what Mr. Binch believes. But apparently the rumors of Wardenclyffe have managed to persist and travel across the ocean and catch the attention of the Reich. Makes one wonder what information they may have. Binch seems like a nice guy. Why wouldn't he tell us the whole truth? He's a company man. And an Edison man. Obviously it's in his best interests to make Edison look better than Tesla. We'll have to see what your boys come up with down at the library. But it seems to me it's clear what you have to do next?"

"What's that?" Heinlein asked.

"Find out what happened in 1908."

EPISODE 12

"WERE YOU MORE of a Shadow or a Doc Savage fan?" Isaac asked Sprague as they waited for the librarian to bring them copies of the old newspapers they had requested. The Reading Room of the Public Library's main branch was busy, people filling the long tables, and yet the room was quiet and Isaac's voice carried. He felt the eyes of readers fall upon him. Isaac didn't really care. It wasn't every day a person got to meet Walter Gibson, and he was still buzzing with the thrill.

Sprague shrugged. "I don't know. Neither, I guess."

"Really?"

"I was reading Cooper, Melville, Hugo, Verne, Wells. Those guys. Didn't really have time for the pulps."

"Oh." Isaac rubbed his chin. "How about *Amazing*?"

"Very little. I was drawn to *Weird Tales*, for Robert E. Howard and H. P. Lovecraft. That's why I like *Unknown* the most, now."

"Oh," Isaac said again. "Well, my dad owned a candy store, so I got to read all of them every month—as soon as they came out."

"That must have been nice," Sprague said.

"Yeah, it was. Ever been to Park Slope?"

"Nope."

"It's nice."

"I've heard that," Sprague said. He looked up as if he was examining the plaster ornamentation on the ceiling. "You know they built this library on the site of the old Croton Reservoir?"

"I didn't."

"My dad used to bring me here when I was a little kid and they were just finishing building the library. He told me how when he was a boy, he'd written a note, then sealed it in a bottle and thrown it over the wall in hopes it would come out in his faucet back at home. But it never did. When they drained the reservoir, they probably found the bottle stuck in the pipes. I love the history of New York. It's like a story that's constantly being rewritten. The architects who built this library designed everything down to the garbage cans." Sprague checked his watch. "Twelve thirty. Missed my nooner."

"What's that?"

"Cathy and I have a standing appointment to get together every day at noon."

"For lunch?"

Sprague smiled. "No, Isaac. Not for lunch. She'll have to give me a pass today. I don't mind paying up."

Isaac felt guilt flood into him. "I should call Gertie."

"You two do the nooner, too?"

"Um. No," Isaac said. "I just need to talk to her. I kind of left in the middle of an argument last night."

"Uh-oh." Sprague gave him a knowing wink. "Never let a fight fester. It only makes women crazier."

"Really?"

"You're still a newlywed. It's all roses and wine for the first year. Then the work starts."

Isaac looked down at the table. Years of people taking notes on its surface had left deep scratches in the white oak. He traced one of the grooves with his fingernail. "It's been a lot of work already."

"Really?"

"Maybe things would be different if we'd stayed in Brooklyn, near our families. But we're so far away."

"Philly's not that far away, Isaac."

"Yeah it is." He hung his head, feeling miserable. "I don't know what to do. She's just not very happy. I'm not very happy."

"Well, why don't you start by remembering what it is you have in common? What do you like to do?" Sprague looked concerned for him.

"We like to go to the movies."

"That's good. What else?"

Isaac slapped his palms on the table. "The real problem is she hates science fiction!"

"What?"

"She doesn't like sci-fi. She won't read *Astounding* or *Unknown* or *Amazing*. She doesn't even read my stories when I get them published. Oh, she'll pretend to. She'll be polite about it. But I know she doesn't read them. She just doesn't like sci-fi. How can I be married to someone who doesn't like sci-fi?"

Sprague looked at him for a long moment in disbelief and then burst into a fit of laughter that turned heads from one end of the Reading Room to the other. He stifled himself and leaned in to Isaac. "Lots of people don't like sci-fi, Ike," he said. "It's okay if she doesn't. I don't think it's grounds for divorce. Doesn't mean she doesn't love you."

"I know."

"Look." Sprague sat back and pulled some coins from his pocket. "There are some payphones out back by Bryant Park. Why don't you go give her a call and tell her you're sorry? Set up a nooner for tomorrow."

Isaac took the coins. "I should. Yeah. I guess I should." He stood up.

"I'll wait for the newspapers."

"Okay." Isaac paused. "But don't call me Ike."

He found the phones outside and had the operator connect them, but Gertie didn't answer, so the operator refunded his money. The smell of the nearby hot dog vendor made his stomach gurgle so he wandered over and bought one with some of Sprague's change. Then he sat down on a bench to eat.

An old bald man sat on a bench opposite him across the pathway. He pulled crumbs from a brown paper bag, his hand trembling, and scattered them for the few pigeons that strutted in front of him. When he looked up at Isaac, he smiled as if Isaac was sharing in the experience

with him. Isaac hated pigeons, but he nodded back to be kind. He finished
the hot dog as quickly as he could while trying not to make eye contact
with the withered man opposite him. When he looked up, the old man
was gone. Isaac wandered back into the library and found Sprague finishing a conversation with a librarian, who scurried away as he approached.

Sprague had several old newspapers spread out in front of him. "Ike,"
he snapped, "just in time!"

"What's up? Did you find something?"

"Not really. I don't know. Maybe. You have to put us in touch with
Hugo Gernsback."

"That's an impossibility."

"You know him, right?"

"Look, Gernsback really has it in for some of my friends."

Irritated, Sprague waved away that little detail. "He knows who you
are, right?"

Isaac swallowed hard. "I guess so."

"Come on, let's call him."

"Why?"

"We need to see him. Right away."

"Why?"

The newspaper flying toward him was Sprague's response. Isaac realized the article Sprague wanted him to read was Tesla's recent obituary.
"Did you know he was one of the last people to see Tesla alive and one of
the first to see him dead?" Toward the end of the article, the name "Hugo
Gernsback" leapt out at him as the one in charge of making the funeral
arrangements.

Sprague quickly skimmed through a phone book the librarian had
brought for him, found the number he was looking for, and scribbled it
down on a notepad similar to Isaac's. In fact, a quick glance showed him
that Sprague used it for the same purpose; the pages were covered with
possible titles, suggestions, and scraps of dialogue.

"Let's go call." Sprague stood up. "You hungry? I could do with a dog."

"I could eat," Isaac replied, following the tall man as they headed back
outside. At the phones he took the number Sprague had ripped from his

notepad and thrust upon him. His hands were shaking as he held the phone.

"Gernsback Publishing." The voice of the man who answered was rough and tinged with a vague Continental accent. Because of years of listening to kraut villains on the radio and in the movies, Isaac had become conditioned to react poorly to the slightest hint of a Prussian inflection. The chill spreading through his stomach was instant and painful, even though he had already been afraid to speak with Hugo.

"Um . . . Mr. Gernsback," he began. "This is Isaac Asimov calling."

The pause was long. Very long. Isaac knew the man was on the other line because he could hear the breathing.

"Do you remember me?" Isaac asked, irritated at how high and squeaky his voice sounded.

"Of course I remember you, Mr. Asimov. Part of that Wollheim's gang."

"Not really a gang, Mr. Gernsback."

"I don't publish scientifiction anymore, Mr. Asimov," he said, using the term he preferred because he had created it. "I'm out of that business. You boys put me out of that business. So I can't buy your stories."

"I'm not calling about a story, Mr. Gernsback. I work for the Navy now. I'm calling you about Nikola Tesla."

"Ah," Hugo replied. "So now that he's dead, the Navy wants to know about his Death Ray."

The chill of fear left Isaac's body, replaced by a rush of adrenaline. "Did you say Death Ray?" he repeated loud enough for Sprague to hear as he approached with the hot dogs.

"Isn't that what you want to talk about?"

Sprague's head was rapidly bobbing up and down.

"We want to talk to you about the Death Ray."

"Who is 'we'?"

"I'm with Sprague de Camp. He works for the Navy, too."

"He's a good writer."

"Okay." For some reason Isaac didn't feel like this information needed to be shared with Sprague. "We're in the city today. We'd love to meet with you."

"I can meet you at the New Yorker Hotel on Eighth Avenue in half an hour."

Recalling Tesla's obituary, Isaac said, "That's where Tesla died, right?"

"No, Mr. Asimov, that's where he lived. And that's where he was murdered."

"Murdered?" Isaac watched Sprague's eyes widen.

Hugo sighed. "I only have an hour for lunch, Mr. Asimov. How many questions you have answered is entirely up to you." He hung up.

The New Yorker Hotel was an immense building of brown rectangles, stacked one on top of another.

"This building has its own coal-fired steam generator in the basement," Sprague said. "Ironic that the inventor of alternating current would have chosen to live in one of the few buildings in the world privately powered with direct current."

"It looks like it could almost blast off," Isaac replied.

"You see spaceships everywhere, don't you?" Sprague said.

"Well, not everywhere," Isaac replied.

Hugo Gernsback stood stiff as a ramrod, waiting in the center of the lobby in spite of all the available chairs. His suit was brown, tailored to disguise his stout frame; the ensemble was neatly topped with a checkered bow tie. What hair he had was slickly plastered across the top of his head with Brylcreem. To Isaac, he appeared the exact same age he had been when Isaac had met him at the World Science Fiction Convention of 1938, as if he hadn't aged a day since. Hugo Gernsback, Isaac decided, would always look fifty-five years old.

Even though Hugo Gernsback made Asimov nervous, he also felt possessive of him since he knew the man and Sprague didn't. "This is Hugo Gernsback," he said, introducing Sprague, "the man who created *Amazing Stories* and science fiction."

"And this is Isaac Asimov," Hugo Gernsback said, as he shook Sprague's hand. "Part of the gang that ran me out of science fiction."

"Maybe if you had paid my friends for the stories they wrote for you they wouldn't have felt like taking you on."

"Maybe I made a mistake coming to meet with a GhuGhu follower."

"I was a Futurian. Not a GhuGhuian."

"Okay," Sprague said quickly, stepping in between the two men. "Mr. Gernsback, I've been reading *Radio-Craft* for years. The 'Popular Electronics' column helped me to get my electrical engineering degree. I'm a big admirer of yours."

Hugo Gernsback cleared his throat and his chest seemed to expand.

Sprague continued, "Now, I understand this hotel has five restaurants. Is the tavern agreeable to you?"

"I think the tavern will be fine," said Hugo Gernsback, after sizing up de Camp and finding something about him acceptable.

As they followed him into the restaurant, Sprague leaned down and whispered, "What the hell is GhuGhu?"

Isaac responded by shaking his head and muttered, "Later."

At the table, Sprague ordered a cup of coffee while Isaac and Hugo Gernsback both agreed on turkey club sandwiches. "You got room for that?"

Isaac nodded. "So what?"

Sprague shrugged. "Good thing they've lifted the rationing for restaurants." He turned to Hugo Gernsback. "You're out of the science fiction business."

Hugo Gernsback gave a curt nod. "I've been out since *Wonder Stories* was stolen from me in 1936. Who cares? Who cares about science fiction stories now when the world of science today is more exciting than the fiction of tomorrow? Science fiction was an accident anyway."

"What do you mean?" Isaac asked through a mouthful of food, happy that his sandwich had arrived so quickly.

"I had space in my old *Science and Invention* magazine but no articles to fill that space. So I put in Jules Verne's 'Off On a Comet' to fill out the magazine. It sold out. Then the people started writing letters. Oh, the letters! We want more of this scientific fiction, they cried. More, more, more! So I started writing stories and buying stories until I had so many stories and so many readers I had to start *Amazing*. And then the readers became writers became fanatics." He stared harshly at Isaac. "They destroyed the club I created for them and started their own. A safer place, they called it. A place for their dreams."

"You wouldn't hold free elections for the management of the club and you revoked the memberships and charters of people who didn't agree with you," Isaac protested.

"It was my club."

"It became *our* club."

Hugo Gernsback smiled patiently at Sprague. "The science fiction fanatics are a revolutionary breed. It took me a long time to figure out why they are so excited by their little fantasies. For any other fan of literature, there is a long and vast history to explore and examine and debate. This science fiction is so new that there is no history to invest with knowledge. Only a future to be written. That is what they fight for. An unwritten future. Ah, but television is my future, at any rate. Not publishing little science stories. It is too bad, though."

"What is?" Sprague asked.

"There are more good writers today than there were in the days when I had *Amazing Stories* and *Wonder Stories*. Like you"—he indicated Sprague, completely ignoring Isaac—"and, of course, Robert Heinlein."

"Yes, well, he's working with us on this Tesla investigation," Sprague said, stirring milk into his coffee and taking a sip.

"Ah." Hugo Gernsback nodded. "Well, that is why we're here now, isn't it?"

"Yes, it is," Sprague said. "Isaac said you know about the Death Ray."

"We jokingly called it a Death Ray. Tesla's teleforce weapon. His greatest failure. I met Tesla about thirty years ago when I was a young man and he was already beginning the downward spiral that would lead to his lonely end here in this building. Of course, I didn't know that then. What I knew was that I was in the presence of the man who had invented radio. Not that Italian scoundrel, Marconi. In this I feel that the Supreme Court will vindicate Tesla by invalidating Marconi's patents. I wish Nikola had lived to see this.

"You know I helped pay his bills here in the last few years. A few of us, his friends, who understood his genius, felt his contributions to mankind deserved some response. He deserved so much more."

Hugo Gernsback neatly folded his napkin along precise lines visible only to him. "The teleforce weapon. He began working on it in the early decades of the century. The truth is that Tesla understood that in the end it took only a small step to transform electromagnetic radio waves into electromagnetic energy, which could be used to destroy ships and planes hundreds of miles away. It would require a tower, easily a hundred feet tall, to create the ionized energy."

Sprague gave a low whistle. Isaac realized he had a mouthful of food he had forgotten to chew. He forced it down and asked, "Like the one at Wardenclyffe?"

"Of course you know about Wardenclyffe," Hugo said. "There are many questions about Wardenclyffe still to be asked. And answers that may never be found."

"Tesla appeared to believe that something terrible happened in June of 1908 in connection with Wardenclyffe," Sprague said. "Do you know what that might be?"

Hugo Gernsback appeared not to have heard. "Tesla's most important work was lost to us years ago. A tragedy. It certainly contributed to the decline of his state of mind."

"What do you mean?"

"Tesla lived for many years at the Waldorf-Astoria Hotel. He even designed his own vault in the hotel's basement to house his most valuable papers and ideas. But after numerous failures, he was asked to leave the hotel under the most humiliating conditions and was never allowed back in to empty his vault. When the building was torn down in 1929, he was devastated."

"The old Waldorf on Thirty-fourth?" Sprague asked, flicking a speck off the tablecloth as if it was of great importance. Hugo nodded.

"But Wardenclyffe?" Isaac asked, staring wistfully at Hugo's uneaten sandwich half. "We've heard it was designed to be a broadcast communication station sending radio and, someday, television signals around the world."

"There's more to it, isn't there?" Sprague leaned forward.

This, then, was the grand plan for Wardenclyffe. Not to send radio signals around the world, but to send power. The earth and sky would become the conducting circuit, and with some simple modifications, each home, each building, anybody, anywhere would be able to receive free electricity. As much as they wanted, simply by plunging a spike into the earth, or raising an antenna.

"The first test was on June 30, 1908. Tesla had given a case of equipment to Admiral Peary that would receive the signal. Tesla believed that through frequency modulation he could narrowly direct the signal to any point he desired. The publicity that he would receive from the association with Peary's race to the North Pole would benefit his work greatly and perhaps allow him to free himself from J. P. Morgan's purse strings. He would have to wait to know for sure until Peary sent back word, but the wait would be worth it. Instead . . . instead, the next day he discovered how wrong he had been. About everything."

"It didn't work?" Isaac asked.

"All too well. He told me that it was only a small mention in the paper of the day, but he knew what it meant. It was near the back where they post international news of dubious interest. The report was that there had been an explosion in remotest Siberia—a region known as Tunguska. The impact registered on seismic counters across Europe and generated atmospheric disruptions that were detected as far away as California. Because of the isolated distance of Tunguska from, well, anywhere civilized, the reports on the scale of the explosion were sadly lacking in detail but for one, which was incredibly relevant to Nikola. The time of the blast, as measured by those scientific instruments, was moments after he himself had thrown the switch at Wardenclyffe. It wasn't until nineteen years later that the first expedition explored the region. What they found was that eight hundred square miles had been destroyed in an instant by a force of astounding power."

"Jesus Christ," Sprague said in a low whisper, his eyes wide.

"The report indicated that there were probably as many as eighty million trees knocked down. But Tesla didn't need to wait the nineteen years for the proof. He felt—he knew—he was responsible. And, of course, before he could implement the changes necessary to correct the equipment, Morgan pulled the plug, incensed that the broadcasting station he was paying for would instead provide power he couldn't charge people for.

During the Great War, the government had the tower torn down so that it couldn't be used as a landmark by any possible invasion forces. And Tesla was ruined. So, whether Wardenclyffe could have eventually been used for a Death Ray we will never know."

"Do you believe that's what happened? That Tesla caused an explosion in Siberia?"

"I believe it's possible. Tesla was trying to harness elemental forces. What's more important is that Tesla believed it. And others have made the connection between Wardenclyffe and Tunguska as well. Foreign interests, perhaps. In the last years of his life, Nikola felt he was constantly being followed by spies. I fear he was right."

"Why do you think he was murdered?" Isaac asked.

"One day he sent me a letter, posted to Samuel Clemens, which was subterfuge on his part to throw off the spies, he claimed. In his note he told me he had discovered that his vault of secrets—what he called his Catalan Vault, for reasons all his own—still existed. That the flooding in Greenwich Village he'd read about in the paper proved it. If he could enter it, he could retrieve his Wardenclyffe work—and the world might finally be ready for it. Obviously, he was raving.

"The next day he sent another envelope, with only this in it. No explanation where it could be used." Hugo Gernsback set a large, rusty key upon the table. "The following day I received a call from the manager here. Nikola Tesla was dead. He had been found in the morning by a chambermaid.

"His body had been taken to the Frank Campbell Funeral Home, so I rushed there. I felt a death mask had to be made to preserve his likeness for posterity. I met the funeral director, who took me to the body in the embalming room, and we set about preparing the materials. As I caressed my friend's face for the last time, I noticed a slight mark around his right ear and on his fingertips, as if he'd been charred by a flame. When I pointed it out to the mortician, he shrugged and told me only that he had said as much to the police but they said that this was an eighty-three-year-old man and he must have had an accident, maybe, and that was all. He said that the marks were only suspicious, not definitive, and old people often had strange marks on them at the end. But I've spent my career around electricity. I know what electrical burns look like. Ironic, I know. Nikola Tesla, electrocuted."

Hugo Gernsback pushed his plate away from him with one hand and placed the other over his mouth.

"Are you all right?" Sprague asked.

"Yes." But his voice was hoarse. He took a deep breath and pulled himself together.

"You think spies got to him?"

"I don't know. We live in perilous times. There are enemies everywhere. And Nikola had his share of them. But I will go to my grave believing he was murdered."

Sprague picked up the key and examined it with interest. "Do you think I could borrow this? I'd like to show it to someone and I'll make sure you get it back tomorrow."

Hugo looked suspicious for a moment and then softened. "I don't see why not."

Sprague pocketed the key and the three men sat there in silence for a few moments. Then Hugo Gernsback withdrew his pocket watch, glanced at it, and cleared his throat politely. "I have other matters to attend to."

"Of course you do," Sprague replied. "We appreciate your time."

At that, Hugo Gernsback rose and nodded curtly toward Sprague. "I would be happy to publish your work if I ever get back into science fiction."

"I'd be thrilled."

Hugo then peered down at Isaac. "I could even see publishing yours."

"Really?"

"You've become better." Hugo Gernsback straightened himself, then slipped efficiently past the other tables and out of the tavern.

Sprague began to instantly scan the room for their waiter. "We need the check."

"What're you going to do with that key? We don't know where it goes," Isaac said, deftly moving the remains of Hugo Gernsback's sandwich onto his plate while Sprague scanned the restaurant.

"Yes, I do," he replied.

"You do?"

"Tesla's lost vault? It isn't lost anymore."

"It isn't?" Isaac nearly choked on the dry turkey.

"It may still exist. And if it does, I know where it is."

EPISODE 13

HEINLEIN WAS WORRIED about Gibson. Since they'd left the Rainbow Room his friend's limp had grown further pronounced; he leaned heavily on his cane even in the elevator back up to the office at the Empire State Building. More than that, he seemed tired, cloaked in his own private aura of darkness and sadness. His trademark vibrancy seemed dissipated and the stillness that had replaced it was deadening. As Gibson lowered himself into one of the unused chairs before the metal desk, Heinlein couldn't help but notice his sigh of relief.

"How're you doing there, Walt?" he asked. The two men were alone as Hubbard had gone off in search of a bathroom and the two younger men had yet to show up.

Gibson shrugged and stared out the window. "It's good to be out."

Heinlein had a seat on the small sofa. "Since you have some time off from *The Shadow* are you working on anything else?"

"No. Not really."

"Walter Gibson not writing? What is the world coming to?"

Gibson's smile was thin. He rubbed his hand on his leg. "Honestly, I haven't been myself since the car accident."

"You don't have to tell me anything about it."

What little smile there was faded away. "I was driving from Maine to Florida for the winter. I had spent the day trying to finish a story in time to make the mail, so I got a late start. It was dark by the time I started out. Raining. I don't know if you've ever driven in Maine before. There isn't a straight mile anywhere in the state. But the plain fact of the matter is that I was driving way too fast. My mind wasn't where it needed to be.

"The boy had been out for some late-season fishing and got caught in the rain. That's what they figured later on. That's why he ran out of the woods. I didn't see him until . . . Well, it was too late."

"Oh, Jesus."

"I never had the chance to stop. I swear—" his voice broke and he choked on the words. "I've lived through it a million times since. It's the first thing I think about when I wake up and the last thing I think about before I fall asleep. I never saw him. One minute, the road was wide open and then there was this . . . thud. I went off the road and into the trees. I got out of my car and as I ran to the road I just kept saying, please let it be a deer. Please let it be a deer. But it was a boy, and his name was Jack. That's what he told me when I reached him. I tried to get him to tell me where he lived but he was crying and afraid about how much trouble he was going to get in. I couldn't see any houses, the road was so dark and empty. I was just praying to God that a car would come by and help me. His little body was all twisted around. I was in the ambulance corps in France during the last war and I know you're not supposed to move someone in a situation like that unless you have to, but I couldn't just leave him lying there. No help was coming.

"I picked him up and I could tell he was broken in so many places. I couldn't believe it. I don't even really remember what happened next. I was running through the night, trying to find someone. I saw some lights at last and I was finally able to find a farmhouse. The people were nice and they knew Jack and they called the police and the fire department. His parents didn't have a phone, so the husband got into his car and drove out to get them.

"I couldn't let go of Jack's hand. I just kept holding on after we laid him on a bed. I was telling him stories about Houdini and magic and I knew it was helping him, I just knew. Even after the cops came and the doctor and they told me he must have died instantly, I couldn't let go. I knew they were wrong. He had talked to me. Told me his name was Jack. Smiled at my stories. Then his parents arrived. They were tired old farm folk, stoic and hard. I think I even remember Jack's dad saying how it must have been the boy's fault for being such a fool as to run into the road before a car. I couldn't believe it.

"The police took me out to the scene of the accident. It was pretty obvious to them what had happened. They were actually very sympathetic to me. Everyone was so nice to me. I just wanted someone to put a bullet in my head.

"They brought me to a hospital. Clinic, really. My leg, my hip, my back were messed up. Got my car towed in to a gas station. Judge held a little inquest, said it was an accident, which it was. But it was my fault. The downside of having a vivid imagination is that it can blur out reality, I guess. That's what happened to me. I was so busy thinking about my next Shadow story, I forgot to pay attention to where I was and what I was doing." Gibson expressed the air for his lungs in a great breath, puffing out his cheeks as he did so. At the same time he ran his hand through his silver hair.

"I'm so sorry, Walt," Heinlein said quietly. "I had no idea." The sense of empathy was so acute his chest physically ached. The murder of his business partner years ago in an ill-advised silver mining venture reminded him of the shock and horror of a sudden, violent death. He knew the anguish of responsibility, the guilt of surviving, to an extent, but not like this.

The sound of someone gently clearing his throat caused both Gibson and Heinlein to turn. De Camp was leaning against the doorjamb, his hands thrust deeply into his pockets, dark eyes trained on Gibson. His tall, lanky frame was all odd angles of awkward elbows and shoulders.

"I heard your story," de Camp told Gibson. "I didn't meant to eavesdrop, but I heard it."

"It's okay." Gibson shrugged. "Doesn't change anything."

"I was in a car accident about ten years ago," de Camp said. "I was driving out west with my brothers, we were at a ranch, having some fun on my dad's dime. Too much fun. I lost control of the wheel, we spun out. Flipped. In a convertible. My brother, Chase, was killed instantly. I was barely scratched." He entered the room, putting a gentle hand on Gibson's shoulder. Gibson raised his for a moment, as if to brush it away or hold it there. But de Camp lifted it as if he hadn't noticed and sat on the corner of the desk in front of Gibson.

"I bet you feel like you want to die. You probably thought about killing yourself a million times. But one day it's not going to be the first thing you think of when you get up and not the last thing you think of before you go to bed. I promise you that."

Gibson nodded. "Maybe."

The three men were silent for a moment. Then, Hubbard in the door-way, carrying a box filled with coffee cups. "Jeez," he cried. "Who died in here?" He handed Gibson a cup, nodding at his sly smile, and then passed one to Heinlein. "I didn't know we were expecting company," he said, guardedly eyeing the third and last cup, then de Camp.

"It's all right," de Camp replied, declining the coffee. "I'm Sprague de Camp."

Hubbard shook his hand while giving his uniform a casual once-over. "You're with the Navy?"

"I'm with Campbell's group," de Camp said with a nod.

"Oh. You're a writer?"

"A good one, Ron. He's in *Unknown* this month. Sprague, this is Ron Hubbard."

De Camp's change was immediate and remarkable. He drew rigid and his cheeks flushed. "The writer."

"That's me." Hubbard held out his hand.

"I know who you are." De Camp refused to extend his hand. Hubbard stared at him. "Did I miss something, fella?"

"You know."

"I swear I don't." Hubbard seemed completely oblivious. Even Heinlein wasn't sure why Sprague was upset—he couldn't imagine that the two men had ever met before. He turned to Hubbard. "De Camp's a big fan of Lovecraft."

Hubbard's bushy red eyebrows arched up in surprise. "Howard Lovecraft?"

"Yep."

"We were at his funeral," Hubbard told de Camp. "The three of us. Did he tell you that?"

"No," de Camp said, smoothing his hair back.

"That's where we met. It's a good story," Hubbard said. "Remind me to tell you about it sometime. If these guys'll let me. Remember how he showed up after his funeral?" Heinlein gave him a subtle gesture, cutting him off. Hubbard shrugged and took a sip of his coffee, then asked, "I can get reimbursed for this, right?"

"Sure," Heinlein agreed, and handed de Camp his own cup. "Where's the kid?"

"Ike? He's down in the lobby."

"He's that afraid of heights?"

"I guess so."

Heinlein shook his head. "Everyone's got something, I suppose."

"What'd you find out?" de Camp asked.

"Nothing really new. Edison and Tesla didn't like each other much. There might be spies interested in Tesla's work. Tesla ended up being a few watts short of a lit bulb. Oh, and he blew it at Wardenclyffe."

De Camp looked crestfallen. "Oh, you heard about the explosion?"

"Wait. What?" Gibson asked, suddenly interested.

"The explosion."

"What explosion?"

"The Wardenclyffe explosion that blew up Siberia."

Heinlein glanced from Gibson to Hubbard. "You better start at the beginning."

De Camp related to them the details of the lunch with Gernsback. Then he presented the vault key to them with a dramatic flourish.

Gibson took it and immediately topped de Camp's presentation by swiftly making it vanish, then reappear over and over again. "How do you know where the vault is?"

"Are you a New Yorker?" de Camp asked Heinlein.

He shook his head. "Californian."

"You?"

Hubbard said, "I was born in Montana, but then we traveled all over the world. Singapore, China."

"I am a New Yorker," Gibson interrupted him loudly.

"Then do you remember what building stood on this very spot before they tore it down to build the Empire State Building?"

Gibson thought for a moment, scratching his silver hair. Then his face brightened and he looked up. "The original Waldorf-Astoria Hotel."

"Where Tesla lived for many years. And where he had his vault built. The vault where his secrets were locked away when he was exiled from the old hotel. A place he didn't know still existed until days before he died," Sprague said excitedly. "Right here, below us. In the basement of the Empire State Building."

"Binch said that the last thing he heard about Tesla before he died was that he had caused a commotion in the lobby here," Gibson reminded the others.

"Really?" de Camp asked. "Hugo Gernsback said that Tesla had found the vault. He must have been trying to get back in."

"How did Tesla find out it was still there?" Gibson asked.

"Because of the flooding."

"Flooding?"

"In Greenwich Village. He read about it in the papers. You see, when they were first digging out the foundation for the Waldorf they discovered an underground river down there. They couldn't dam it so they had to build a structure around it—a tunnel for it to flow through. When they tore the Waldorf down they still had the problem of the river. So the river tunnel was left in place, and every so often, during a heavy rain, it will flood into the basements of old village homes. I think Tesla's vault must have been built into it. It would have been nearly permanent. And it would have survived the destruction of the Waldorf and the building of this skyscraper."

"How do you know all this?" Hubbard asked, his voice dripping with skepticism.

"Al Smith was a good friend of my father's. He told us a lot about what went into this building."

"The old governor of New York was a friend of yours?"

"My father's. He was also the driving force behind getting this building built. He needed something to do after his career in politics flamed out. My father said he basically needed a project to make him rich after years as the last honest politician in America."

"Well," said Heinlein, clapping his hands together eagerly, happy to dispel the earlier gloom, "this place is the New York headquarters for the U.S. Army. It's crawling with armed troops looking for spies and saboteurs. So who's up for breaking into the basement of the Empire State Building?"

Hubbard said, "How're we going to get down there?"

Heinlein flashed his badge. "We've got artistic license."

"Okay," Hubbard replied, tucking his folder of pulps under his arm. "Where do I get one of those?"

Amid the stream of soldiers flowing through the burnished bronze lobby, Isaac Asimov, in his ill-fitting suit, stuck out like a palm tree in a wheat field. He was happy to see them and was introduced to Hubbard, who, Heinlein noted, feigned as much ignorance of Asimov's writing career as he had of de Camp's. The young man blanched a little at the suggestion that they head into the basement in search of Tesla's vault, but in the end, as long as they were going down, not up, he agreed to the quest. The group followed de Camp through the long corridor that connected Fifth and Sixth Avenues. Beyond a bank of elevators they turned left at an intersection that led to administration offices. As they walked, de Camp grandly described the opulent elegance of the old Waldorf-Astoria—how two great buildings had been awkwardly joined together to form uneven floors, the great staircase which had swept visitors into a grand hall, the parade of New York's high society.

"How do you know so much about this place?" Hubbard asked.

"I was an escort during debutante season," he said, as a matter of fact. Then, when the blank looks from the others showed they needed more explanation, "Deb balls? Coming-out parties? The social event of the season? Hm?"

"He's definitely not in the pulp racket for the money," Hubbard whispered to Heinlein after de Camp turned away.

"Not the Navy, either." Heinlein envied the tall young man, his officer's uniform—even though de Camp was only a lieutenant, Heinlein missed a uniform's snap of implicit authority. He was the team leader, but de Camp was the one leading the motley group—a limping middle-aged man and three slouches in cheap suits; they looked like a group of administrators on an official tour. Which, Heinlein realized with a shock, was why they hadn't been stopped. The impression they gave off was one of the few things that actually struck fear into a military man: civilian bureaucratic importance. Stopping a politician could lead to a world of nightmares for a soldier. Lucky for them, no one realized that politicians would wear better suits.

The far west corner of the 33rd Street side of the building abutted the enormous loading dock. The doors were less ornate and solid-looking, more functional in nature, reflecting their status as entrances for custodians and administrators. One door was clearly marked with a graphic of descending stairs. De Camp tested the knob and found it locked. Pointing to Heinlein's badge, he asked, "Does that open locked doors?"

Heinlein shook his head, then jerked his thumb toward Gibson. "But that does."

With a theatrical flourish, Gibson held several thin pieces of metal between his fingertips where there had been only thin air an instant before.

"What're those?" Asimov asked.

"Lock-picking tools. Houdini told me to never leave home without these and I never have. You wouldn't believe the jams these things have got me out of."

"I would," Hubbard muttered.

Gibson double-checked the corridor to make sure it was clear, then leaned over the doorknob. After a few metallic clicks, he smiled. "Abracadabra." The door slowly opened to reveal a staircase.

"Well," Hubbard said, craning his neck to look past Gibson and Heinlein, "it's going in the right direction. Down."

"Come on, guys, let's get out of the hall." Heinlein led the way down the stairs. Hubbard, last to follow, shut the door behind them. The staircase turned at a landing and led to a concrete floor. He could hear the deep rumble of the elevator machinery far off down the corridor.

"That'll be access to the loading dock," de Camp said, pointing to a door to their left. "We're looking for a sub-basement. Where the boilers and incinerators are."

The brightly lit alleyways below the building were almost as populated as the halls above, but instead of military personnel, the uniforms down here reflected the status of housekeepers and laundrymen. "Let's find it quickly," Heinlein said. He had his doubts that their official demeanor would mean as much down below, and indeed, after turning a few corners, he heard a man call out and knew they had been meant to hear it. He stopped, turning to face a heavyset janitor in a brown jumpsuit.

"Where do ya think you're goin'?" the janitor asked. "What are ya doin' down here?"

"Official inspection," Gibson said, stepping forward to confront the janitor with a powerful, commanding voice. "These men are direct from Franklin Roosevelt's office in Washington, D.C. They're here on official business. I'm giving them a tour of the facility. Do you think we'd have found our way down here without proper authorization? Anybody important enough to be notified was. Were you?"

"I guess not."

Gibson drew himself to his full height and stepped toward the janitor, the crown of silver hair falling just below the man's jawline. "Then obviously you didn't need to be notified. We're trying to find the sub-basement but I think I turned wrong. Can you show me the way before I get in trouble for getting President Roosevelt's advisers lost?"

"Uh, sure," the janitor said. "Just make the next left and it's two doors down on the right."

"Thank you," Gibson said. "Follow me, gentlemen!" He slid past the other men, whispering to Heinlein as he did, "We better hurry." Heinlein was pleased to see that, at least for a moment, his friend was his old self again. He followed Gibson as the older man rapped his cane happily against the floor and turned a corner.

They followed the janitor's directions until they came to a door that simply bore the word HEATING. Heinlein gave a nod and Gibson stepped up again. Soon they were through the door and heading downstairs again into a darker, more humid arena. The descent was lengthy, as the vast room held the immense pieces of industrial equipment used to deliver power, water, and heat through the great building.

"How much time do we have now, do you think?" Hubbard asked, last to come down the stairs, folder still tucked under his arm.

"I think the real question is, how much trouble do you think we're going to get in?" de Camp replied.

"What are we looking for?" Heinlein asked, impatient.

"Al Smith told Father that they always knew they might need access to the old structure below the building. We should look for a cover, like a vent or a grate or something."

"Or a manhole cover?" Asimov asked. He was standing in the near corner, looking at an object beneath his feet.

"Exactly!" de Camp cried, leaping to his side. "That's it exactly."

They gathered around the iron square set into the floor, inscribed with the image of the Empire State Building and dated 1930—the year the foundation was laid. A set of hinges bordered one side. Heinlein knelt and examined four holes molded into it. He hooked his fingers through two of them while de Camp did the same with the other two. Straining and grunting, they boosted the lid up.

"It's spring-loaded," Heinlein groaned.

The others leaped to the edge and helped ease the lid until a metallic click echoed through the room and it locked into its open position. Once the hole was clear, Heinlein rose to his hands and knees and looked down, aware that the others were looking over his shoulders.

"Dark down there," Hubbard said. "Anyone got a flashlight? Walter?"

Heinlein's eyes adjusted and after a minute he said, "There's a ladder." He looked up at the others. "I'm going down."

He swung his feet over the ledge and let his toes find the first rung. Then he gingerly rose, supporting himself on the rim of the hole, letting more and more of his weight rest on the metal pole until he was convinced it would hold him. "Here we go," he said, trying to sound nonchalant, but hearing the nervous tightness in his own voice.

Heinlein began to descend. Each time his foot left a perch, a panic nearly overcame him until it found the next rung. He looked up and saw the concerned faces of his friends hovering around the glowing opening above. Down he climbed, the iron cool under his hands, the air growing more humid, the sounds of the great machinery becoming faint. Finally, his searching foot found the firmness of a hard floor. "I'm down," he shouted.

Lit only by the light from above, Heinlein could see the tiles on the floor, the arch of the ceiling, the columns—the lost remains of a golden age. He stood on the brink of a deep pool of clear water which bubbled out of a tiled dome at the far end of the room; the tiles were visible at the bottom, ten or so feet below the surface. The water then flowed through a shallower channel, across the entire length of the room, disappearing in darkness somewhere beyond the edge of the light. Set deep into the wall behind him was a heavy iron door, covered in thick red rust. He ran a hand over its cool surface, feeling the rotten iron crumble under his fingers. "Is this it?"

"Could be," de Camp said breathlessly, having descended the ladder quickly. He fished around in his pockets until he came up with the key. In the meantime, Gibson, followed by Asimov, worked their way slowly down the ladder.

De Camp inserted the key into the door and gave it a twist, grinning as the tumblers fell smoothly into place with a satisfying click. The ancient hinges shrieked in agony as he gave the heavy piece of metal a strong shove.

At that moment, Heinlein heard a shout from above and something briefly obscured their source of light. Something heavy clattered against the ladder and then splashed into the water.

"Christ! It's Hubbard!"

Heinlein leaped to the stream's edge. Hubbard was facedown, just beyond grasp. As he reached for the man he heard a grating squeal and looked up in time to see the spring-loaded cover crash shut with a thunderous *clang*, plunging the room instantly into the most intense blackness he'd ever known.

EPISODE 14

HIS LEGS HURT.

He was lying on a floor in the dark.

Why?

Other body parts were beginning to ache. His head throbbed.

He was cold and wet. Where was he?

A voice in the darkness. His?

Were his eyes open or closed?

"Ron?"

What the hell?

"What . . . the . . . hell?" His voice sounded funny.

"He's alive." That was Bob Heinlein, he recognized the voice.

"Are my eyes open?"

"Yeah. We're in the dark." Heinlein again. He sounded worried. "Are you okay? Are you bleeding anywhere? Anything broken?"

He moved his hands slowly over his head and body. "I'm okay." Struggling to sit up, he felt hands helping him into an upright position. His probing fingers found a lump on his head. "Damn."

"You fell. Into the stream."

"I did? Damn! I lost my mags."

Heinlein helped Hubbard to his unsteady feet. His suit was soaked and clung to his skin. "Isaac? You there?"

"Yes."

"Can you climb on up there and see if you can move that lid?"

"Up?" Hubbard could hear the fear in the young man's voice. "In the dark?"

"Oh, for Pete's sake," Heinlein retorted. "I'll do it myself. Walt—you got your lighter on you?"

The response came in the form of a metallic ring that echoed in the hollow space and a fitful burst of flame that flickered from the Zippo now visible in Gibson's fingers. In the glow cast by the lighter, Hubbard could see Heinlein scaling the ladder.

I fell from there, he thought. Christ. Lucky to be alive. Lucky to not be broken. Hubbard rubbed his head. "Sure would like to get my hands on the sonofabitch that clocked me." Walter nodded solemnly. "Any blood?"

"No."

"Well, that's a plus." In the dim glow he could see Ike's pale, frightened face. "You look worse than I feel, kid."

Heinlein had climbed into darkness and Hubbard could hear him grunting with exertion while the old iron ladder creaked under the strain. "It's jammed, or wedged!" he said, his voice filled with bitter frustration. He clambered quickly back down to the floor, his face slick with sweat. "I can't budge it."

"You mean we're trapped?" Isaac's voice was so high it was nearly feminine. "What about calling for help?"

"Who's going to hear us over the boilers up there?" Heinlein responded with a shrug.

"I can't believe this!" Hubbard snapped. "A few hours with you, Walt, and now I'm stuck in a secret basement beneath the Empire State Building. You know, I still won't go anywhere near Chinatown thanks to you. Hell! I won't even eat Chinese food!"

Gibson's light suddenly wavered and the room grew dim again as he turned away from them to explore the wall. "Hey!" he exclaimed, finding something mounted on the wall near the doorway where the other man still stood.

"What is it?" Heinlein asked.

Gibson fiddled with something and a low hiss filled the air. He brought the lighter close and suddenly a bright flame burst forth, illuminating the room. Stepping back from the glowing wall sconce, Gibson grinned. "They always forget to turn off the gas."

"Well done, Walter!" Heinlein clapped him on the back. "Where there's light, there's hope."

Gibson, still grinning with a mysterious pride, tapped the fixture, indicating Heinlein was to take a closer look at the logo on the lamp.

"'Gibson Gas Fixtures & Works, Philadelphia, PA, USA,'" Heinlein read, then turned with delight to Gibson. "The family business?"

"We built 'em to last." Gibson's grin was contagious. "Wish my old man knew about this."

"You walked away from a good business like that to write pulps?" Hubbard asked.

"Who wants to live in their father's shadow?" Gibson countered.

Now that they had light, Hubbard could see the whole of the space they had become trapped in. The great hall was longer than it was wide, running north and south along the block under the west side of the Empire State Building. The walls rose to curve up into a grand ceiling in a seamless flow in an interlacing pattern of milky white that seemed softly illuminated from within. The ladder they had descended rose up to a hole cut into the ceiling tiles. The floor was littered with broken pieces of ceramic and mortar that had fallen from the walls and ceiling over the years. A stream of clear water lined on either side by a bank of carved granite stone cut directly through the center of the length of the room, cascading from an elevated pond on one side of the hall and vanishing into a dark, low arch at the far end. Hubbard didn't want to think about what would have happened had he missed the aqueduct and landed on the floor.

"The Catalan Vault!" the man whose name rhymed with "Plague" said, looking up, his face filled with wonder and joy. "A lost Guastavino!"

Sprague! Sprague de Camp! That was the man's name, Hubbard realized. "Who?"

"Rafael Guastavino. The great architect."

Now that he could remember who he was, Hubbard could also remember that he was growing tired of the younger man's condescending tone, even though he had no inkling what he was talking about.

"He created this technique you see here of layering terra-cotta tiles to create these arches. They support themselves without an underlying structure. The subway station at Grand Central, the atrium of the Natural History Museum, even Grant's Tomb were projects of his design. And here—at the Waldorf-Astoria. This is marvelous. That curve in the ceiling? The style is known as the Catalan Vault. I'd heard about it growing up, but until I realized that Gernsback was talking about it, I never thought it was something I'd see."

"Well," Heinlein said, framed in the dark doorway, the gas flame illuminating half of his face perfectly while leaving the other half in darkness, "as long as we're going to die down here, let's find out what for."

They followed him into the darkness, Hubbard noting the heavy steel door as he passed by. Gibson quickly found another gaslight, and as another yellow flame burst to life, Hubbard leaned forward to see what wonders the room held. "Incredible," he said, his shoulders falling. "It's empty."

The chamber was about as big as a ship's cabin. The walls were lined with barren shelves. Whether they were metal or wood was indeterminate because of the thick layer of the dust of dozens of years that covered them.

"Not quite." Heinlein walked to the back of the room, each footstep leaving a distinct mark, like a cartoon character or the Invisible Man would leave behind. The solitary object tucked away in the back was covered by a gray tarp, also nearly buried under the dust. He flipped the oilcloth back and a cloud of choking particles filled the air, settling, then sticking to Hubbard's wet clothes until he felt like a chimney sweep. Heinlein sneezed, then shrugged. "Sorry about that."

They all stepped forward and stood around the object under the tarp. The brown steamer trunk showed signs of age and travel, the faded leather straps fastened shut with brass clasps. Inscribed in silver on a small plaque on the lid was the single word: ROOSEVELT.

"The *Roosevelt* was Peary's steamer on the North Pole Expedition," Hubbard explained to de Camp, pleased to have some information to contribute.

The young man, however, seemed unimpressed. "I know."

Gibson conjured his pieces of metal again and in a few moments both latches were unlocked. Heinlein took a deep breath and slowly lifted the lid of the case inside. Hubbard heard his sharp exhalation and leaned forward to see if it had been one of relief or exasperation.

The seal of the box had been tight enough to protect its contents from the dust. A flat layer of polished, burled wood rested several inches below the lip of the trunk. Embedded into the panel were several different gauges, bronze rings holding clear glass over them, shiny needles designed to point to the ornate numbers all pinned to zero. Below each gauge were small brass strips engraved with words like "Volt" and "Signal Strength." Under the gauges was a long thin horn, like a small coronet, with an arrangement of switches and knobs beside the fluted end. The center of the case was bisected by a thin strip of brass topped by a small ring. On either side of the strip were sealed glass compartments— each of which was filled with a different-color liquid. Heinlein pulled on the ring, and the strip, the top edge of a square panel, slid out easily. The brass edging contained a glossy opaque tile, the milky color of jade. He handed it to Isaac. "Know what that is?"

"Let me take it out to the light," the boy said.

In a compartment on the right side of the case was a coiled-up length of cable wire attached to a long spike. Hubbard reached a hand to stroke the warm, almost glowing metal of the cable. "It's gold."

"The best electrical conductor," de Camp offered.

"I know that." Hubbard pulled his hand away.

Heinlein noticed something affixed to the lid of the trunk. He pulled back a thick brown leather book. He opened the cover and Hubbard could see the handwritten notes inside.

"This is it!" A look of sheer joy crossed Heinlein's face. "Tesla's journal!" He flipped through it, page after page of notes, diagrams, and mathematical equations. "Oh my God! It's all here. Fellas, if we can get this back to Philly, we could figure out what Tesla was really up to." His eyes glittered feverishly. "This will solve the Wardenclyffe mystery."

"That's a good if," Gibson said. "Otherwise we're just going to be another part of the Wardenclyffe mystery for somebody else to solve someday."

Hubbard jerked a thumb back to the bigger hall. "Why don't we douse the flame, let the gas fill up, then ignite it with the lighter and blow the lid up there clean off?"

"Are you nuts?" the kid asked. "Don't you understand the formula for gas density?"

"Uh, no?"

"Seriously? Density equals mass divided by volume? You've never heard that?"

Why were they all so intent on making him feel stupid? "What does that mean?"

"It means we'd suffocate before we ever built up enough gas to do anything."

"And even if we could survive that," de Camp added, "a basic energy equation shows that the shock wave would kill us even before the roof collapsed on our heads."

"Well, let's dam up the stream and just float up and let the water pressure pop the top off!"

"Are you kidding?" the young man asked, incredulous. "The hypothermia would kill us."

"Before we drowned under the ceiling."

"I was kidding," Hubbard snapped at them. "The problem with you two is you're too smart for your own good. That goes double for your stories!"

"So you've read my stories?" Asimov looked pleased.

"Sure. You're the guy ruining science fiction with too much science and not enough fiction."

"Knock it off, Ron," Heinlein said, walking toward the door, tucking the Tesla book into his bomber jacket as he did so. "De Camp, what do you know about Minetta Stream?"

De Camp and the others joined him by the bank of the aqueduct. "Minetta comes from its original Lenape Indian name, Manetta. Manetta was the evil serpent who had made every effort of mankind futile since the beginning of time until finally he was driven to the ground by a great hero. Until it was buried by the Waldorf-Astoria it was known to the New Yorkers of the day as Devil's Stream."

"Real helpful," Hubbard muttered.

"This spring here used to feed into a pond. When they drained it, they found hundreds of skeletons of animals that had gotten stuck in its muck and drowned—even a human or two. So the water is strong. It runs downhill along Fifth Avenue into Greenwich Village, where it's diverted into the Hudson."

"So it follows a man-made conduit all the way?"

"Yes. But it's old."

"Oh, you've got to be kidding me," Hubbard said. "Come on, Bob!"

"The water is only a little more than waist-high. The channel is deep enough for us to stand in with just enough headroom."

"Wait a second. Let's hear from the brain trust to tell us how we'll die."

Asimov and de Camp looked to each other and then shrugged at the same time in silent agreement.

"Hypothermia again."

"Yeah, probably hypothermia."

"Well, I'm already wet, so let's get moving before I dry off."

"We've got to take *that* with us, too," Heinlein said, tossing his head in the direction of the trunk.

"I . . . I have an idea," Asimov stammered nervously. "I could wait here with the case and then you guys could come back for me, and it, once you get out." Hubbard hadn't realized until just that moment how scared the kid was. "I'll just wait here. I don't think . . . I can go down there."

"You have to." Heinlein put his hands on Asimov's shoulders.

"I'm . . . sorry, Bob. I don't think I can."

"Hey, Ike," Hubbard said.

"Don't call me that!" Finally a flash from the kid of something other than fear. Anger.

"Okay, Isaac. Look at it this way. All we're going to do is just take a stroll down Fifth Avenue," Hubbard said. "Sure, it's fifty feet below, but you've been on Fifth Avenue a million times in your life. We'll just count off the streets and stores as we go. And before you know it, we'll be down at the White Horse."

"White Horse?"

"Where do you kids go for drinks after writing?"

"Drinks?"

"Fine. First one's on me. Literally, it seems. But you can do this."

De Camp and Heinlein disappeared back into the vault again. The pair reemerged carrying the light trunk easily by the leather handles on either side. They set it down by the edge of the stream. Gibson, meanwhile, occupied himself with wrapping strips of oilcloth from the covering around the head of his cane.

"Okay, so what's next after Altman's?"

"I'm not sure."

"There's a great delicatessen that has the best pastrami in the city just across the street on Thirty-second. We'll be close enough to smell it."

Heinlein sat down on the bank, took a deep breath, and slid in. The flowing water buffeted him a little until he could catch his balance. "Cold," he said, his voice thin and tight.

"You get used to it," Hubbard said, watching as de Camp lowered himself in next. He joined Gibson by the trunk and helped hand it down to the two men in the water.

Gibson went in next. "Hope I can keep my tobacco dry," he joked. Hubbard turned to Asimov. "You ready?"

The boy hesitated for a moment. Then he took a deep breath. "Okay." Without another pause he dropped to his rump, then in another moment was in the water, bobbing up and down and sputtering. Though the sight was comical, Hubbard suppressed the giggles by jumping into the water himself.

"Goddamn! That's not cold, that's arctic! Takes me back to the fishing creeks of my youth."

"They say this used to be a pretty good trout stream," de Camp said.

"I couldn't give a . . ."

"Hubbard!" Heinlein shouted. "Grab the case."

The trunk was bobbing easily between the two men. Gibson picked up his cane and held his lighter to the oilcloth, which quickly caught fire. "Should give us about twenty minutes."

"Your leg okay enough to take the lead?" Heinlein asked.

Gibson nodded. "I'm taking the water cure. Feel like a million bucks."

"Okay, Rockefeller. Lead us onwards unto the Devil's Stream."

Hubbard put his hand on Asimov's shoulder. "Lower Fifth Avenue. That's what we'll call it, all right?"

"Sure."

"Good man."

"My wife's going to kill me," he said.

"You're a married man?"

Gibson bent under the arch at the far end of the room and the running water pushed gently against the rest of them, making it easy to head toward him.

"Yeah." Asimov nodded. Then he gave an utterly surprising laugh.

"What?"

"I was mad at myself for not inviting her to come to New York!" The kid ducked under the arch as Hubbard braced himself against it until he was through. For a moment he was alone, standing in the waters which still flowed in the Catalan Vault under the Empire State Building. "Too bad," he muttered to himself. "You could have really shown her the sights."

Was that good enough? "Really taken her downtown."

Almost. "Instead of taking her on the town, you could be taking her under it." That one was pretty good. He'd have to remember it when he got around to writing about this.

"Ron! You coming?" Heinlein's voice sounded scarily distant.

"Hell," said Hubbard, stooping to get under the arch. "I am!"

EPISODE 15

ISAAC COULDN'T GET the word "hypothermia," nor its pervasive, irritating accompanying facts, out of his head. He couldn't see his hand in the dim light provided by Gibson's torch, way too far ahead for his comfort, but he didn't need to know that he had the shivers. "Stage One," he muttered, when the body temperature drops from its normal 98.6°F to anywhere between 98° and 95°. The blood vessels in his extremities were contracting, sending vital heat back into his organs. He touched his thumb and his forefinger together several times. The sensation was reassuring, both because he hadn't yet gone numb enough to no longer feel it, but also because the inability to complete the action would be a sign that he was heading into Stage 2.

The water swirled and gurgled just below his belt, pushing incessantly at his back. What was thigh-high for Heinlein meant the tip of Isaac's necktie was getting wet. The ceiling above continued to gently curve overhead. No one spoke, everyone continuing to concentrate on taking just another next step in the right direction.

"Did you say something?" Sprague asked, his voice sounding thin and strained.

"When a sailor's ship is sunk and he goes into the drink, it's not the sharks that he's got to worry about," Isaac said. "It's not the salt water or starvation or heat exposure, either. What he's really helpless against, and what'll kill him faster than anything, is the hypothermia. Seventy degrees or below. It's my Philadelphia project."

"A way to beat hypothermia?" the red-haired man behind him asked, a voice in the darkness. Isaac knew of L. Ron Hubbard, mostly through the man's cowboy pulps he had read in his father's candy store. But he also knew that Hubbard had moved early and forcefully into the sci-fi pulps, had seen his name in *Astounding* as early as '38 or '39. Isaac and his friends had always maligned his appearances as a those of a hack without a feel for real science. "Because that would really come in handy about now."

"Uh-uh," Isaac replied. His teeth had just started chattering. Another bad sign. "I'm trying to figure out a way to get them out of the water quicker. Rescued. A man in the water, wearing all blue except for a little orange life vest, is going to be almost impossible for a plane to spot, let alone a ship on the seas. But if he had something highly visible that spread out around him and covered a couple of square yards, that would make it easier to spot him. A fluorescent gel or dye that doesn't dissipate in water. That way he can be rescued before Stage Two sets in."

A loud splash from up ahead as Sprague stumbled in the water, dropping his end of the case. Buoyant, Isaac could see it low in the water, bobbing gently. Sprague emerged from the water, sputtering and disoriented. He sluiced the water from his face and hair.

"Loss of muscular coordination," Isaac said, as Sprague regained his footing and grip on the box.

"Not funny, Ike," Bob snapped.

"Irritability, too," Isaac muttered, as the men ahead of him began to move forward again. "And I wasn't trying to be funny."

"Hey." Ron clapped him reassuringly on the shoulder, but using the motion to urge him forward at the same time with a gentle push. "What happens in Stage Three?"

"Death," Isaac replied.

"So, no Stage Four then?" He could almost hear Ron's grinning. "Good to know."

They began following the stream again. Isaac could feel a gentle slope to the bed, almost imperceptible, but just enough to make each footfall less sure than the one before it. Soon the tiled ceiling gave way to rough, natural stone, carved by years of the water's endless Stygian flow. This was where the excavators, the New Yorkers known as groundhogs, had stopped work. At the same time, the floor began to grow uneven and slippery. A force-field generator, something on a belt, would be useful now. It could create a bubble of protection around him, pushing the waters back, keeping his head safe. But if it pushed water away, surely it would keep oxygen out and his carbon dioxide in, and he would suffocate. Which would be like drowning. He heard himself whimper.

"Hey, Ike," Sprague said, in a bright, conversational tone that wouldn't have been out of place over a cup of coffee.

"Stop calling me that," Isaac said, forgetting, for a moment, about drowning, which might have been Sprague's intent.

"I've been meaning to ask you. What was that thing that Gernsback was asking about?"

"What thing?"

"GhuGhuism. Tell me about it."

The water was now over Isaac's belt. He could no longer ignore the fact that the stream was growing deeper. "It's a religion that my friends Johnny Michel and Donald Wollheim started. A religion for fans of science fiction."

Ron grunted behind him.

Isaac didn't care if the writer was making fun of him or not. Not really. "It was a joke," he explained. "Sort of."

"Do tell." A note of interest appeared to poke through Ron's dismissive veil of jaded indifference.

How far had they gone since Sprague had slipped? Half a block? "Hugo Gernsback realized from the amount of mail he was receiving after starting *Amazing* that there were thousands of fans out there. So, he started the Science Fiction League. A correspondence club for those of us who wanted to prove that it was literature—knew that it could be important. We wanted to protect science fiction. Was that a rat?"

"Keep walking, Ike," Bob said. "Keep talking."

"Lots of fans joined up. I did. It was just so uniting. I mean, you think you're the only person in the world who likes this stuff and then you find out that there are others out there who like it, too. And Hugo Gernsback published the names and addresses of members in the League so we could write each other. People in different towns could find each other. Like Freddie Pohl found me in Brooklyn."

"Pohl?" Sprague asked. "The writer?"

"Yeah. He's also my agent." For a moment Isaac forgot what he was talking about. His mind was beginning to race in wild directions and he recognized the sudden burst of mental energy as symptomatic of the mountain of anecdotal testimonies of sailors rescued from cold seas the Navy had provided him with as research material.

Stage 2.

He began speaking rapidly, as if the jaw and lip and tongue action could provide some warmth to the rest of his body—but mostly it was a nervous reaction to the realization that he really was going to die down here and Gertie would never know. "So, Freddie's group was spread out through Brooklyn and Queens. It wasn't really his group. It was Wally Sykora and Donald Wollheim and Johnny Michel. They called their club 'the Futurians.'

"Michel had an idea, a belief, that science fiction could really, ultimately, become a political movement. Almost that the people who most wanted to imagine the future should bring about the future. He was very serious about it. Even presented a speech once at a small science fiction convention in Philadelphia called 'Mutate or Die' in which he called for more direct political involvement from the fans. But, y'know, most fans just like what they like, and otherwise they're pretty different from one another.

"So Wollheim suggested that maybe why Michelism was receiving such a poor reception was because fandom actually had more in common with a religion than a political movement. Christ, it's really getting deep isn't it?" His feet had momentarily left the bottom and he had half-bobbed, half-floated for several yards.

"Go on about the religion thing." Ron sounded out of breath.

"GhuGhuism, Wollheim called it. GhuGhu was a giant beetle that lived on the side of a mountain on a planet called Vulcan and controlled Wollheim through mental manipulation—using him to spread the gospel. For all intents and purposes, Wollheim was to be considered GhuGhu himself on earth. Wollheim and Sykora and Michel even created something like a Bible and went so far as to write up tenets of belief and obeisances and named saints in other cities from the Science

Fiction League rosters. It was all a huge joke, of course. But at the same time, Wollheim was angry at Hugo Gernsback because he hadn't been paid for a story he'd written for *Amazing*. And he began accusing Hugo Gernsback of not letting the membership have a more active hand in the management of the club, so Hugo Gernsback publicly revoked his membership. Actually put a notice in the magazine. He didn't have to do that. It was all silly and meant nothing up until that point. But that was like a shot fired at us.

"Well, we didn't want to be in a club without Wollheim, and we were outraged for him, so we left and started our own club. And we wrote all the other clubs, because we had their addresses, and we got them to leave the League, too. Well, without all that dues money pouring in, Hugo was put out of the science fiction club business in a matter of months. And there were all these new clubs all over the place. At about the same time, Campbell took over *Astounding* and *Unknown* and we had more reading choices, better reading choices, and a whole different market to sell to, and then Hugo Gernsback was out of the science fiction business altogether. But it wasn't really because of GhuGhuism. That's just Hugo Gernsback taking it out on me. Because Wollheim was my friend, I helped kill the Science Fiction League. But I was never Ghuish."

He was really swimming now. The torch ahead was doused as Gibson lost the room to hold it over his head. The black that flooded through the tunnel even as the ghostly spots of light left on his retinas by the firelight still bobbed and waved before Isaac was like the darkness one finds in between dreams. "Hey!" he cried out. "Hey!" He held one hand up and out of the water, almost slowing himself down by dragging it along the ceiling just in front of him. Isaac prayed that there were no stalactites.

He could hear the voices of his friends up ahead, farther away than he would have liked, their words indistinguishable. Hollow echoes.

"Hey!" he tried again. There was a sound from not too far behind. Ron, swimming.

"There must be other feeders into the stream," Ron gasped. "It's picking up speed. Goddamn, I've always hated the idea of drowning."

"I don't want to drown."

"I almost drowned once when I was a kid."

"We're not going to drown, are we?"

"Hey, did your GhuGhu answer prayers?"

"No."

"Too bad. We could use the ear of a not too busy god about now."

"I'm an atheist."

"Even now? I admire you, kid."

"You?"

"I've got an angel watching over me. A redhead. I've been told she'll protect me."

"You don't really believe that, do you?"

"Not until about ten minutes ago. But the way things are going, we might find out if there is a God together."

Bob called back to them. "You fellas all right?"

"What's going on?" Isaac yelled back.

"The tunnel's narrowing!"

"Thank you, Oh master of the obvious," Ron sneered.

The waters rushed them forward. "Do you hear that?" Isaac asked.

"What?"

"It sounds like a . . . a . . . a rumbling. Like a subway. You don't think we're near the subway, do you?"

"That's something else. It's something up ahead."

"Light!" Isaac cried. "I see light!" Indeed, far ahead the black seemed to give way to a lesser gray. "Bob!"

But there was no answer. The sounds he had mistaken for the presence of a subway began to grow into a roar, even as the waters grew choppier. He was positive that if he could see, there would be whitecaps.

"Damn!" Ron hissed, sounding farther away again.

The gray-green glow suffused from what appeared to be the tunnel's end, but it could by no means be misconstrued for daylight. The distant, seemingly round opening was bisected neatly in two—the upper part illuminated, the lower dark with water. He could see the bobbing heads of his friends as they struggled to navigate the case. Isaac tried to find a hold on the right-hand wall of the tunnel, his fingertips scraping against a rough surface as they successfully slowed him down a bit. Typing was going to hurt for a few days. In spite of his situation, he had to smile a little. Some part of him actually thought he might yet survive. An instant later, the impact of Ron's body colliding with his knocked the last bit of good humor from him. Together they tumbled back into the stream, toward its termination point.

As Isaac surfaced, he heard voices shouting, unsure of the direction. There was water in his eyes, in his ears. A hand clutched at the collar of his jacket, pulling him to the wall. The water foamed and leaped around him. His grasping hands, alive and on their own at the ends of his numb arms, found something solid—metal—and closed around it tightly, almost involuntarily. His feet sailed along behind him, pulled by the current flow, but his grip held.

"I've got you, Ike." Bob's voice. Calm. Reassuring. Close.

Isaac opened his eyes. Mere feet from the craggy gap, he was holding on to a metal pipe. Iron or copper, it was held in place by rungs of great brackets which rose up through a wide hole cut into the ceiling. He looked up and could see Walter and Sprague managing to make their way up the pipe and disappearing into the darkness. Bob clung to the first rung above the water, holding on to the pipe with one hand, and Isaac with the other. "You hold on to the pipe," Bob said. "I've got to let go."

He nodded. Bob suddenly extended himself as far as he could, splashing into the water, simultaneously tackling and snagging Ron. Behind him, a repetitive heavy thud. Isaac turned from watching Bob reel in Hubbard to see the Tesla trunk knocking perilously at the stream's terminus, trapped against the lip of the opening caught in a swirling vortex only about three feet away from him.

"The trunk," he shouted.

"Forget it," Sprague hollered back from somewhere above.

He could reach it.

Bob had just pulled Ron to the pipe as Isaac launched himself toward the case. He heard both men calling his name, but the water flung him toward the opening with a speed that made him feel as if he were flying, hurtling into orbit around an alien planet. Both arms flung out in a reflex motion, feeling the narrow wall on either side. His forward momentum was frightening. With a heavy thud, his chest, unprotected by his arms, struck the trunk with full force, knocking an ugly, desperate grunt from his throat.

Jarred loose, the trunk tottered for a second. He reached for it, his fingers touching the leather, before it shot suddenly through the opening like a piece of spaghetti being sucked into a person's lips. One second it was there, and the next it was gone. Like the proverbial cork out of a bottle, the water surged forward, drawing Isaac along. Spread-eagled, he braced himself against the opening as his head was forced through.

Beyond the gap he watched in horror as their prize, pinwheeling end over end, dropped through a curtain of water and air far beyond his reach until it finally crashed onto the rocks poking through the small churning pool of white foam dozens of yards below. Wires, glass, and gears scattered every which way. What was left of the case itself then floated halfheartedly into the stream that flowed away toward the far side of a great cavern (for that's what he was peering into) before submerging once and for all beneath the dark waters. For a long moment Isaac remained suspended against the opening, peering into the vast subterranean chamber, the walls and ceiling coated with some kind of phosphorescent luminescent glow. Here were stalactites and stalagmites, great growths of colored crystals and spatterings of glittering ore woven through fields of oversized fungi.

He was yanked back into darkness and cold. Bob and Ron had him, commanding him to kick, swim, fight for his life. He grabbed the pipe again, the vision of the cavern still in full flower before his eyes.

"The case," he coughed, after a moment. "It's lost."

"You shouldn't have gone after it," Bob yelled at him. "I was going to get it."

"Leave off him, Bob," Ron said, breathing heavily.

Suddenly, light—like those nearly divine shafts of light one sees driving across farm country when they cut through distant clouds—fell upon them.

"Thank you, Walter B. Gibson," Bob sighed. "Okay. Up you go."

Isaac climbed the rungs up the pipe as if they were a ladder. He could feel the vibration of water flowing up the tube. The hole he climbed through was rough-hewn, drilled out quickly in order to drop the pipe and anchor it, but not suited for regular maintenance. It grew wider, like an inverted cone, indicating that the people who dug this had run out of the patience required to maintain consistency. Bob and Ron were below him. He looked up and could see the substructure of an old building—planks, mortar, old hardwood—then a hole above, hands reaching for him, drawing him up, helping him to his feet on a concrete floor.

That they were in a basement was obvious by the dust, boxes, and stairs which only led up. The hole in the floor that the two men followed him up through was apparently usually covered by a cast-iron hinged door that Sprague and Walter had managed to force open. The pipe continued to rise up until it merged into the ceiling above. Soon they were all standing, dripping wet, but alive.

"I'm sorry about the case," Isaac said to Bob, at last.

Bob shrugged. "How was I going to get it up the pipe, anyway? Besides"—he pulled an object from beneath his shirt, wrapped in oilcloth from the outside of the case—"at least we still have this." He unfolded it gently, and revealed Tesla's journal, still dry. He grinned.

"Oh, and I've got this," Isaac said. He pulled the green piece of glass framed in thin brass from his pocket. Pleased, Heinlein gave his shoulder a graceful squeeze.

"Thank God," Sprague said.

"Thank GhuGhu," Ron corrected him.

After surviving the adventure of the past few hours, it seemed funny to Isaac as they stood clustered around the door at the top of the stairs, knocking politely until a very surprised custodian opened it. They offered no explanation as they sloshed past him into the lobby of 2 Fifth Avenue, the great arch towering over Washington Square Park visible just outside the doors.

"Well," Walter Gibson said. "The Village. I'm practically home. That's convenient."

Exhausted, they followed him across the lobby, still barely able to place one foot in front of the other, heading for what warmth the setting

sun could provide, each of them ignoring the merry burbling of cold
clear waters cascading from the top of the large Art Deco fountain standing in the middle of the floor.

EPISODE 16

"ARE YOU AT Walter Gibson's now?" Leslyn asked, her voice full of such
intimate concern that he could feel the tensions and aches that had
seemed to cluster at the spot where the back of his head joined his spine
drain away. It struck him how much he had been afraid of angering or
upsetting her, of spinning her off her delicately perched roost, so that he
had held back much of his adventure in its retelling. The terrifying trip
through Minetta Stream became an almost humorous stumble through
a New York sewer.

"No." He cast his eyes about the Italian marble floor, the aged oak
wainscoting, the great velvet curtains, the chesterfields and china on
permanent display. The room was like an exquisite museum display, New
York rich, *fin de siècle*, everything perfect and perfectly in place. "I'm at
de Camp's grandmother's house on Seventy-fifth Street."

"Sounds quaint," sarcastic now, not quite believing him.

The clock on the end table which also supported the phone he was
using was gilded and accented with elephant tusk ivory. Or rhino tusk.
Or sperm whale penis bones. De Camp had pointed out numerous ex-
amples of all three. "Quaint," he agreed. "Gibson couldn't put us up for
the night. I think he was done with us. De Camp said his grandmama had
rooms she wasn't using, so we came up here. Boy, he wasn't kidding. You
should see this place."

"You couldn't have come home?"

The exhaustion in every muscle, sinew, and tendon was nearly electric. "No way I could drive home. I barely got us up here."

"If you say so," she said. He could almost feel the phone growing
physically cold as a distance that was more than physical set into her
voice.

"What does that mean?" He couldn't even hear her breathing. "Are
you still there?"

"Yes."

"What do you mean?"

"If you needed to go to New York and go whoring around with your writer buddies, you could have just said so."

He thought of the black water and smiled grimly. "Don't be crazy."

"I am crazy. You've got the commitment papers to prove it. I understand if you don't want to be around me. I wouldn't want to be around me, either."

He had to be careful now, he was entering Leslyn's mine field. She was trying to draw him into a fight; a doctor had told him that when her moods were upon her, she would act provocatively. It was almost as if she needed someone else to share her emotional turmoil—to experience what she was feeling. Alcohol only made her worse. Heinlein shook his head. That was the wrong way, unfair way, to put it. Alcohol only made her problems worse. Not her. It wasn't her fault.

When he had first met her, in Los Angeles, her pale skin—she hated the sun—striking against her bohemian-style tight black cashmere sweater, the highball glass, icy cold and full of gin, pressed against her flushed face, he had been instantly attracted to her aura of jaded sexuality. She spoke with a lazy slur, drunk or not, as if either way she couldn't be bothered to offer full support to her vowels and consonants and left them to fend for themselves. Leslyn was an archivist at Universal Pictures and claimed to have actually seen more of the studio's movies than anyone else alive. She'd had some inchoate ambition to write for the movies, but had never taken the first formative steps, trying to get work in the story department as an assistant, for example, which would have even paid her a little bit more. He'd never seen her pick up a pen to write a word of fiction. But when she was fully engaged and impassioned, she could tear a movie apart to its essential elements like no one he'd ever seen before. Themes, motifs, references, archetypes, Leslyn could divine these in any picture, even the monster movies, where he only saw plot and characters. Unfortunately, the mental razor she used to slice W. C. Fields out of *The Bank Dick* and place him into a cultural pantheon as an American Falstaff was the same blade she'd turn on her husband to cut at his heart and soul. And depending on how bad she felt, or how much alcohol she'd been able to find, she could be as dispassionate about the dissection of her husband as about a movie.

He could tell by the lack of outright belligerence that she hadn't been drinking. That was good. The New Jersey sanitarium had cost him a fortune, everything he'd had since he'd begun rebuilding his life after having lost it all in that ill-fated silver mine investment. If it couldn't cure her of her dramatic swings (and one of the reasons he'd pulled her was his adamant refusal to authorize electroshock treatment as the next step in her treatment), it had apparently loosened alcohol's choke-hold on her.

"I still want to be with you," he said.

"Sure," she replied. "It's really easy for you to say that when you're not here, Bob."

"I told you all about that. I'm here on work."

"I know. There's a war on. It's your job. Save the world. I'm not trying to stop you. In fact, I'm saying I don't want to stand in your way."

"You're not in my way."

Asimov stuck his head over the landing to see if the phone was available—his bushy eyebrows knit tightly together over his thick glasses, running into each other. Bob turned away from him and dropped his voice. After a moment, he could feel the withdrawal of the younger man's anxious, twitchy presence. Elsewhere he could hear the low murmur of de Camp in conversation with his grandmother, virtually bedridden, he had claimed. Her voice rose loudly for a moment, thick and polluted, filled with recrimination about how de Camp's old man had abandoned his obligations and run for shelter upstate in Great Falls. De Camp's tight response, followed by a directive that she lower her voice while they had company in the house, implied that she had been complicit in the abandoning. Their voices then grew quiet. From down a hall he could hear the rattle and clink of bottles and glasses being rifled through—Hubbard's boldly announced quest for the bar had apparently paid off and now its conquest had begun.

"Are you still there?" Her end had grown so quiet.

The strike of a lighter carried over the line. "Are you?"

"I'll be home tomorrow."

"Ah, tomorrow," she said. "Who knows if the answer to the question, 'Are you still there?' will be the same tomorrow."

"Come on, Les," he snapped. "Knock it off. I'm exhausted."

"Of course you are," she said, suddenly sounding sympathetic. "I know you are. That's what I've been telling you. I know you are." A long inhale and exhale of smoke. So familiar the sound that he expected to smell the thick, piercing aroma waft past his nostrils as it would were they in the same room. "I wish you were here. I wish we could make love right now."

"I know." The bed was the one place where they could still seem to make each other happy. Or at least less sad.

"We could pretend," she said, lowering her voice to a more animal purr.

"I'll be home tomorrow."

"I meant right now."

"On the phone?"

"We could."

Asimov was pacing overhead.

"I can't," he whispered.

"Please," she begged. "Please, Bobby. I really want to. I need you to."

"It's just . . . not the right time."

"You're exhausted."

"Yeah."

"And you'll be home tomorrow."

"That's right."

"Okay. Good night, Mr. Heinlein." She never called him that, and the sound of his name pronounced like that made his head snap slightly. The young lady at the naval yards, the scientist, his scientist, had been the last one to call him that. It had been playful then. Virginia. That was her name. What an inopportune moment for her to spring to mind, he thought. "Good night, hon," he replied quickly. He waited for a moment longer, heard the exhale of her smoky breath grow faint as the phone receded from her mouth, and then the click as it settled into the receiver.

For a few seconds he drove the handset into his forehead, grinding the smooth, cool Bakelite against his skull. Then he moved to slam the phone down, stopping himself only at the last moment by remembering he was a guest in someone else's home and this phone didn't belong to him. He replaced the receiver, as gently as he could—so softly as not to even make a click. And yet the instant his hand was lifted, he could hear Asimov's approach, the swift clatter of his heavy feet on the stairs.

"It's all yours," he murmured, stepping aside.

"Thanks," Asimov said, grabbing for the phone as if Heinlein was going to snatch it away from him.

"Calling the wife?"

"I'd like to."

"Do me a favor. Don't tell her about the . . . y'know, please?"

"Oh no, I wouldn't. Besides, she's going to be mad at me."

"Yeah? Funny. Mine was, too."

Asimov's eyes snapped wide open with a surprise so genuine that Heinlein found himself intrigued. "What'd you do?"

"Said I was sorry and I'd see her tomorrow. What else can you do, right? Take it like a man."

Heinlein noted that Asimov's brow began to unfurrow a little. He patted the kid on his shoulder.

"Tell you what, on our way back tomorrow we'll stop at one of those little farm stands off the turnpike and pick up a huge mess of fresh flowers for them. Uncle Sam's treat. What do you say?"

"She'd like that." His face brightened considerably.

"I bet she would. I know mine will," he lied with a grin.

Heinlein left Asimov, phone in hand, similar smile on his face, ready to talk to his wife, and wandered down the hall, unsure of where he was going, but mesmerized by the rich, strong-jawed history of the Sprague and de Camp lines as evidenced by numerous paintings of ancestors, the last of whom on the wall nearest the kitchen predated the republic by a century or so. From the luxurious styling of their clothes it was apparent some had contributed to, participated in, and profited from its inception.

The door to the kitchen, equipped to serve a full restaurant, stood open. Heinlein could hear the radio broadcast: the Yanks were beating the Athletics. That would be bad for morale back at the Navy Yard. The native Philadelphians, who handled services like feeding the military personnel on the base, grew notoriously surly and slow when their sports team, especially the Athletics, lost, and particularly to the Yankees. Sticking his head in, he received baleful glares from the elderly woman who had answered the door and appeared to take care of Mrs. Colonel Sprague, and an old man, apparently Mrs. Colonel Sprague's chef. Not welcome here.

He backed down the hall again, turning toward the opposite staircase when he realized he was dangerously close to overhearing too much of Asimov taking his lumps. Heinlein didn't know the kid hadn't even told his wife he was heading out on a mission. He was glad he'd commandeered the phone first. Asimov was going to be a while. And Uncle Sam was going to have to buy a lot of flowers tomorrow.

Heinlein stopped at the landing on the second floor. De Camp had given them a quick tour, but the layout up here was different and he couldn't recall which room was his. There was one—well, for lack of a better word he'd have to say wing, for that's how the hallway appeared— to starboard, and another to port. He reasoned it was always easier to tack to the starboard side and turned to the right. Besides, the hallway was dimly lit as opposed to the utter darkness of the other wing. After today, he couldn't bring himself to walk into the black.

He remembered that his door was at the end of a corridor so he walked in what he felt was the appropriate direction, his feet sinking deeply into a Persian runner that was still thick, plush, and comfortable after decades of use. Asimov's voice was finally out of earshot; even what passed for the kid's whisper had carried farther than Heinlein would have thought. It was nice to have a little privacy.

The door past his right shoulder suddenly flew inward with a force powerful enough to muss his hair. Badly startled, his knees buckling, he leaped to the other side of the hallway, throwing himself into the doorjamb. A great bulk filled the newly open doorway, blocking the light. Whatever the monster was, he knew he didn't have the strength or acuity to fight it. He was done for and he wasn't as sad as he thought he might have been.

"Where's my milk?" the creature snapped. By milk, Heinlein was pretty sure it meant his warm blood. It was shorter than he was, but its girth expanded beyond the door frame. Corpulent, wrinkly, covered in a gray fuzz, hungry eyes glittering at him through a frayed curtain of white hair; if there was a mouth there, a leering maw, he didn't want to see it. "Milk!" it croaked again, as if his blood, his beating heart, were its birthright.

"Ray!"

Heinlein couldn't bring himself to take his eyes off the huge beast, but its head swung toward the end of the hall where he had thought his room awaited and from where the call came again. At the second call, he snuck a look.

"Ray!"

De Camp strode rapidly down the corridor, holding a steaming highball of white liquid before him. He wore an expression of irritation and embarrassment, as well as a sumptuous red dressing gown and blue silk pajamas that were obviously tailored since they fit so well. Heinlein had never even considered tailored pajamas. Now he thought how amazing they must feel.

"Bob." De Camp nodded at him while handing the horrible brute its treat. "This is my grandmama, Ray. Mrs. Colonel Sprague, they call her."

"How do you do?" Heinlein asked, as brightly as he could considering only a moment ago he had contemplated his death at her hands. "Ma'am?"

She replied by slurping down the milk in great, loud gulps, while fixing him with a baleful eye. When she finished, she belched loudly, proudly, then dragged the sleeve of her gray flannel nightgown, ancient, still tufted with red thread remnants of what must have once been embroidered robins or roses, across her lips.

"Ray!" Sprague snapped at her.

Another belch. One Heinlein could smell: roast beef, milk of magnesia, castor oil.

"Sorry," her grandson apologized while she glared balefully at the two of them. "She's ninety-three years old and thinks that confers upon her a certain invulnerability to the conventions of society and civilization."

"That's okay." Heinlein shrugged. "I just got lost looking for my room."

"Masher," she hissed at him. "Pervert."

De Camp shook his head in pained surrender. Then he pointed back to the landing. "It's down the other way."

"Degenerate."

"Ah. Is there a light switch down there?"

"Deviant."

"It's a little hard to find, but it's on the wall on the left just past the corner. Want me to show you?"

"Rapist."

"Murderer" crossed his mind. She forgot murderer. "I'll find it. See you tomorrow. Good night, Mrs. Colonel."

He left de Camp trying to squeeze her back into her lair and made haste for the landing. Asimov was still on the phone and obviously making little progress. Instead of looking for the light switch and finding his room, he trotted down the staircase and headed for the smell of scotch.

Hubbard was sprawling in an overstuffed leather sofa and gave Heinlein a languid wave as he entered the library. Which, Heinlein noted, looked like a movie set. It was ringed with books from floor to ceiling and even had a ladder on wheels affixed to a brass rail running around the entire collection. There were pedestals with huge volumes open to pages that hadn't been read in ages. Busts of authors and composers sporadically kept books apart from each other. Heinlein wondered if a bust of his head would ever find a space on a shelf like this and then realized that, well, no, because he had yet to actually write a novel.

There had been a few attempts. But getting a clever idea to last over several hundred pages wasn't enough, he'd found. Short stories left a lot to the imagination; novels filled the imagination.

Hubbard had discovered a trove of liquor in the bar. He'd arranged four bottles on the floor next to him, and four glasses, all overfilled. Also, water and ice and more glasses were handy but untouched. He fondly tapped each bottle as he introduced Heinlein to them: "Angus Dundee, eighteen years. Dalwhinnie, ten years. Royal Lochnagar, twenty-five years." There was a lecherous tone in his voice that made Heinlein wish Hubbard had been the one to accidentally wander into the clutches of the Mrs. Colonel.

"No White Horse?"

"Feh!" Hubbard picked up the last bottle and rescued it comfortably on his chest, staring at it with awe. "Glenfiddich. Founder's cask, 1847. Signed by William Grant his self." Heinlein understood the reverence in his eyes. "I broke the seal."

"Should you have?"

"I had to." Sitting up, he filled one of the empty glasses for Heinlein, added a dash of water, just a splash, and handed it over.

Heinlein was drunk on the aroma before the liquid gold even touched his lips. It was molten sunlight, spreading from his stomach into his central nervous system, rising up his spine into his brain, imbuing it with a vision of a world completely and utterly at peace. "Good," he managed, sinking into a club chair.

"Hell it is." Hubbard sighed. He lay back down, his head on a pillow, picking up the book he had set aside and resting it on his chest. It was obvious he had no inclination to read at this point, but he seemed to like the security of a book nearby. "Did you know that the alternating current motor appeared to Tesla in a vision? In fact, he says that most of his best ideas appeared to him fully formed. He could see these things floating in front of his eyes. Do you think people really experience visions? Or is it a sign that they've become insane?"

Heinlein took a longer, more lengthy sip, letting his eyes wander over the library until they came to rest upon Hubbard again. As the liquor continued to spread into crevices of his body he had heretofore been unaware of, a touch of anger crept along with it. "You can't—" and pointed, unable to find the word.

"I told you. I had to."

"You can't read that book," Heinlein finished his thought.

Hubbard held up the leather-bound Tesla journal with only limited interest. "What? This?"

"Yes."

"Seriously?"

Heinlein gestured for it but Hubbard didn't comply.

"Why not?"

"It's the property of the Office of Naval Scientific Research."

Now Hubbard sat up. "You are serious."

"I need the book, Hubbard."

"Bob, I . . . Jeez. I'm in the goddamn Navy."

"It's government business."

"Maybe I'll join up with the Office of Research."

"I don't think you'll pass the security clearances. You've been court-martialed." He held out his hand.

"Christ." Hubbard tossed the book to him as if it didn't matter, but Heinlein knew it did. "You're always one for following authority."

Heinlein didn't answer because it was uncomfortably close to the thought that had occurred to him while wading through the stream. He couldn't actually convince himself that Hubbard was a spy, per se, but the timing of his appearance could be misconstrued by Slick and Scoles when he reported on the day's events. To come in here after all else that had happened and find the man reading the Tesla journal was enough to place him firmly in the line of authority's suspicion.

Hubbard rose unsteadily, letting the bottle of Glenfiddich drop to his side. "I know what this is really about."

"No, you don't."

"If that's what you want to tell yourself."

For a moment, Heinlein thought that physical conflict was on the man's mind; he felt physical strength flow through him, if only Hubbard would throw the first punch. Instead, he hoisted his glass to Heinlein. "You are a true hard-ass, Bob. Nothing wrong with that." He took a long sip. "But you shouldn't have come down so hard on the kid for losing that case. You'd have never gotten it out of there no matter what you think. And he was scared shitless." Hubbard walked past him, still swinging the bottle. "Hope the book is worth it to you." He paused in the doorway. "By the way. Page eighty explains why we found the Peary case in the vault. It wasn't returned to Tesla because it never left."

"What?" The rage turned cold in an instant.

"Peary never took it. His expedition fell behind. In fact, he didn't even depart until after whatever happened in Tunguska. Tesla never sent him the signal because he was still here in New York." Hubbard sauntered out of the room, chuckling to himself. Heinlein fought the urge to throw his glass at the back of his red head. Instead, he drained the glass. He heard Hubbard loudly wish Ike a good night on his way up the stairs. "Don't call him Ike," he muttered to no one in particular. "He doesn't like it."

Heinlein looked at his empty glass and wanted more of the golden essence that had been abducted from its proper place in the library. He knew that no matter how good the others that Hubbard had left behind were, they would pale in comparison to what he'd finished. Still, he figured, any port in a storm. He carried his glass over to the sofa and took a seat. There was no way he was going back upstairs, may as well be comfortable here. He poured himself a glass of the Royal Lochnagar. It wasn't bad. It just wasn't an insight into the divine.

He lay on his back, feeling his bones settle into the sofa. He opened the Tesla journal and began to read.

EPISODE 17

"THIS IS IT?"

After the long drive on Route 25, through the drearily repetitive farm country and tract house lots it ran past, and knowing they were heading toward the ocean, Hubbard had expected something more, well, extraordinary. He'd made as many Gatsby and East Egg versus West Egg jokes as his wit could conjure up ("Watch out for yellow cars!" "Is that billboard staring at us?"), but nothing seemed to penetrate the dismal gloom of the other three men. Whether it was the rain, or exhaustion from the travails of the day before, Hubbard couldn't be sure. Furthermore, he had a sneaking suspicion that none of the other of his fellow writers had actually read Fitzgerald. Then again, their names on mag titles sold better than any book with Fitzgerald's name on it, so why would they care? Finally, he had settled into the rhythm of their funk, growing silent. After all, it wasn't his job to provide entertainment. As Bob had pointed out the night before, he didn't really have any job with them at all. He was just along for the ride.

But, be that as it may, he had expected Wardenclyffe to be something more after all he'd gone through to see it today. The building was much smaller than it should be, he thought, as they got out of the car. It sat alone in a field of sea grass and scrubby maples fronted only by a parking lot where they had come to a stop. The pavement was cracked like the moon's surface, with thick clumps of weeds culpable for its destruction. The jagged remains of several other buildings, once part of the compound, somehow managed to remain standing—like an old drunk in a dive at the end of a long evening—at improbably listing angles.

The bricks of the main building were still vividly scarlet. On either side of the pair of great doors were four arched windows; behind the glass, black emptiness. The angle of the roof was low and its smoothness was interrupted in the middle by a square belvedere with a smokestack rising above it.

"You say a famous architect built this?" he asked.

"Stanford White." Bob nodded.

"Just looks like a small factory to me. And this is where he supposedly blew up Siberia?"

Bob kicked a stone loose from the mud with the toe of his shoe.

"I just expected more from a mad scientist."

He watched Bob squint into the misty drizzle, as if trying to perceive something that lay behind the fine gray curtain.

"You know"—Hubbard nodded his head toward the general direction where he thought the ocean might be—"we're not all that far from Haimoni Island."

The mention of another time and place jarred a wry grin onto Bob's face. "Lester Dent would have loved this place."

"Norma, too."

"Yeah."

"Want to take a look around back?"

"Sure. Hey, fellas, we're going around. Want to come?"

Asimov was still sitting in the car. Hubbard wasn't sure that he wasn't sulking. "It's raining," he muttered through the open window crack and didn't move another muscle.

"Fine," Hubbard said. "You're on spy watch."

De Camp shrugged and climbed out. Bob tapped on the window and

Asimov rolled it down. Hubbard saw him slip Asimov something and heard him say, "Make yourself useful."

Bob had already begun to walk, so Hubbard turned from the car to follow and let de Camp catch up when he could. He followed Bob around the building, still surprised that this one-story structure was supposed to have been involved in global energy and communication transmission in any way, shape, or form, let alone harbor potentially devastating weapons technology. In the field behind Wardenclyffe, Bob was pacing off the distance between two of four old concrete anchors. He held out his arms up in front of him to form a triangle toward the sky. "This is where the tower stood. It rose up here high over the building. Like Shoreham's own Eiffel Tower, but built entirely of wood, even down to the pegs."

Rotten planks the size of railroad ties covered the ground at the center of the four points. "That's the pit, right?" Hubbard asked, at the same time warning de Camp back with a raised hand.

"One hundred fifty feet, straight down." De Camp nodded.

"Why, I wonder?" Hubbard shook his head. "This whole place—it's a monument to not making sense. Like Easter Island."

"Imagine what he could have done here if Morgan had just let him finish. It might have changed the world. Maybe there's a parallel universe where he succeeded. In that place, every living person on the planet receives free power."

"Maybe war would have ended, too," de Camp said. "If this could have been used to destroy fleets of ships or planes, or cities from afar, who'd want to go to war against that? No one could ever launch an invasion armada again. The Blitzkrieg would have been stopped with the push of a button."

"If it worked," Hubbard reminded them. He could tell by the look that passed between the two other men that for them it was mostly a foregone conclusion. "I've been having a hard time believing that a smart man like Morgan wasn't able to figure out a way to make money off this, even if it wasn't apparent at first or as easy as hanging a meter. I mean, if I spent ten minutes thinking about it, I could probably figure out some way to charge. Maybe Morgan decided he was being hustled?"

"Maybe Morgan lacked the particular vision," Bob said.

"Why don't we go see what's left inside?" Since this conversation wasn't going anywhere, at least he could take the credit for leading them to the inevitable. As they left the remains of the tower and trudged through the mud toward doors nearly identical to the ones at the front (or was this the front? Hubbard couldn't be sure), he asked de Camp, the obvious authority on all things New York, "Why is it called Warden-clyffe?"

"An investor named John Warden had a fancy resort near here called Wardenclyffe-on-Sound. I suppose there are cliffs around here some-where but I don't really know the lay of the land. At some point he moved into Tesla's New York orbit, and when he heard that Tesla needed land, I guess he figured the Wardenclyffe World Wireless Center had a nice, highly profitable ring to it."

"Sounds like a good deal," Hubbard said.

"You know what's odd?" de Camp said as Bob put his hand on the door.

"What?"

"Most abandoned buildings like this—the windows are all busted out. This building—they're all intact."

"Look around," Bob said. "You need kids to bust windows and there's no kids for miles around."

"Kids seem to always find a window to break." De Camp was more concerned, not less. "Who owns this place?"

"It's deserted." Bob twisted the knob and the door opened.

"Guys"—de Camp looked over the shoulders of Hubbard and Bob as they stood in the doorway—"this place is not deserted. It's empty be-cause it's Saturday. But it's sure as hell not deserted."

"It looks like some kind of lab," Hubbard said. The main part of the open room was filled with long rows of tables covered with big jars of chemicals. More containers of liquids and powders sat on the many shelves lining the walls. He followed Bob inside. The ceiling was higher than the impression the exterior gave. Great swaths of black duvetyn, flame-retardant velvety fabric, pinned to the walls kept light from seep-ing in, or out. Half of the great space that had stood open in Tesla's time had been crudely divided by a wall, which shared none of the skill and craftsmanship now apparent to Hubbard in the rest of the building.

"Maybe someone's still trying . . ." Bob's words trailed off before he could give voice to his hope.

Hubbard flipped some light switches and a crimson bulb mounted over the door set into the middle of the newer wall blinked on. In its glow, he could read the word stenciled on the wall above it: DEVELOPING. "It's a lab, like I said. A film lab."

De Camp picked up several envelopes from the desk by the door. "Peerless Photo Products," he said, tossing them back.

Bob walked deeper into the room, staring around for some clue that Tesla had once been here. He gave a futile shrug and was about to speak when they all heard a surprising but distinctive sound from the far end of the building.

"Plumbing still works," Hubbard said. "Maybe Tesla flushed Siberia down the crapper."

A door in the far shadows swung open even as Hubbard finished speaking and a young man, wearing the plain uniform shared by security guards everywhere, appeared. Clearly assuming he was alone, he whistled as he continued to tuck his gray shirt into his gray pants. Jutting out from his armpit was a rolled-up magazine.

Bob cleared his throat and the boy leaped, startled. He grabbed his magazine and waved it at them. "Hold it right there! Don't you move!"

As he was still quite distant from them and they had a good chance of outrunning him, Hubbard asked, "Is that thing loaded?"

Bob stepped forward and held up his hands. "Easy there, buddy. We're not here for trouble. We thought the place was abandoned. We just opened the door a moment ago. There wasn't even a car in the parking lot."

"My mom drops me off on Saturdays. Are you some of those Tesla freaks?"

"Yeah! That's it exactly. We just wanted to see if it was for real."

"You guys cause me more trouble." By now the kid was close enough that Hubbard could count the pimples on his face. Younger than Asimov. Probably still in high school, ready to enlist after finishing his senior year. "Now I gotta call the cops."

Hubbard caught a glimpse of his mag and smiled: *Unknown.* It was worth a shot. "Look, kid. I'm L. Ron Hubbard, the writer. Ever hear of me?"

"No."

"I've been in that mag. And lots others, too."

"Really? I never heard of you."

"Believe it. And this fella here. His name is Bob, sorry, Robert Heinlein. Robert A. Heinlein. Ever hear of him?"

As if hearing a far-off church bell, the kid tilted his head and concentrated. "He don't write no more."

"That's right." Bob nodded. "What's your name?"

"Chad. Who's that guy?" His eyes had narrowed with suspicion.

"Sprague," de Camp said with a shrug. "Sprague de Camp."

The kid's squint dissolved into wide-eyed awe. "*The Castle of Iron,*" he whispered.

"Him you know?" Hubbard asked, turning to see if de Camp stood in a new light. "Really?"

"I'm so glad you wrote a sequel to *The Mathematics of Magic,*" the kid continued.

"Well, it wasn't my idea, really. My cowriter had the idea."

"Fletcher Pratt?"

"Yeah, him."

Who? Hubbard mouthed to Bob, but the response was a shrug.

"You know that part where Harold Shea and Thor fight the frost giant?"

"Yeah."

"I love that."

"Well, thanks."

With the mention of the name Harold Shea, the tumblers suddenly clicked in Hubbard's head and in a sucking instant he realized why de Camp had treated him with such high-handedness.

Harold Shea.

Like every author in the *Astounding* and *Unknown* stable, Hubbard had received one of Campbell's urgent letters requesting a story be written based on an idea he was providing herein in the body of said letter.

In this particular case, Campbell had a character he'd presented in several earlier issues of *Unknown* (issues provided for reference) and he'd like Hubbard to work him into a story. The character had a knack for dropping out of the real world and into lands based upon various mythologies. Could Hubbard do something with Harold Shea?

Hubbard went right to work and had a story in mind by the time he sat down at the Smith Corona. No need to actually read the accompanying mags. Campbell wouldn't have given him the job if he hadn't thought Hubbard was the right (and only) man for the job. Campbell hadn't asked for a rewrite, and in August 1941, the story was published. Hubbard hadn't given a thought about it since the check cleared months earlier.

Then, in September, Campbell printed the letters. They were unanimous in their utter disgust of Hubbard's treatment of the (beloved? who knew?) Harold Shea. Really, it was Campbell's fault. Campbell should have stressed the importance of the character. Regardless, there were already other stories to write, and he'd had bad reviews from the fans before (though never quite at this level of outrage), so he'd forgotten all about it. Until right now. Not that he really cared, but he could imagine how upset de Camp must have been to see another, more accomplished writer take possession of a character he had created. It was the literary equivalent of a land snatch; in other words, a shooting offense. For all de Camp knew, Hubbard might have begged Campbell for a writing project. Anything. Might have even suggested taking a crack at someone else's character.

(Is that what he'd done? He kind of remembered pestering Campbell about needing work. His memory was so damn fuzzy on points like that.)

"So, Chad," de Camp said, as if they were old foxhole buddies. "We're just going to go on about our business and leave you to yours."

Heinlein opened his mouth to speak, but de Camp shot him a look that silenced him.

"Unless, if it's okay with you, you know of any old stuff, Tesla's stuff, around here that you could let us just sneak a look at?"

Chad looked at his rolled-up magazine. "There's nothing."

"Ah, well." De Camp quickly removed his government-issued pen and notepad and began to scribble. "If you remember anything, why don't you give me a call? We're working for the Navy, and it would really help us out."

"Really? The Navy?"

De Camp stopped writing but didn't look up from the paper. "The Scientific Research Station at the Navy Yard in Philadelphia. It's important work." He snapped the notepad shut. "It's a mission."

The kid twisted his magazine until the cheap paper fibers would twist no more. "There's some things in the basement. You might want to see those. And then there's the tunnels."

"Tunnels?" Hubbard groaned.

"You don't have to come," Heinlein snapped.

He was really starting to feel like the odd man out—especially now that he knew why de Camp had been mad at him. He already had an idea what had ticked Heinlein off, but he wasn't going to try to bring it up again. He'd danced around the outside of it last night and even that had just seemed to get under Heinlein's skin.

"Help me move this table," the kid said. De Camp and Heinlein took one side and he helped the guard with the other, and together they gently moved the table and all its contents aside to reveal a wooden trap door set into the floor. Then the youth bent down, grabbed the brass ring at the top of the hatch, and swung it open. Inside, all was darkness.

"Damn," Hubbard sighed. "Another black hole."

"Nuh-uh!" Chad knelt down and reached into the black, feeling around until he found what he was looking for and a light went on.

"Thanks, GhuGhu." He could see a plain concrete floor below. "Somebody ought to stand lookout," he said, as Heinlein hurried down the flight of stairs that had appeared in the light.

"You can if you want to." Bob's voice emerged from the opening. De Camp made it obvious that he wasn't going to sit around by dropping into the hole as soon as Bob had disappeared.

Hubbard looked at the kid, who was getting ready to descend. "Hey, fella. You ever read the Harold Shea story 'The Case of the Friendly Corpse'?"

"Yeah." The kid made a face of disgust. "That was awful. You write that?"

"No. Why?"

Chad shrugged and started on down the stairs. "I thought you said you were a writer."

"I heard it was pretty good, was all." He was pretty sure the kid was out of earshot.

"It wasn't."

Hubbard looked out the window. The rain had let up a bit and he could see Asimov reading in the car. There was no other sign of anyone who could hit him on the head, and so, with a reluctant sigh because he really couldn't help wanting to see what was downstairs after all, he trotted down the stairs and caught up with the others.

The basement was as deep as the floor above it was high, and still open even as the other had been divided. It was sparsely filled with a few pieces of ancient, gutted mechanical equipment that wouldn't have been out of place in a tool and die shop. But what really caught Hubbard's attention were two great sealed iron boxes seated next to each other and rising almost to the ceiling, each as deep and wide as a car. The tops appeared to be sealed with round rivets each as big as an egg.

"What're those?"

Bob shrugged. He banged on one; the sound was heavy and muffled, no hollow echo. Either the metal was very thick or the enormous box was filled with something.

Hubbard looked up and could see spots on the ceiling above each box; they appeared to have been stopped up in a more recent era with wood that didn't match. "Cables fed in from above and probably plugged in here," he suggested. The others nodded, affirming the best theory going.

"There were coal generators on the first floor," Heinlein said quietly. Hubbard realized he'd spent some time with the Tesla journal. "These might be some kind of transformer or capacitor. Maybe even a battery. This place did sit empty for a few years. I suppose that vandals and thieves made off with everything they could when Tesla was locked out, and before Peerless took over. But they couldn't carry these or even figure out a way to take them apart." He turned to Chad. "You said there were tunnels."

"Over here." The kid led them some yards down the big room to an iron door that seemed to be of about the same placement as the one they had entered above.

While the rest of the complex seemed as light and indefensible as a church or school, this barrier meant business, and its business meant to keep people out. The hinges and rivets were of the same thick style that went into the creation of the boxes, probably forged at the same time. Bob gave the handle a halfhearted shake, as if he knew it was going to be locked even before he touched it.

"Only the president of the company has the key," Chad said with a sad shrug.

"Ever seen it open?"

"Oh yeah. Once a month he opens it up and they, uh—" Suddenly he clammed up.

"What?"

"Well, there's a big hole at the end of the tunnel. Huge, enormous. It's so deep you can't even see the bottom with a flashlight. Once a month the processors take all the chemical stuff left over from developing all that film and carry it down here and . . ."

"What?"

"They dump it."

"Into the hole?"

"Yeah. There's a ledge at the end so no one can fall in—kind of a low wall. But it's still really dangerous, so we can't go in unless we're all together."

"That's going to be a huge mess for someone to clean up someday."

"Yeah," said Chad. "Oh, by the way, don't nobody light a match."

"What else is down there?"

"I've seen other tunnels that lead off the main one, but I'd never go down them."

"Has anyone?"

"Some guys have, I guess. I hear they make a ring all the way around the big pit. You can see other ledges across the hole." He pointed to the four corners of the earth.

They heard above them the sudden clatter of hurried footsteps. Hubbard swore to himself under his breath, afraid of this new round of trouble.

"Guys! Bob!"

Hubbard relaxed. Asimov.

"Down here, Ike . . . Isaac," Bob called back. He motioned for the others to follow him.

Isaac was waiting for them, eagerly bouncing from foot to foot. In his hand he held the Tesla journal, the object that Bob had passed him through the car window. "Crocker?"

"What?" Bob asked.

"The Crocker Expedition."

"What are you talking about?"

"Peary's expedition was delayed and he didn't take the case."

"Right," both Hubbard and Bob replied.

"But there was another expedition. The expedition was led by a Professor Keeler, director of the Lick Observatory in San Francisco. They went to a small observatory in the Aleutians to witness some kind of once-in-a-lifetime solar event. In its day the expedition was almost as famous as Peary's. This one was called the Crocker Expedition, in honor of William Crocker, who financed it. Coincidentally, Crocker occasionally gave Tesla some funding."

"So?" Hubbard asked.

"So?" Isaac looked at him like the answer was obvious. "So? When Tesla found out Peary wasn't going to be able to leave on time, he needed someone else who could help him make headlines. The Crocker Expedition left on time, in January 1908. By June 29, 1908, he would have been right where Tesla wanted him to be."

"The night of the experiment."

"Right. Now he never spoke to Tesla, but Tesla included a snippet from a letter he received in December. He apologized for having had to leave Tesla's device behind but that it would be safe in the islands until he could return to get it and demonstrate its wonders to the world. But"—and here Isaac paused for dramatic effect—"evidently he was never able to return."

Heinlein's mouth had slowly fallen open and he hadn't even realized it. Hubbard had never actually seen Heinlein more surprised. Asimov seemed pleased by the effect of his dramatic pause. "There's another case?" he asked, only because no one else seemed able to.

Isaac nodded. "There's another case. A case full of 'wonders.'"

EPISODE 18

THE DISCOVERY OF the sub-basement under the Empire State Building had filled Heinlein with a thrill that was rapidly superseded by the elation he felt when he found the case. That had given way to the terror of the tunnel and then the crushing loss of the case, mitigated only by the safety of the journal. But when Hubbard found that the Peary expedition hadn't participated in any experiment, that had very nearly been the last straw, the trip to Wardenclyffe merely a formality; just something he had to see. Then Asimov burst in with his news, and Heinlein's heart soared again. There was something to all this; he was really starting to believe that.

Maybe it was the cautious reserve he had proudly learned growing up in Kansas City, but he had been suspicious of the Tesla legend until he entered the Catalan Vault. From that moment on, not only had he wanted it all to be true, he almost needed it to be true. If Tesla's mad dream had come within inches of reality, what could it take to finally make any dream come true, any of his, as well as Tesla's?

He wouldn't admit it to anyone, except maybe Campbell, but until he quit writing, he had spent far more time in the future than was probably good for him. Even before he'd picked up the pen, he'd always felt that there was a better way for people to live together—he just didn't know exactly what it was. Deep down he felt that technology was the answer. That science, be it physical or political, would end poverty, cure ills, eliminate war, create peace, answer truth, and lift humanity toward a destiny that lay elsewhere—in space, amongst the stars.

As a boy, he'd lay in the tall grass on a summer's night and, listening to the crickets and bullfrogs, focus on the twisted spiral of the Milky Way above. Soon the sky would begin to spin and he would be falling through the stars, whizzing past galaxies. He'd enlisted some boys from the neighborhood to help build a rocket ship in the field other kids used as a baseball diamond. It didn't matter that they were eight. Or that the rocket ship was made from wood. He'd attacked it with the same intensity and belief he'd later brought to stories and now devoted to Philadelphia. He'd spent time at the library trying to understand the physics of inertia and momentum, the laws of gravity, the speed of light. All he'd learned was that there was so much to learn before he could begin to know. And when the older boys from the neighborhood destroyed his spaceship and beat him up for having the audacity to display his intelligence proudly, he knew only that he'd start again. There was time to learn. His rocket ship would fly someday.

Until then he'd keep it to himself.

Except, when rocket ships flew in his stories, they didn't seem silly at all—and the only beatings he took were from the occasional disgruntled fan. He'd started writing only five years ago. On paper, his dreams almost seemed plausible. And not just to him. Two years ago, fans from coast to coast had voted him the best science fiction writer alive. And that's when he walked away from it all.

True, the war had called, and provided him a reason to put his focus elsewhere. But after a party in West Hollywood, the end was inevitable. Someone had asked him what he did. When he replied he was a writer, the fellow asked what studio employed him. His reaction when informed that Heinlein wrote science fiction for the pulps was jarring. It was as if, until that moment, the guy hadn't realized it was actually possible for a writer to have lower work than writing screenplays. Pulp science fiction. It was like being beaten up in the field for his dreams all over again, yet instead of hands it had been done with a look.

That was it. Heinlein didn't want to do it anymore. It all suddenly felt so frivolous. Especially in the days after Pearl Harbor when everything changed. How could he go back to writing about artificial robot hands when the Japs could launch an attack on his little home in Los Angeles at any time? How could he inspire anyone when he was so uninspired?

How could he write about the promise of tomorrow when tomorrow only promised more woes with Leslyn?

Campbell had called soon after the war began—as if he'd known that Heinlein's last attempt to rejoin the Navy had ended, once again, in rejection. He didn't want a story (well, he did, but he knew he wasn't getting one), he wanted Heinlein in Philadelphia. For Heinlein, who had already been thinking about getting out of Los Angeles while the Jap attack threat was growing day by day, the offer seemed fortuitous. He desperately wanted to find a way to prove himself in war. And the idea of being among the smartest people Campbell could get his hands on, of working with them to turn imagination into reality, kept him up for nights. The only problem he could see was Les—and how to tell her that he was going to go, with or without her. In the end, he didn't have to. She'd tried to kill herself with a bottle of vodka and a bottle of sleeping pills.

He'd been in the garage he'd converted into his office. Writing; or thinking about writing. Only when the sirens kept wailing outside had he poked his head out to see what was happening. Turns out one of their neighbors, a friend of Les, had come round for coffee and, seeing her sprawled on the floor of the kitchen, called for help. Of course he knew why she'd been so upset as to try suicide—she'd felt she'd betrayed her husband, when, in fact, it was only another disappointment to him, one he had thought he could live with. Even so, as he held her cold hand in the ambulance on the way to Mount Sinai, he found himself wishing that the neighbor hadn't decided to peek. It would have been a simple end to the endless cycle of vomit and fighting, hangovers and apologies.

When she revived, she complacently agreed to come east, to the sanitarium at Morristown. She'd even seemed eager to try another cure. Les still felt she had to atone . . .

"Give me a hand up," he said now to Hubbard, indicating the old iron tanks. There was about two feet of space above them and Heinlein wanted to take a look at their top sides.

"Really?"

"Is it too much to ask?"

Hubbard laced his fingers together to make a sling. Heinlein stepped into it, put his hands on Hubbard's shoulders, and launched himself up. Closer to the ceiling he could see the ancient hinges and seam above what appeared to be a pair of cargo doors that once must have opened into the yard above so the metal cases, and other large pieces of equipment, could be lowered down. He felt Hubbard shift below him and give him a boost, which helped him slide on top.

"I'm good," he called down, then wished he hadn't opened his mouth at all. The big tanks were covered in years of dust: he'd sucked in the last decade's worth and ended up coughing so hard he thought he'd pass out. "Okay," he wheezed, after a few moments, tears streaming down his face. The TB had cost him so much. He should have had his own ship by now. A destroyer, perhaps, maybe even a battleship, or a squadron. This should have been his war, on the sea.

When his vision cleared, he saw several small iron handles, almost like those found on a kitchen cabinet. They were attached to a thin strip of metal running down the seam between the two tanks, which were otherwise fastened so tightly together that even a knife blade wouldn't slide between them. Reaching out, he tried to loosen one of the wing nuts that sat at either end of the metal strip, clamping it in. It didn't turn. The pain in his fingers flared, only causing him to clench his jaw and try harder, until it felt as if his knuckle might snap. He wanted this.

The barest hint of give was all he needed. He pinched again, and the nut began to twist at last. It felt so good he laughed at his ridiculous victory. The other nut gave him almost no resistance at all, as if he had somehow proven himself with the first one. Finally, he pulled on the handles.

The panel, about three feet wide, slid out in hinged sections, collapsing down toward him like a Japanese fan each time it seemed as if it would hit the ceiling. It was as if he were pulling a sword from a stone. It slid smoothly, as though oiled, but the seal was tight and the screech of metal grinding against metal was accompanied by the pungent odor of rancid fish.

"Ike?" he called. "Sorry. Isaac? You still got that square from the case on you?"

"The green one? Yeah."

"Attaboy. Let me see it."

He stopped pulling the lattice from between the tanks, letting it fold down on one of its hinges on the dust-covered top. A thick black liquid oozed off it. Each row was formed of six empty square holes spaced evenly apart. Asimov passed up the green tile and Heinlein pressed it into one of the hollow squares. When it clicked into place as if it had always belonged there, for the first time in a long while he could almost put the regret of not being more involved in the war behind him.

Heinlein passed the frame, with the smooth square still firmly in place, for the others to examine. Then he eased himself backwards until he was able to slide off and let his feet find the floor. Dusting himself off, he turned to find the other men examining the piece. "So, boys," he said. "What do we have here?"

They looked at him, each ready to speak but more ready for someone else to, as if each only had a part of the answer.

Heinlein patted the cool metal plate. "Okay, we've got two compartments, filled with some kind of conductive material." He sniffed dramatically. "A kind of oil, I think."

"That's the dielectric medium!" Asimov blurted out—the first, or rather, second, to put it all together.

"And when these green tiles are all in place between the two tanks, it keeps the fluids separated. I'm guessing these are some kind of nonconductive material."

"A capacitor." De Camp nodded.

"Jesus. Will you look at how big these things are," Hubbard said. "How much static electricity could these things store?"

"An incredible amount," Heinlein said. "The generators upstairs pumped electricity down into here where it would build up until Tesla was ready to send it down the tunnel to the tower. The case we found had just one of these tiles, separating two small fluid chambers. It must have been a smaller capacitor. The effect of piezoelectricity from this could theoretically cause a reverse microphonic effect. The tile in the case would vibrate, creating audio. Maybe even electricity." He popped out the green tile. "We need to figure out what this is."

"A mass spectrometer could analyze it," de Camp said.

"You don't have one in Philly?" Hubbard asked.

"We're more of a practical applications lab than a research lab," Heinlein said. "What we really need is a top-notch chemistry lab." He turned to Asimov. "Like the kind you find at the very best universities."

"Yeah." the young man nodded proudly. "There's a mass spectrometer at Columbia."

"How do you know that?" Hubbard asked.

"Because I'm getting my PhD there," Asimov snapped, causing Hubbard to blink in surprise.

"You're getting a PhD from Columbia and you're writing pulps?"

"So?"

"So, nothing." Hubbard shrugged. "The pulp racket has really changed."

"Yeah," Heinlein said. "The writing is actually getting good. Looks like our days are numbered, right, Ron?"

Hubbard shrugged again, but not before Heinlein caught the expression of genuine alarm cross his face. It was obvious he was concerned about his place in the pulp food chain, maybe for the first time in his writing career. Heinlein could sympathize, though he wasn't jealous. But it was obvious the new crop of pulp writers, the kids like Asimov and de Camp, were in it for the love of science fiction, whereas Hubbard, and to some extent Heinlein himself, were in it for the easy money. Of course, every now and then Heinlein liked to kid himself that he was actually good. Maybe even the best.

For now.

"What do you think, Isaac? Can you get over to your old lab?"

"Sure, I can call my old professor once we get home. Maybe I can go back next week or the week after."

"I was thinking today."

"What?"

"We're under some pressure here, Isaac. If this technology did, in fact, create some kind of death ray, we could end this war with the push of a button. Need I remind you that if our little funhouse doesn't come up with something soon, you're probably going to be drafted and there's nothing we can do . . ."

"I'll go today," Asimov said, comprehending the urgency.

They had bid farewell to Chad, the security guard, with a promise to send a case of every Street & Smith pulp. It was de Camp who showed them how to navigate through Queens to an elevated station, where they left Asimov shivering mournfully in the rain spattering upon the open platform. For a moment, Heinlein had thought Hubbard might jump out to join him, but the other writer gave no indication of leaving his seat in the car. In spite of the storm, they made it back to Lansdowne in a few hours, grabbed a quick lunch at a joint called Walt's Steaks. Heinlein dropped de Camp off at his house, swallowing a tinge of envy as Catherine rushed out onto the porch to greet him with a kiss that threatened to merge her body into his.

"Damn," Hubbard murmured. "How's Leslyn?"

"Is there somewhere I can drop you, Ron?"

"If you're heading to the base I guess I can see if they've got a bunk for a landlocked sailor."

Heinlein gritted his teeth and drove. His badge and Hubbard's naval ID got them onto the base; soon they had parked and were walking past the great ships docked in the harbor. Ron, hearing music, stopped to look for its source. Upon sighting the Officers' Club, he clapped Heinlein on the back. "I'm going to grab a drink."

"A little early for me."

"Sorry, Otis. Serving officers only." And with a wave he vanished into the building, the door closing with finality.

Finally alone, Heinlein headed down the road toward his facility, ignoring the gulls who berated him for not providing them with easy sustenance. He felt a twinge of guilt for not going home. At the same time he couldn't face the darkness that he knew would engulf him as soon as he entered his house. So, almost without another thought, he opened the lab door. The place was thinly populated this late in the afternoon, but he waved at the people toiling away. Not wanting to talk, he put his head down as if deep in thought, and walked into his office. A stack of pink slips showed the phone calls he had received. Colonel Tom Slick had called twice. General Scoles had left several urgent messages as well. The final message was a request for a call from Mr. Binch. He had to think about that one for a few moments before he remembered the General Electric executive. Wondering what all the callers could want from him, he sat down.

He was on his back, staring up at the ceiling before realizing that he'd hit his head and that the loud crash ringing in his ears had been his chair bursting apart. As he struggled to roll over and stand, he heard voices just outside his office, then people entering. He closed his eyes against the pain.

"Bob?" Slender Walb was speaking. "You okay?"

Hands were helping him up. He rubbed the spot on his head that ached, hoping the action would make the stars go away.

"I'll go get some ice," he heard a woman say, her voice receding along with her footsteps.

"How about a medic?" Walb asked, concerned.

"No." He squinted through one eye. "No medic. Just a bump on the head." He willed the other eye open. The chair had fallen apart into each of its component pieces. "What happened?"

"Some of those sailors got in the other night and played a prank on us. Guess they wanted to finish the fight they never got to have."

"What'd they do?"

"They removed all the bolts from the chairs. People were falling on their asses all day long."

"Didn't think they'd got into your office," Meisel added.

"Who knew they had it in them?" he said. The pain, like most head bumps, was quickly fading away, though the goose egg would last for several days no matter how hard he rubbed it. It was a shame he was losing so much hair up top. The thick pelt of his youth would have protected him. Now he was down to a fine layer of single strands; someday he might just shave the whole thing. "Damn," he muttered. He looked around at the faces staring at him. "I'm okay," he told them. "Thanks. Anybody got a chair I can borrow? A real one?"

Jack Bullen rolled in a chair from one of the lab stations just outside his office. Heinlein kicked the rubble aside, put it behind his desk, and sat down. "Anything else?" he asked.

Walb cleared his throat, his Adam's apple jumping up and down like one of the balls in his cylindrical pressure chamber experiments. Heinlein looked at him, and then realized that there was a man standing behind him who he didn't recognize.

The stranger was easily the shortest man in the room and probably always was, no matter the room. His head was bald and polished, highlighting an ugly scattering of freckles. He wore a crisp white lab coat that fit him so well Heinlein wondered if it was possible to have a bespoke lab coat. "I'm Dr. Reinhart," the man said, as if the name should mean something.

Heinlein leaned back in his new chair and put his arms behind his head. "Other than a chemobotanist I wasn't really expecting any more scientists."

"Nevertheless," Dr. Reinhart said, "I am here."

"What's your specialty?"

"Administration."

"That's a science?"

"Mr. Heinlein . . ."

"Captain."

"Not for some time, Mr. Heinlein. Some changes have been made. At the top. In Washington. It's been decided that your department hasn't really produced any, shall we say, results. I'm here to change that." His voice was like a scratch on a record.

Heinlein rocked back and put his feet up. At least now he knew why Scoles had left messages for him. "The things we're working on take time. You can't expect results overnight."

"You've been here over a year. You've spent nearly two million dollars on personnel and equipment. What do you have to show for it? A plane rudder that doesn't freeze at high altitudes."

"Those planes were death traps. We saved lives."

"You're supposed to win the war, Mr. Heinlein. I'm here to see that you do."

Heinlein stared out the window. In the distance he could see the small destroyer escort the crew at the barracks had been waiting to outfit making its arrival. It could be identified only by its numbers now: *DE-173*. The ship would receive its name when it was fully fitted out after receiving its commission. Until then it wouldn't even be referred to as "she." It was a small vessel, as Navy ships went, only about 200 feet long, built to provide support to convoys and larger ships. The cannon-class vessel would have been built in Newark before being finished here. The ship would be fast; its innovative diesel-electric tandem motors made it agile and easy to handle as well—as indicated by the very small crew, perhaps six altogether, that was negotiating it from the deep channel of the river to its berth near his lab. Trim but deadly was how the sailors referred to this line.

Two batteries of 40mm cannons which could shell shorelines, as well as ships several miles away, were fastened to the foredeck, flanked on both sides by smaller antiaircraft gun boxes. On the rear deck was the heavy rigging for lofting the garbage can–sized depth charges overboard. This weaponry would be completed by torpedo tubes below the waterline—the two systems working in tandem to accomplish the ship's primary function, which was to sink the U-boats hunting in wolf packs throughout the oceans.

Reinhart continued, "Where is the big stuff? Where are your force fields, your jet packs, your radar jammers? Where are your death rays?"

He held up his hand and interrupted the man. "You see that ship there?"

The little man's mouth snapped shut as if he'd never been cut off before.

"We're going to make it invisible to radar."

"How?"

Heinlein waved away the details. "Recent discoveries in the field of electromagnetism."

"I want to know about them."

"It's in here." Heinlein tapped his head. "I haven't written them down yet. An administrator couldn't be expected to understand."

"I have degrees in physics from MIT."

"That's impressive. But still. I'm working on it."

"When?"

"Soon."

"I want a report in my office first thing Monday morning."

"Sorry, first thing Monday morning I'll be in General Scoles's office having you reassigned."

"We'll see about that." Reinhart spun around on his heel in a move that reminded Heinlein of nothing so much as Charlie Chaplin imitating the great dictator. "This is not a club for your science fiction writer friends," he snapped.

"Half these guys aren't writers," Heinlein retorted. "They don't even read science fiction."

Reinhart didn't pause. "Monday morning."

"Unctuous little shit," Heinlein muttered, watching through the window as Reinhart strode through the lab. His lab. The other men were still standing in his office.

"What are you going to do, Bob?" Meisel asked.

In response, he rose slowly from his chair, picked up the chalk, and wrote a few words upon the chalkboard, hitting it hard and underlining the words with an emphasis that snapped the stick.

"I don't know."

"And what if that doesn't work?"

"Then somebody's probably going to put a uniform on you and slap a gun in your hand and point you at some Nazis." Glumly, the men filed out. After they were gone, Heinlein put his face in his hands.

"I brought you some ice," he heard the soft voice of a woman. "For your head."

Virginia stood in the doorway, dressed casually in black slacks and a white linen shirt. With each little move, her reddish-brown hair caressed her shoulders with what seemed to be a life of its own.

"You're out of uniform," he said.

"It's Saturday," she replied, with a wry smile that made a dimple appear in her right cheek.

"Thanks," he said, beckoning her to bring the ice toward him. "I could use that."

She entered his office, eyes quickly taking in the mess, the papers, the pulps. "I hate to say it, but you could use a woman's touch."

"It's been a busy time."

Virginia bypassed his open hand and instead, placed the cloth filled with ice against his head herself. "Is that the spot?"

He took her warm hand, feeling the soft skin, and moved it ever so slightly. "Like that," he said.

She sat on the edge of his desk, leaning forward to hold the pack. Her legs brushed against his. "How does that feel?"

"Good." He nodded. "It feels good."

"Do you want some aspirin?"

"No. This is fine." He realized he was still holding her hand. Her eyes were green, but he couldn't remember whether he had noted that the first time he'd met her or not.

She looked at the words he'd written on the chalkboard. "'Make the damn ship disappear'?"

"Heinlein's folly." He took the ice bag from his head and returned her hand to its owner. "It's okay," he reassured her.

"Are you sure?"

He nodded.

"Is there anything else you need?"

Heinlein could hear the lonely call of a distant gull from the direction of the water, demanding and insistent. "Yes," he said. "Have dinner with me."

EPISODE 19

ISAAC WAS DRENCHED to the bone for the second time in as many days and he was not happy about it. He felt as if he hadn't even thoroughly warmed up from the dunking in Minetta Stream. And now he was sneezing. Which meant he was going to get sick. He just knew it.

It was tough going up Broadway to 120th Street with the rain pouring down this hard but trudge he did because . . .

Well, the answer to that was interesting, wasn't it?

He'd been on the phone to Gertrude for almost two hours last night trying to make her understand that he didn't want to be in New York, even though Sprague's grandmother's place was incredible—like something out of a fairy tale.

He smiled to himself in spite of the rain. He'd finally said something right last night and made her happy. He'd told her that he didn't want to be in New York at all. He wanted to be with her. And that was true. After surviving the sewer—for that's what he felt it really was—it occurred to him that there was nowhere else he'd rather be than home with his wife, preferably in bed. He hadn't actually meant to say it to her, it was embarrassing, but it just popped out of his mouth.

Funny thing was, telling her that had made her happier than he'd heard her in months. Since they'd moved to Philadelphia, actually. It had left him thrilled. He'd wrapped up the call by telling her that he couldn't wait to see her tomorrow and that he'd show her how much he wanted to be with her. Tomorrow.

Which was today.

Now he couldn't even bring himself to call her and explain. He knew he was going to have to, and it had better be soon. But it was going to be hard to tell her that Bob had only asked him to, hadn't even really insisted. Of course, his job really did depend on it. So he knew that he was going to have to figure out how to tell her in a way that made it seem that what he was doing was really important. Not just that it was something that Bob wanted him to do.

He couldn't bring himself to admit to her last night, and she had only pressed so far, but he was still starstruck by Bob. Isaac had already wanted to write science fiction before he'd read Heinlein; in fact, he'd published a few stories. But when he read "Life-Line" in *Astounding*, he'd made a mental note to remember the author's name. Said author's subsequent contributions were dazzling. When Heinlein had revealed in print two years ago that his stories fit into a comprehensive view of the future, and supported it with a nifty illustrated timeline to help readers keep track and sort the connections, the scope of the effort made Isaac's brain feel small. And for someone who prided himself on always being the smartest person in the room, it was an unsettling sensation.

It wasn't just the interesting threads which connected the future history stories that inspired Isaac. It was the fact that the stories were just so damn well written. It was safe to say that much of what Isaac had learned about the English language came from the pulps. He'd read enough of them to know at a certain point that the writing was uniformly terrible. That hardly ever mattered, though. What mattered was that the stories were exciting. Fun. Readable. For example, he knew who L. Ron Hubbard was, and he was absolutely certain the man was only feigning ignorance of Isaac's works; they'd been published in the same mags, for Christ's sake. Ron was a punch line to the Futurians for his propensity to write so badly. And so much of it. When westerns had been popular, he wrote about cowboys riding the open range. When the newsstands cried out for adventure stories, Ron discovered lost cities from the heights of the Andes to the depths of the Atlantic. Already kind of famous—to pulp readers—he'd dived headlong into sci-fi, with predictable results. As a writer, he was terrible. They all knew it. But everyone, Isaac included, loved Ron as a storyteller. Nothing pretty about his writing at all. Yet he told a ripping yarn. And until Bob came along, that was good enough.

Before Bob, and before the three-year run he'd begun with "Life-Line," then "Requiem," the nearly thirty other stories and novellas, and especially "Methuselah's Children," all Isaac had wanted to be was a pulp science fiction writer. After beholding that streak, Isaac had realized he wanted to be a real writer. He could now clearly see the difference between what was pulp and what was real, and he could never go back. It was true that he didn't have Bob's natural grace with words, his poetic skill, but he was much younger, too, and he wrote more. There was time to learn. He'd asked John once what Bob's magic was and the ed had replied, "Feelings." Isaac was still trying to figure out what that meant.

If it hadn't been for Bob, Isaac would never have attempted to write *Foundation*. Probably. That would have been a shame because those stories were the first he'd ever written that were actually better than okay. He could still remember the tingle of excitement that started at the top of his head and spread down his spine as he realized, on the way to pitch Campbell an entirely different story, that it would be fun as hell to cast the fall of the Roman Empire as an interstellar saga. Campbell had agreed with him instantly, as fast as he'd ever seen Campbell agree to anything with anybody. It was Bob's future history that gave Isaac the confidence to try something in science fiction that he'd never seen before—which, given how much Isaac knew about science fiction, meant it probably hadn't been done before.

It saddened him that Bob wasn't writing anymore. Bob had simply told him that all those stories had paid off his mortgage and he didn't need to write another word. Isaac couldn't imagine not writing; he wrote every day. If he wasn't writing, he was unhappy. He'd do it all day if he could make a living at it. But he was no Walter Gibson.

He made the right turn onto a tree-lined path, then another left past the statue of the scholar's lion. Happy to get out of the rain, and happier to be back at Havemeyer Hall, his home for years, Isaac ran up the steps and into the building. Dry, warm, and safe—but it always was. No classes today so the halls were nearly empty. But he knew Dawson would be here. Dawson, the scientist whose research team Isaac had joined as a PhD candidate, was rumored to live in Havemeyer, so he would probably be around. On the other hand, Asimov could only hope that Urey, the one person he didn't want to run into, was out freeloading on the lecture circuit.

As a registered student on a deferment, Isaac still had free run of the building. In minutes he was on the second floor and opening the door to Dawson's lab.

The sole person in the lab was Lloyd Roth, still as tall, gawky, and awkward as ever. "Isaac the A!" he cried, the owlish protrusion of his eyes greatly magnified by the heavy glasses that kept him out of any service, and harm's way.

"Roth." He grasped the man's hand, happy to see a familiar face. "How's it hanging?"

"Like it's made of aurum." Roth smirked. "What brings you back? Is the war over?" From his slightly worried expression, Isaac could tell that he was seriously afraid he might have missed this news. Roth was as single-minded as they came. Isaac had seen him forget to bathe or eat for days on end, and once he had entirely missed the High Holy Days in spite of repeated reminders from Isaac, the other Jew in the chemistry department.

"No. Still plenty of fight left in Hitler."

"Ah, good. No, that's not what I mean at all."

"I know."

"How's your bride?"

"She's terrific."

"Is she? That's good." He waggled his eyebrows, which looked like two bushy caterpillars trying to climb up a bowling ball. "I've got a girl now, too."

"Yeah? That's great."

"You know what's great?" He leaned close in order to conspire and confide. "Regular sex. That's really good."

"I *know!*"

"I'm going to ask her to marry me."

"That's good." Isaac looked past Lloyd to the black metal cabinet nestled against the wall. The face was covered with alternating rows of columns and dials and switches. Attached to the left side was a long cast-iron tube with an opening panel in the bottom. "Is anyone using the Missus?"

Lloyd shook his head. "Not in weeks. There aren't enough students around to use it these days. On account of the war."

"Figured that," Isaac said. "Listen, I need to analyze a sample. Do you think Dawson would mind?"

"Not at all," a familiar voice said from behind. The professor was about the same age as Heinlein, and managed to look almost as cocky leaning against the door. "As far as I'm concerned, you're still my research assistant. So, what are we researching today?"

"This." Isaac withdrew the square panel and placed it on the desk. He was struck again by its strange green-tinged milky quality. Professor Dawson picked it up and eyed it without comment, then handed it to Lloyd, who began examining it eagerly, but offered no suggestion either.

"It looks intriguing," Professor Dawson said, chewing on his pipestem in a casual manner which Isaac took to indicate that his mind was churning at its most furious pace. "Where'd you come by this?"

"I can't actually tell you. I'm sorry."

"Don't be. Loose lips lose ships, or something like that, they say. The texture is nearly ceramic, but it has the heft and density of a metal. Also, there's an intangible quality, an evanescence to it, that bears examination. Dr. Roth, would you do me a favor and prepare a sample solution for ionization and then run it for us? I'd like to say I did my part for the war effort."

"Dr. Roth?"

"You've been gone nearly a year, Asimov. If you'd stayed, you'd be a doctor by now as well. Dr. Roth is one of the few colleagues who didn't answer the clarion call of glory."

"Oh, I'm hardly in this for the glory," Isaac said.

Professor Dawson scrutinized Isaac in a way that made him feel sorry for stray molecules under his microscope. "Come with me," he said at last. "I want to show you something."

"What?"

"The future."

Lloyd was already deeply enmeshed in grinding some dust off the plate and Isaac would only slow him down, so he shrugged and followed the professor, who led him down the hall toward the steam tunnels. Isaac wasn't as familiar with the legendary underground network as most of the other students of the sciences were. Even though he'd attended Columbia for nearly seven years altogether as an undergrad and grad student, he'd always lived at home and spent most of his time in the labs of Havemeyer, never exploring the mazes below the school.

Instead of growing cooler as they walked down the staircase, the heat and humidity rose until Isaac was loosening his necktie. As they walked along, the professor kept up a running commentary updating Isaac on the current whereabouts of all his classmates, a few of whom had been consigned to foxholes in Europe, which terrified Isaac. After making their way along several corridors separating small rooms, at a particular intersection, they turned left and Isaac knew they were headed toward Pupin Hall, the physics building. Isaac was aware of a deep, powerful vibration that grew even stronger as they apparently walked toward its source. At a locked door that appeared to have been installed much more recently than anything else Isaac had seen belowground, the professor pulled out a key and paused. "You do have government clearance, right?" Before Isaac could gulp out an answer, he laughed and unlocked the door.

In the center of the low, wide room were two great round discs of equal size, one suspended directly over the other by a thick axle. Each disk was about three feet thick and as wide around as a taxi cab. Anchored on one side of the floor and rising like a bridge over the two discs, squeezing between the top one and the ceiling before anchoring on the opposite side, was a round duct as thick as a man and wrapped in insulation. In front of this aluminum-covered rainbow was a sign that could be lit up if needed but was currently off. Still, Isaac could read the words:

MAGNET ON
KEEP WATCHES AWAY

"The cyclotron," he said with awe. He'd heard rumors about experiments that had taken place here, but it was off limits to, well, everybody.

"Indeed. The atom smasher." Dawson's eyes gleamed as he nodded. "Harold Urey's reward from the university for winning the Nobel Prize. And now that Fermi and Dunning have gone to the west, he gets to play with it. He even lets me at it every once in a while. We're part of a project. Like yours in Philadelphia. But our part is in Manhattan. Among other places."

"But why does a chemist need an atom smasher?"

"Those physicists, they're good with the numbers and the big math, but when it comes to actual work, separating U-235 from U-238, you still need a chemist."

"You're helping Urey enrich uranium? Why?"

"Why do you think, Isaac? To do what you dream of. To create the future. To save the world. I wish I could tell you what we're doing."

"It's really impressive." He ran a hand over the smooth disc, imagining that he could feel a small electrical tingle.

"It is. You could come back and join us, Isaac. Come join the team."

"I've got a job, though."

"As good as this?"

"Professor, I'm not even sure what this really is. Maybe . . ." Before Isaac could explain further, he heard voices coming from the tunnels leading toward Pupin Hall. "We should go."

But Professor Dawson took his arm and held him fast. In another moment, two men that Isaac recognized, Professors Booth and Urey, had entered the room, deep in discussion. Urey looked up as he sensed the presence of the others in the room. "Dawson?"

"Professor."

"Who's that with you? Is that Asimov?"

"Hello, Professor Urey," he said.

The glare was withering, and without acknowledging him further, Urey turned to continue speaking with his companion.

"I was trying to convince Asimov to join our team."

"Why would you want to do that?"

"Because he's brilliant."

"Professor Dawson, you may be aware of some hidden potential for greatness in your protégé, but as we've discussed in the past, his refusal to commit to science completely, his decision to dilly-dally as a pulp writer, will only be a hindrance to a serious scientific career."

"Da Vinci was both a scientist and an artist," Isaac said, and instantly wished he hadn't.

"I've seen your research and read your stories. You, Isaac Asimov, are neither scientist nor artist." And with that note of finality, Urey turned his back to Isaac and Dawson, to inspect something of great importance on the cyclotron.

"Come on, Asimov." Dawson pulled him gently from the room.

"He never liked me." Asimov was morose as they walked back toward Havemeyer.

"He expects a lot of you. We all do. How many other Nobel-winning scientists do you know personally who show any interest in you? Other than Urey, of course."

"I'm a good scientist. I like chemistry a lot and I'm doing good work."

"It could be great. You could be great. If you so chose."

"Do you think he really read my stories?"

Soon they reached Dawson's lab. Lloyd was carefully monitoring the multitude of dials on the front of the black case. "I just put the sample in," he called out, as if their presence was now as annoying and distracting to him as it had been to Urey. "Come back tomorrow and I'll give you your results."

Isaac felt his heart bounce off his stomach. "Tomorrow? I was hoping for later today."

Lloyd waved a hand at him without looking up from the gauges.

"Tomorrow's Sunday. Are you sure you'll be in?"

"Why would I leave? You can stay here, too, if you want. There are cots in the closet."

"No." Isaac sighed. "I want to go home."

In Park Slope his mother had shrieked when he opened the door, and his kid sister, Marcia, and little brother, Stanley, cheered with happiness. Judah, his father, hadn't risen, but from the way he looked over the day's newspaper, Isaac could tell he was pleased to see his son as well. And after dinner, while the two women were in the kitchen cleaning up, he'd said as much. After trying several ways to engage Isaac about his current mission, Judah stood up and said loudly in the direction of the kitchen: "I think I left something in the shop."

"What? What did you leave that you have to go out now?" Isaac's mother shouted over the water running into the sink.

"Something. I have to get it. Isaac's coming with me." He nodded toward Isaac, who knew better than to protest or resist.

"Oh, don't take him, Daddy," his sister squealed.

"He has to help me."

Within moments they were walking down the familiar tree-lined street. People called to him, or his father, waving, smiling, asking after health, family, and fortune. Judah reached the storefront and knelt down to unlock the gate. Isaac helped him slide it up—the crashing noise good to hear again.

"You know I was robbed last month?"

"No, Dad! I didn't. What happened?" Isaac felt terrible for not having been there, for not even knowing about it.

"A fella walked in with a gun. He pointed it at me. I gave him the money. That's how it's supposed to work, I hear."

"You have to get an alarm. Or a gun."

"Ach. Either of those would have winded up getting me killed. It's better to just give him the money. This is Park Slope. Not Tombstone, like in those cowboy magazines you're always reading."

"Dad. I haven't read westerns in years. Sci-fi, remember? Science fiction. I read it. I write it."

"Mm." Judah turned a single light on in the store; enough to see by, but not enough to alert the neighborhood that their candy fix might be available. He looked out the window. "I used to watch you play stickball from here."

"Ugh. I was lousy at stickball."

"Still, I watched. Every game. It was the only time I prayed since your sister was born. I prayed for you to get a hit."

"I got a few hits."

"One hit. And then the police came and everyone ran home before you could take your base. I thanked God for that one hit."

"Why did it matter so much?"

"I just wanted something to come easy for you. So you could fit in. Be at home here."

"I guess it wasn't my game."

Judah sighed. "I miss having you around."

"I know, Dad. Once the war's over . . ."

"Ah. The war. When it's over, you and Gertie will find a home somewhere and have children and we'll see you when you can find the time."

"Dad."

"Is there a good temple in Philadelphia?"

Isaac realized that he hadn't invited his parents down once in the time since he'd moved there. He and Gertie had been up to see them, but they'd always spent the nights at her parents' apartment. "Temple Beth Zion is just down the street from our apartment." He'd never been inside, but it was reassuring to stroll past on their way to Rittenhouse Square.

"That's good."

"Why don't you come down sometime in the next few weeks."

"There's so much to do here."

"Well, I'll talk to Mom about it."

His father shrugged. "It's good to see you now. I'm glad you came. I miss my boy."

Isaac rubbed his father's shoulder. "I miss you too, Dad." He could feel his father grip his arm.

After a moment, Judah pulled away. "I've got something for you." He headed to the darkness of the back of the store and Isaac heard him fumble for something.

"Wait a sec, Dad." He reached for the switch panel.

It took a moment for his eyes to readjust to the light but several seconds for his brain to adjust to what he saw. On the three walls of the store, high above the racks and shelves, were framed issues of every *Astounding*, *Amazing*, and *Wonder* that carried a story by Isaac Asimov.

At the far end of the room, Judah cleared his throat, as if he were embarrassed.

"You redecorated," Isaac said.

His father ignored his obvious pride and walked back, clutching an object in his hand. He shut off the lights and the dozens of images of space and the future disappeared in an instant. A gentle hand ushered Isaac out of the door. After pulling the gate down again, they walked back down Sixth Avenue. Soon they reached the steps of the brownstone. Judah paused here and pressed the mysterious object into Isaac's hand. "I'm glad there's something that comes easy for you," he said.

Later that night Isaac lay in his old bed in his room, which his mother had left virtually untouched. The shelves were lined, the floor stacked, every surface covered with the books and pulps he had collected for years. He passed the object his father had given him from hand to hand, past pondering it, the strange things happening far below the surface of Manhattan, the lonely building at the end of Long Island, life in Philadelphia, the pitfalls of marriage. He was beyond all that. There was a story beginning to take root at the back of his head. He knew there would be a robot in it. Isaac thought long enough to know that he wouldn't forget about it by morning, that in fact it would continue to grow in the fertile ground at the back of his mind as he slept.

After some time, he carefully placed the pink Spaldeen ball, which his father had left in the store to recover after Isaac's only hit and kept safe for so many years, on the nightstand next to his bed.

EPISODE 20

HUBBARD WAS A little vague on the events of Saturday night, but he knew that he was in trouble when he woke up to see Heinlein staring at him through the bars of the brig.

"Things don't usually get out of control at the Officers' Club," Heinlein stated in a flat tone.

He rubbed his hands over his face, feeling the rasp of stubble. It'd been days since he'd shaved; could hardly pass as an enlisted man, let alone an officer. "Sorry to drag you out of church."

"It's not Sunday," Heinlein said. "It's Monday morning."

"Crap. I ended up at the Shore Leave Saloon. Know it?" His right fist hurt, and the fingers were skinned just above the first knuckles.

"Sure."

"Don't go there."

"I wouldn't be caught dead there."

"The MPs tell me they dragged you across the Navy Yard sometime last night screaming that all they had to do was get ahold of me and I'd fix everything."

"Really? I must have gotten you confused with Clarence Darrow."

"Dammit, Ron." Heinlein pressed his forehead against the bars. "I'm trying to maintain a low profile here. I've already got eyes all over me. The last thing I need is to have a drunk screaming my name all over the place."

"I'm not a drunk, Bob. You know that." He craned his neck back and forth; the tendon cracks were loud and satisfying.

Heinlein sighed and beckoned to someone beyond Hubbard's range of vision. A walking muscle wearing an MP suit stepped to the bars. The flesh around his left eye was ringed with black and purple.

"That's some shiner you got there, sport."

The MP glared at him. "You should know, sport. You sucker-punched me."

Hubbard looked down at his fist, the raw skin. "I didn't know I had it in me."

Heinlein cleared his throat. "I've made a deal to get you out without charges." He looked at the MP. "One punch."

"That's all I'll need," the guard confirmed.

"Wait, what?"

The soldier's key was already jingling in the lock as Heinlein turned away, saying, "I'll wait for you outside."

The side of his face felt as if it had been loosened from his skull, and the light of the morning sun was so bright he had to squint out of his one good eye. Through the bleary haze he could see Heinlein leaning against the side of his car. He staggered down the steps of the Military Police building, while probing his teeth with his tongue for any missing soldiers.

"One punch," he muttered, as Heinlein opened a car door for him. "Thanks."

"Better than another court-martial."

He slid into the car, ready to deal with his hangover.

"Hey, Ron."

"Hi, Ron?"

Their voices from the backseat were nearly in unison. "Great," he muttered. "Frick and Frack. Where are we off to now?" he asked Heinlein, who was climbing behind the wheel.

"New Jersey," was Asimov's chipper reply.

"Why?"

"It's a mystery to us, too," de Camp said, as the car began to roll.

"A lot happened while you were up the river."

"Yeah?"

"Isaac, tell Ron about our green tile."

"It's an oxide of barium and titanium," Isaac began, his voice filled with excitement. Too much, in fact. "It would make for the most amazing dielectric . . ."

"Save it," Hubbard said, closing his eye. "Don't talk 'til we hit Trenton."

"Hey, Bob," de Camp said quietly at some point in the journey.

Hubbard wasn't sure if it was right away or hours later. "Is Reinhart really in charge now?"

"So I'm told."

"But why?"

"Apparently we are considered something of a security risk."

"Us? Who would think that of us?"

"The FBI, for one."

"Why? What did we do?" Asimov sounded afraid. "Are we in trouble?"

"Not yet. But thanks to Campbell and Cartmill . . ."

"Cleve Cartmill?" Hubbard asked, halfway to sleep and irritated that he wasn't all the way. "What the hell did he do? What the hell could he do? He's about as threatening as a Pekinese."

"Evidently he has a very dangerous imagination. The G-men are interested in some of the things Campbell's been encouraging him to write. They're also interested in Campbell. Which, by extension, means they're interested in us. They wanted to close us down completely, but since we're Scoles's pet project, the compromise was Reinhart. He's got scientific training and he works for the Feds, so he's perfect as far as they're concerned."

"The perfect spy," de Camp said.

"Well, he's not a spy if he's out there in the open. He's more of an informant. He's just going to require some special handling."

"I like the sound of that," Hubbard grunted.

"What are you going to do?" Asimov asked.

"*We* are going to keep him very busy."

"How?"

"We're going to prove the value of what we're doing, and what we've learned. We're going to dazzle him with the awesome power of electromagicalmagnetism and send him back to the District of Columbia with tales of our inevitable, immanent victory over the Axis."

"How are we going to do that?"

"There's a plan coming together. But the one thing we're not going to do is tell him anything about Wardenclyffe." Heinlein turned the wheel and the car began to bounce on some rougher road. Then he pulled to a stop, gravel crunching under the tires. "Or about this guy."

They had entered a clearing, about a couple of square acres, in the middle of a scrubby wood. Beyond the road they had taken in he could see a development of low, ugly, unoccupied houses under construction. The car had kicked up a tremendous amount of dust; as it cleared, Hubbard recognized the man in a tailored suit walking briskly across a field toward them. "Hey," he said. "It's Binch!"

The small man approached as if the dust cloud were no annoyance at all. Hubbard and the others climbed out of the car.

"Who's that?" Asimov asked.

"Don't know," de Camp said with a shrug.

"Our friend at General Electric," Heinlein whispered to them. "Ixnay on the ardenclyffeWay." He raised his voice. "Hello, Mr. Binch. Thanks for your call."

"Greetings, Mr. Heinlein. Thank you for coming. I told you I had something of great importance to show you. Gentlemen, this is hallowed ground. This is where the future was created," Binch exclaimed, holding out his arms and indicating the wide, empty field. "Welcome to Menlo Park. The former site of Thomas Edison's laboratory. You're standing on the exact spot where the light bulb and the phonograph were invented. This, as far as science is concerned or will allow, is hallowed ground."

A gust of wind swept the curtain of dissipating grit from the sparse meadow. As it lifted, it seemed to pull a long white monolith up from the ground, though in fact it was only revealing the great, tall spire, topped by a spherical dome, which towered over the field.

"What the hell is that?" Heinlein asked, as the others were too busy staring.

"That," said Binch, "is the Edison Monument. A tribute from some of those closest to him that the work that happened here would never be forgotten."

"You know," said Hubbard, "it looks a little like the Tesla tower. Only the cap isn't big enough."

"Turns out it doesn't need to be so big," Binch replied with a slight smile. "Nikola was already convinced that on the second go-round a much smaller globe would suffice. His next tower would also be taller, close to one hundred fifty feet high, and thinner. A fifty-foot diameter would suffice. The building materials we had in 1933 were far superior to 1908, as well, and that made a huge difference, though the interior is still built completely of nonconductive materials."

"You've got to be kidding me," Heinlein said, one hand clasped tightly against his jaw. He took several tentative steps toward the obelisk, as if any sudden movement might scare it off.

Binch pointed to a small wooden barn, barely standing, at the edge of the meadow. "Why don't we get out of this sun and I'll tell you about how I finally convinced Thomas Edison that what Tesla had started deserved to be finished."

While they fell in line behind the old man, Heinlein had a hard time pulling himself away from the attraction of the tower. "Does this . . . work?"

Binch stopped, looked up at the tower, then to Heinlein, sharing some secret communion with him, as if only the two of them could really see it. He shook his head. "No." He began walking again. "Christie Street, here, was the first street in the world to have electric lights. You can still see the train tracks from Edison's electric train, which ran up and down the avenue here. That's his old house down there at the corner. The tower is standing directly on the spot where his laboratory once stood. This building here," he said, as they reached the front door of the blue barn, "was the toolshed."

"You'd never know anything happened here," Hubbard said.

"Sad, isn't it?" Binch opened the door. "This is where Edison harnessed electricity for the good of mankind, but now there's not even a caretaker." He flicked the light switch on and off a few times. "Sometimes there's not even power."

"Did you work here?" Asimov asked.

"I'm not that old, son. By the time I left Tesla's operation and joined Edison's, he had been in West Orange for at least a decade."

There was plenty of light streaming through the windows into the nearly empty barn. The heat was intense. Instantly, all five men had removed their hats and were fanning their faces with them.

"Why didn't you tell me about this last week?" Heinlein asked, his face clouded with excitement and concern.

"I didn't know who you were, for certain. There are lots of people who want to know about Tesla and Wardenclyffe. I try to answer as many questions as I can. But when I meet with people, as I did with you, for instance, I'm meeting you as an officer of the General Electric Corporation and I have an ethical obligation to act in the best interests of my company. But I asked around about you and people seemed impressed that Robert Heinlein and company had paid a visit. You have a lot of fans around the laboratories of GE."

"Glad to hear that."

Hubbard cleared his throat, but the old man must have been hard of hearing for he didn't mention Hubbard's fans at all.

"I wanted to meet you again, not as an employee of GE but as the keeper of the flames of Edison and Tesla. I've carried their secrets for a long time now. But I'm getting old. My chance for success, for implementing their vision, is fast fading. But you, with the resources of the United States Navy behind you, might prevail."

"It's not exactly as if GE is a mom-and-pop operation," de Camp said.

Binch stared at him, then daubed at his forehead with a red silk handkerchief. "In fact, it's more like a grandma-and-grandpa operation. It's not known for its imagination but for its methodical approach to practical research. A project like Wardenclyffe doesn't fit that model. Though Tom disagreed in the end."

"Did you steal Tesla's work for Edison?"

"No. No. No. Tom had little interest in Tesla's research when I first came to work for him. He had plenty of work for everyone and didn't need to compete with Nikola anymore at that point. Through the years I'd mention what we'd done at Wardenclyffe to Tom. And as I proved my value and loyalty over the years, he began to listen."

"Why didn't you just drop it?"

"I couldn't. Do you realize what we could do if what we had tried to do at Wardenclyffe worked? It would have changed the world."

"Edison could sell a lot of light bulbs," Hubbard said. "Why wouldn't he be interested in that?"

"Tom was always proud of the fact that he'd never manufactured a weapon."

"So the tower could be used as a weapon?" Heinlein asked.

"Absolutely. With some slight modifications and manipulations to the equipment, the same energies that could be sent through the earth could be sent through the air and destroy not just a single plane but a fleet of planes, at a distance of over a thousand miles. Had we been able to build it, no country would ever be attacked from the air. The London Blitz could never have happened.

"I spent years trying to recreate, as much as I could recall, the works of the Wardenclyffe project. I tried to speak with Tesla about it, but it was difficult. He felt I had betrayed him and I suppose he was right about that. But when I left him, I was young and had a family to care for, and he was clinging to a ship that was sinking and he refused to bail. On the other hand, I'm not proud to say that I took the lifeboat. But I never forgot what we were going to do there. I still believed in it.

"Finally, I took all that I recalled and laid it before Tom. I explained what I knew, apologized for what I couldn't recall. But that was where Tom's genius lay, being able to see the missing pieces. I knew that once he began to think about the puzzle, he would almost be helpless until he had solved it, and I was right. Or maybe he'd never really forgiven losing the circuit wars to Tesla and wanted to get inside his thinking. Whatever the reason, he began to mull it over. On several occasions he'd pull me into his office to discuss this theory or that. He showed me his designs for a more modest tower—a test site, actually—he believed in endless testing while Nikola always felt one had to go for broke every time. In contrast to Tesla's version, Edison's did not need to power the entire northeastern corridor first time out of the gate. We talked about how to build it. Even talked about where. And then, just like last time, it all came to an end."

"What happened?"

"Tom died—October 18, 1931. He left me his papers on the subject and established a fund so that I would have enough money to pursue it further. And that's exactly what I did. I approached the leaders of the township of Raritan with an offer to pay for and build a monument to Thomas Edison, right here at Menlo Park. Well, of course they saw visions of tourists coming from all over to pay their respects to Tom and spend their money in town buying souvenir light bulbs. I had the tunnels dug and the tower built in two years."

"Tunnels?" Heinlein asked.

"Oh yes," Binch replied. "The tower was only one part of the device. I recreated here almost exactly the network of tunnels and the great hole under the tower through which the electricity traveled downwards. Help me with this cellar door, will you?"

Why me? Hubbard asked himself, as he leaned down to give the iron ring a tug. There were three other men just standing there. Why had the old man picked on him? It took some effort, but a gaping hole in the floor finally revealed itself with an upward rush of cool, mildewy air.

"Sorry," Binch said. "I haven't been here in a while."

He led them down a flight of stairs. Once below, he lit a kerosene lantern that looked as if it might have been the last relic of the original facility. "If we were up and running, I'd have the diesel generators going to provide electricity to the tower and down here. But I've let the tanks run dry."

"Why didn't it work?" Heinlein asked.

"I don't know. All I can figure out is that Tom and I must have overlooked some critical elements. I remembered all I could, but it wasn't enough. Tom contributed what he could. Still. I don't know. I was hoping you boys could tell me."

"Us?"

"There must be something you could discover. I'd let you see all of my papers, Tom's papers. Give you full access to everything here. Just think, Mr. Heinlein, if you and your team can get it to work, you could end this war."

"We could stop the super-bombers," Asimov whispered.

"The what?"

"Nothing," Asimov muttered, shrinking under Heinlein's harsh gaze.

"And then, once this war's over, imagine what we'd have given the world."

"Yeah," Hubbard said. "You'd be in line for a hell of a promotion."

"Mr.—I'm sorry, I forgot your name?"

"Hubbard. Lafayette Ron Hubbard."

"Right, Mr. Hubbard. I'm already a stockholder in the General Electric Corporation. Money is not my motivation. Redeeming the reputation of Nikola Tesla in the eyes of the world is."

"You're trying to atone," Heinlein said softly. "For your betrayal."

"I'm only sorry I wasn't able to bring it off in Tesla's lifetime. But of course, his mind was so far gone by the end of his days I doubt he'd have even been able to appreciate what I was trying to do for him. He barely recognized me the last time I spoke with him."

Heinlein patted a table full of oscilloscopes. "May we look around?"

"Be my guest. I haven't been here in three years or so. I'm afraid the local wildlife may have nested in some of the equipment. There's a lot that would have to be replaced. It's possible, though. I could even have GE run a high-powered line in here in a matter of days if I wanted to."

As they explored the generators, cables, and machinery, Heinlein questioned Binch. "What happens when you crank it on?"

"It creates some very interesting lightning effects at the top of the tower. But it's only effective in scaring the farmers."

"What do you think the problem is?"

"I'm not Tesla."

"Fair enough. None of us is, either. I'm certainly not an electrical engineer by any stretch of the imagination. So bear with me as I talk this through. The generators create the electricity. Then the mechanics of the tower generate the proper resonance before the energy is driven down into the electric level of the earth's crust or bounced off the upper atmosphere. By adjusting the frequency, the direction and range can be accurately projected."

At this new information, de Camp caught Hubbard's eye, who cautioned him to stay silent with a simple gesture.

"That's a very good description of the process, Mr. Heinlein."

"Please, call me Bob. There's something I'm missing, Mr. Binch."

"What's that?"

"This tremendous amount of electricity. I'm assuming it's more than the generators can create, am I correct?"

"Yes."

"So, is there a capacitor of some kind which can store the energy until it's built up enough to the required level?"

Binch indicated a bank of metal cases the size of refrigerators sitting side by side against the wall. "The capacitors."

"And what are you using for a dielectric?"

Binch flipped back a couple of latches on top of one of the capacitors and withdrew a lattice of metal that Hubbard instantly recognized as nearly identical to the one Heinlein had pulled off the top of the tank at Wardenclyffe. "Nitrogen suspended in a porcelain vacuum." He proudly tapped on one of the clear glass tiles that were intact in each of the frame's slots. "Tom's best guess of what Nikola must have been using. You wouldn't believe how much thinking went into this."

Heinlein nodded thoughtfully. "And where's your receiver?"

"Sorry?"

"When we last met, you told us of the receiver that Peary had taken with him on his expedition. The one that would prove the tower worked when it received Tesla's signal."

"I could never build one that worked. Whatever I missed in creating the tower was also lacking in the receivers."

Heinlein nodded. "Well. I guess that's enough."

"Don't you want to look at the pit?" Binch pointed to the long corridor that terminated in darkness in the distance.

"I owned a silver mine once. Once you see one hole in the ground, you've seen them all."

"What do you think about what I've done here?"

"I think it's an interesting monument you've built to some interesting men," Heinlein said, with an empty shrug. His early enthusiasm seemed to have waned, though Hubbard couldn't for the life of him understand why.

"But can you make it work?"

"I don't know, Mr. Binch. I'd like to take it back to my bosses and see if they'll even give me the permission to look into it. If they agree, then I'll put it before my team and find out what they think. But we've got a lot of projects going on right now, so I'll have to see."

After poking around for a little while longer, Heinlein suddenly but politely bid their guide a good day. Upstairs, walking back to the car while Binch watched their receding backs from the shade of the barn, de Camp complimented Heinlein. "You certainly played that like a cool customer."

"Hm?"

"Pretending that you're not interested. That you don't know if it can work."

"I don't know if it can. But I certainly don't want to share what I know with him yet."

"You're a suspicious sonofabitch," Hubbard said.

"From my time in politics," Heinlein replied.

"He's using the wrong dielectric material," Asimov said, climbing into the front seat. Hubbard pulled him out and sent him to his place in the back. "There's no way his capacitors can build up enough charge."

"There's a lot to repair even if it could work." Heinlein started the car. "It'd take weeks. Which is about all that we have left at this point." He looked up to the top of the monument for a long time, then, finally, began to drive.

Hubbard dozed again on the way back to the Navy Yard while the others chattered about theoretical stuff he couldn't give a crap about. "That's the bar we ended up at," he yawned at one point, as they drove toward League Island. The others were silent. So silent, in fact, that Hubbard was certain they had been discussing him while he slept.

Heinlein pulled the car to a stop in front of what was obviously an administrative building. They looked the same on every base Hubbard had ever been on. "Ron, wait here a minute," he said, leaping out of the car and running into the building.

"See you, Ron." Asimov climbed out, too.

"Have a good trip," de Camp said.

Hubbard barely grunted as they left. He was finally alone in the car and might actually be able to get back to sleep. He rubbed his head. It was still sore where he'd been hit . . .

Hit?

Good trip?

His eyes popped open.

Heinlein was exiting the building accompanied by a small, tight Army officer wearing fancy cowboy boots instead of government issue. They both hurried into the car.

"This is Colonel Tom Slick," Heinlein quickly said, by way of introduction.

"Nice to meet you. Bob, head over to Hangar Four."

"That's way out on the far end, right?"

"Yeah, that's where he's waiting."

"Who's waiting?"

"Sorry, son," the colonel said. "You'll find out in a minute."

Son?

"Bob here tells me you're currently unassigned?"

"That's correct."

"Sir."

"That's correct, sir." Shit. A hard-ass. He sat up in his seat.

"Well, consider yourself on assignment now."

"For what? Hey, Bob. What's going on?"

Heinlein refused to look him in the eye.

"A secret mission," Slick continued. "We're lucky to have you. And lucky to have a pilot in town heading to California who's a friend of mine. I'll owe him a favor after this."

"Hey, Bob!"

Slick continued talking as if he were chatting about the box scores. "Of course, I could use a trip to the Pacific Islands, too. I'd almost go if I weren't needed elsewhere."

"What the hell?!"

Heinlein braked the car hard in front of the immense hangar, and both he and Slick popped out as if the car's momentum had thrown them out. Hubbard followed, shouting at them over the powerful roar of the Mustang warming up on the tarmac.

"You can't send me to the Pacific! I don't have any clothes or money!"

"We'll have everything ready for you before you're in California. Clothes, money, itinerary," Slick said, approaching an extremely tall pilot who was performing a last-minute inspection on his aircraft. "Hello, Lieutenant Stewart!"

"You're sending me to the Aleutians." Hubbard spun around to Heinlein.

"We need you to find that case, Ron," Heinlein said, meeting his gaze at last. "It's the final key to the puzzle. Find it and bring it back."

"What the hell? Build a new one!"

"There's too much about it we don't know. I'm going to try to turn Menlo Park on. But I need that case to make sure I'm doing it right."

"You can't do this to me."

"Why not? You did it to me."

"What do you mean?"

Heinlein leaned in close. "I know you slept with Leslyn. Back in L.A. I know all about it."

Hubbard's mouth went dry. He had always suspected that Bob knew, but had never expected to be confronted about it. "So, it's an open marriage for you but not for her?"

"You took advantage of her. You knew she was sick."

"You're sending me off to get rid of me? To get me killed? Because your wife got drunk one night while I was around and you weren't?"

"No. I'm sending you on this trip to help us save the world. In spite of the fact that you slept with my wife behind my back, which sent her over the edge so she almost killed herself."

"I won't go."

"It's not up for discussion. You've been ordered. By Colonel Slick—and John W. Campbell, Jr. If you want a future in the military or in the pulps, you'll do it."

"Hubbard," Colonel Slick said, walking up with the tall pilot, "consider it an adventure."

"This . . ."—Hubbard pointed to the plane—"this is a goddamned rocket to the morgue!"

"Maybe you should just buck up and follow the orders of your superior officers," the pilot snapped, suddenly turning around and drawing himself up to his full height, which enabled him to look quite down on Hubbard. The pilot's voice was unmistakably familiar, his face even more so, save for the fact that Hubbard had only ever seen it by the silver glow of the movies. "Is he going to piss and moan the whole way to California?"

"He'll be fine, Jimmy. Trust me. Right, son?"

"Yes. Sir."

"You owe me one for this," the pilot said in his trademark Midwestern twang—a lilt that had mesmerized audiences in the film where he had played that idealistic young senator. He seemed more grizzled and masculine in real life, flint-eyed, steely. And tall.

"Are you in such a hurry to get back to training your rookies in Idaho?" Colonel Slick said.

"You know I'm sick of that."

"Well, I hear there's a bomber group out of Sioux City that might be heading to England soon for combat operations."

"Yeah?"

"I hear they're looking for an operations officer. Why don't you drop in on your way back to Idaho from California. Ask for Colonel George Reynolds. He's a friend of mine. I'll let him know you're coming."

The pain of his hangover, the punch, the road trip, the roar of the Mustang—it all melded into one golden blur in Hubbard's head. He rubbed his skull, the back of it still sore from where he'd been hit in the basement of the . . . He gripped Heinlein's arm. "I just remembered something."

"Ron . . ." Heinlein tried to jerk his arm away.

Hubbard wouldn't let go. "Look, I'm not trying to get out of this. I'll go. But I'm trying to tell you that I remember something now. Back in the Empire State Building, when I was getting ready to climb down the ladder; there was someone there. I saw his shoes. He went for my folder—the one with the pulps. Before I could look up, he hit me in the head with something.

"I didn't fall accidentally. I was knocked off the ladder. You have to be careful, Bob. There's somebody on your trail."

"I'll be careful." He brushed Hubbard's arm off. "You too."

"You know this is a lost cause, don't you?"

The movie star turned to Hubbard and said, "Those are the only ones worth fighting for." Then he turned and, with lengthy strides, headed toward his plane. Hubbard had to run to catch up. After all, he knew when he wasn't welcome.

ISSUE 3

THE COLD ELECTRICITY OF DREAMS

EPISODE 21

GINNY'S BUNSEN BURNER was set so low that the flame sputtered, repeatedly threatening to completely die. The heat had to be as low as possible, but the irregularity was becoming a real distraction. She gave the throttle the tiniest tweak and the flame steadied—at least enough so she could continue to distill the mineral oil without completely boiling it away. There was a noise from Bob's office, causing her to instinctively look up. False alarm. Walb had accidentally stepped on one of the model ships by the executive offices, but she could see through the blinds that Bob was still absent. That was fine. She didn't need to know his every movement or whereabouts. He didn't really owe her anything. He was a married man and he had his own life.

She just would have liked to see him, that was all. She hadn't seen him since she'd let him take her out for a dinner.

Her eyes dropped from his silent door back to her worktable. Before her were a variety of large jars nestled amongst a number of healthy potted plants: the components of her experiments, as well as the fruits of her labor. In one of the glasses was a gallon of liquid designed to repel insects from Africa to Europe to Asia. The only problem was that there were so many different kinds of insects, sensitive to so many different scents, that the only substance she could come up with smelled so abhorrent that no soldier would put it on to test it. Still, she'd continued to try to work to reduce its odor until Reinhart had asked her, begged actually, to stop. Then she'd turned her attention to plant extracts, to see if there were any useful applications for highly concentrated oils.

She liked being here at the lab. It was better than the bakery in New York she'd been working at before Eleanor Roosevelt had convinced the Navy to launch the program that had finally given her a chance to serve her country, Women Accepted for Volunteer Emergency Service. Ginny had signed up on the very day the WAVES began accepting applications. Because of her degree from New York University, she'd been selected for officer training and sent to the Naval Reserve Midshipmen's School at Smith College. She'd loved the drilling and lectures in naval history. And because of her years as a figure skater, she excelled particularly at the physical education aspects, always placing first in any athletic competition.

The mineral oil vapor wafted through ever finer series of glass and copper coils surrounding the beaker, which was suspended over the flame, until it vanished as it vented out the top of the tubing. The chalky scent was as familiar to her as her own perfume. In fact, she'd inhaled enough of her own special blend over the years that she probably exuded it. Probably one of the reasons she always attracted lab types.

"What are you up to?" Sprague de Camp, one of Bob's favorites, dropped his long frame into an available chair by her table. She enjoyed his personality; he seemed to take a lot of pleasure in his life.

"I'm distilling plant essences," she replied. Then, before she could stop herself, she added, "Have you seen Bob?"

"Not today."

"He's awfully busy, isn't he?"

"I like to think of Bob as a bit like Jason from Greek mythology."

"Really?"

"I've always been bent toward the classics. I can't help it. Bob is captain of the ship, *Argos*, looking for the Golden Fleece, and we're his Argonauts."

She thought of the letters over the lab door, and smiled. "You're not really a science fiction kind of guy, are you, Lieutenant?"

"I'm really more of a fantasy guy," he replied bashfully.

"So, do you believe in magic?"

"Maybe a little."

"So, who are the rest of your Argonauts?"

"Well, Asimov is Orpheus, with his deep thoughts. Meisel and Bowen are the Boreads, Calais and Zetes, because they're always in such a hurry. Walb is Telman, the strategist. Brinley is Philoctetes for his quick comebacks, like an archer's arrows."

"Who would you be?"

"Me? I'm Heracles, of course."

"Were there any women among the Argonauts?"

"There was indeed. There was the huntress Atalanta."

"Oh," she exclaimed. "I like the sound of her."

"The virgin huntress, Atalanta, I meant to say."

"Oh. Any other women?"

"Among the Argonauts, no. But there were plenty of women along the way to the Golden Fleece. Um"—he paused and blushed—"things don't go so well for a lot of the women in the story. But that's how some of those classics are, y'know?"

"So you like to think you're all on some Greek adventure. That's cute."

"The quest for the Golden Fleece is more than a quest for adventure. Ares, the Ram, represents the symbol for iron. The real quest of Jason was not about trying to discover an old skin. Jason and his friends were seeking intellectual knowledge—they were searching for the way to turn iron into gold."

"Alchemy?"

"Exactly. They were warrior-scientists, traveling throughout the Mediterranean seeking all the knowledge of the day. Gold."

"That's what we're looking for," her voice dropped to a conspiratorial whisper. "Gold?"

He leaned in close. "It's only my personal metaphor," he whispered back. "Helps me deal with . . ."

"Lieutenant de Camp!" Dr. Reinhart bore down on them and they sprang apart.

". . . this," de Camp said in her direction.

"I know what you mean!" She couldn't help herself, but in Reinhart's presence she always subtly checked to make sure her blouse buttons were closed all the way to the top.

De Camp nodded at the man but remained seated. After all, Reinhart wasn't his superior officer, only his boss.

"I understand you haven't been running any more rudder control tests even though the new compressor has been delivered."

"I've been working with Bob on some different things."

"I thought so." Reinhart ran a finger along the black slate surface of her table, leaving a thin trail as if his fingertip oozed slime like a snail. "I don't really have the allocations for whatever this project is."

"It comes directly from General Scoles."

"Perhaps it does."

Ginny felt his eyes crawling over her body, even though she wasn't looking at him.

"But I don't have any orders from Scoles about this. So, as far as I'm concerned, you need to be back in the weather room instead of taking trips to see Broadway shows."

"That's not what we were doing in New York."

Reinhart smiled. "So you were in New York. See, I already know more from talking with you for five minutes than I do spending an hour with Heinlein."

De Camp bit his lip.

"If you want to tell me anything else, I might be able to offer some more assistance."

"Bob's the one who knows everything," de Camp said with a shrug, though there was a tight quiver of anger to his voice. "You'll have to speak with him for another hour or so."

"Like I said." Reinhart noticed the slime on his finger and wiped it on his lab coat. "If you want to cooperate with me, I'll cooperate with you and Heinlein."

"I'm just doing my job," de Camp said.

"In fact, that's exactly what I expect of you. Nothing less, and certainly nothing more. As of tomorrow, I want you back in your weather room and I want to see experiments proceeding apace and I want reports on those experiments and I want results. Otherwise, there is a war on, you know, and a good officer is always a valuable commodity."

De Camp snapped to his feet, towering over Reinhart, who took a defensive step back. "Only a coward would think for a second that threatening to send me into combat would scare me as much as it scared him."

Reinhart took another step back, putting a hand on the lab table to steady himself. "I . . . I wasn't. But you are here to do a job and I expect you to do it. Until I'm informed otherwise by General Scoles, consider yourself assigned to, well, your original assignment." He lifted his hand, rubbing his fingers together before holding them up to his nose and sniffing. Turning to Virginia, he said sharply, "You need to clean up your workspace, Miss Gerstenfeld. There's oil all over it." Then he turned, smoothed his coat, and walked away from them with official purpose.

"Sonofabitch," Sprague said, then added, "Pardon me for swearing like a sailor."

"It's okay, Lieutenant. I'm in the Navy, too."

He grinned.

"Is this going to upset Bob?"

"Him? He's a big boy. He can handle Reinhart. Meanwhile, looks like I'm heading back to the icebox."

"Doesn't sound so bad in this heat."

"Anything's bad if you have to do it ten hours a day." He looked at her tabletop. "Did you spill something?"

"No." The surface of her table was covered in a radiant sheen. She ran her finger through it, tracing a path much as Reinhart had done. "It's my mineral oil. It's condensing on the surface."

"What are you doing, exactly?" Sprague seemed more than merely interested.

"I'm pumping mineral oil through the coils around the jar to keep my plant essences from boiling out because I can't adjust the burner well enough. I guess the heat transference and the pressure is atomizing the oil into the air."

"It's invisible." Sprague held his hand over the opening of the tubing. After a moment he pulled it away. His palm was shiny with a slick of clear liquid. Next, he crouched down to look beneath the beaker at the flame itself. "Will you look at that?" Then he pursed his lips and whistled as if it was the best way to communicate that he was impressed.

The flame still flickered as it had all morning, but now it seemed surrounded by an almost solid orb of light the size of a baseball, a holy glowing corona.

Sprague shot up. "Come over here," he commanded, rushing several tables down the row. Quickly, she trotted after him.

"What is it?"

He placed his hands on her shoulders and spun her around, back to facing her table. Her table sat by one of the windows and all around it, the air seemed to shimmer as if a doorway to Wonderland or Oz were about to open.

"Yani," Sprague called to his engineer friend who spent his days working with mirrors, crystals, and lenses in an attempt to reproduce the Claw of Archimedes—a parabola capable of focusing the sun's rays so as to blind or even burn out the eyes of oncoming kamikaze pilots.

The man lifted his head from his toils, eyes hidden behind the tinted goggles that protected him from constant solar exposure. "Yes."

"Swing the Claw around and point it at the far wall there," Sprague indicated.

"Why?"

"Does it matter? Come on."

Yani did what was asked of him. The claw prototype was as large as a dressing mirror, but it pivoted on a stand scavenged from a large floor fan.

Ginny saw the concave surface gleam as it caught the available sunlight. Then she gasped. In the shimmering air above her desk, the light seemed to solidify into golden gossamer. "What's happening?" she asked, as the other men in the lab began to drift toward the sight like children drawn to a cotton candy machine.

"Irradiant lighting," Sprague said with a slight, gleeful laugh.

Bernie Zitin joined them, unable to take his eyes off the hovering image. "It's like an invisible movie screen," he said. "What's your medium?"

"My own blend of mineral oil," she said.

"That explains it," the biologist said. "Mineral oils have a high level of refractivity."

"That's right!" she exclaimed. "We use oil immersion techniques in our microscope sometimes to increase the resolution."

"Looks like you've figured out a way to suspend it in thin air," Bowen, the engineer, said. "A combination of the right fluid, the right temperature, and the right amount of pressure."

"It's incredible," Sprague said. "You can barely see any haze at all."

"Watch this!" Yani called, as he plucked a large crystal from his wooden box. He held the crystal in front of the big bowl and in an instant, the golden beam over her table transformed into a nearly solid rainbow. The room grew silent, as if everyone were afraid that simply speaking would make the vision disappear.

Ginny clapped a hand to her lips. She felt a pressure on her shoulder squeeze ever so slightly and thought it was Sprague until she smelled the Old Spice and heard Bob's warm voice in her ear. "It's beautiful."

"I know."

And then his hand slipped away. She turned slightly so she could see him without losing sight of the rainbow. "I'm glad you got to see it."

"I wouldn't have believed it otherwise," he whispered. "You're the first one to really make something wonderful here."

"But what's it good for?" she asked.

"Look at them," he said, nodding toward the cheering lab rats. The only other time she had seen them so united was the day of the near riot.

The image flickered and shivered and then drifted away like a cloud breaking up after a storm.

"Oh, that goddamn Bunsen burner!" she cried, but no one heard her because they were all applauding. And they weren't applauding for Yani and his Claw of Archimedes, they were all turned toward her, and she felt the pride in her chest and Bob was grinning at her and shaking his head.

"You make rainbows," she heard him say, over the din. "In the middle of war, you make beautiful rainbows and liquid gold."

EPISODE 22

THOUGH GERTRUDE DIDN'T quite know what to make of Isaac's story about wallowing trapped in a river under Manhattan last week, she was happy to have him home. His absence last week reminded her how much she hated his being away; it made her worry about how she would get along were he to be drafted. At the same time, she was surprised by how much she had come to depend upon him in such a short time. Actually, it was something more than that. She just really liked the way her life had opened up since she met him, the things she had learned, the excitement of really being an adult and on her own. With Isaac, of course.

Summer was coming. She could feel it on the breeze. Even though she was in the wrong city, she couldn't help singing "How About You?" under her breath as she walked down the sidewalk toward City Hall. Although Isaac had gone to work this morning sore at her, the beauty of the day made it hard for her to feel sorry for herself. Gertie didn't think he had much of a right to be mad anyway. If she didn't want him putting his *shmeckel* in her mouth, then she shouldn't have to. And if she didn't want to put herself on her hands and knees in her own bed so he was looking at the back of her head while she stared out the window at nothing, well, then, she didn't have to do that either if she didn't want to. If she had to do sex—and she knew that was part of the deal of marriage—she at least wanted to see her husband's face and not his belly button, or the variety of curtains in the building across the street. Sex was so odd.

Still, she knew Isaac was mad. And she wanted to figure out a way to make him happy, so it was time to run errands. The first stop was Reedmor Books, on Walnut. The musty smell of old literature tickled her nose, made her sneeze. She thanked the wild-haired chubby old man who owned the shop for the courtesy of his blessing, then went to the magazine rack. Isaac had told her that Reedmor had the best selection of pulps in the city. She wanted to pick him up some of the latest issues. But more than that, she was going to read them. If she could show more interest in his science fiction work, she knew he would be pleased.

Those mags were easy to find, on the first row of the display case. Gertie had heard of *Unknown*, *Amazing Stories*, *Astounding Science*

Fiction, so she plucked those up instantly. Then she selected *Startling Stories*, for its cover of animals entering, two-by-two, a rocket ark. *Thrilling Wonder Stories* promised a story of a bare-chested man with a sword defending a woman in a torn, diaphanous gown from some kind of monster, so that went into the pile as well. The artist had really captured the lovely woman's expression, a combination of excitement and dread, and something else that she couldn't quite put her finger on, something in the fiery eyes.

She looked up from the mag in her hand at the shelves in front of her. She had never really taken in the pulps in their entirety before. There were so many of them. And most of them featured women in danger. Some of them were on the verge of being rescued, but most of them were about to be, well, violated was the only word she could think of, by some kind of menace. A flush crept up her cheeks as her eyes fell upon the top row—the mags hidden behind the others. The titles alone made her feel guilty: *Spicy Mystery* and *Speed Mystery*. *Spicy Detective* and *Speed Detective*. *Spicy Adventure Stories*. These women, they were in their underwear, the lovely styles of which she'd never seen before. She could imagine Mrs. de Camp owning clothes such as these. Some of them were bound or under the control of a man much stronger. As she looked at the young blonde being presented at a slave auction to fierce-looking Arabians, a surprising warmth flowed downward from just below her navel.

In a few minutes she was at the counter, where the chubby old man had to stir himself from the stool to tally up her purchases. He didn't say a word as he thumbed through the science fiction mags, and then the large stack of spicy mags she'd placed below them. She felt judged, though he said nothing. "These are for my mother," she said self-righteously.

"You sure she wouldn't be more comfortable with the censored versions?"

"Hm?" She found it hard to look him in the face. Instead, she focused on the star he was tapping on in the upper-right corner of *Thrilling Love Stories*.

"They didn't cut out the dirty parts. If your mother wants those versions, they look the same but have these stars."

"No." She shook her head. "She'll take the uncensored ones."

"Okay." He shrugged, then tapped a name on the cover as he handed over the unstarred replacement. "Robert Leslie Bellem. You're going to like him."

"My mother," she corrected.

"Of course," he replied. "That'll be three dollars."

Back on the street she tucked the plain brown bag into her purse, walked quickly away from the store, and her brisk pace led her swiftly to one of the few things she liked about living in Philadelphia, living near Wanamaker's. There were so many things in the immense department store she had never even thought of owning before, never even knew existed, like the black Parisian fishnets she held in her hands. She didn't even own a garter belt. She'd never really owned anything fancy.

It wasn't as if her parents were strict, or went out of their way to protect her from a world they perceived as dangerous or cruel. But like most families, making it through the last dozen or so years—which encapsulated most of her conscious life—had been a mighty struggle every single day. And the light at the end of that endless tunnel—filled with saving, scrimping, moving to the next town where there were rumors of work, going hungry at night, eating meat only a couple of times a month, praying hard, crying, listening to the radio, being afraid—had been the funeral pyre of an entire world at war. So she bore her parents no bad feelings for not exposing her to chenille. All the same, it was exciting to discover it for herself now, and there was part of her that was glad she had waited until she was older because it meant more, and made the day exciting. There was also part of her that was grateful to Isaac for having made it possible.

She put the stockings down and wandered to the balcony where she could look down over the Grand Court, three tall stories below. People who actually had money to spend wandered across the wonderful white marble floor. Wanamaker's was fun, a museum where everything was for sale. A rattle overhead startled her and she looked up to see the pneumatic tube anchored to the ceiling shake as a canister inside whizzed toward an unknown destination elsewhere in the great building. After happily watching the shoppers sweeping along on the main floor as if they were in a Busby Berkeley movie, swirling colorfully to the bouncy strains of "We're in the Money" provided by the live organist, Gertie decided to acknowledge the growling in her stomach. It was time to meet Isaac. Their friend, and Isaac's agent, Freddie, now simply Pfc Pohl, was passing through Philadelphia to board a ship to Italy, and they were getting together for a lunch at the Automat. She was ready for some macaroni and cheese.

Gertie never noticed the man, she had turned so quickly. His shoulder caught her solidly in the cheek and she staggered clumsily into a table of handbags, scattering them.

"God, miss. I'm so sorry," the man said, helping her to right herself.

"I didn't see you coming," she replied, eyes closed against the pain, the shock of the impact.

"Are you okay?" But the concern in his voice sounded false, almost as if he were bored or exasperated. "Let me help you with your bag."

She opened her eyes to see a thickset man, bending down. "I didn't realize I dropped it."

The man handed it to her, then replaced the other spilled bags. His face looked like an old scuffed and cracked leather satchel that had been left to rot in the sun. "Here you go."

"Thank you," she stammered. Embarrassed at how she had clutched the bag back from him, she ducked her head and slid past him, almost making a dash for the escalators in her haste to get away. In moments she found herself scurrying across the ground floor, approaching the revolving doors just beyond the information counter. She stretched out her hand to push her way through when a hand clamped painfully down just above her wrist, causing her to shriek, while bringing her up short. Instead of the man she had expected, the stranger who had bumped into her earlier, her forearm was being gripped by a taller male, with long limbs like a spider and the sallow gray face of a dour undertaker.

Still holding her arm, the man thrust his hand into the handbag looped around her shoulder.

"Hey!" she cried, attracting attention.

The man kept his eyes focused squarely as he began to pull an object from the purse. The fishnet stockings.

"I didn't take that," she stammered.

"Come with me, please." The man pulled her out away from the door. At the same time, the short man she had bumped into earlier passed her on his way out. As he entered the door he tipped his hat and said, "Goodbye, Mrs. Asimov."

"Wait!" she cried after him. "That man there, he . . ."

How had he known her name?

The man holding her arm squeezed it. "Mrs. Asimov, you need to listen to me very carefully. You have two choices. Either talk quietly with me here for a few minutes, or let me call store security over and tell them I've caught a thief. A lingerie thief."

"How do you know who I am?" she asked.

With his free hand, he reached into his jacket and pulled out a slim leather folder. He flipped it open to reveal a War Department card with the name ROSS DUGAN printed under the photo. "I'm with the Counter-Intelligence Corps," Dugan said, releasing her arm and putting the ID away.

She massaged her wrist. "What do you want?"

"I want to know about your husband."

"Isaac? Why? What has he done?"

"Is it true that he is part of a Socialist organization?"

"I don't know what you're talking about."

"Is he or is he not affiliated with a group known as the Futurians?"

"The Futurians? They're not Socialists."

"Michel. Sykora. Merril."

"Merril? I don't know any Merril."

"Judith Merril? Her married name is Zissman. Judith Zissman?"

"Oh. I don't know anything about any of their politics."

"How about a man named Cartmill? Cleve Cartmill."

"No. Why?"

"They are Socialists and Communists."

"So what? This is America. They can be whatever they want."

"We're at war, Mrs. Asimov. There are enemies both within as well as without."

"These are Isaac's friends! They're just writers. There's nothing dangerous about them."

"Marx was just a writer. Hitler wrote a best-seller. Writers can be the most dangerous participants in a society. Especially ones who write about the future. It's a small step from writing about it to trying to bring it about."

She put her hand over her mouth. "Oh my God," she whispered. "You're crazy."

Dugan ignored her. "Since your husband began working for the U.S. Navy, do you know if he's had any contact with these people?"

"I don't know."

"He took a trip to New York last week. Did you know this?"

"Yes."

"His whereabouts are unaccounted for. Could he have met with any of the Futurians and perhaps given them information he might have come across in the course of his work?"

"You're accusing him of spying? You don't know Isaac. He loves his country."

"Not enough to fight for it, though."

"How dare you!"

"Maybe you should consider other reasons why he went to New York, then."

"He went for work."

"Did he? Mrs. Asimov, I hate to put it to you this way, but could your husband have been meeting a lover?"

Gertie stared at the man's pockmarked face for a long moment, letting her disgust with him truly sink in. Then she flung the fishnets at his chest so hard he had to take a step back. "Go to hell!" As he stumbled awkwardly backwards, she strode past him to the door, not caring at all whether or not he grabbed for her, half wishing he would so she could start screaming and screaming. But nothing happened, and a moment later she was out on the sidewalk, not even waiting for her eyes to adjust to the light before walking as fast as she could away from the department store. It occurred to her that Dugan, or his partner, might be following her, but she didn't care. There was nothing to hide. All the same, once she made the left onto Chestnut Street, she increased her pace nearly to a trot. And that's when the tears came.

She leaned against the front of a haberdashery and let the sobs catch up with her. She couldn't believe what Dugan had said about the Futurians. They weren't dangerous. They only wanted to talk about their silly stories. Occasionally, Michel might get a little political about how slowly the world was going in making a better tomorrow happen. But trying to change the government? Acting as spies? Using Isaac as a conduit to some Bolshevik masters?

Ridiculous.

Gertie rooted around in her purse until she could find a handkerchief to clear the tears from her cheeks. Her racing heart was beginning to find its way back to its normal pace. She took a deep breath. The Automat was within sight.

The man's insinuation was almost as ridiculous as Isaac's excuse—that he'd discovered a secret cavern under Manhattan. But Isaac was her husband. She had to believe in him, and that meant believing him.

She entered the Automat, her head held proudly high, as befitting a Blugerman, an Asimov. The gleaming chrome of the coin-operated cases around the restaurant set off the fullest variety of appetizers, entrées, side dishes, and desserts imaginable. Half the patrons in the restaurant were in uniform. More than half of those had receding hairlines, less than half of those had mustaches, and by process of elimination she found Freddie Pohl sitting by himself at a table for four, nursing a cup of coffee between slightly trembling hands. He grinned when he caught sight of her and stood to give her a hug.

"Hey, are you all right?" he said, stepping back from the embrace. "You're shaking."

"I just had a traffic scare," she said. "I'm so sorry I'm late. Is Isaac here, yet?"

"No." Freddie held her chair out for her. "He's running late, too. A little odd, I thought, since ten minutes early is five minutes late for Isaac."

Gertie quickly looked around the restaurant to see if somehow she had missed him, but there was no sign of Isaac. "How's Doë?" she asked.

"Good." Freddie rubbed his hands together. "She's okay."

"She must be upset about you leaving."

"She's not happy about it."

"How was your basic . . . ?" Before Gertie could finish the question, her gaze fell upon an object she hadn't noticed before. Opposite from her, a small satin clutch rested on the table. "Is Doë here?"

Freddie swallowed hard. "No."

A shadow fell across the table. Gertie looked up, hoping, almost praying, to see Isaac.

"Judith?"

Gertie had always described the woman taking her seat next to Freddie as tight. If one were to pull out her hat pin she might completely unravel from head to toe.

"Hello, Gertie," Judith said, with her patent disinterest. Gertie didn't know if it was reserved specifically for her, or whether it was the attitude she took with anyone who wasn't a science fiction writer. "Didn't know you were coming."

"Isaac said we were meeting with Freddie. I didn't know . . . What are you doing in Philadelphia?"

"I came to see Freddie off. It's what Futurians do for one another."

"But what about Doë?" Gertie turned to Freddie.

"I said goodbye to her," Freddie said with a shrug. "And Judith knows Philly."

"But she's your wife. Didn't she want to come?" Gertie felt as if the room were spinning. "Oh. Does she know Judith is here?"

"Doë understands my relationship with Judith."

"But she's married."

"Marriage is a dying institution." Judith sighed. "In fifty years no one will be getting married at all. It's completely inevitable."

"But you're married too!"

"And just because I'm a woman doesn't mean I shouldn't have the right to come see a friend off to war."

"Gertie." Freddie placed his hands upon the table. "I think you're misreading the situation here."

Gertie turned to look at Freddie, whose handsome face was pulled tight with embarrassment. "Freddie, I think you're the one misreading the situation."

"Oh, Gertrude," Judith sighed, as if mollifying a child.

Where was Isaac? This was turning out all wrong. She never should have bought the mags, touched the stockings; never should have wanted what she couldn't have. "I can't believe you're having an affair."

"It's not an affair," Freddie said. "That sounds so sordid. Isaac would understand," he added, as if that would make it all right.

"Oh no he wouldn't, Freddie! You Futurians. Honestly. Just using your little club as an excuse to drop your pants with whoever, excuse me, whomever you feel like."

"It's not like that," he protested. "This is something that happens on an intellectual level. Doë knows that she can't give me *everything*."

"Are you so sure that you are all Isaac needs?" Judith added.

Gertie rose, the feet of the chair shrieking as they skidded back. People turned to look at her. "I hope you're safe in Italy, Freddie." The tears began to roll down her cheeks again. "I really do."

She pushed her way out of the restaurant, ignoring Judith's last little looks of triumph, and fled home in a fog of tears. Her apartment, so quiet, felt safe and she collapsed on the bed. The tears were gone and she stared at the ceiling for a long time. Finally, she must have fallen asleep, for when she heard the rattle of keys in the lock, the room was infused with rich amber sunset light and the shadows had grown long.

Isaac cleared his throat in the hallway and entered the bedroom, coat already off, loosening his tie. "Hey," he said.

She watched him as he hung up his coat. "You stood me up."

"I'm sorry about that. Bob had us all work through lunch today. I tried to call you but you must have left early. Did you see Freddie? I can't imagine him a soldier. I hope he'll be okay."

"He'll be okay," she said, turning on her side away from him.

"Anyway, I'm awfully sorry."

"I want to go home," she said.

"What? You are home."

"I want to go home to Brooklyn."

Isaac paused in the middle of taking his shoes off, letting the one in his hand drop to the floor.

"What are you saying?"

"I don't like it here and I want to go home."

"But I need you here."

Gertie took a deep breath. "Are you having an affair?"

"What? No! How could you even think that?"

She sighed.

"I love you. You're the one I love."

"Nothing lasts forever, Isaac. Did you see another woman in New York?"

"Hell, no."

"Maybe marriage isn't for you. As someone who writes about the future you must know that it's an archaic institution that'll be dead in fifty years."

"What are you talking about? What did Freddie say to you?"

Rolling over on her side again, she thought there might be tears again, but there weren't.

"I want to go see my parents."

"Okay," he said. "We'll go this weekend."

"No, Isaac. I'm going tomorrow."

"For how long?"

"I don't know."

"What does that mean?"

"It means what it means, Isaac. It means I don't know. I don't know how long I'm going to need, but I just need some time away from all this."

"From me?"

"From you! From Mr. Heinlein. From the future. I just need some time."

"What can I say to stop you?"

"I don't know, Isaac. You're the writer. Think of something."

Instead, after a long while of just staring at her or the wall, he got up and finished undressing in silence. Then he left her alone in the bedroom. Soon she heard the familiar *click-clack* of the typewriter keys. The sound made her grit her teeth. Even tonight, when she really needed him to curl up beside her and stroke her hair, he couldn't bring himself to stop writing. He did have another lover, she knew then. But it wasn't a woman. It was his damn typewriter.

EPISODE 23

"HOW ON EARTH are you going to make a ship disappear?" Ginny asked while lightly dragging her red nails through the sweat-moistened thicket of his chest hair.

"I can't tell," Heinlein replied, his voice thick and drowsy.

"C'mon. I work for you. I ought to know."

"You've seen the posters, doll. 'Loose lips sink ships.'"

"I'm not a spy!"

"That's exactly what a spy would say."

"I'm not."

"Why would a spy ever seduce the head of special projects at the Naval Research Station? No, there'd be nothing to gain by that."

"If that were true, I'd be in bed with Reinhart."

"I don't think you're his type."

"What do you mean?"

"I mean that his kissing your ass doesn't move him up the ladder. Whereas with me, it just makes us both feel good."

"Fine," she said. "I'll find out sooner or later."

He fluffed one of the pillows, trying to get it just right so he could fall asleep.

"I hate a mystery. You can ask the nuns. I made them crazy questioning how Mary got pregnant. Or asking why scientists couldn't dredge up the Red Sea at low tide to find Pharaoh's chariots. I can make you crazy."

"I have the patience of a saint, m'dear. You can torture me if you want, but all you'll get is my name, rank, and serial number."

She drummed her fingertips on the skin over his ribs. Heinlein opened his eyes a little, squinting at her. Other than Virginia, there was nothing to see in the small hotel room he had rented; she was the main attraction—spirited, funny, and intellectually curious about science. Naked, he couldn't help but feel that she looked like one of the perfect, dangerous dames from a Norman Saunders pulp cover, all curves in action. Her body was long and athletic, with the kind of generous full breasts he loved on a woman but had never really been able to get his hands on before, despite years of trying. But there was something else about her that attracted him even more.

Ginny Gerstenfeld was a Republican. He'd found that out at their first dinner, three nights ago, when she'd mentioned how she'd raised money for Taft. He'd almost laughed at her naïveté, but then she'd questioned his own worldview by asking how many conservatives he actually knew. He'd had to concede that his circle was filled with liberals, Democrats, Socialists, even Communists. Most artists were, he'd found; after all, they were the enlightened ones. And he'd been very happy with that arrangement. But how challenging was that? she asked. Not very, he replied. And as she continued to chip away at his assumptions, he'd found that he really wanted to get her into bed.

A sigh escaped him. This was going to be a huge world of hurt, but he didn't care. He'd never felt such a complete attraction to a woman before—he couldn't even fathom it. It was if all the laws of physics were at play, from electromagnetism to gravitational pull, all happening on a quantum level at the speed of light.

"What's wrong?"

"Nothing."

"You're thinking about your wife."

"I wasn't, actually."

"It's okay with me," Ginny said. "I understand you're married. We're at war. Things could change at the drop of a dime. We've got to take our happiness wherever we find it and whenever we can."

"Are you happy?"

"Tremendously." She slid up on top of him and kissed him. "Are you?"

"Absolutely. Infinitely."

"Do you know the story of Jason and the Argonauts?" The morning light was creeping softly through the curtains. She rested her head on his belly.

"A little."

"Do you know what happens to Jason, at the end?"

"He becomes a constellation?"

"His ship collapses on top of him and kills him."

"How very Greek."

She raised herself to a sitting position. "I have to get to work. My boss'll kill me if I'm late."

"I'll give you a pass."

"You're not my boss anymore. Reinhart is."

"Right."

She went about the room picking up articles of clothing, shaking them into some semblance of freshness, and putting them on. "Do you think you'll ever write stories again?"

Heinlein got up and splashed some water on his face in the sink. He wished for a razor. "I doubt it."

"Why?"

"It's a lot of work for a little reward. Being in the pulps. Big deal. Who cares?"

"It's not like there's any heavy lifting involved. That's work."

"Trust me. Writing is work. Hours spent in solitary pursuit, shut away from the world. Forget it. I want to be part of the world. Not sell advertisements."

"Everyone says you're really good at it."

"Everyone?"

"I asked around."

"I'll give you some of my stuff to read. Then you can decide whether I should write again."

"Really?"

"Sure. Why not? But I'm warning you, you'll be disappointed."

"We'll see about that."

Together, they drove back to the base. The security level was as high as ever. Even though they both presented their badges, the MPs explored the car and its trunk thoroughly before waving them through. They parked in the Swamp and as they got out of the car, Heinlein realized he didn't care if anyone saw them together. In fact, he even boldly held her hand as they walked along the street. Since it was early there were few people to notice them, but he kind of wished there were some strangers around to gawk at the gorgeous woman holding on to him. At the door to the lab he pulled her in close for one last kiss.

"Tell me a secret," she whispered.

Her hair tickled his nose and he breathed in the scent of lavender. "I have no idea how to make a ship disappear."

Ginny snickered in a dirty way that made him feel good. He finally let go of her hand and opened the door, allowing them both to enter as professionally as possible. His hand felt empty without hers, his fingers twitched the way they used to when he was in the middle of writing a story and had wandered away from his typewriter for a while but the fingers were still involuntarily trying to keep up with the words flowing through his brain. Writing. Sex. Sometimes the only difference was one of them was harder to do alone.

Walb approached him as he walked across the lab. Heinlein was always impressed with the man's ability to keep his shirts starched. "Bob! I checked out that list for you."

He paused and took the page from Walb's hand. It was the list of names Binch had prepared for them while they lunched at the Rainbow Room. Each of the dozen or so names had a line carefully drawn through it. "Any of them know anything, Tom?"

"They're all dead, Bob. All of them have passed on in the years since Wardenclyffe."

"Thanks, Tom," he said, taking the paper. Reaching Asimov's station, he put his satchel down, slipped the paper inside, and invited de Camp over with a wave. As he waited, he gave the vertically mounted Erlenmeyer flask rotator on the table a casual spin so it went round and round like a carousel. Asimov shifted uncomfortably until it slowed to a stop; he hated it when people played with his stuff. A casual glance showed that Reinhart was in his office. "What've you got?" he asked them in a low voice once de Camp arrived.

"Problems," Asimov said, rescuing his flask from the spinning rotator as it passed in front of him. The kid looked exhausted.

"What kind?"

"Well, I think I may have figured out a way to recreate the barium titanium plates in spite of the fact that there's no mention of how he had his made in that notebook." He looked at them expectantly. "It was not easy."

"So? Sounds like you've done it."

"The problem is that the blend of barium I need is unstable. That means that I lose a lot of it in the process of making it. I'm over my budget as it is and I'm already out of barium and nearly out of titanium."

"Okay," Heinlein said. He turned to de Camp. "Tell me your problems."

"Tesla spoke seven languages. I barely speak English. Trying to map out his wiring schematics so we can compare them to what Binch tried to recapture at Menlo Park is a sonofabitch."

"But you'll get it?"

"I'll get something."

"Good." He turned back to Asimov. "Where does barium come from?"

"I don't know. I'll find out."

"Good man." He gave Asimov a reassuring pat on the shoulder. "Keep it up, both of you."

"Heinlein!"

Reinhart was standing in the door of his office, glaring at him. "Got a minute?"

"Sure." He gave the rotator another spin and plucked up his satchel. "Find out where your barium comes from," he muttered to Asimov. "ASAP. I can't take much more of this clown."

He tossed his bag into his office as he passed by and then entered Reinhart's. The little man had resumed his seat behind his desk. For some reason, the way his white lab coat bloomed out around him made Heinlein think he resembled one of Walb's white rats scurrying around in the cages on the far side of the lab—the ones subjected to sporadic bursts of bright light to discover what atmospheric effects might blind a pilot. "Close the door," Reinhart squeaked.

"What is it?" Heinlein did, and then took a seat. It hadn't been offered to him, but anything that might puncture the man's formality was a welcome thought.

"I've been expecting a report from you for some time now."

"About what?"

"I know this hasn't been an easy transition for you, Bob, but I don't really care. Honestly, I'll be happy to have you out of here. I'd send you to the front if I could, but I've seen your personnel folder, and evidently your health has eliminated you from service."

"What's your excuse?"

"It would be a crime to deprive the nation of my mental abilities." Reinhart twirled his pen and stared at Heinlein as if he were some kind of unpleasant specimen sample. "I understand you were a graduate of Annapolis, too."

"That's right, Doctor. Anything else you want to know about me that you can't find in my personnel file?"

"I want to know how you plan to make a ship invisible to radar."

"Is that what I said I'd do?"

"I'm pretty sure it was. I want to know how."

"I can't tell you."

"Why not?"

"Because you wouldn't understand it. It's magic."

"Show me."

"I'll need a ship. A whole ship."

Reinhart leaned back in his chair, folded his hands behind his head, and stared out the window. "A demonstration?"

"Sure."

Reinhart was silent for a long time. Heinlein couldn't help but notice that the men he had brought to Philadelphia were making more trips than normal past the office here, sneaking looks and shooting him reassuring gestures.

"I'll tell you what," Reinhart spoke at last. "I understand that you don't like me. Don't trust me."

"Good. We're making progress."

"The Navy has a special consultant working for it. A scientist. They go to him for . . . special problems. He has a way of finding answers by asking the questions that aren't being asked. A very unique mind. I'd like you to meet with him. I have no doubt that he can understand where I wouldn't. If he reports back to me on the veracity of your plan, I'll get you your ship. And I won't ask another question until your demonstration."

Heinlein felt his back against the wall. At last he nodded. "Fine," he said. "I'll meet your friend."

"Oh, believe me, he's no friend of mine."

"I like him already."

"Don't try to be so clever with him. He won't appreciate it."

"I'll try and restrain myself. Why don't you set up an appointment in a few weeks?"

"I want you to go Friday."

"I've got opera tickets Friday night. I'm going to see the greatest tenor in the world. Do you know all America is waiting to hear him sing? I'm hoping America meets him halfway. He can sing loud, but not that loud." Heinlein rose.

"Are you mocking me?"

"Honestly? I wouldn't know where to begin. You tell your consultant that Otis P. Driftwood and company will be paying him a visit next Monday. No, better make it Wednesday. I'm off to Europe Tuesday."

"I beg your pardon?"

Heinlein opened the door. "I'll see him Thursday of next week." As he closed the door he began to whistle "Lydia the Tattooed Lady." The little tune caused smiles to appear on the faces of the people who caught it as he passed by. Throughout the rest of the day he would overhear men humming or singing fragments. He sat down behind his desk and put his head in his hands. A few minutes later he lifted it to see who was knocking on his door: Asimov and de Camp.

"What is it?" he asked as they sat in his chairs.

"Missouri," Asimov said.

"What?"

"The barium I need is mined and processed in Missouri. There's a company there that refines it for their fireworks business and the man thinks he might be able to spare us the five hundred pounds we need."

"Jesus. It's going to take five hundred pounds to get a handful of those tiles?"

"The good news is that he can press the tiles for us, too."

"How long before he can get it here?"

"Well, that's a bit of a problem. It appears that the surplus he has is being held for the U.S. government."

"Great! That's us."

"That's what I tried to tell him. But he says he needs authorization from the War Department to release it."

Heinlein rubbed his face and wished again that he'd been able to shave. "Missouri, you say? I was born there." Heinlein smiled. "I want to know how long it will take your refiner to pull his stash together. I'm talking date and hour."

"Yes sir," Asimov said, almost reflexively.

"See, we'll make a military man out of you yet, Asimov."

"What's the situation with Reinhart?" de Camp asked.

"As long as he's not sure if I'm crazy or a genius I've got half a chance of staying around here for a few more weeks."

"So the crazy Groucho routine throws him off?"

"Actually, I think Groucho is a genius. Always have." He waved them out of the office and then picked up the phone. It took him a little while to get the various operators and secretaries to figure out where his call needed to go, but in the end a phone rang in an office in Washington, D.C., and was answered by a hoarse voice, full of confidence.

"Norvell Page, Office of War Information."

"Mr. Page? This is Robert Heinlein. I need your help."

"Hello, Mr. Heinlein. I can be at the Navy Yard the day after tomorrow."

"How did you know where I am?"

"As I said, Mr. Heinlein, I am the Office of War Information."

EPISODE 24

SHE WAS CLOSE.

He could feel her.

Hear her calling.

It was almost as if she was causing the very air in Los Angeles to vibrate. The distance from where he was in Manhattan Beach to where she was in Pasadena was like the space between two supermagnets forced apart—elemental forces of attraction and repulsion surged between them. God help anything that got caught between should one or the other be released.

He couldn't go to her.

He had to go to her.

Sara didn't know he was in town. There had been no conventional contact, no post or phone call. But there was still something in the air. Something that convinced him that she knew he was close.

She came to him in his dreams.

Lieutenant Stewart had landed his plane just before twilight three days ago. The P-51 was not designed for any kind of comfort, only to drop out of the sky like a hawk raining death on Mitsubishi Zeros and Messerschmitt Bf 110s. Hubbard, who prided himself on being up for anything and more, was exhausted. The cockpit was cramped and the pilot kept his own counsel, even during their refueling stops.

At the landing field, cryptic instructions for the next leg of his journey awaited him, when and where to report, little more. Grateful for the chance to decompress, he had checked himself into a fleabag near Los Angeles field and dropped like a stone, the engine's vibration still shaking his bones, the prop roar still clogging his ears. Hubbard had never slept so hard in all his life—night into day and into night again.

And the dreams came.

Sara had appeared to him, so real he felt as if she were really in his room. Her red hair floated around her face the way it did when she swam naked in Parsons's pool with him far below her. She wore a sheer white flowing cloak, something he'd never seen her in before. There was something she wanted him to know but he couldn't tell what. Then she was furious at him for not understanding, her face contorted into rage, eyes glowing red, hands turning into claws. Coming at him for some reason he couldn't fathom. At that point he'd thrown himself out of the dream with a physical jerk that left him awake and afraid in a room he didn't recognize, convinced that Sara knew he was in Los Angeles. And Jack Parsons did, too.

It was late morning as he stared out the window of the cab; a power-ful magic seemed to hover thickly in the broiling air, a shadow filter that dimmed the bright California daylight ever so slightly. Something ugly and alive was trapped in the ether over the city, and it had his scent. The crooked transplanted palm trees whizzed past outside. Nothing looked straight out here. Why had he never noticed that before? The war had been very good to Los Angeles County. The last time he had come out this way, there were actually large fields of untouched land; now there were only property lines and construction sites. At least he had caught a reassuring glimpse of the ocean, even though he'd been heading away from it toward what passed for downtown. They hadn't yet figured out a way to hide the Pacific. In a while, the cab pulled to a stop on South Broadway.

On the sidewalk, the sunlight itself seemed heated to the point of flu-idity, molten rays pouring over him; dead air hard to inhale. After a mo-ment he turned and entered the cooler air inside Clifton's Cafeteria. The familiar decor and tasty scents brought a smile to his face, the memories of many happy discussions with the Science Fiction League replacing the pervasive sense of dread that had been haunting him.

The great hall was several stories high and supported by immense col-umns shaped like redwood trees. More trees ringed the room, and a host of huge stuffed animals culled from the Santa Cruz Mountains peered down at him from every wall. A waterfall cascaded down a rocky out-cropping and flowed into a stream that wound its way past the tables and across the restaurant floor. The staircase to the second floor was carved like the entrance to a great Californian lodge; he made his way up. He walked along the balcony where diners munched merrily on thick slices of ham steak, piles of macaroni and cheese, slabs of corn bread. His stom-ach gurgled. He hadn't eaten in a while.

The Brown Room was nestled amid a grove of ferns set into the giant mural of the Western landscape that filled the wall from corner to cor-ner and floor to ceiling. Below his landing was the great stone fireplace, above the dim doorway an impressive moose head. Hubbard stuck his head into the gloom. "Cartmill? You in here?"

When Cartmill spoke, his voice came from a low place somewhere in the room. "Hello, Ron." His voice was accompanied by the soft squeak of metal grinding on metal.

Hubbard looked down at the pale white face lit by the single candle dripping down the Chianti bottle. "Hey, Cleve. I see you still refuse to oil yourself."

Cartmill backed his wheelchair away from the table, pushing forward to shake Hubbard's hand. The table was set for three, with only scraps left on the plates. "Come on in," he commanded in a no-nonsense tone, indicating that jokes would hardly be tolerated. "What do you want?"

"It's Saturday. I thought I'd drop by and see if the League was meeting. See how you were doing."

"You're not here to gather dirt on me?"

"What the hell, Cleve? I tried calling you first."

"I'm not answering the phone."

"Why not?"

Before Cartmill could answer, Hubbard heard a floorboard squeak, as if someone were hiding behind the swinging doors to the rear of the fake log cabin. Still disturbed about belatedly realizing that someone had recently snuck up on him and rapped him on the head, he felt more attuned to his instincts, and the thick, paranoid atmosphere inside the Brown Room wasn't helping. In an instant, he leaped across the room and jerked the door open, stepping aside as two men stumbled out of the service entrance.

Both were younger than he and Cartmill, somewhere in their twenties, and as different in appearance from one another as two men could be. While the softer, round one lay turtled on the floor, astonished blue eyes large behind bottle-thick lenses, the tall one who had affected a pretentiously suave, movie-star look rose to his feet. "*Salutoj, samrangulo veturanto,*" he said, smoothing out his Army uniform. "*Tradukĵvico tro longa, reprove poste.*"

"Damn, Ackerman. I'm in no mood for Esperanto."

"Sure, Ron," the soldier said, somewhat meekly. "*Mizera.* I mean, sorry."

"How's your brother, Alden?"

"He's in Italy now. Not sure where."

"Hey, help Bradbury up, would ya?" The kid still couldn't get up. "He's about as coordinated as a slug."

As Ackerman gave the young man his hand, Cartmill pushed himself across the room, and if it was possible for a wheelchair to move somberly, this one did. For someone who was usually the life of the party, this present gray attitude came as something of a shock.

"Why all the paranoia, Cartmill? Who did you think I was?"

"Like you don't know." The sarcasm was obvious.

He said it slowly so it wouldn't be misunderstood. "I don't know."

"You've never heard of Ross Dugan? Or Riley Killough?"

"Are they writers? Fans?"

"No." He wheeled his way past Hubbard to look out onto the main floor. "They're a couple of federal agents who have crawled up my rectum to make my life a living hell. They've tapped my phone and turned my postman into a spy. He's always pumping me for information."

"Oh boy." Hubbard had seen this happen before. Sometimes science fiction had this effect on its fans and even its writers. They got in too deep, began to believe in the reality of it all. They showed up at conventions with little ledgers filled with cramped writings on alternative theories of light, gravity, aliens, or government. Sometimes they wore costumes to reflect their concerns. He'd heard of others who fashioned hats of tin or aluminum to deflect beams of interference they'd claimed to have discovered. He often wondered whether the genre attracted this type of personality or if something about the imaginative writing caused some kind of fundamental change in the structures of the mind. What was it about science fiction that compelled its followers to join together, form clubs like Heinlein's Mañana Society, or Asimov's Futurians, or Clifton's Cafeteria Sci-Fi League? It was something more than fanaticism. Baseball lovers were fans. But they weren't trying to win converts, or coming together in tiny apartments the way ancient Christians had scurried toward meetings through the catacombs of Imperial Rome. He was coming to the conclusion that it was something more dangerous—a zealotry.

Not only were fans like Isaac Asimov and Forrest Ackerman and Ray Bradbury forming cultish groups to lay claim to their little piece of the action, they were becoming active proselytizers—spreading the word, literally. Mystery writers often sprang from an I-can-do-that kind of fandom, but these kids had far more passion, a sense of I-have-to-do-it that pervaded their character. Hubbard did it for a buck, as he knew Heinlein did. But they were older. He got the feeling that Bradbury would be writing this stuff even if there were nowhere to publish it.

"Where's your wife, Cleve?" he asked a little nervously. "And your boy?"

"I've sent them away to stay with her mother. It's too dangerous here for them."

Hubbard had a seat at the table and began picking at some pineapple upside-down cake. There were typewritten pages spread out across the table. The League often critiqued one another's stories. He wiped off his fingers and flipped through the pages. "Why are you acting so subterranean?"

"Didn't Campbell tell you what was going on?"

"No. So why don't you fill me in?"

"It's about 'Deadline.'"

"That story in *Astounding*? The one about the bomb? So what."

"My research. Did you know that uranium 235 is highly fissionable? If this element were smashed together with enough force, it could start a chain reaction, unleashing incredible power. God only knows how powerful it could be."

"That's pulp, right?"

Cartmill shook his head. "That's reality. A bomb like that could destroy a city, a continent. The earth, maybe. Who knows? I broke it all down into a story. The aliens who were developing the super-bomb? They were pulp. Window dressing with tails."

"Nice touch." Hubbard nodded. "Aliens disguise the facts."

"That's what I thought."

"The issue came out last week. I got paid. End of story, right? The stuff we write. It's harmless, right? A pastime, right?"

"I guess so."

"The day after the mag is out, we came home to find my house robbed."

"Wow."

"Everything was turned upside down. My wife was in tears. But you know what was weird?"

"What?"

"They left the jewelry and the pin money. The only thing I found missing were the letters between me and Campbell, my research, the drafts of the story. The originals. Gone.

"That night I got a call from a friend of mine who works at Bell Labs in New York City. He said he needed to know how I knew what I wrote. Said people had come to see him. They said I knew things I couldn't have known and they were fingering him as the source. But as we talked, I could hear someone else on the line. Breathing, listening in. My friend heard it too, and warned me to stay off the phone. Said the phones could actually be dangerous. I hung up and haven't made a phone call since.

"The next day, my mailman told me he had read 'Deadline' and wondered where I came up with that stuff. He was very casual about it, saying that I must know some very smart people. By lunchtime I had sent my family away.

"That night, they showed up. There were two men in nice suits wearing cheap shoes on my stoop. Dugan and Killough, from the War Department. Government men, through and through. They probably crap eagle eggs.

"Where did I get my information? How did I know about such top secret materials? I couldn't possibly have made it up. Who was my source? Who did Campbell introduce me to? What access did I have? Did I know this person or that person? Did I know Rovert Cornog? No, of course not. Do I have friends in New Mexico or Tennessee? How about Philadelphia? Did I know Robert A. Heinlein?

"I paused. And they knew I knew him."

A liquid chill ran through Hubbard. "Bob's not your source, is he?"

"There is no 'source,' Ron. No one's slipping me secrets. I'm an educated man and so is Campbell, and we put together the idea for a theoretical super-bomb from *Popular Science* articles and a little imagination. But try telling the War Department that. They think I'm part of some great conspiracy. That there's some great secret out there that I'm spilling to the Nazis. And that Campbell and Heinlein are at the center of it."

"What do you think the secret could be?"

"What do you think it is?" The wheelchair rocked back and forth, squeaking ever so softly. "What is the biggest secret we could be hiding? A secret so big that even the mention of it in a cheap pulp brings the U.S. government into the home of a private citizen?"

Hubbard's mouth suddenly felt dry. "A super-bomb?"

"It doesn't take a rocket writer to see it. I've inspired somebody. I think people want to know if there's more to what I know that I'm not telling. Someone's going to use 'Deadline' as the instructions for a super-bomb. And no one is supposed to know about it. It's the kind of thing people would kill for to keep quiet."

Hubbard rubbed his head, imagining he could still feel the bruise. "Or kill to get their hands on."

"I'm telling you, Ron. My story is going to change the world."

"You really think someone's trying to build an atom-smashing bomb? Based on your story?"

"I'm positive."

"We're just pulp writers, Cleve."

"We're more than that, Ron," Ackerman said. He wasn't much of a writer, but he was a huge fan of science fiction, even going so far as to wear costumes to conventions. "We're prophets of the future."

Hubbard shrugged. "Maybe. I don't know. If you ask me, Hugo Gernsback was a prophet. A science fiction prophet. Campbell, now he could be considered a prophet. Prophets talk about tomorrow, the future. That's what science fiction writers do, too, right? In the unenlightened days before people had widespread access to general science, they turned to religion to understand the universe. Now science fiction is helping to explain a more scientific world. Or maybe faith in science is just another religion waiting to be formalized."

He grinned. This was the kind of League discussion he loved and it felt like old times. "What does religion promise, anyway? That your soul might be liberated from its flesh to roam the sky. Rocket ships are going to take you and your flesh there soon. Religion promises that you might get to heaven or wind up in hell, that God might save you or damn you. Old Testament wrath or New Testament salvation. Well, science fiction offers visions of Apocalypse or Utopia, right, Cleve? Isn't that what 'Deadline' does?

"Religion offers an end to suffering. Science was promising new cures for ailments every day; even the polio that took the use of your legs might be defeated someday. Gods promised life eternal. Science might discover the medical keys to immortality. Maybe our new literature is as close to faith as rational-minded people can bring themselves to experience in an era when science is chipping away at the divine every day. Maybe it fills a mental, emotional, or genetic atavistic craving we have for understanding.

"Hugo Gernsback. There's our Moses, bringing the rules down from on high: Thou shalt use thy imagination. Thou shalt be original. Then Campbell the Baptist came along, bringing convert after convert, sending them out to spread the Word. The fans are the apostles, welcoming the mystery sects into the fold, incorporating their rituals, anointing the local priests at conventions."

"But something's missing," Ackerman said. "What do all prophets eventually prophesy? That someone will come soon who will explain everything to them, the way the universe works, and will take care of all their problems."

"A Messiah." Cartmill nodded.

Hubbard smiled. "John the Baptist thought he was the Messiah until he met a better Messiah. The Messiah, any Messiah, is more than just a prophet. Messiahs are men who carry within them the spark of the divine, transformed by some experience to recognize it. Buddha meditated under the tree until he attained Nirvana. Christ faced the challenges of the unknown desert. Each returned from their transformation with a message that the faithful had been prepared to understand by the prophets."

"It sounds so simple," Cartmill said.

Hubbard looked to Bradbury, the youngest person in the League, a younger writer even than Asimov. Hubbard had met him a few years ago when Bradbury was invited to join the group on the strength of a science fiction magazine he had written and published on his own. He was shy, only coming to life when defending an idea or reading aloud. Hubbard had listened to some of those stories and the kid had potential to be very good someday; his stories spoke of loneliness with a poetry that even Heinlein rarely achieved. "What do you think, Ray? Are we prophets? Are we creating the future?"

Bradbury cleared his throat, and when he spoke, Hubbard could barely hear him. "I'm not trying to create the future. I'm trying to prevent it."

Hubbard took some time to grab a tray of real food from the steam line, wolfed it down, then finally bid what was left of the League goodbye.

"Where are you off to now?" Bradbury asked.

"I could tell you. But you're already in enough trouble."

"Funny guy, Hubbard."

"Yeah," he said, wishing he was joking. Back in the heat, he caught a cab, and then relaxed.

Prophets? Please.

Hubbard had read Cartmill's work. At best he was a roadside revival tent minister.

Though the Port of Los Angeles was not a military base, it served no larger purpose these days than to supplement the flow of troops and equipment to the Pacific from San Diego. As he got out of the car, watching soldiers stream through the gates, much as they had in San Diego and Philadelphia and through the streets of New York, he was stunned by the impact of the immense scale of the war they were involved in. The concept of just how large a number the word "millions" represented was suddenly conceivable, and it was sickening.

At the water's edge, among the many warships bristling with armaments, he could see the stocky profile of the attack-class transport, the *Funston*, that Heinlein's instructions had told him to rendezvous with, its single smokestack belching black diesel smoke as the engines warmed for imminent departure. Even as he fell into the security checkpoint line behind the others, he could see the tugboats circling it, and as gulls swooped through its rigging, a whistle gave off three earsplitting blasts, indicating that unmooring was to begin. He began to worry that he had spent too much time with Cartmill.

The line was moving quickly with only a half dozen or so sailors and merchant marines ahead of him when he felt a tap on his shoulder.

"Wait your turn, buddy," he snapped.

"Lafayette Ron Hubbard?"

He turned his head to see two men flanking him from behind. One of them looked like a shaved gorilla. The other was tall and thin and looked like an accountant. They wore dark suits and Cartmill had been right about their shoes.

"The writer?" he replied, eyeing the head of the line and the crowd beyond it. "One of my favorites." He took several steps forward as another sailor was admitted.

"A moment of your time, please?"

"I don't know who you are."

"I'm Mr. Killough," said the gorilla. "And this is Mr. Dugan. We'd like to talk to you about your visit today with Mr. Cartmill."

"Never heard of him."

"You came all the way out here to see him," the tall one said.

"Look, Abbott, Costello. I've been on leave. Where I go and who I choose to visit is my business. Look, you guys were pretty sharp at following me and sneaking up behind me. You wouldn't be the type of guys to clock someone on the head while he was, say, minding his own business or climbing down a manhole, would ya?"

Killough exchanged a confused look with his partner. "Mr. Hubbard . . ."

"Lieutenant Hubbard," he corrected the talking ape. "I'm a serving officer in the U.S. Navy. Why aren't you in uniform, pal? A little over the weight requirement, I'm guessing." Another sailor passed muster.

"You've also been in recent contact with Robert Heinlein, Socialist, and Isaac Asimov, Trotskyite."

The *Funston* whistled again, urgently. Hubbard snorted. "Socialists and Trotskyites? C'mon, gentlemen. Why not just come out and call me a Nazi or Jap-lover while you're casting aspersions?"

"How about John W. Campbell? Is that a name you're familiar with?"

"Sure."

"How?"

"I see his name on a check every once in a while."

"Lieutenant, I don't think you appreciate the situation you're in."

"Sure I do, pal. I'm in the military. There's always a situation."

"We're with the War Department."

"Aren't we all in one way or another?" He flipped his ID to the sentry, who checked it against papers on a clipboard. His heart began to race as the pages were flipped back and forth. "But there's one difference between you and me."

"What's that?" Dugan asked.

"My name's on the list." The MP nodded with satisfaction and handed Hubbard back his wallet. "And yours isn't." With that, he began to run.

"Hey!" the hairless simian shouted, but they were tangling with the MPs by that point.

Hubbard pushed his way into the milling throng of American youth, ignoring their cusses and shoves. Breaking free, beyond the sight of the sentry post, he dashed as fast as he could, keeping his head down, zigzagging through troops and pallets of cargo, uncertain as to whether he was being followed. The gangplank of the *Funston* was being raised: with a tremendous leap, he cleared the distance from the dock, scrambling to the ship's deck before the astonished eyes of the duty officer.

"Lieutenant Hubbard. Reporting as ordered." He snapped off a salute that was slowly returned.

"Hubbard?"

Struggling for breath, he turned to the dock to see if the two government men had followed him, but there was no sign of them in the crowd. "That's right."

"You're a little late."

"Looks to me like I'm right on time."

"Well, that's true. Kind of surprised to have a passenger on board this run, but word came right from Washington that we were to have a berth prepared for you."

"Isn't that something?"

With another tremendous whistle of escaping steam, the casting off began and the ship was pulled away from its mooring. Hubbard began to breathe easier.

"As requested, we've stowed your cold weather gear."

He began to grin as the gray water rushed in to fill the void between the hull and the dock. The familiar oaths of sailors starting a voyage filled the air. A sense of well-being flowed through Hubbard as he turned his eyes toward the blue of the ocean. He was heading back to sea, he thought with a grand thrill, the albatrosses above crying out as if cheering him on. "Wait a minute. Cold weather gear? What the hell am I going to need that for in the South Pacific?"

The duty officer looked taken aback, then grinned as if Hubbard was having a joke at his expense and he got it. "I don't know where you thought you got your ticket punched for, Lieutenant," he said. "But this boat? It's headed for the Aleutian Islands."

"Islands, right," Hubbard said. "In the Pacific."

"Lieutenant," the other officer said, as the great engines roared to life, the ship lurching with acceleration, "the Aleutians are Pacific islands, all right. But they're in the North Pacific. Beyond Alaska."

EPISODE 25

"THERE'S SOMETHING I'VE been meaning to ask you," Sprague said to Isaac while they spooned down their stew in the nearly empty mess hall as quickly as they could. They had about fifteen minutes left before whistles blew and the enlisted men piled through the doors.

Isaac's heart was pumping blood through his body with such force he was worried about a sudden attack of hypertension. He peered over his shoulder at Corporal Brinley, one of the model-ship war game enthusiasts who was helping prototype methods of degaussing ship hulls so as to render the magnetic triggers of enemy mines and torpedoes useless, still on KP. He'd spent a long night manufacturing a nearly perfect replica of the *DE-173* to add to the miniature armada navigating the lab's floor. On his way out he'd been shoulder-checked by one of Olson's men heading toward the genuine article. When the MPs had arrived, the model maker was airing out his knuckles while the carpenter was collecting teeth off the sidewalk. By lunchtime of that same day Brinley had found himself passing out silverware behind the lunch counter. Catching Isaac's eye, the large man nodded and grinned back. Isaac's head snapped back to Sprague. "What?"

"What the hell was the Science Fiction Convention War?"

Isaac cleared his throat. "Really?"

"Yeah."

He flicked a few specks of powdered salt from his jacket cuff. "The World's Fair was about to start in Flushing Meadows. Did you make it?"

"No. I wanted to, but I was in California."

"The Dawn of a New Day. That's what it was called. And it was amazing. If half the things I saw there come true, then in about twenty years we're all going to be watching television sets in our air-conditioned homes, far from cities, traveling to work on diesel electric trains.

"When the Fair was first announced, the Futurians saw that it was going to be a beacon to our kind of people; the fans were going to come from all over to catch a glimpse of the 'World of Tomorrow.' Fred Pohl, Johnny Michel, and Don Wollheim had the idea of hosting a convention that would coincide with the Fair. The biggest convention ever. One that would unite the world of science fiction: a World Science Fiction Convention. The Futurians announced it to all the mags, sent letters to all the fanzines, sent emissaries to other clubs and smaller conventions. The response was hugely positive. The actual organization not so much. The Futurians could always be distracted by wine."

He jumped at the sound of Brinley placing a bin of silverware near the plates. The clatter sounded like a tin roof collapsing. "We're going to get our teeth handed to us."

"No we're not. Just relax. Go on with your story."

Isaac tapped his spoon against the rim of his empty bowl. The crew outfitting the *DE-173* was closest to the mess hall and the first to enter when the whistle blew. They had timed it. He looked nervously out the window, then cleared his throat. "Another thing we were really good at was making enemies. I guess some people think we're a little arrogant sometimes. Some of those guys were watching for a moment of weakness, and when the Futurians took too long showing any progress, because Michel, Pohl, and Wollheim had kind of let it slide, they pounced. Wally Sykora, who had actually been in the Futurians before I joined, and Sam Moskowitz, who had always been part of a rival club, let it be known that the Futurians had abdicated, and now they were the committee in charge of the first World Science Fiction Convention. Ha-ha, right? These science fiction fights are so big because the stakes are so small.

"These guys were serious. And they were organized. They got it all put together before we knew it. Booked Caravan Hall, sold tickets, invited speakers, the whole nine yards. Frank Paul was the guest of honor."

"Good cover artist."

"I was pretty excited because either way I was going to get to go to a big convention right in my own town. But it really rankled Wollheim."

"I can imagine."

"So he and Pohl and Michel got together and wrote up a manifesto challenging the authority of Sykora and Moskowitz, mimeographed it, and got all set to cause a huge commotion on the floor of the convention. I tried to talk them out of it. But Wollheim, in particular, always thought that science fiction was a political platform dedicated to using science to uplift humanity. That had to be the real purpose of the convention. And if it had been his convention, maybe it would have been. But it really wasn't anymore. It belonged to the fans. The hundreds of fans who showed up from all over the country, the world even. Just as we had hoped. My friends should have just kicked back and enjoyed what they got started, but . . ." He shrugged.

"We arrived to find that the Futurians were to be barred from the hall. They called it the Exclusion Act. It didn't apply to me because I was a professional pulp writer by that point. So I went in. From inside the hall I could see the Futurians come off the elevator, yellow manifesto pages in hand. Sykora and Moskowitz were there to greet them with hall security. I saw a huge burst of yellow papers, like a banana peel blizzard.

There was some shouting, some pushing. But in the end no punches were thrown because, y'know, science fiction fans, after all.

"By the time I caught up with the excluded Futurians at a coffee shop across the street, they'd wised up. Instead of trying to crash the World Con, they'd host their own. A counterconvention. Where *all* would be welcome. The venue was at the only place that would have us—the Young Communists' League headquarters in Brooklyn. People came. Lots of people. Not enough to sink the World Con, but enough to have fun. And that's exactly what we had."

The shrieking steam whistle lifted him right out of his seat.

"Here we go," Sprague said with a grin. "Wait'll we tell the mad scientists about this one."

The double doors to the hall burst open, and, as anticipated, the crew of the destroyer escort swaggered in, confidently boisterous, Olson at the lead. They headed toward the front of their line as if it was their God-given right. Asimov kept his head down, focusing on his empty bowl, dividing his furtive glances between Sprague and the sailors.

Brinley served each of them a bowl of stew, grinning good-naturedly at their haranguing, which was not at all good-natured. As they slid their trays of food down the row, he made sure none of them forgot their silverware. Meanwhile, from the far corners of the base, dozens of hungry men and women, more and more every minute, were taking their place on the lunch line.

The petty officer and his crew had a seat at a table, en masse. Olson was promising big excitement tonight after the shift at the Shore Leave Saloon. At the same instant, he dunked his spoon into the stew. "What the hell?" Olson cried.

The liquid in his bowl began to foam violently and spew steam. He lifted his implement from the small tempest and held it before his eyes. Only a twisted fragment of softened metal remained. Before he could utter another word, the bowl before him cracked open with a violent pop, spewing meat and potatoes across his lap. Several other members of his crew were dipping their spoons into their meals and watching in hypnotized amazement as their bowls, too, frothed, then blew chunks of stew into their faces. Within seconds, the entire table, and all the people at it, were drenched in food while the rest of the mess hall erupted in laughter at their misfortune.

Olson rose angrily and approached Brinley. The MPs on duty quickly stepped up, as the big man smiled and said, "If you want some more, back of the line." Even though dozens of others had sat down and were eating their stew with no incident, the line of hundreds wound out the door.

"Time to act casual," Sprague said, rising.

Isaac rose as easily as he could, but not before noting that, as Olson stood helplessly while meal after meal passed him by and plucked mealy potatoes from his red hair, Brinley was carefully setting aside the small box containing the few remaining spoons that Isaac and the rest of the mad scientists had spent long hours last night molding. They hurried out of the mess hall together.

"Christ!" Sprague was wiping the tears from his eyes as Isaac joined him on the sidewalk. "Good thing they didn't put those spoons in their mouths!"

"Nothing would have happened. People aren't hot enough," Isaac said. "The spoons were coated with an alloy of bismuth, lead, tin, and some other things. The alloy has a melting point of one hundred and seven degrees. The stew was hot enough to dissolve the outer layer, releasing the highly reactive potassium powder into the water base of the stew. That's all. I wouldn't let anyone get hurt."

Sprague clapped him on the back and laughed. "You know, Isaac, you just disproved an ancient adage."

"Which one?"

"That revenge is a dish best served cold!"

Isaac smiled at that. Sprague grandly held the door open for him and he entered the lab, his head held high.

"What's for lunch?" Walb asked, on his way out.

"Asimov surprise," Sprague replied. The others in the room, Heinlein's originals, shared looks of approval.

"Maybe I'll just grab a hoagie," the scientist muttered, slipping through the door.

Isaac looked around. "Good. He's out."

"Who?"

"Reinhart. He's been bugging me for a demonstration of my dye, but I haven't been able to get it to work."

"What happens?"

"It. Doesn't. Work."

"Okay. Anything I can do to help?"

"Really, Sprague? You didn't even know that potassium explodes in water. How are you going to help me get my molecules to bond?"

Sprague shrugged. "Don't let it go to your head, Ike."

"Don't call me that."

"You got it, kid." With a smile he sauntered off to his table. Isaac almost wished he could help Sprague out, but he didn't seem to need it. It wasn't nearly as difficult as trying to get one liquid to remain on top of another liquid and not be dangerous. The problem he had run into with the oil-based solutions he'd tested was that a sailor in the water was prone to inhale a certain amount of that water, along with any substance floating on top of it. And oil in the lungs was bad news.

"Asimov!" Bob stepped out of his office and approached his lab table. "You busy?"

"I've got work." They hadn't told Bob about the retaliation operation. He hoped he wasn't in trouble.

Bob cleared his throat, almost as if he were embarrassed about something. "Would you be in the doghouse with the missus if I kept you late?"

"She's visiting with her folks this week."

He visibly brightened. "Ah! That's great. Come with me then."

"Where are we going?"

"I've got to go visit Reinhart's consultant today." Isaac could tell that whatever Bob wanted to talk to him about, as he got closer to bringing it up, he got more uncomfortable. His hands were thrust deep into his pockets, his head was down, a lock of hair swinging loosely over his forehead as he swayed from foot to foot. "The thing is, you're Jewish, right?"

"Occasionally."

"Well, some of the, um, powers that be think that having a Jewish, um, person . . ."

"Jew's fine, Bob. I'm a Jew. Not a Jewish person."

He exhaled hard. "Right, so. In this particular situation they want a Jew to come. To meet the special consultant."

"Who is?"

"I don't know."

"Are we going back to New York?"

"No. New Jersey."

"Okay. If you think it'll help. I only barely speak Hebrew or Yiddish. I speak a little Brooklynese. If that makes a difference."

Bob scratched his head as if he were unsure. "I don't know. I don't think so."

Isaac leaned in a little. "If you're worried that there's some other secret form of communication we Jews have, there isn't. At least not that the Elders of Zion have introduced me to. Yet."

Bob laughed nervously. "So. Let's go?"

"You know, one thing I kind of appreciate about the military is that, as an institution, it doesn't really give a hoot as to whether I'm a Jew or not," Isaac told Bob as they made the long hike toward the Swamp, where the car was parked. "After people get over who's Irish, Italian, or Jewish, everyone just seems to blend into a martial beige. Which is a big change from Columbia. I'm one of five Jews in my class. There were five of us in each of the other upper classes. Only five, each year. And still hundreds apply and hope."

"Must make you feel pretty good to be one of five," Bob said, as they reached his car and he unlocked the doors.

"Who doesn't want to be singled out? But as a matter of policy, restricting admissions because your God doesn't work with my God is a shame."

"Not my God. I don't have one. I'm an atheist."

"Think of all the brilliant people who are being denied a good education. Think of the damage it's doing to the nation, not to educate the best to the best of their ability. Is that smart, I ask you?"

Leaving League Island behind, Bob headed down a network of unfamiliar roads, overtaking streetcar after streetcar in his apparent haste. Before long, the cramped brownstones and row houses gave way to larger lots and stately homes. They pulled to a stop across the street from the largest mansion in the entire neighborhood. The grounds alone covered a whole block. Numerous chimneys rose from the different wings. Bob shook his head. "You know whose house that is?"

"No."

"Remember how Walter Gibson said he still had a home in Philadelphia? That's it."

"It's the biggest house I've ever seen."

"Growing up in a Gothic place like that sure can make you understand why he's got such a thing for the shadows."

"I guess so."

After a few more minutes, Bob put the car in gear and drove on. He seemed to be mulling something over so Isaac let him drive for a while, until they were clear of the city.

"So," Isaac said, when he finally felt it was okay to speak, "we should get the wives together again. That was a fun night." Then he remembered how it had ended and clamped his mouth shut tightly.

Bob's laugh sounded as if it came from deep within. Isaac had never heard him laugh like that before. It was infectious and even he began to chuckle, though he wasn't quite sure what was so funny. Bob wiped tears away from the corners of his eyes. "Ah, thanks, Isaac. I needed that. The wives. Right. All of them."

Isaac wished for a phone. He wanted to call Gertrude as soon as possible. They drove on for a long while, listening to the latest war bulletins on the radio. The Sicilian advance, what the reporter called the greatest amphibious operation in history, had begun: 160,000 Allied troops were finally marching in Europe. It was as if the war had finally really started.

A little over an hour passed before Bob spun the wheel, cruising past two brick posts and entering a broad, elm-lined boulevard. Their new surroundings were so elegant and immaculate, the buildings so stately and refined, that Isaac felt as if he had entered a kind of status oasis. The grounds were filled with a number of young men, hustling from one point to another much in the same way that the base personnel did, but it was obvious from all the lightweight cotton and seersucker suits that they were not in the military and probably never would be.

"Princeton?" Isaac asked, suddenly alert. "We're at Princeton?"

The car came to a stop after following a winding path and Bob nodded at Isaac that this time he was welcome to get out of the car. The building they approached reminded Isaac of Independence Hall in Philadelphia. Gertie and he had visited it one Sunday afternoon. The Continental style was similar, the same red brick, the same white tower on top. Only this version was much larger. He swallowed hard as he read the brass plate outside the door to be sure where he was, though he already knew.

The Institute for Advanced Study.

His knees felt weak.

"You okay?" Bob had him by his elbow.

"Yeah. Yeah." He struggled to regain his composure. "I think this is going to be a good day to be a Jewish person."

"Why?"

Bob confirmed his appointment with a secretary. She led them down a long hallway, to the door of a nondescript office, just another brown panel in a long corridor of brown panels. There was no indication on the exterior whether a special consultant to the Navy waited inside. Only a simple plaque on the door read PROFESSOR OF THEORETICAL PHYSICS. She knocked, opened the door slightly, and spoke softly. A moment later she opened the door wide, then stepped out of their way.

The man behind the desk was older than they were, maybe as old as Isaac's father. It was hard to tell. His bushy silver hair made him seem wizened, yet youthful at the same time. He quickly but carefully set the issue of *Amazing Stories* he had been reading on his desk and leaped to his feet. As he flew around to greet them, his shoulder scraped a blackboard and his sweater erased a line of equations in a single swipe, though he appeared enthusiastically oblivious.

"Isaac Asimov and Robert Heinlein here in my office!" he said in a delightfully light European accent. "It's so nice to meet you."

He grasped Isaac's hand and shook it with such great warmth that Isaac almost instantly felt at ease. The man's eyes were bright and the light in them sparkled with happiness.

"It's a . . . a pleasure to meet you, too," he croaked. "Professor Einstein!"

EPISODE 26

"DR. REINHART IS a prick."

Heinlein laughed. He had found it hard at first to be in the presence of a legend, but as they talked through some of the challenges facing his team, the legend had become a man, warm and earthy. Isaac sat to his left on the old leather sofa, while Einstein had pulled his office chair from behind his desk and sat across from them. On the small table between them sat three cups of dark Viennese-roast coffee, *"mit schlag,"* as their host had ordered.

"I'm so sorry to hear that the two of you have to report to him, a man of no imagination and less knowledge. A pity. No university or corporation will have him, you know."

"Well, leave it to the Navy to find a place for him," Heinlein said.

"Ah, yes, the Navy." Einstein folded his hands together behind his head. "They call me a special consultant and ask me lots of questions, as if I'm an Oracle. Albert, can Hitler defy gravity? Albert, can Hitler create a super-bomb? Albert, can Hitler invent a death ray? Albert, can we go back in time and kill Hitler as a young boy? Is time travel possible?"

Heinlein watched Isaac shift uncomfortably in his seat. He felt a little like squirming himself.

"Is it?" Asimov asked eagerly. "Is time travel possible?"

"Of course it is! Of course! We're all time travelers, traveling into the future together."

"Oh." Asimov sat back, visibly disappointed. Heinlein shot him a look that implied he should keep his mouth shut.

"As if I know the mind of Adolf Hitler, I say to them," he grumbled. "What they mean to ask is, is this possible? I say to them, if he has it he will use it, and you will know. Until then, concentrate on Hitler's bullets, that's what I say. And they always leave disappointed. Because, really, what they've come to ask is, Albert, with all your theories, why have you not created for us a weapon? Why can you not help us kill more and better? Can you imagine that that's actually someone's job? To find out more efficient ways to murder in the name of war?" He sighed. "I've already given too much, unleashed too much. Such a shame that the first practical application of my work . . ." He stared into the palms of his hands as if he had written something there and then washed it away before remembering it. "I couldn't work on it if I wanted to. Would you believe, I'm considered a security risk?"

"Really?" Isaac looked amazed.

The bushy eyebrows rose comically. "They say I'm something of a leftist," he said with a sly wink. "European, you know. And a Jew." He turned to Heinlein. "So, as you say, the Navy found a place for me. This is for the better, anyway. I wouldn't work on it if they asked me."

"What is 'it'?" Heinlein wanted to know.

Einstein drew a finger across his mustache, staring at a point on the floor, and Heinlein realized he hadn't heard his question. The professor pulled himself out of his chair and approached the blackboard. Picking up a piece of chalk, he tapped it against the slate for a few moments and then quickly filled in the letters and numbers his shoulder had erased, though Heinlein wasn't sure if they were the same figures as before or new ones. Seemingly satisfied, he put the chalk down and took a step back like an artist, taking in the whole of a new painting. His lips pursed and he uttered a dissatisfied cluck. Then he turned and caught Heinlein in his gaze.

Heinlein felt a jolt of energy run through him as the intensity of the dark eyes bored into his skull. Gone was the twinkle that had cheerily lit up their conversation; now two dark fires of forged obsidian pinned Heinlein in his seat. In a blink Heinlein saw something else and understood—for one moment he saw the incredible focus of a mind pulling with all its force at one single thread of the fabric of the universe, and the incredible isolating lonely sadness of that challenge. Then, as easily as if he were sliding on a pair of slippers, the professor slipped into the more familiar garrulousness and Heinlein was relieved for him. He had read enough about Einstein's work to be able to claim he knew and understood special relativity. But that glimpse into the depths of the man's mind was vastly humbling. He knew nothing. Understood less. In Einstein's eyes he saw a man whose utter comprehension of an aspect of the universe was so complete it was beyond mental or physical or spiritual definition. Heinlein, meanwhile, couldn't even find a simple word to describe the utter knowingness he had just seen.

Einstein coughed into his hand, clearing his throat. He circled around his chair and took a seat again. Then he leaned forward, eagerly, and Heinlein could see the childlike sparkle in his eyes once more.

"Tell me," he asked the two of them, "about the future."

"Well, you're the expert," Asimov said.

"Not at all," Einstein said. "I don't have the imaginations you two have." He turned to Heinlein. "It seems to me I haven't read a story of yours in quite some time."

"That's true," Heinlein agreed. "I gave it up."

Einstein made a face quite like a pout. "Why?" Could a genius pout?

"I felt silly." He gave Asimov an apologetic look. "After Pearl Harbor, writing about rocket ships and aliens seemed so frivolous. I couldn't do it anymore."

He expected the doctor to call him ridiculous, but instead the man nodded thoughtfully. "I understand."

"You do?"

"I understand. It can be hard to keep the imagination engaged in such dark times. But you have to keep in mind that the future you imagine helps create the future we live in."

"What?"

"There are those who think that the universe does not exist but for our observing it. That's philosophy, not physics. I believe that the moon is there even if no one is looking at it. You and I may perceive it differently, but it exists nonetheless. It is not the uncertain effect of observing that changes the nature of things, but the effect of participating that influences a reaction. By this I mean to say that it is not your attempt to predict the future that will make the future you predict come true, but it is the act of influencing the future which will make it real. There is no uncertainty to it."

"I'm not sure I follow."

"It's simple, really. Do you realize how many scientists and engineers I know who even now are working to bring your dreams to life? Inspired by you, they are designing rockets to the moon that you and I see. They are motivated to make your visions of robots and computers and space travel a reality. Walk into any lab anywhere in the country today and ask who's heard of you. You will be proud to see your influence."

"But our ideas are inspired by science."

"Does the dog wag the tail or the tail wag the dog? Who can know for sure? Men want to build the future you write about. You, and Mr. Asimov here. That is cause and effect. And that is the true nature of the universe. So you should write, Mr. Heinlein, and have a hand in creating the future."

Heinlein swallowed hard, unsure of what to say.

"Imagination is the secret weapon that will destroy Hitler. And the next Hitler. And the one after that." He glanced at his pocketwatch.

Heinlein knew his time was limited. "Professor, do you know anything about Nikola Tesla?"

Einstein's smile faded somewhat. "The electromagnetic wizard," he said with a smirk.

"Ever meet him?"

"In fact, I did. In 1921, during my very first visit to America, I was introduced to him at a reception at the Marconi Transoceanic Transmitter at New Brunswick here in New Jersey. As you can imagine, since he felt Marconi had stolen the idea for radio from him, he was not in a very good mood. However, I think he was paid to be there, he always needed money. And I flatter myself to think that he might have wanted to meet me. But that may have contributed to his foul disposition, as well. In his eyes, I was nothing but a mere theoretician, I could make up anything I wanted to. While he was a practical inventor who had to put his hypotheses to the test each time he turned on a switch. I saw no cause for competition where, apparently, he may have."

"What do you think of his work?"

Einstein studied his hands for a moment. "Tesla believed that the universe, from gravity to life itself, is subject completely to the laws of electromagnetic energy. For him there was nothing else. You have to understand that electricity as something that man could control was still relatively new when Tesla started to experiment with it. It is true that he contributed useful technology to the world. But useful theories? Not his area of expertise, I'm afraid."

Heinlein nodded to Asimov. "Okay, then." He stood up. "You've been more than generous with your time. I don't want to keep you from the rest of your day."

Einstein rose as well. "It's entirely been my pleasure." He extended his hand and Heinlein took it; not so much a shake as a warm clasp. "May I make one more point before you go?"

"Of course."

"Come. I'll walk you to your car."

They walked through the building toward the parking lot. "I have to warn you that there are dark times ahead."

"But you were saying the future is bright?" Isaac asked.

"Cause and effect, remember? For all the light that we are bringing into the world, the darkness will be equal to it. The darkness is ignorance. Fear of science. You see, once upon a time, science made sense to people. Newton says that gravity makes apples fall, people see an apple fall and they can understand that. It helps explain their world to them. Then, I say gravity is an effect of the curvature of space and time, and suddenly that stops making sense to them, even though that's the way it is. It's not like they can see space and time curve the way they can see the apples fall.

"But we haven't stopped there. For our science to explain the universe we need black holes, subatomic fragments, cats that may live or die if a box is opened, and many other things that can't be seen. They require faith. Perhaps more faith than believing in God and angels and those other things that science mocks because they can't be seen require.

"So you see? We ask of people to believe us because we can do math. But why should they believe in what we ask them to? Maybe we're asking too much of people. I think we frighten them. Ask them to have too much faith. And that fear will lead to darkness. If we're not careful. If you don't help us be careful."

They were halfway back to Philadelphia when the professor's mesmerizing effect apparently wore off Asimov. "He wasn't being completely honest with us, you realize?"

"What do you mean?"

"I've been around academics long enough to know that when they say they're not being competitive, that's exactly when they're being competitive."

"I'm impressed! I don't usually expect that kind of perception from you when it comes to people."

"Why not?"

"I don't know. You don't really write about, y'know, emotional stuff. That's okay. It's not your specialty."

"I know about emotions."

"I wasn't saying you don't."

"You think I'm some kind of robot or something?"

"Hey, that's not what I meant at all. I was complimenting you on your powers of observation. I didn't realize Einstein was obfuscating."

Asimov had turned away from him to stare out the window.

"Isaac?"

"Hm?"

"Why do you think he did that?"

"I think he feels threatened by Tesla's work. You know, anyone whose career is based on creating theories has to live with a certain level of fear."

"Fear?"

"That their theory will be disproved by research. When that happens, everything comes to an end. Funding, work, adulation, reputation. An inventor can always go back to the drawing board. A theorist only has the board."

"So you think he may feel threatened by electromagnetic theories because there's been more practical application?"

"Well, I think he may be more worried that someday someone like Tesla will throw a switch and prove him wrong."

"About what?"

Asimov looked out the window. "It won't matter."

They finished the journey mostly in silence, driving onto the base as the sun was setting. Heinlein knew there was a predicament the minute the lab came into view. De Camp, Scoles, a few others, sat dejectedly by the front door. Ginny was among them, and when she saw him climb out of the car she gave him a wry wave and a little wink. Walking toward the building he could hear someone pounding on the door.

"What's going on?" he asked her. With a toss of her head she deferred to de Camp.

"Olson and his boys," he said with a sigh. "They welded the doors shut."

"All of them?"

"The windows, too."

"Christ! Who's in there?"

"Just a few of the guys. It's late. Most everyone's gone home. We were over at the base exchange."

"Who?" Heinlein demanded.

"Walb. Bullen. And Reinhart."

"Dammit."

"What are they retaliating for? I thought they retaliated. The stunt with the furniture?"

All eyes turned to Isaac, who cleared his throat and looked away. He held his chin high.

"What did you do?"

"There may have been a touch of . . . escalation," he said.

Before he could even begin to vent his spleen upon the young man who stood before him with his chin held high in defiance, Ginny spoke: "Bob. There's also a man in there who came to see you. From Washington, D.C. He went straight into your office."

"Who?"

"I don't know. I'm not a secretary and he didn't say. But, Bob," she said, with an edge of caution, "he was wearing a cape."

"A what?"

"A cape? Black, with a red velvet lining. Like Bela Lugosi. Like he was going to the opera."

Heinlein laughed. "Finally! Some good news. Let's get this damn door open. It's hot as hell out here, so they must be roasting in there."

"What do you want us to do?" de Camp asked.

"I think we're going to have to break some windows, boys. What do you say?"

"This is government property. We could get in trouble."

"Christ almighty, Asimov. Half the sailors on this place have declared war on us, we're a rat's whisker away from being shut down, and you think breaking a window will get us in trouble? Trust me. We're already in trouble."

He returned to his car and removed a tire iron and a length of rope from the trunk. At the window he could see the worried faces of some of his friends. With a couple of quick strikes, Heinlein shattered the two center panes of glass. "Hey, fellas!" he said to the men inside as he began to loop the rope around the struts. The response to his greeting was desultory. By the time he returned to the car, de Camp had the other end tied to the bumper. Heinlein climbed into the driver's seat and gunned the engine. The car surged forward, he felt a sharp jerk and then a bounce. De Camp uttered a sharp whistle and he hit the brakes. A quick check in the rearview mirror showed that the entire window frame had been pulled out of its setting and now lay shattered on the tarmac. De Camp and Asimov were helping the sweat-drenched staff out into the open air. It was irritating to note that Reinhart had been the first one to evacuate.

"Send a couple of guys over to the machine shop and borrow an acetylene torch. Get that door open," Heinlein said to de Camp. Then, ignoring Reinhart, he boosted himself over the window ledge and into the lab and headed toward his office. The lab smelled of dirty laundry and the heat caused him to break out instantly into a drenching sweat. He took off his jacket, loosened his tie, rolled up his shirtsleeves, then opened the door. "Hello, Norvell."

"Hello, Robert." In spite of the heat, the little man sitting on the couch was dressed in a black three-piece wool suit. The cloak Ginny had described lay neatly folded next to him. In his hands he held the scale model of the destroyer escort de Camp and Brinley had created. The top of his head was bald, but he had drawn some long strands from the tufts over his right ear in a failed attempt to cover it. "It's nice to see you again."

"You didn't have to come all this way." Heinlein sat on the edge of his desk. He had met the man once, in passing, at the third World Science Fiction Convention.

"I don't mind. There's a lot of interest in your work here where I come from. I thought I'd see for myself." Norvell Page's voice had the sound quality of a dirty needle being dragged across a phonograph.

"Hope you're impressed." He swept his hand toward the empty lab.

Norvell Page smiled. "I hear you're out of the pulps."

"I hear the same about you. You're not writing *The Spider* anymore?"

"The adventures of Richard Wentworth have always been told by Grant Stockbridge, and they always will be. With or without me."

Heinlein knew how much the hero pulp writers resented having to publish under pen names. Walter Gibson, forever hidden behind Maxwell Grant as the creator of The Shadow. Kenneth Robeson accepting all the glory for Lester Dent's Doc Savage. Sometimes Heinlein would use a pen name as kind of a lark, to try out a different style or so as not to compete with himself when being published by two different mags at the same time. But it had never been forced upon him by a publisher. Anonymity to a writer, especially a successful working writer, was galling. "So, you're really getting out?"

"I'm not getting out, I'm being left behind." He set the ship model down and crossed his arms in front of his chest.

"By whom?"

"By you. And by Asimov. And by Campbell. You guys came along and turned something that was just meant to be entertainment into something a lot like literature. And my fans have grown up to be your fans. The irony of evolution. Something always gets left behind. Hero pulps are atavistic now. Superman, The Batman, Captain Marvel, Captain America have accomplished what no villain ever could. They've killed The Shadow, Doc Savage, and The Spider."

"It's not as bad as all that. You could write for Campbell. See your own name in print for a change."

Page gave him a rueful look; the pain in his face was obvious. The man was in mourning. "I had my own monthly mag. I destroyed the Empire

State Building but saved Manhattan. I defeated armies. I foiled plots. Publishing a few shorts every now and then? It wouldn't be the same."

"Maybe after the war . . ."

"Ah!" Page clapped his hands together, and by the force of impact changed the subject, at least as far as he was concerned. "The war! I've arranged the Missouri store of barium ore to be processed and released to you per Mr. Asimov's specs."

"That's terrific, Norvell! Really swell news."

"But first I need a favor in return. Quid pro quo."

"Of course. It's to be expected." He had hoped that there would be no strings attached. "Whatever you need."

"We captured a U-boat in the North Sea. Apparently it was just heading out on a mission to Tokyo. A cargo mission."

"What kind of cargo?"

"Gold cylinders. The gold is used to shield what's inside. I need one of your scientists to examine the canisters."

"Bring them over. I'll get a team right on it."

"This isn't for you, Robert. I need them delivered to the Naval Station in Norfolk, Virginia. It's a little closer to home, under somewhat more adult supervision.

"The canisters, and some of the other weapons pulled from the U-boat, are currently stored in a warehouse at the Brooklyn Navy Yard. As you might imagine, there are a number of different departments, yours included, that might like to take a peek inside the latest example of Nazi technology and see what they might have in store for us. The debate rages on in the corridors of power. However, the people who will owe me a favor if I deliver this to them are the kind of people I want to have owing me a favor. That's my stock in trade these days. Favors."

"You want me to steal Nazi weaponry?"

"No. I've already stolen it. I just need one of your scientists to safely escort it to Norfolk by the Friday following this one. In return, I'll have your barium waiting for you there."

"I'll send a truck," Heinlein said with a shrug.

Page shook his head. "Stay off the roads. There are spies everywhere."

"What am I supposed to do?"

"Use your imagination." He rose, and with a flourish a matador would envy, the cape was dramatically fastened around his shoulders. Heinlein wondered if Page was aware that it made him look even shorter.

Page handed Heinlein the model. "Nicely done," he said. "Looks just like the one out there. Looks like it's about ready for a shakedown cruise." He nodded the few strands of hair still fastened to the top of his head toward the destroyer escort at its mooring. "I can see myself out."

Heinlein replaced the ship model, and when he looked up, Page was gone and Reinhart was standing in the place he had occupied an instant earlier.

"Heinlein!"

Heinlein braced himself for a fresh barrage of insults to issue forth from his plum-faced supervisor.

"I got a call a little while ago from our special consultant. Directly from him."

"Oh?"

Heinlein recognized Reinhart's expression. The man was amazed. "He was quite impressed with you. And with Asimov. Told me you had some great theories that needed researching and I was to assist you in any way possible. Any way. Anything."

"He did?"

"Hmm. I want you to tell me what you're up to, Heinlein. I want in. We can help each other."

"You're supposed to help me, right?"

"Right."

"Where's my ship?"

"I've already cleared that. You can have that one."

"The destroyer escort?"

"Yes. I can't wait to see your first successful test. When do you think that will be?"

Heinlein watched the gulls circle the great radar array on top of the destroyer escort. "Friday after next," he muttered.

"Okay." Reinhart rubbed his hands together. "What else do you need?"

Heinlein walked around the desk and toward Reinhart as if he were thinking seriously about the offer. "What else do I need? What else do I need?" He nodded as the answer arrived. "I need you to stay out of my office," he said, closing the door on Reinhart.

EPISODE 27

"DAMMIT, LES," HUBBARD muttered to himself. "You said you had an open marriage. There's not supposed to be payback in an open marriage."

He had never sailed this far north, and in these latitudes the ocean was unlike anything he'd ever seen. Gray and churning, the water seemed to have a solid plasticity as it heaved and undulated, rocking the heavy vessel in unexpected directions. The roiling landscape, the unsteady motion, the thick smell of diesel smoke which the wind seemed to force down into the ship instead of blowing out to sea had laid waste to more than half the sailors and most of the marines. Belowdecks smelled like vomit and fear. If it hadn't been for the persistent driving rain, Hubbard would have slept on deck. Instead, at night, he buried his nose in his wool blanket and tried not to let the moans of sick, weakened men penetrate his mind as he waited for sleep to fall and the dreams of his comforting flame-haired angel to arrive.

The first couple of days, he'd tried to write. Unable to find a typewriter, he'd settled in the galley with a notebook and pen, but the pitching and yawing made it impossible to keep the nubbin on the paper. On the third day, when he'd finally found a rhythm that could work, the words failed him. After four days, all he'd been able to put together were a couple of halfhearted short notes to his children, ending both with a promise that Daddy would be home soon, although he knew there was no chance of his returning to Bremerton, Washington. Even though somewhere in the back of his mind he still clung to the romantic idea of Polly stoking the home fires while he set off in search of adventure and fortune, he knew she'd never let him warm himself by the hearth again. He'd asked too much of her, done too much to her, abandoned her too many times. He expected her to ask for a divorce every time he opened a letter from her. It hadn't happened yet. But it would.

The ship was full of secrets and no one was telling anyone anything about their mission. People were furtive, scared, whispering. Haunted men looked past each other or through one another; eye contact could start a fight. Other sailors had written tales of voyages like this one, he recalled. Strange seas upon which a man traveled alone in spite of his shipmates. The other sailors cut him a wide berth. Even among the alone he was isolated. A Jonah.

Shortly after dawn, he huddled against the starboard side, slightly protected from the hail that seemed to pelt the port side harder than where he stood now, his hands thrust deeply into the pockets of the leather jacket he had been given, so as to keep his arms pinned closely to his sides. In the distance he could occasionally see the crags of a snow-covered mountain, its peak hidden by swirling fog or volcanic smoke, drift by like an iceberg. But of course that was an illusion; the islands merely stood silent watch as the ship cruised past. Once he understood where he was bound, he'd looked up the destination in the set of encyclopedias in the small ship's library. The Aleutian chain was nearly 1,200 miles long, extending out from the mainland of Alaska like a curved tail, and it was along the south rim of this arc that they traveled.

For the past few hours the skies had been filled with the sound of faint buzzing. Infrequently, in the gaps between the clouds, he could see black shapes like the great crows which had ventured out from the distant islands to roost inquisitively in the rigging. Bomber squadrons, charting the same course the *Funston* was on. An advance force. On all sides he could see plumes of black smoke seemingly rising from the ocean's surface. At some point during the night they had fallen in with a convoy.

"What the hell is going on out here?" he said out loud. "This looks like an invasion fleet."

"It is."

Hubbard hadn't realized he had company. The Seabee scanning the horizon at the rail nearby was short and burly, a heavy coating of beard climbed up his cheeks. A thick leather strap around his neck supported the expensive camera in his hand. A thick book was tucked into his pants, but Hubbard couldn't see the title. The Seabee squeezed off a couple of shots of a passing island. "We're invading America."

"What do you mean?"

"You heard about Dutch Harbor, right?"

"One of the shithole islands out here that the Japs attacked last summer. Guess they got lost on their way to L.A."

"The Japanese had a very good reason for attacking." He pointed out to sea. "These islands are strategically the most important pieces of property on earth."

"What do you mean?"

"You need to understand the spheres of influence here. If Japan controlled all this, they could attack Russia on one side, or launch against Canada and America on the other, all the while defending Tokyo. That's why they struck out for Dutch Harbor. They tried to take out our naval base there."

"Yeah, but we beat 'em back."

"Not really. What you haven't heard, what no one knows, is that the Japanese are still in these islands."

"You're shittin' me."

"In fact, I shit you not. Imagine what it would do to morale if Ma and Pa back home found out that Tojo had invaded, and holds to this day, American territory. It would cause a panic, no matter how far the continental U.S.A. is from this place. The Japanese are on our land, at our back door, doing God knows what, building God knows what, making God knows what plans.

"This is the biggest secret operation in the history of war. Those bombers are softening them up for the attack that's going to drive them out of the islands once and for all." The Seabee snapped off a few more shots. "There's a secret history to every war. And we're in the middle of one."

"How do you know so much about it?"

"I have the ability to become invisible."

"What?"

"I can blend in. Disappear. No one notices me until I want them to. Then I just listen."

Hubbard laughed.

"How long do you think I was here before you noticed me?"

"You've got a point."

A new phalanx of heavy bombers crossed overhead from the west. The Seabee pointed them out. "Those bombers are returning. We're not too far from Kiska now."

From a great distance they could hear the rumble of thunder without end.

"Kiska." He'd never felt so afraid.

"We beat 'em off of Attu a few months ago, around the time of Guadalcanal. Everyone heard about Guadalcanal. No one heard about Attu. Took three weeks to take a tiny island in the middle of nowhere. They charged out of the hills at dawn on the last morning, screaming 'Banzai!' and attacking with rusty bayonets and knives beaten out of tin pots. The bastards fought to the last man."

"You were there?"

He nodded. "Three weeks of hell. Thought I was clear of the islands after my furlough. But here I am again. Guess the powers that be really want me to die there. If I were you, I'd stay with the ship as long as possible."

"What about you?"

"Me? I've got to build a runway or dig graves. I'm not sure which yet. I'll know in a few hours. You be careful . . . ?" An eyebrow was raised quizzically.

"Hubbard," he told the man.

"They call me Herbie." He scratched his beard. "There's a story writer named Hubbard. Ever hear of him?"

"Can't say that I have. Any good?"

"If you like his kind of stuff, yeah, I guess so. Pulps, y'know?"

"Something wrong with the pulps?"

"They're okay for what they are. But if you want big ideas, you've got to look elsewhere." He held up his book.

Hubbard read the title aloud: "*Science and Sanity: An Introduction to Non-Aristotelian Systems and General Semantics.* Sounds like fun."

"It is for me. Korzybski really has the mind figured out."

"How so?"

Herbie just smiled and handed the book over. "Find out for yourself."

"But this is yours."

"I'm not going to need it out here." The boom of a particularly loud explosion rolled over the waters. "A sound like that can travel over fifty miles across open ocean. The human voice can travel ten."

"Didn't know that." Hubbard examined the book.

"Did you know that the natives call these the Rat Islands?" he said. "Rats. The only things living out here. I hate the ocean. If I never see the ocean again, I'll die happy. You know what I'd like to see right now more than anything?"

"What?"

"A desert. A lovely, dry, brown desert full of hot sand." Then the Seabee sauntered aft, pausing once to take a photo of Hubbard staring toward a smoking island rising for only an instant on the horizon before fog rolled over the deck and hid land, ocean, and man from the lens.

Drawn by the distant clamor, the men of the 7th Infantry began appearing on deck, the few wiseacres quickly silenced by sudden flashes in the fog, like lightning on the surface of the ocean. Hubbard tried to count how many cigarettes were lighted up in the first minute but gave up in a hurry.

The convoy worked its way around the leeward side of the islands toward the north. Bomber squadrons spun like pinwheels overhead and Hubbard thought he could see the ordnance dropping from their holds. Other troop transports were already making landings on the beach, men and vehicles pouring ashore. There were destroyers, with their escorts, in a natural harbor lobbing shells far into the sky to disappear into the clouds, only to be followed long moments later by ominous booms from the far side of the mountainous island.

"It's all high ground," one of the soldiers muttered, indicating the cliffs.

Several miles away Hubbard saw one of the destroyers (he wondered who its namesake, *Abner Read*, was) jockeying toward a better shelling position. He was admiring the speed with which it tore through the water when a great geyser suddenly erupted from its stern. For an instant he thought that maybe the ship had thrown a propeller, but as the rear rose out of the water as if kicked, fire and smoke belched forth from a gap that had been just below the waterline. The noise and force of the explosion hit him with enough power to make his heart vibrate in his chest.

The klaxons on board the *Funston* began to wail as sailors hung over the sides to look for the telltale wake of the torpedoes they were all shouting about. The *Abner Read* slammed back into the water like the breaching orcas he used to watch from the porch of his home on Puget Sound, listing horribly to starboard. Men spilled off its deck, or leaped, into the cold gray water. Still others faced their fears and grabbed the hoses needed to fight the fires that raged below. He felt the *Funston* surge forward as the engines roared, the sharp turn throwing him off balance, making him grab for the rail. Other ships were diverting as well.

He could see smoke just below the waterline, flowing out of a gash that must have been about fifteen feet long. By now there were forty or fifty men in the water; some had had the time to grab life vests, but most didn't. In the cold water, they would only have minutes before hypothermia set in. He'd lost his footing in a spring river once, knew how ice-cold water could grip a man's chest in an instant and squeeze until he couldn't breathe.

Hubbard was amazed at the efficiency taking place amidst the chaos. The *Funston* was launching lifeboats already while the destroyer's escorts aimed powerful water cannons at the flames. Cargo netting had been dropped over the side, and the men who could clambered up to safety. Frightened, cold, bloodied, they flopped on the deck like a strange catch of fish. Someone handed Hubbard a stack of blankets and he went about distributing them, helping the victims wrap themselves.

"What happened?" he asked one of the men.

The man looked at him with the eyes of a dog who doesn't understand why it's being whipped. His teeth were chattering so hard he couldn't speak; his head snapped to the right again and again with the effort to form words.

"It just blew," he heard another man say.

Hubbard turned to the man who was huddling under a blanket that someone else must have laid across his shoulders. He'd already managed to get his hands on a cigarette. "It just blew."

"Was it a torpedo?" Hubbard asked, casting an anxious eye out to sea.

The man shrugged. "What does it matter?"

"They could sink us."

"If they sink us, they sink us. I already dodged my bullet for the day. I was standing right by the door to the oil tank. I got blown clear off the ship."

"She's breaking apart!" someone shouted from the deck above, and the cry ran down the line. The gouge Hubbard had seen before was spreading, spreading like a rip in a cloth across the aft end of the ship. Then, pulling away with a great roar, the entire rear end of the *Abner Read* fell into the ocean with a tremendous splash. The lower decks of the ship were engulfed in flames. The water cannons from several escorts were instantly directed on the fire. Its inner bulkheads must have been shut in time, for though water poured into the gap and the vessel rode low, it didn't appear to be sinking. He hoped the men who had had the foresight and courage to do that deed had lived.

There were a lot of men in the water. With a dawning sense of horror, Hubbard realized that many of them were dead. Whether from the explosion or the frigid water, he couldn't tell. But the officers on board the *Funston* had seen it too; from the bridge they were directing the rescue boats toward live objectives, using the ship's speakers. Lifeboat after lifeboat returned and men either climbed up the netting if they could, or if they were too injured, were hoisted up with pulleys or cranes.

Handing out the last of the blankets, Hubbard moved forward, scanning the open waters for the telltale sign of a periscope. He knew what to look for.

"Over there!" he yelled to one of the lieutenants, scanning the seas with his binoculars. "That's it over there!"

The officer glanced at him, then turned his glasses in the direction Hubbard was pointing.

"See the U-boat?" Hubbard was breathless. He could hear others behind him passing the word of a U-boat sighting.

The young officer lowered his glass. "Albatross," he said, dismissing Hubbard with a scornful tone.

"Are you sure?"

"It's just bobbing on the surface. Yes, I'm sure."

"It was there!"

The officer grabbed Hubbard by the front of his shirt and slammed him against the bulkhead. "Listen! There's enough to worry about out here without you screaming about U-boats. There was no U-boat. There never was. If you say that word again, I'll have you thrown in the hold for the next week. There's no U-boat. Now say it."

Hubbard felt the officer's authority override his, felt the suspicious eyes of the other sailors behind him. "There's no U-boat," he said softly. "Never was."

The officer let him go. "Now stop trying to be a hero." The officer and the others all turned their backs on him. He slipped away, down the deck.

There was no U-boat. Never was.

By noon, the *Funston* was heading in to shore. Smoke still poured from the *Abner Read*, but several fleet tugs had stabilized it. The troops were ordered below to prepare for disembarkation. Hubbard's orders were that he was to remain on board the ship, but he couldn't wait to get off. So, when the ship docked, he staggered off, his landlegs as unsteady as those of all the other soldiers, and walked toward the beach. The rise to the mountain range began about a mile from the camp. The bombers continued to disappear over its top, discharging their loads. Down the shoreline where it swiftly rose to cliffs, artillery cannons boomed again and again, lobbing shells over the mountains. A tent city was rising to his right, smoke from hundreds of stove fires rising to the heavens.

The troops were happy to be off the ship at last. The man in front of him carried a guitar case. To the side of the wooden pier a camera crew, consisting of an operator and a director, filmed the landing, the director yelling again and again for the troops to stop grinning at the camera. Hubbard wasn't smiling. The island was cold, and once he stepped off the wooden planks of the path, his feet sank into a slushy mix of ice and mud. The cries of carrion birds filled the skies.

The wounded were taken off on stretchers to the medical tents. He was close enough to hear their screams and smell the blood in the air. He stumbled away toward the edge of the camp. An endless line of soldiers slogging through the mud up trails toward the mountains flowed past him. Jeeps and heavier equipment struggled through the half-frozen mush.

"I thought I told you to stay on the ship."

Hubbard turned to see Herbie, the Seabee, a shovel over his shoulder, sauntering up the path.

"I didn't want to get shot out of the water by a U-boat."

Herbie shook his head. "She hit a mine."

For some reason that didn't make Hubbard feel any more confident about staying on board.

"Are you heading up?"

"Nope." The Seabee twirled his shovel. "No graves to dig yet. Landing fields, I'm told. Which I'm taking as a good omen." He joined Hubbard in staring up at the mountains. "How do you feel about being so close to the Japanese?"

"It's strange."

The Seabee nodded. "That's the word for it. Where are you heading?"

"The highest point on the island. That's where you'd put an observatory, right?"

"Yeah."

"I haven't hiked a mountain since I was a kid in Montana. I'm going to head up the trail to that peak there. I'm going to have a seat up there, and I'm going to watch the battle. I've never seen a battle before. Even if no one's going to ever know about it, someone ought to remember it."

"What about the Japs?"

"Fortunately, that seems to be our territory. Even so, I'm armed."

"Well, the sun's not going to set too much this far north. You'll probably be safe up there. I still think you're better off on the boat."

"It's just something I have to do."

He shook the man's hand and set off. In his backpack he had K rations, blankets, a lighter, canteen, a pistol, and bullets. The trail rose rapidly and he walked alongside soldiers for much of the way. The land was utterly treeless, covered only with a scrubby moss. In spite of the chill in the air, the swirling mist was muggy. Hubbard couldn't imagine the weather patterns that occurred in this part of the world.

Finally he reached the path he had chosen to lead him to his private peak and he split off from the troop column. The climb was steep but steady. Sometimes he found himself having to clutch at the scrub grass to keep from sliding backwards. When he looked back and realized the landing area had been reduced to the size of a busy anthill, he was surprised at how far he had gone. The harbor was full of ships and more steamed toward it. There was another landing site far to the south. He could easily see the smoking hulk of the stricken ship and he wondered what the butcher's bill would be in the end.

The ridge he had spotted earlier was just ahead. About fifty yards. It was around this point that he realized he had a better chance of slipping and breaking something and dying unaided up here than of confronting a Japanese warrior. With that thought firmly lodged in his brain, he lost his footing and slipped. He slid rapidly backwards on his belly, fingers scrabbling to find some purchase. The backpack slid away from him and he heard the clatter of his gear scattering. His knee bounced off something sharp, sending him over onto his side. Hubbard caught a glimpse of a small scrub bush and desperately reached for it; as his hand grasped a thorny branch, his skid ended.

He lay there, trying to catch his breath. The pain in his knee was white in its intensity and he wondered if he had shattered it. In spite of the pain, he flexed it and was relieved not to feel anything crack or rattle. Easing up on his elbows, he surveyed the situation. His backpack had disappeared somewhere down the slope. The only thing he could see was the blanket caught on some rocks above him. He had fallen about seventy more yards, but the summit was still attainable. The thought of turning back, even after his fall, never crossed his mind. There was only going forward.

Hubbard struggled to his feet, gritting his teeth against the fire in his leg. It could still support his weight, which was a relief. He limped up to recover his blanket. Then, making sure his right foot was securely planted, he swung his other leg forward and began heading up in a slow, steady gait, always keeping the weight on his right leg.

A warm breeze greeted him at the summit. It was, as he had hoped, a safe and secure vantage point. He looked down on the smoking surface of an alien moon, scarred with uncountable numbers of craters, still spouting with flame-tipped geysers that made the ground rumble. Far to the left he could see the swarm of American troops assembling on a plateau overlooking the valley into distinguishable geometric patterns, squares and arrowheads.

On a flat patch of land, what must have once been an old cabin had been reduced to nothing more than a pile of stones and smoldering wooden beams. The heat was oddly comforting. For decades, the structure had stood, empty, waiting for someone to explore its mysteries. This morning, the Army Air Force had obliterated it.

Hubbard sank onto a vaguely comfortable boulder with a sigh. From here he could see the curve of the earth, the islands in the distance, clouds so close he could touch. In spite of the thousands of men nearby, friend and foe, he was alone.

"I am in the wilderness," he said to the rocks and trees and wind. "I am in the wilderness."

EPISODE 28

"IN THE END, the robot felt nothing. He wasn't programmed to."

Isaac's fingers ached as he dragged them from the typewriter keys. He usually took satisfaction in being able to write the words "The End" but not this morning—the action felt somehow flat. There was no one to celebrate those two little words with. He'd tried to ignore how the striking of the typewriter's hammers had echoed around the apartment all night long. Now he realized that the silence was even worse.

Robots. He'd been writing about robots because that's all he felt he could relate to. Campbell always told him to write about the emotions of his characters. Well, he'd found a way to solve that problem. He pushed back from the kitchen table, and when he stood, his knee joints creaked, convincingly in need of oil. His positronic brain was still firing words at his fingers but he knew it was time to shut down for a while. Circuits frying were a genuine concern in models like his.

He wandered the quiet halls of the apartment, reaching the bedroom. The bed was still made. Gertie had been off visiting her mother for a week now. She'd left in tears. Isaac had been on a streak of work and words ever since. But he hadn't felt much, didn't even know what to feel. And that's where the robot story came from. At least Campbell would be happy. Isaac was pretty sure he'd like the new stuff.

He slept on the sofa for a few hours. For some reason that didn't feel as lonely as being in the bed by himself. After the sun was up he showered, got dressed, posted the story, then caught the train to the Navy Yard. No hassles at the gate, which was a refreshing change of pace. There was no reason to hurry as he strolled along Constitution Avenue. It was already too bright, too hot, too humid.

The lab offered no relief. The maintenance crew was taking its own sweet time in getting around to unsealing the windows. Fans helped push air around, but it was only the same unpleasant oxygen being moved from one side of the room to another. Isaac gave a few unenthusiastic waves to some of his coworkers before sitting down at his table. The contents of one of the conical Erlenmeyer flasks he had filled a few days before with ammonia and phosphate had separated unexpectedly. A thick sheet of bright orange oily sludge floated on top of a clear liquid. The vague aroma of alcohol wafted out of the open neck. He picked up the bottle and gave it a spin, the top layer breaking up into thick gelatinous globules. He put the flask down, the orbs still swirling gently in the circular current, and placed his head in his hands.

"You okay?" Sprague asked.

"I was up all night writing."

"That'll do it."

"I think Gertie's left me." He said it so suddenly he surprised himself.

"Oh brother." Sprague pulled his chair closer to Isaac's. "What happened? Did you have a fight?"

"I didn't think so."

"You always have to know if you're fighting with your wife. Sometimes you can just be talking and it's a fight. Was that how it was?"

"All I did was miss lunch. Now she's going to divorce me."

"C'mon. Hold your horses. No one said anything about getting a divorce. Did she say divorce?"

Isaac shook his head.

"Did you say divorce to her?"

"No."

"So no one's talking divorce."

"But she left me."

"Where'd she go? She went to her mother's, right?"

"Yeah."

"See, that tells you she doesn't want a divorce from you."

He felt a tiny surge of hope in his chest. "Really?"

"Absolutely."

"How do you know?"

"If she were even thinking divorce, she'd have kicked *you* out of *her* home. No woman ever wants to admit defeat to her own mother."

"But Philadelphia's not her home."

"The apartment is. And what she wants is for you to make her feel welcome there."

"I don't understand."

"Look, a woman lives to be adored, to be appreciated, but above all, to be desired. If she's left, it's because she wants you to bring her back."

"You think so?"

"I swear to God. I'm not saying to go in there like a caveman and club her over the head and drag her home. But I am saying if you show up and make a grand gesture that shows how much you want her back, and how you'll stop missing lunches and dinners and staying up all night writing . . ."

"Well . . ."

"Okay, I don't know if that one matters so much. But if you'll let her know that the home she's making for you is home for both of you, you'll find you'll both be happier in it."

"Is that what you did?"

"Hell, no. Never happened to me and Catherine."

"Then how do you know?"

"I had a lot of experience under my belt before I met her. You married kind of young and I'm guessing that being a science fiction prodigy wasn't exactly catnip to the ladies of Brooklyn."

"I did just fine."

"I'm just saying that sometimes, in the absence of experience, you have to rely on emulation. Did your parents argue a lot?"

"Sometimes. Not a lot."

"Did your dad fight like you do?"

"He doesn't fight and neither do I," Isaac said proudly.

"I see. Did your parents kiss a lot?"

"Don't be gross."

"I don't mean any disrespect, Isaac. Just suggesting that maybe you should look around for some inspiration to help you be more, just a little more, romantic."

"From who?"

Sprague gave him a long look, the same way Isaac had seen him scrutinize an experiment when it didn't work as it was supposed to, and then he smiled. "You'll know it when you see it, I guess." He picked up the flask Isaac had been toying with earlier. "This is something," he said.

"What is it?"

Isaac looked at it. The globules had re-formed into a rubbery sheet again. Intrigued, he dipped a glass stir rod in, then withdrew it. The slime clung to the rod like fluorescent tar. "That's the damnedest thing."

"What?"

"Yesterday I spilled orange Nehi in. It seems to have coagulated . . ."

The front door to the lab suddenly burst open, the metal clanging against the wall with a sound that reminded Isaac of the gong from the opening credits of *Gunga Din*. Outlined in the bright light were three figures.

"Those guys!"

"Crap!" Sprague said.

The three shadows resolved into the extremely solid shapes of Gallinsky, Cafferata, and, finally, Olson—men of the *DE-173*.

"They wouldn't hit a guy with glasses, would they?" Isaac muttered to Sprague, pushing his heavy frames up his nose.

"I'd take those glasses off if I were you," Sprague whispered back.

The trio of sailors pushed their way past the scrawny, awkward scientists and engineers and took up a position with one on each aisle of Asimov's table, and Olson on the far side. He pointed a meaty finger at the two of them. "What'd you do to us?"

"What do you mean?" Isaac asked, innocently removing his glasses and wiping them with his tie.

"We're all of us pissin' blood. There's a line outside the infirmary. Only the doc says it ain't blood."

"Guess you should have left our Nehi alone, huh?"

"What was that?"

"Someone's been swiping our soda every week. I put a little something in it to find out who. And look who it turns out to be!"

Olson flew around the table and grabbed Isaac by the lapels, yanking him up on his toes. "Listen, you little snot . . ."

"You might not want to get your heart rate up." Although Olson didn't let go, he could feel the sailor's grip loosen just ever so slightly.

"Why not?"

"If I were you, I'd want to keep my blood pressure even, too."

"Why?"

Now his heels were touching the floor again. "Ever hear of nitroglycerin?"

"God! Is that what you gave us?" Olson released Isaac and took a soft step back.

"No." He smoothed his ruffled jacket and put his glasses back on. "I didn't give you anything. You just happened to drink some soda that had phenolphthalein in it."

"And that's like nitroglycerin?"

"I just think you should walk carefully for the next day or so. And be careful what you drink from now on."

"When this is over, I'm going to find you and pound you into a bloody pulp."

"No, you're not."

Isaac and the others spun around to see Bob standing in the doorway of his office.

"You're petty officer on the *DE-173*, right?"

Olson nodded. There was no resisting Bob's tone of authority.

"You know that's my boat now, right, sailor?"

"Yes, sir."

"That means, Mr. Olson, that until that ship is commissioned and you get further orders, you and my friend Mr. Asimov here are coworkers, as far as I'm concerned."

"Yes, sir."

Bob's whole bearing was charged. Isaac had seen him take plenty of ribbing for his aborted naval career, how he ought to be commanding a squadron instead of scientists, and he was always good-natured about it. Until now he had never seen Bob as an actual officer, the top graduate in his class at Annapolis, a man capable of ordering others to fight to their deaths. He stood ramrod straight, not blinking, staring at Olson with a steel coldness. "These pranks and retaliations are over as of today, do you understand?"

"Yes, sir."

"How about you, Asimov?"

The precision glare fell upon him, catching him off guard. "Sure, sir. Bob."

"How seaworthy is your ship?"

"Almost ready. It can practically sail itself, in fact."

"Good. I've got a mission for you. We're going to take her on a shakedown cruise. We're going to test the degaussing system out. Do you understand?"

"Yes, sir."

"We'll be using a skeleton crew. You. Me. Your men. You tell the men who come with us that if they do their jobs, I'll have a couple of cases of rum and whiskey for you all, plus I'll buy all the drinks at the Shore Leave for the rest of the weekend. Sound acceptable?"

"I guess so."

"Fine. We'll leave before dawn next Friday—a week from today. Expect to be back after sundown."

Olson turned to follow his orders, but Heinlein stopped him with one raised finger. "And Olson, just so you know. Phenolphthalein isn't anything like nitroglycerin. It just turns your piss red. You're not going to explode. But don't ever steal our pop again. Next time you might. Understand?"

"Yes, sir."

Isaac watched the sailors leave. As soon as the door shut, he turned to Bob, but Sprague spoke first.

"Jesus, Bob. What are you messing with?"

"I'm testing our degaussing system. Didn't you hear me?"

"But it's not working yet."

"Don't worry about it. Just keep working on Tesla's journal."

"There's not much about Wardenclyffe. Though it's interesting that it looks like the Crocker Expedition wasn't in the Aleutians in June 1908 after all."

"What?" It was as if a dark cloud fell over Heinlein's face. "What do you mean?"

"They never made it to the observatory there. Bad weather. Seems that in late May they turned south to the Tonga Islands."

Heinlein's shoulders slumped, and he dragged a hand roughly down his face. "Jesus Christ. Why didn't you tell me?"

"It's not that big a deal."

"Maybe not to you. But it sure as hell is to Hubbard."

"What do you mean?"

Isaac put his glasses back on and stared at Heinlein. "Yeah. What does that mean? You told us Ron went back to California."

"What did you do, Bob?"

Bob's gaze was less steel-forged, but no less riveting than when he had confronted Olson. "I did what I had to do, and so is Ron."

Sprague pointed to the waters beyond the buildings. "Is he out *there*? Looking for the case? Bob! What the hell are you up to?"

"Settle down," Bob said calmly. "There's a bigger picture here, Sprague."

"Tell me what's going on." Sprague's voice rose.

"I can't."

"You've sent Hubbard halfway around the world on a wild-goose chase. There's a good chance he'll get killed out there. Who's to say you won't get one of us killed trying to recreate Wardenclyffe. You are not Nikola Tesla. You're not even Thomas Edison. You're just a pulp writer. We're just pulp writers."

"It's more important than that, Sprague. I'm sorry you don't see it."

"Well, I don't. And I'm sorry about that. I can't help you, Bob." Sprague turned his back on the both of them and strode angrily through the lab, disappearing into the bright daylight that filled the doorway.

"You going to walk, too?" Heinlein turned to Isaac.

"I guess I'm in," Isaac said.

Surprisingly, Bob put a hand on Isaac's shoulder. "Thanks, buddy."

Isaac looked through the windows at the far end of the lab. The ship looked small beyond it, resting at its berth on the river. He was glad he wasn't going to have to set foot on it. He liked ships only a little less than airplanes.

"I need you to help me out next week, too."

"Sure. What can I do?"

"I need you to go to New York. The Navy Yard on the East River in Brooklyn. I need you to examine some cargo while I arrange transportation for it. I'll meet you there before noon."

"Okay."

"Thanks again." He scratched his chin. "I've gotta figure out how to get a message to the Aleutian Islands. Why don't you take the rest of the day off. Go home and see your bride."

"Gertie," Isaac quietly corrected him. Then he looked down at the orange slime he had accidentally created. "Maybe in a little while," he said, but Heinlein was already gone.

It was hours after everyone else, Bob included, had left that he finally put down his equipment and headed back home to his apartment. His heart jumped with happiness for a moment when he found the door unlocked and the lights on. But a cursory tour around the apartment showed him that Gertie had not, in fact, returned, and that he, in a cliché of the absent-minded scientist, must have forgotten to lock the door when he left in the morning.

EPISODE 29

THE EXPLOSION HAPPENED at some point behind him as he walked down the thick, muddy trail that had been created by the endless wheels of artillery equipment. He felt the blast like a hot hand, shoving at his back, slapping at his ears. Then he was facedown, the cool mud actually soothing against his inflamed skin.

He just lay there. It wasn't that he couldn't move, he just didn't want to.

Someone behind him had wandered off the path and triggered a booby trap. The island was riddled with them.

By the time he'd made his way down from the mountaintop yesterday, the scouts had returned with the word. Unbelievable at first, but others confirmed it: there were no Japanese on the island. They had been there, all right. Hundreds of empty tents flapped in the chill wind. The campfires had gone cold days or weeks before. The refuse pits reeked with the most ungodly smell. On the beach at the far side of the island, Hubbard had found a picture of a woman in a kimono holding two small children. How much of a hurry had their father been in to evacuate the island to have left behind such an important memento? he'd wondered. Maybe the soldier felt it was fine to leave it behind because he was going home to see them. Or maybe he'd known his life was going to end soon and didn't want something that would make him regret losing it.

He couldn't tell whether the screaming he heard was his or not. Either way he wished it would stop. He just wanted to be left in solitude with his pain.

How many men had fallen in incidents due to the explosive devices left behind by the enemy? Thirty, forty? Then there were the injured. Scores of them.

"Lafayette?"

"Leave me alone."

"No."

The smell of moss and brine tickled his nostrils. It was a pleasant scent to accompany a death.

"Lafayette."

"I'm dying."

"We all die."

"But I'm dying now."

"You're not."

He knew her voice. "Sara?"

Silence. The screaming had stopped. Now, instead of the earthier fragrance he had grown accustomed to, he smelled a hint of jasmine in the air. Sara wore jasmine.

His fingers found purchase in thatches of scrub grass and he pushed against it. Laser bolts of pain shot up from the small of his back, where the brunt of the explosion had slammed into him. With a groan, he sank back into soothing muck.

"Don't do that."

"Just go away."

"If you don't get up, you'll miss your plane. Do you want to be stuck here? Or sent somewhere else?"

"I want to go home."

"Bob won't let you go home. You have orders."

"Brand-new orders." As he forced himself up, he felt the grip of extra hands helping him. He brushed at them.

"Easy, buddy. Easy, Lieutenant."

His eyes gradually found a way to focus on the grime-streaked face of the medic attached to the unit Hubbard had been assigned to follow back to the base camp. "Where's the blood coming from?"

"You're not bleeding."

Hubbard indicated the medic's hands that had just been upon his back. "Blood."

"You got hit by Antinori."

"Why'd he do that?"

"He didn't mean to. He stepped on a land mine. You got splattered."

Looking around, he could see several pieces of what moments ago was a large man. Other members of the squad were stumbling to their feet. It appeared he had only been down for a few moments. "He was right behind me."

"Guess his number was up."

"I think I'm deaf."

"Your hearing will probably return. Most likely."

He rubbed some of the water and slime from his face. "What am I doing here?" he muttered.

"Yeah, Lieutenant." The medic rested on his haunches. No one seemed to be calling for him. "We were wondering the same thing about you. What *are* you doing here?"

"Secret mission." Hubbard rose, unsteadily supporting himself against the medic, who rose alongside him. "Can't talk about it."

The man handed him his helmet. "Too bad you're leaving." He was barely out of his teens and had a friendly, open face.

"Why's that?"

"The men were starting to think you were bringing them good luck. Having to get you back to HQ meant they got off the beach and some hot food. Even if it's just mess hall crap." He looked around at what was left of the other man. "Of course, if this keeps up, they might start thinking of you as a jinx."

"Got any aspirin?"

The medic pressed a couple of tablets into the palm of Hubbard's outstretched hand.

"What a waste, huh?"

"Of aspirin?" The young man looked confused. "I've got plenty. Morphine, too, if you need an ampoule."

"All this." He indicated the view down the trail back to the beach, partly littered with Antinori's remains. "All the men. All the equipment. All the fucking effort to get here. And because of what? A rumor."

"Better than fighting," the medic suggested.

Hubbard shook his head dismissively. "What a joke. I'd laugh if it weren't so pathetic. Somebody will probably get a medal for this mess." He dug a furrow with the toe of his boot. "Who was he?"

"I don't know. Neither of us were with the unit for long. I heard he was from Pennsylvania, though."

The soldiers of the squad began the ugly business of retrieving what they could of the man's body, gently placing him in a dark green wool blanket. Hubbard picked up the dead man's helmet, which lay in a puddle near the path. A faded Bicycle playing card was stuck in the headband.

Hubbard flipped a corner back to see the red ace of diamonds. He was considering the relevance to Antinori when the cool metal was suddenly plucked from his hands. Startled, he looked up. The grim corporal gave him no explanation. None was necessary. Each of the other men of the unit, in the midst of their horrible task, would stop periodically and give Hubbard long, dark, questioning stares.

He began to walk, past the remains on the blanket, weaving past the dozen or so troops who had grown still on the path as he passed. Soon he was alone on the trail, climbing over the ridge, and tears were rolling down his cheeks. That's what had caught the ire of the soldiers and why they had grown so uncomfortable in his presence. Hubbard hadn't realized he was crying, didn't feel any accompanying sadness or shame because in truth, he felt nothing. He apparently had no control over the situation, though he tried to make the crying stop. Yet he continued to weep helplessly as he stumbled, unaccompanied, up the path toward the camp.

The flow must have ended eventually as no one in the mess tent seemed to pay him any mind. On the other hand, Hubbard wasn't sure how he'd come to find himself seated at a table with a steaming cup of hot coffee in front of him. He had no recollection of passing the sentries, making his way here, getting the drink, sitting.

Startled, he turned to a man who sat not far away to his right. "Excuse me," he asked. "How long have I been sitting here?"

"Not long," the man replied. He had an equine face, with a head topped by a mound of copper hair, far redder than even Hubbard's. The wrinkles around his eyes revealed his age; the man was a lifer. "Twenty minutes or so."

"God." Hubbard rubbed the lump at the back of his head.

"Took a bump?"

"Yeah. I guess so."

"That can happen."

"This is a disaster."

"You mentioned God."

"Hm?"

"Can you imagine that this is all part of God's plan?" The man turned to a more comfortable position for a long chat, and Hubbard saw the Star of David, and the chaplain's insignia on his uniform.

"I don't know about God, but I'll tell you what I've been thinking." Hubbard took a sip of the coffee; as long as it was in front of him, he might as well enjoy it. "When I was a boy, my mother and father took me to the county fair. Ever been to one of those?"

"Sure. I'm from Indiana."

"Okay. This was in Montana. I'm sure yours was exactly the same. It was late summer, early harvest time. The country air was filled with the scents of fresh hay, popcorn, and healthy manure. After riding some rides and watching a few singers, I found a game on the midway that really captured my attention.

"All you had to do was toss a ring around the neck of a goldfish bowl and you could win that goldfish and the bowl. I don't know why I was so caught up in the game. I had pets. I didn't really like fish. I think I just wanted to win because the game looked winnable. I had two dollars on me, my allowance for the week. My father had done me the *favor* of saving it up for me and handing it over at the gate. I tossed ring after ring. Some bounced to the left, some to the right. Some lay a little on the top, and some almost nestled the way they were supposed to. But none of them ever popped around the neck of the bowl. Five cents for three tries. I spent my entire allowance. At the end of it I had no fish, no bowl, no money."

"The rings were too small."

"That's what my father said. But others were winning. Part of the carny's routine was to show that the rings fit before he gave you the very same rings. No. The problem was that I just wasn't any good at it. But I really wanted to win. I thought about it all night. Ran it in my head like a movie, memorizing the heft of the ring, practicing the wrist movement to get the right trajectory. I thought I had it cracked. So I broke into my piggy bank, found another two dollars, and went back the next day. Same carny. Same situation. I could not win to save my life.

"I ran out of money again. Blew it all. I was just devastated. I begged the carny to let me try again. Made a real pest out of myself, yelling a little. Instead, he said to me, 'Look, kid. I know you tried really hard. I don't do this for just anyone, and if you tell anybody else, I could lose my job. You hear me?'

"Well, I was so excited, even though I didn't know what he was going to tell me, I promised him I could keep a secret.

"'Okay,' he said to me. 'I'm going to give you a fish.' I practically jumped for joy, I was so happy. Even though I hadn't won, I felt like I had earned that goldfish. Then he said, 'But I can't just give it to you.'

"'What do you mean?' I asked him.

"'Well, you don't want one of those fish.' He patted the traveling trunk he was sitting on and said, 'The good fish are in here. I put 'em out at night for the grown-ups and I can charge a dime instead of a nickel. They're beautiful, these ones, with great flowing fins and a color of orange you only see at sunset. They're bred in China, used to be special for the emperors only. I think you've earned one.' He winked at me and I totally understood and wanted one of those fish more than I'd ever wanted anything in the world. 'Thing is,' he continued, 'I lent the key to my buddy, Finn. He's down at the freak show. You go and tell him Dusty sent you to get the key. Then you come right back here, I'll pop open the chest, and get you one of these beauties. How's that sound?'

"It sounded pretty great to me.

"'But don't you come back here and bother me without it. I got a business to run.'

"I ran, well, I ran as fast as lightning, as we say in the pulps. As fast as the wind. I ran to the freak show tent to look for Finn. But the show had started and kids my age weren't allowed in, so I had to wait. Then a man came out and I asked him if he was Finn, and he said he was, but before I could continue he started barking up a new crowd.

"Well, I wanted that fish, so I kept interrupting until he finally paid attention to me. I told him I was looking for the key.

"'Ah, the key to the midway,' he told me.

"I shrugged and told him I didn't know that's what it was called.

"'Sure,' Finn said. 'It'll open up all sorts of wonderful things here.'

"Well, can I have it?"

"He grinned. 'Patty who runs the hot dog concession came by and got it just a little while back,' he told me. 'All you gotta do is go find her.'

"So I was off and running again. There were eight hot dog vendors on the fairgrounds, which covered twenty-two acres. Somehow I couldn't find Patty until I'd been to all eight of them and then back to a few again, and finally I found Patty, who I'm sure had been there the first time I visited."

"Let me guess. Patty had given the key away."

"Yep. I was nine years old. I ran all over that fair from one carny to the next until I just gave up and went home. I was brokenhearted and empty-handed, and you know what?"

"What?"

"It did not occur to me at all that they had sent me on a fool's errand. I was too ashamed to tell anyone for the longest time, and when I finally told my scoutmaster, he told me the cruel facts of life. Told me I was a sucker. I hated that feeling. And since we got here to this damn island, I feel like a sucker all over again. Only this time the key to the midway is the Japanese fighting man."

"What's the goldfish?"

"I guess, staying alive."

The rabbi nodded thoughtfully. "So who's the carny? The president? The general?"

Hubbard shook his head and pointed skywards. "The man upstairs, Chappy. Your boss."

"Well, it wouldn't be the first time God tested someone for reasons known only to Him. And it wouldn't be the first time that it seemed ridiculous to the person being tested."

"I was never any good at tests. Didn't I just explain how I couldn't get a ring around a bowl?"

"Sometimes I think Moses must have felt his mission was getting a little futile around the seventh or eighth plague. I've often wondered if the thought ever crossed his mind, 'Hey, how many plagues am I going to have to bring down here before I get some results?'"

"It took him a while, but he figured out the right one."

"I'm not saying that what we're doing on this island is akin to Moses in Egypt. But it is a test for all of us. Even you."

"But what's the point?"

The chaplain held his hands apart. "To get the goldfish!"

The sound of a ship's horn rolled in from the harbor. Hubbard looked at his watch, but the face was cracked and the hands had stopped at 11:47—the time of the explosion. "What time is it?"

The chaplain checked his wrist. "Two twenty-five."

Hubbard tossed down the rest of the coffee. "I've gotta catch a boat. On my way to the tropics."

"Empty-handed and brokenhearted."

"You have no idea." He stood up. "Been nice chatting with you, Chappy."

"Likewise. Thinking about popcorn and manure took me back to my boyhood. Want to take any reading materials along with you?"

"What have you got?"

"What do you like? I've got the Bible, the Torah, the Book of Mormon, the Lankavatara Sutra—that's about Buddhism, in case you didn't know. I've also got several copies of the Koran, just in case, but I've only met one Muslim soldier in my whole career and he had one already."

"I'll take one," Hubbard said.

"Which one?"

"One of each. I've never read any of them, except a few parts of the Bible."

"I wish I had more souls like you."

"No, you don't, Chappy. You really do not."

A little while later he trotted down toward the bay, his bag a bit heavier than it was this morning when he'd packed it. He couldn't wait to get aboard the USS *Ulysses S. Grant II* and start the run down the North Pacific line. The far-off sound of an explosion made him pause for a moment.

Another soldier had just lost his search for the key to the midway.

EPISODE 30

"DO YOU WANT me to have sex with her?" Leslyn asked. She sat in the armchair with the high back that made her seem small, almost childlike. The cigarette dangled from her fingertips so lightly that he thought this time she might actually drop it. "Because I suppose I will if you want me to. Though it seems so tawdry. So French."

"That's not what I want." He rubbed his hands through his hair. There was so much less of it these days. He could easily feel his scalp.

"She could move in. We could share a bed together or you could pick which of our bedrooms to come into each night like a Mormon."

"This isn't about her," Heinlein replied. He hunched on the edge of the loveseat on the other side of the coffee table, which was covered with movie magazines. "It's not even really about you. I only told you about her because you wanted to know who. But she's not the why."

"I always knew you were going to punish me sooner or later, but I just figured you'd leave me. I never thought it would have been anything so perverse as asking me to become a lesbian. But I suppose of all the things it could have been it's not the worst."

"I didn't!"

"Are you sure it wouldn't be easier if you just stuck me in another sanitarium and forgot about me? No, I suppose you might want to get married again someday. Though I wouldn't recommend it. I don't think it's really your cup of tea. Do you?"

"Do I what?"

"Do you want to get married again?"

"So," he sighed. "That's where we are."

"Yes." She looked away from him, toward the kitchen, saying something under her breath.

"Excuse me?"

"What if . . ." Leslyn put the cigarette down and rested her hands, open, upon her knees. Tears began streaming down her face, as if she had suddenly reached the end of her reserve of coolness. "What if I can't leave you?"

He rose and went to her, crouching by the chair and taking her hands. Heinlein had started the conversation right after work while it was still light out. Now, though the sun had set and the room had grown thick with gloom, her wet eyes glittered in the remaining light.

"But it's too late for that," she said, smiling bravely and stroking his face. "You should go."

He handed her his handkerchief and she daubed at her eyes and nose.

She placed her hand against his cheek. "We never did make much of a marriage, did we?"

"I've seen worse."

Leslyn heaved a sigh as if pushing a weight off her chest. "Well, divorce is very fashionable right now. Rita Hayworth, Ava Gardner. Of course, she's practically a kid. But still." Leslyn tossed the handkerchief onto one of the mags. "Fix me a drink, would you? I could use a stiff one."

"I don't think it's a good idea."

"It doesn't really matter what you think anymore now, does it?"

Heinlein walked to the sidecar and poured a glass of vodka, her usual. As he reached for the water to thin it a little, she spoke. "Don't do that."

His fingers fell away from the bottle. He handed her the glass and she took a long slow sip that drained half the glass. She closed her eyes for a long while and finally looked up at him. "Why are you still here?"

He packed two suitcases and the typewriter, everything he had, throwing them into the car. All the while she sat in her chair, smoking the cigarette, rising only every so often to refill her glass. Finally, he stood under the arch to the living room. His heart pounded behind his breastbone and he felt as if he couldn't breathe. Heinlein knew he could take it all back right now, change the course he had set out upon, she would let him. Her eyes said as much. But then she closed her eyes and he turned away.

There was no reason to stay in Lansdowne. He got into the car, drove to the Franklin Hotel, downtown near Independence Hall, where he checked himself in. After hanging up his few suits and throwing his other belongings into drawers he sat on the edge of the bed for about a minute before he realized he might go crazy if he had to spend any time alone with himself.

The hotel's bar was small but well appointed. He had a seat, nodding politely at the burly man nursing a drink on the next stool.

"What'll you have?" the bartender asked.

His eyes fell upon a ceramic jug. "I'll have some of that Michter's rye."

"You sure? It's a bit steep. I think it's been in the collection since before Prohibition."

"Then it ought to be pretty good."

The liquor was both sweet and peppery, and flowed through his central nervous system, instantly releasing the muscles in his back that had kept him from relaxing and loosening the band across his chest that had made breathing so difficult. "Ah," he sighed. "That's the taste that kept George Washington in the fight."

"Scotch drinker myself," said the man on the stool, rattling the cubes in his glass. He pointed a thick, hairy knuckle at Heinlein's drink. "What's the celebration?"

"Not a celebration." Heinlein shook his head. "My wife just showed me the door."

"Sounds like a reason to celebrate to me." The man had a manner of speaking through slightly pursed lips.

"You a married man?"

"Hell, yes."

"Happily?"

"I guess so. As happy as any man can be. Don't get me wrong. Some days it's great. I love coming home to a hot meal every night. But I hate it that she has to know where I am every minute. I have to call her no matter where I am or what I'm doing." He looked at his watch. "It's almost time."

"You're not from around here?"

He shook his head. "D.C."

"Ah, the source of the other half of my problems."

"You work for the government, too, huh? What do you do?"

Heinlein gestured for another drink. "Try to figure out where imagination ends and reality begins." Then he grinned. "Trying to make pulp trump reality."

"How's that going?"

He took a long sip from the new glass. "I'm having one of those days where nothing goes right, y'know? I'm literally trying to make the impossible possible and I feel like I'm trying to do it all by myself. I've got a boss who's a pencil-pushing bureaucrat who doesn't understand the first thing about what I'm trying to do. Half my team is feuding with some guys who are going to kick their teeth in. My best man just quit. The thing we're working on is so complex that some of the best geniuses in the world haven't been able to crack it and I'm not even a scientist!"

"You're not?"

"Hell, no. I'm just a writer."

"Anyone I've heard of?"

"I doubt it."

"Don't be so sure. I read a lot."

"'Magic Incorporated'? 'Waldo'? 'Methuselah's Children'?"

The stranger shook his big head. "Nope. Never heard of them. What else?"

"Not much."

"How's that pay?"

"Not bad."

"I should get into that."

"Yeah?"

"Sure. I got lots of stories from work."

"What do you do?"

"You could say I'm a kind of special researcher."

"Sounds interesting."

"It sure is. For example, my partner and I, we're researching whether some people with access to certain government secrets may be passing those secrets along to one another."

Heinlein emptied his glass slowly. Then he put it down so that it fit perfectly on its ring of condensation left on the napkin. "Do I know you?"

The man slid off the bar stool in a single, methodical flow, his hefty girth pressing against Heinlein's arm.

"Easy, buddy."

He leaned forward, the faint scents of sweat, Old Spice, and whiskey clinging to him. "You don't know me, Mr. Heinlein," he whispered. At the same time Heinlein felt something hard jab him in the kidneys. "But

I know who you are. Now why don't you stand up, nice and easy, and let's you and me go have a chat."

"But we're having a little chat right here."

"We can't talk about what we need to talk about in a place like this."

"And what's that?"

"You committing treason against the United States of America."

"Maybe you should meet me in my office tomorrow with the general I work for and, oh yeah, my lawyer." He motioned for another drink.

The man poking him in the back with what had to be a gun waved the bartender off.

Heinlein rapped the glass on the bar. The bartender walked over with the bottle and filled it, in spite of the glare from the man standing behind. Heinlein swung around on his stool, forcing the big man to take a step back and slip the gun, which Heinlein caught a glimpse of, into his coat pocket.

"Look, Heinlein," the man said. "You're going to have to leave here eventually. The way I see it, there's a couple of ways you can go. I can knock your head against the bar and carry you out like you're a drunk. Now the problem with that is I can give you a concussion, or break your head open and get blood everywhere. I've even seen men die from that. If they got weak skulls."

"What else you got? You gonna shoot me?"

"Only if I have to. Another way is you get up and walk out of here with me, I drive you down to my office, and you, me, and my partner talk for a while."

"No chance of you just leaving me alone, huh?"

The man shook his head.

Heinlein considered for a split second throwing the rye in the man's face, but that would probably only tick the fella off and be a waste of some good booze. He downed it quickly. "Let's go then." He stood. "After you."

"C'mon," the man said.

"Okay." Heinlein slipped past him.

The bartender cleared his throat. "The Michter's ten bucks."

Heinlein quickly threw a thumb back toward the big man. "He's buying."

With a disgruntled sound, the man reached into his wallet, pulled out a bill, and plunked it on the bar.

"Each," the bartender said. "Ten bucks each. I told you it was expensive."

"He's got it," Heinlein reassured the bartender.

The big man chewed his lip for a minute and pulled some more money out.

"Don't forget the tip," Heinlein said. "I'm a good tipper."

"You're pushing your luck."

Heinlein shrugged. "I'll get you back later," he told the bartender, who returned with an exasperated nod as if he had known all along that it was going to be a light night and mightn't have bothered coming in at all. As he walked across the barroom he felt the big man walking behind him. He hated the sensation of being followed. "What's your name, pal?"

"Killough," he heard the man say.

"I've got some Irish blood in me, too."

"Well, ain't that good for you."

As he led the way through the lobby, he tried to divert toward the front desk.

"Where you going?"

"I wanted to leave word where I'm going. Where am I going?"

"Don't worry about it."

"I need to see if my wife called."

"I thought she gave you the boot."

"She might have forgiven me."

"You're a regular Groucho Marx, ain't ya?" He felt the pressure of the gun in his back again. Even though he didn't think the man would shoot him down in the lobby of the hotel, he had no reason to believe that he had an innate sense of decency either. Plus he'd seen more than his share of guns accidentally discharging to want to press his luck.

"Actually, I've really come to appreciate the genius of Bugs Bunny."

"I'm a Mickey Mouse man, myself."

"Of course you are."

A revolving door would have made escape an easier matter, but only a pair of glass doors stood between them and the street. Heinlein made to hold the door open, but Killough shoved him ahead onto the sidewalk toward a Pontiac parked beside the curb.

"This yours?" Heinlein asked, peering through the window.

"Yeah. Get in."

He turned back to face Killough. "Uh-uh."

"C'mon, don't make me—"

Heinlein threw his clenched fist toward the man's prominent cheekbone. He was blocked by a beefy forearm that appeared to rise out of nowhere.

"I wish you hadn't a done that," Killough said.

Heinlein caught a glimpse of the man's other hand coming around from the left. The hand which held the gun. A thought crossed Heinlein's mind that he was about to be pistol-whipped. Cupids and carrots exploded through his brain. The sensation of being able to tell up from down and left from right vanished with most of his consciousness. From his crumpled position he found himself muttering something repeatedly, and he hoped he was saying it loud enough for Killough to hear. "Of course you realize this means war."

There was a car ride, he was pretty sure of that. By the time he found himself stumbling up a flight of stairs, full consciousness was returning along with an even fuller pain. Killough bounced him through a door into a dingy office, government issue. Heinlein caught a glimpse of city outside a grimy window—he hoped it was still Philadelphia, but he wasn't sure.

"Is that him?" someone asked.

"Yeah. Heinlein."

"Put up a struggle?"

"Nah. We had a drink and everything."

"So, what happened?"

"Can't hold his liquor."

"Put him over there."

He was pushed down into a desk chair, Killough's beefy hand clamped over his wrist, and before he could pull away, something snapped painfully around it. A handcuff shackled him to the chair. "Seriously?"

The other man was as tall and lanky as the first was squat and beefy. Standing beside Killough, he looked like one part of the weariest, most rumpled pair of traveling salesmen one would ever find on their front stoop. "My name's Ross Dugan," he said.

"What's up, Doc?"

"Oh, he also thinks he's a comedian," Killough said by way of explanation. "Or a cartoon."

"You know, Heinlein, there's nothing funny about this," Dugan said.

"Maybe not to you," he replied. "But I'm having a world-class day."

"His wife kicked him out."

"Did you get a chance to talk to him about anything actually important?"

"Well, not about Cartmill."

For the first time, Heinlein felt the fluid sensation of fear flowing through his lower torso. He had known that this was trouble of some kind, but he'd assumed it had more to do with the shenanigans at the Navy Yard than anything else. Norvell Page's warning to him that his work might attract attention rang in his ears. Or else it was still the chimes from the pistol-whipping. "Cleve Cartmill?"

"You know him?"

Dugan tossed a mag at Heinlein. He made no effort to catch the pulp, letting the *Astounding* issue featuring "Deadline" slide to the floor.

"You read that?"

"Yeah. It stinks."

"I ain't no critic," Dugan said with a shrug. "But there's a lot of other stuff in that story that we want to know about."

"The bomb stuff," Killough said. "Where'd he get all that dope?"

"I don't know. Ask him."

"We did."

"So?"

Riley and Killough looked at each other, then back at him. "We think you're passing along information to him. You're getting it from Campbell." The smaller of the pair withdrew a large brown envelope from his satchel. The mailing stamps had been blacked out and the end crudely ripped open. Heinlein recognized it immediately and a jolt of adrenaline flowed through him as he realized just how much trouble he could be in. "Tell us about Robert Cornog. Why did you send him this weapon info?"

"He's a pulp fan."

"If you won't talk about them, then tell us about Isaac Asimov. He's a known Communist."

"Asimov? He's no Communist. I don't think he even knows who the president is."

"He's affiliated with a political organization known as the Futurians, which has registered a number of Communists. He also has connections in the scientific community. Maybe he's using some kind of code in his stories." Riley tapped some papers on his desk. "Are robots a metaphor?"

"For what?" Heinlein asked.

"For information."

"What information are you guys talking about?"

"You're going to tell us you're not aware of how accurate the details are in Cartmill's story?"

"It's science fiction, fellas. Fiction."

"Hitler could do a lot with what's in there. Maybe build a super-bomb of his own."

"I don't know anything about it."

"Come on. We know you've been in touch with Lyman Binch at General Electric, and Hugo Gernsback. Why are you passing sensitive materials to Robert Cornog? We know you're looking for information about Tesla. Does this go back to him? Did Tesla come up with a super-bomb?"

"I don't know what you guys are talking about."

"Nikola Tesla left a lot of unanswered questions."

"I'm sorry you never got the chance to ask him."

"Oh, we did," Dugan said. "We did. We just didn't get the answers we needed."

"Wait a minute," Heinlein said. "You were the guys tailing Tesla?"

"*Da,*" Killough said. "I got as much Russian in me as Irish. The old sonofabitch was writing letters to the Russians about super-weapons. That's why we got put on him."

"If Tesla knew something about super-bombs, then you need to tell us."

"Especially if you been passing that along."

"I don't know anything about super-bombs! Honestly."

Dugan scratched his head. "I don't believe him."

"Neither do I."

Heinlein looked out the window. Light gray streaks were breaking through the blackness of the sky. Dawn was imminent. It was Friday morning. "Guys, you gotta believe me. If I knew anything about Tesla's super-bombs, I'd do my duty as a patriot and tell you."

"The thing about patriots," Riley said, "is that they're a lot like Christians. They all think they got the secret."

"I don't have any secrets."

"We all have secrets, Mr. Heinlein. I'll tell you one of ours and then we're going to sit here and talk things over until you tell us one of yours."

Killough stood up and removed a small leather sack, like a deflated baseball, and holding it in one hand, he let it smack gently into the palm of his other. Heinlein could hear the buckshot rattling inside the casing. "Why don't we get down to brass tacks. You're a writer. You know where that expression came from?"

"No."

"My old man always said that the old soldiers had brass tacks in the soles of their boots. It meant that you were all the way down to the bottom of something."

"Oh."

"Course, my old man also said it when he was going to kick me because the last thing I was gonna see was gonna be the brass tacks in his shoes. You can use that in one of your stories someday if you want."

"I don't really write anymore."

"Oh." He took his coat off and began rolling up his sleeves. "That's too bad."

EPISODE 31

THE ISLE OF THE DEAD made Sara tingle. Barefoot, naked under her sleek red velvet robe, she shivered. It was hot enough in the attic temple for tiny droplets of sweat to appear between her breasts, nearly exposed by the gown's open neckline, but she was still cold.

She could envision the painting that had inspired the composition; a copy of it hung over Parsons's great bed. She had never asked him who painted it, or when; she only knew of it what she saw in it. An unsteady rowboat moving across waters still and black. The tiny vessel was making its way toward a small mountain that rose vertically from the dark sea. Rising from a small lagoon, the rowboat's destination, was a copse of great cypress trees like the ones shading her father's cemetery in San Gabriel. Carved out of the spires of the rocky mass on either side of the entrance to the lagoon were a pair of ancient mausoleums. An oarsman propelled the tiny boat forward, while a stoic figure shrouded in white stood in the center, behind a coffin destined for its final resting place amongst the ones beyond hope.

The ominous violins of the accompanying Rachmaninoff piece perfectly captured the vessel's doleful approach. As the rhythm gave way to a more elegiac, sweeping melody, the wood of the stairway began to creak. Her breath quickened in excitement. The Perfect Magician and Companion of the Holy Royal Arch of Enoch had arrived.

The windstorm that had disabled the mansion's electricity just before sunset had been taken as a sign that the forces of Horus had gathered and that it was time to respond with the next level of the Babalon Working. Sara looked around the room at the ones who had assembled in the Lodge, now draped in robes and illuminated by the red and black candles.

The Deacon—her sister, Helen—stood by the Font of Incense on the opposite side of the room, wreathed in the thick, heady ribbons of sandalwood smoke, slightly swaying as if intoxicated by their fumes. To her left and right stood each of the two Children, the recent initiates who had followed Sara up the stairs, friends of Parsons from JPL. Behind Sara stood the People, eight members of the Lodge who had achieved various levels. Only the Scribe was missing, now that the Perfect Priest had appeared, nude, at the head of the staircase.

He gave her a nod and she moved slowly toward the High Altar, an old oak table covered in black and orange fabric, and encircled by a thick gold-threaded rope. Taking one end of the cord, she walked around the altar three times until the coil fell to the floor and the symbol of the Agape Order was revealed. "The Kundalini serpent has been released," Sara, the Virgin, said.

"It is time for the lustration of the Perfect Priest," the Deacon intoned dreamily.

Sara lifted a small golden pitcher from the altar, and a candle, and approached Parsons. His naked body, nearly hairless, glistened in his own sweat. His eyes were dark and motionless; only the rising of his lance as she approached indicated his humanity. She poured a thin stream from the pitcher over his chest, whispering as she did, "I consecrate you with the oil of the earth." Then she circled him, letting drops of molten candlewax drip down his back, the skin quivering. "I consecrate you with the fire of the sun." She returned to stand in front of him. Leaning forward, she drew her tongue from his thorax to his lips, tasting the salt of his sweat and the oil. "I consecrate you with the waters of the ocean." Pursing her lips, she blew gently down the moist trail she had just left. "I consecrate you with the winds of the sky." She stepped close to him, placed her fingers around his warm lance, and moved her hand back and forth as slowly as she could, making the eleven strokes last, making Parsons groan. Then, before he could climax, the Deacon sent the Children forward to encircle him with his robe, while she stepped back, suppressing a smile at how easily she had rendered the Master helpless.

Helen gave her a dour glare. She knew Sara hadn't particularly wanted to fondle Jack's erection, that it was part of the ritual. Her sister had always been jealous of the power Sara exercised over men, particularly her willingness to use that power. Helen was jealous because she had never been their father's favorite. Sara was. In their quiet apartment, behind roadside markets, in the field behind their building, he had taught Sara about her power. She, Sara, not Helen, had been Father's favorite. Just as she was now Jack's favorite.

But the Scribe was the only one she truly wanted. Only Ron.

She moved to stand before the veil that hung behind the altar. On the table before her were an ornate, bejeweled dagger and a piece of parchment upon which had been written the Enochean symbols of the zodiac, which had been smeared with a variety of Parsons's fluids during the three previous sessions of the Working. The paper was held in place by a heavy plaster statue of Pan—one of Parsons's proudest possessions. He claimed that the Great Beast, Crowley himself, had given it to him when they first met in London.

She began her next part: "I charge you earnestly to come before me in a single robe. I who am all pleasure and purple and drunkenness of the innermost sense desire you. Put on the wings, and arouse the coiled kundalini within you. I am the blue-lidded daughter of Sunset. I am the naked brilliance of the voluptuous night sky."

Parsons crossed the floor, his lance protruding awkwardly beneath his robe. When he reached her side, it was her turn to remove her gown. She let it fall to the floor, standing naked before the assemblage. The delicious thrill of the power over their attention made her shiver. Proudly, she lifted her chin, defying them to be as bold as she was.

"Beautiful art thou, O Babalon," Parsons began, speaking to the room as well as to her. "For you have given yourself to everything that lives and your weakness has subdued their strengths. For in that union, they understood. Therefore you are named Understanding. O Babalon, Lady of the Night."

She bowed her head to him, then turned and slipped behind the veil.

"We call to the will of our Scribe across the astral plane while his body traverses the oceans of this material dimension. We know he is here with us tonight as we reach the end of our Congress. I know he invokes the eight Working in our absence."

Peeking through the veil, she watched as Parsons lifted the dagger and plunged it through the parchment. Then he raised the dagger, with the impaled piece of paper, to the candle, setting the edge on fire. The parchment burned evenly, turning to a blackened crisp that landed on a golden plate. Next, he picked up the statue of Pan. He caressed it for a moment, fondly. Then he raised it over his head, and without hesitating a moment longer, dashed it upon the floor in front of the altar. Pieces of the god scattered across the floor and a small cloud of dust drifted through the room.

She turned to sneak a glance at Helen. Her sister hated her. Jack had divorced her for Sara when she was only sixteen years old. And yet Helen had been unable to leave the Parsonage, and Jack's orbit. It didn't even bother Sara if Jack occasionally wound up in Helen's bed again. She enjoyed having Ron in hers more, and she'd made that clear. It was the way of true will. Parsons appeared above it all.

Though she wasn't sure if, right before Ron left, the Perfect Priest hadn't shown some signs of mortal jealousy toward his Scribe. It had come as a surprise when he asked her to represent the Virgin in the Babalon Working, and she was not at all comfortable with the tone in his voice—it was almost as if he were ordering her or there would be repercussions. It made her recall her father's threats, the ones she had almost forgotten.

The spectral tune came to an end, and the record needle bounced in the exit groove over and over until one of the People called out, "Wait a minute!" and went to start the song over again. Meanwhile, the smell of smoke from the parchment embers grew thicker than the incense.

She sighed. Her least favorite part of the Gnostic Mass was approaching. As much as she enjoyed some aspects of playing the Virgin, there were others she had long grown weary of. As she had been applying her makeup earlier and donning her robe, the thought played through her mind that perhaps she might convince Ron to set up a new home, just the two of them. She'd even thought of convincing him to ask her to marry him.

Parsons waited for the music to renew the mood before he began his recitation. "You are Venus, the love and light of earth. The wealth of kisses, the delight of tears, the barren pleasures never born. You are the shrine at which I desire. Devour me with your intolerable fire."

It was her turn. "I am the Grail and the glory now," she said, in a disinterested, rote tone. "I am the flame and fuel of your heart. I am the star upon thy brow. I am the queen. I am the ocean of love that will swallow you. Life, death, love, hatred, light, darkness, return to me."

He cleared his throat with an insincere cough.

She had to say the invocation twice. "To me!" she dutifully commanded. Then she lowered herself to her knees.

The veil parted and the Perfect Priest slid his lance through until it hovered before her face. She looked at it for a long moment.

He cleared his throat again, expectantly.

Sara couldn't stop herself from doing what happened next. She raised her hand and flicked at the lance with her finger, smiling as he grunted. Then she moistened her lips. This was how the magick happened, after all.

She heard someone cough. The smell of smoke was growing even stronger.

"Jack?" a voice called out.

"Not now," he said, his lance waggling in syncopation with his voice.

"Jack!" Helen this time.

The lance withdrew. "What?"

"The Lodge is on fire!"

Sara poked her head through the veil. One of the parchment embers had apparently lodged in the silk bunting that hid the attic ribs and orange flames were beginning to crawl up the fabric. Cries broke out amongst the People. Robes fell to the floor like fall leaves, revealing a variety of street clothes, from suits to dresses.

"Dammit!" Parsons cried.

A hand reached through the veil and grabbed her wrist. "Get up, whore!" her sister snarled at her.

"Virgin," she replied proudly, allowing her sister to pull her to her feet.

Helen thrust the robe at her as a piece of burning cloth fell upon the veil, igniting it. "Look"—she pointed toward Parsons's back as he descended the stairs—"there goes our Perfect Priest. Leaving the whores and virgins to fend for themselves."

By then, Sara had tied the sash around the gown and followed her sister down the stairs. She could hear people yelling from the first floor. Sara paused and closed the door behind her. It could at least delay the spread of the fire.

The people of the Parsonage had gathered on the lawn as Sara and Helen, holding hands, emerged from the building. Flames leaped from the windows of the attic, holes began to yawn through the roofing tiles. In the distance she could hear the sirens of Pasadena's bravest.

Parsons took her hand. "This is a sign that Horus wants to defeat us," he said solemnly. "The Scribe is in great danger. We need to finish the sanctification of our ritual. We need to make ourselves clear."

A breath of wind tossed her hair, and she pulled her hand back from Jack to brush it from her eyes. "You know, Jack," she said, drawing the sash tightly around her waist, "I'm actually feeling perfectly clear."

"But what about the Goddess?"

At that moment, the roof over the Lodge collapsed in a burst of sparks and flames.

"I think I'll be all right," she replied.

EPISODE 32

THREE DAYS TO run down the North Pacific line to the Hawaiian Islands, and the sky had stayed cloudy and low the whole way. At least when the waters turned from slate gray-green to a deep creamy blue he knew his journey was reaching its destination.

Hubbard had spent most of the time in his bunk, blinded by the headaches the mine blast had brought on. It wouldn't have surprised him one bit to discover he had a concussion. It would serve them right, Heinlein and all of them, if he died of brain damage out here, miles from any-where, and their precious case went undiscovered.

When he'd been able to rouse himself to any kind of action (even heading to mess felt like a huge effort), he'd paged through the religious materials the chaplain had blessed him with. His family never had much use for religion, per se, but his mother had always said that a church was the quickest way to be welcomed into a new community. So, as they fol-lowed his father from post to post, they'd sung the hymns with Luther-ans and Methodists and eaten the sacred bread of Catholics and Mor-mons. Mother's tactic had been to visit the particular church in their new location a couple of times in order to make friends. Then, once she had ingratiated herself into sewing circles and coffee klatches, their Sunday mornings—or in the case of the Seventh-Day Adventists of Columbus, Ohio, Saturday nights—were theirs again to do with as they pleased. Which usually had more to do with fishing than the Gospels.

As he grew older he came to feel that his exposure to this patchwork of Sunday School spirituality left him like a speaker of many languages with no country to call his own. For instance, even though he was now in his thirties, he'd never been able to shake a nun's description of a sin as a black stain on the heart, despite the fact that he now knew she had only been conveying a potent metaphor for guilt. He still found himself wor-rying how dark his organ had become. At times like these he would grow angry with his mother for having placed him in situations where it was stressed how much mortal peril his soul was in without ever letting him stick around long enough to learn how to save it.

He'd tried to read the Bible before, but found it hard going after the adventures of Moses. He found it hard to see how lessons learned by desert shepherds had much relevance to a species that was about to launch itself toward the heavens. He flipped through the other books with waning interest, but all he came away with was an agreement that maybe the Buddhists had it right. The contemplation of nothingness could lead to exalted states. That's what these books were to him—pages of nothingness. It wasn't the information they contained that led a pil-grim to a higher state, it was the act of contemplation itself. The only book which seemed worth keeping was the book on general semantics that the Seabee had given him.

Jack Parsons understood the innate joke in religions. That's why he took so much pleasure in debasing and subverting them. But Parsons, and even Crowley, weren't so much revolutionaries as they were re-actionaries; drawing on ancient, alternative rituals instead of creating something new in response to the world around them. What place was there going to be for a god (or devil) created in the time of shepherds, goatherds, warriors, and peasants who were afraid of the change of sea-sons, and plagues, and what lay over the horizon, when all those things could be explained away now? And though the angels may have been a glory to see, they did not shake their wings as a Mustang did. What mysteries remained that science was not on the verge of answering? If heaven lay beyond the clouds, would rocketmen discover it? Who would give a crap what followed death if death itself could be conquered by ge-netic medicine in a few years? All people wanted was to survive here and now as free of pain and guilt as possible, which would in turn allow them to achieve as much of their dreams as they could imagine. That's what churches really sold.

An end to their fears.

Usually he slept like a baby on ships, but he'd had no peace on this one. Sara came to him again and again, but with fire in her hair. She grew progressively more horrifying with each visit, sometimes appearing as if from beyond the grave, sometimes passionately alive, always hovering above him out of reach. Each manifestation more real and horrifying every night. Whether she aroused his desire or his dread, he'd awaken drenched in sweat, heart pounding as if he'd been running. He couldn't understand what she was angry about, but he wondered if she was okay. Parsons hadn't seemed particularly upset that Hubbard had been with her, but Parsons could be a tough man to get a bead on.

The Babalon Working. How serious was he that its occult magick could actually work? Where did the goofiness end for Parsons? In the past the rituals had been kind of fun and perverse parties, usually in-volving a lot of wine and some women. But Hubbard had never actually seen anything that even resembled something inexplicably supernatural. Parsons claimed nevertheless that things had happened, that they had introduced change in the world. But maybe the effect of the rituals on Parsons was more subtle and internal. Was it possible that Parsons believed he'd changed the world because he'd succeeded in changing his perception of it?

Hubbard disembarked at Pearl Harbor, almost too distracted by the thoughts whirling around his head and exhausted by the nightly visitations to appreciate the lush sawgrass and sea-salt–scented fragrances of the air. The other sailors hit the dock with whoops and cheers. Hubbard moved slowly and stiffly, as if compelled to advance by rusty mechanical gears set in motion long ago. There was no concern anymore about what would happen next. A communications officer was waiting for him at the bottom of the gangplank with orders and travel arrangements; the shadow of Heinlein's hand stretching far over the ocean, tightening the snare Hubbard was trapped in.

At the airfield the pilot asked him if there was anything he could leave behind to lighten the load. Without a word, he dropped the duffel full of heavy weather gear and the copies of the Bible, the Koran, the Torah, and the Book of Mormon. Let some other traveler find spiritual and material warmth. The Korzybski he kept. He was led to the C-46, hollowed out and filled with cargo, except for a few empty passenger chairs. Nearly exhausted, he fell into the hard seat by the window.

A few minutes later, as the pilot fired up the engine, the door opened to admit one more passenger. A thin, handsome man wearing spectacles clambered aboard and dropped into the seat next to him.

"Gotta love being in the belly of the whale," he said, as he fastened his harness. The man was dressed as a civilian, in khakis, cotton shirt, and tie. He was lighting a cigarette even as the rattling *clink* of his belt buckling still hung in the air.

"What?"

"The whale. It's what the crews call these Commandos. Because they're big and fat. But they can haul anything, fly over anything, land anywhere, and take a real pounding." He spoke confidently fast, in the East Coast manner, as if his good education were a foregone conclusion. Hubbard passed on the cigarette offered in friendship.

The plane began what seemed to Hubbard an uncertain journey down the short runway. The blue Hawaiian waters beckoned invitingly at the rapidly nearing tarmac's edge.

"I'm Hugh Cave." The man tucked the cigarette between his lips and shook Hubbard's hand, as if he were accustomed to riding out the rumbling, bouncing, lurching acceleration of the whale on a daily basis.

"I'm . . ." The whale took an ungainly bounce to the left but continued moving forward.

"You're Hubbard, right?" Cave had to shout over the engines. It was almost as if their roar were being channeled into the hollow interior.

"How'd . . ."

"I'm a friend of John Campbell's." The man grinned, the cigarette clenched between his teeth.

The earth disappeared and sparkling ocean raced along mere feet from Hubbard's porthole.

"Relax," Cave shouted. "These things only go down when they're shot." As if on cue, the plane at last began to climb skyward, trading one shade of blue for another.

"I used to hate flying, too. But psychiatry really helped me out there. You should try it sometime. I know a great analyst back in the States."

"You're a writer?" Hubbard sputtered, desperately trying to place the name.

Cave shook his head. "Used to be. Now I'm a reporter." He grinned. "Just finished a book about the PT boat crews at Guadalcanal."

"A real book?"

"Uh-huh. Beginning, middle, and end. The whole package. Even got a few facts in there. Now I'm working on one about the pilots who are plowing the fields out here. You know, I saw you give a talk at the Knickerbocker Hotel years ago. Something about world domination."

"When I was president of the Writers Guild?"

"Were you?"

"I was."

"That must have been it, then."

Hubbard could see Oahu receding rapidly, other islands appearing like vast blots in the distance.

"We're going to Tonga?" Cave had to shout in Hubbard's ear to be heard.

"I can't tell you that."

"That's the only place this whale flies. The islands are still under the protection of the British Empire. We fly in some supplies every week for the Brits, and they release our hospitalized soldiers and sailors who've recovered enough for a trip back to American soil." With a nod of his head he indicated stacks of boxes behind them. It was now apparent that what Hubbard had assumed were shelves were, in fact, jury-rigged bunks fastened to the hull of the plane. "I'd hate to have to come back in this thing with a massive, bloody head wound," Cave expounded.

"The Eel!" Hubbard cried suddenly. "Justin Case!"

Cave smiled slyly. "I figured you'd put it all together sooner or later."

"He was supposed to be the next big thing. Then the war started and it put the mag, and The Eel, out of business. And put me in the ass-end of the world."

Hubbard had a distinct recollection of him now, from his time back in New York. Scrawny, withdrawn, nervous tics, not at all like the confident, boisterous fellow chatting amicably with him. War had the strangest effect on people.

"What do you know about Tonga?" Cave asked.

"It's in the middle of nowhere. And I'm betting I can't get a martini there."

"It's definitely in the middle of nowhere. But with all the Brits, you'll find plenty of gin for your martini. No olives, though. Or vermouth. But the best gin I've ever had."

"That's something."

"Tonga's an interesting place. Lots of little islands, mostly volcanic. The Tongans have a monarchy, a king right now, and unlike Hawaii or the other Polynesian islands, their monarchy has never been overthrown or destroyed by the imperialists. You're not wandering into a lost world of primitives here. The missionaries have been out here for generations now so you'll probably bump into Jesus more than you will old Tangaloa Tufunga, their original God."

"No scalping or headhunting?"

"Not anymore. Pretty civilized. It's a very formal society, so watch your manners, and you can never say please or thank you too much."

"Okay."

From the plane's cruising altitude Hubbard could see the long V wakes of ships heading to and fro cutting into the surface of the earth. He knew that they were behind the protective curve of the Allied shield, but nevertheless he hoped that none of those ships below were Jap aircraft carriers preparing to throw Zeros at their exposed belly.

After a while longer, Cave stopped talking and Hubbard fell asleep. He awoke sometime during the night. The plane was refueling on a piece of rock called Kanton Island. The troops there had barely any right to call themselves American. They wore only cutoff shorts and staggered out of their tent-lounge completely drunk, more prepared to fight than help. It appeared to be some kind of long-standing ritual with their hosts and the pilots, as they fired several good-natured shots over the heads of the island drunks. Once the sentries had returned to their revels, the pilots handled their own refueling chores. Then they were airborne again, though Cave recommended that Hubbard keep his feet off the floor until they were at least a thousand feet in the air in case the ground crew fired off a few drunken shots that might penetrate the hull.

Sometime midmorning they landed again, this time on the gorgeous American Samoa. Hubbard's back ached and his hips popped loudly with each step. They were fed some roast chicken with mangoes and papayas from what appeared to be a perpetual grill that cooked all day and all night by the runway.

After dark, the plane touched down on a strip of smooth dirt lined on either side by torches.

"Welcome to Nuku'alofa," Cave grunted, the trip having taken its toll on him as well. "The capital of the Kingdom of Tonga."

"What day is it?"

"It's Thursday night."

"All right. Now what?" Hubbard was grateful to feel the ground beneath his feet. "The way this trip is going, I half-expected Campbell to meet us here personally."

"The barracks are this way." The pilot pointed out the tin-covered half-shell buildings ubiquitous to the U.S. military's presence across the South Pacific. They trudged along behind, and once they had been checked in, Hubbard stumbled to an empty cot. In spite of having slept on the plane, he was exhausted and fell fast asleep.

Sara, surrounded in flames, kept him from resting. He woke up feeling as if the plane had landed on his brain, staggered out of bed and into a shower, then shuffled across the field toward the mess hall.

Cave handed him a plate of the Army special, the shit-on-a-shingle biscuits and gravy dish served for breakfast in every branch of the armed forces. He made himself eat as much as he could, but it was the Samoan coffee that really helped him wake up. Deep, rich, and smoky, he felt it was the first decent thing he'd come in contact with in ages. "This almost restores my faith," he sighed.

"In what?"

He shrugged and had another sip. "Anything."

Cave stirred some sugar into his cup. "You've been playing your hand real close to your vest," he said, watching the milk whirlpool swirling, "which is good, I guess, and what you have to do. But now that we're out here, I was hoping you could tell me a little something so I can help you out."

"I can't really tell you anything."

"How can I help you, then?"

"I don't know. I guess I need to meet someone who knows a little bit about Tonga history."

"How far back?"

"Turn of the century?"

"Which century? This one? That's nothing. I was afraid you might be looking for something before they switched from an oral tradition and began writing stuff down. And since that was about three hundred years ago, I guess we have nothing to worry about."

"Okay, so where do we start?"

"Let's head to school."

They borrowed a car from the motor pool and drove through some lush mountainous jungle that circled the outskirts of what could be called a city, though no building rose higher than two stories. Then in about twenty minutes, after driving through several idyllic villages, they passed a stone lion perched atop a gatepost that guarded a long, low building which a red and white sign identified as TONGA COLLEGE. Inside, Cave asked for the librarian. They were directed to a small library, and Mr. Tu'amelie Faaitu'a.

"Do they speak English?" Hubbard asked.

"Probably better than you," Cave replied.

Mr. Faaitu'a was a thickset Polynesian with skin the color and gloss of fine leather. He wore a Western-style buttondown shirt and a long white sarong. "May I help you, gentlemen?" His accent combined the relaxed rolling tones of all island men along the Pacific rim with the authoritative snap of British supremacy. Hubbard was happy not to have had this man for one of his teachers.

Cave turned to Hubbard. "It's your show."

"I was wondering if you had any information about the Crocker Eclipse Expedition of 1908? They may have left something behind that could be important to us now."

"Really?" Cave asked. "They sent you halfway around the world to ask about some stargazers?"

Hubbard shook his head at Cave. "It's as good a starting point as any. Do you have any records?"

"Well," Mr. Faaitu'a replied, "I doubt if the expedition made a big enough impression on anyone for it to be recorded, though I'll check the island newspaper."

"Oh." Hubbard knew he sounded disappointed.

"But, it was only thirty-five years ago. There will be people around who were alive. I'll inquire as to whether anyone recalls this event. If anyone visited this island and left something here, I'm sure somebody knows about it. Though as there are one hundred sixty-nine islands spread out over five hundred square miles in the kingdom, it can take a while to get the word out."

Hubbard stared out the window. Down the hill and off in the distance he could see the cobalt blue of the ocean. He was in a far corner of the world, and one of the least important people in it. Whatever his destiny was, he wouldn't find it out here. "So be it," he sighed. "Take as long as you need. I've got nowhere else to be."

"Mr. Hubbard," Mr. Faaitu'a said with a laugh, "everyone in these islands is related to everyone else. And we do have radio. It should only take a few hours."

EPISODE 33

ISAAC PACED UP and down the hallway for a long time. Every now and then someone who lived on the floor would enter the corridor, either from the elevators or the staircase heading toward their apartment, or on their way out to enjoy the morning air. When these people appeared, Isaac would stop his circular stroll and studiously examine a light bulb as if he were an electrician in the middle of an investigation of paramount importance to the survival of the building. Finally, as if compelled by a surge of positronic energy, he lurched forward and knocked rapidly on the door of Apartment 17D. When the elderly woman who opened the door gave him a stern glare he tried to ignore it and said, "Hello, Mary. I'd like to speak to my wife."

She glared at him with a mother's hatred. "I don't think she wants to see you."

"I'd like to talk with Gertrude Asimov."

She sucked air through her teeth. "I'll see if she's here," his mother-in-law said, then shut the door on him.

"Tell her I'm in a hurry," he told the oak panel. He heard some murmuring but couldn't tell how far from the door it was and couldn't distinguish any words. He put his ear to the door just as it opened again, causing him to stumble a few steps into the Blugermans' home.

Even though the Slope was only a few miles away, Isaac had spent very little time in the Heights, what Brooklyners called downtown. It was an even more alien world to him than Manhattan had been, at least until he started dating Gertie. She lived with her parents and her brother in a modern apartment building in the area known as the Fruit District because their street, Pineapple, ran parallel to Orange and Cranberry. The slope of the streets toward the East River and the enclavelike nature of the area always confused Isaac and he managed to get lost every time. Even today, when he was on a mission and time was of the essence, he'd managed to get Montague and Joralemon confused and turned at the wrong time.

Now, standing in the living room, he looked from Mary, still stern, to nod at an exasperated Henry sitting in his favorite chair by the radio, then saw Gertie at the door to her bedroom. In a light cotton skirt paired with a white blouse, and with her hair was down, she looked more girlish than he had seen her look in a while.

"Hi," he said.

She leaned against the edge of the door, rocking it gently, as if unsure which side of it he was going to be on when she closed it. "Hi," she replied. "It's early."

"I, uh"—he looked at his watch—"I . . ."

"You came here and the first thing you do is check the time?"

"Daddy, please."

"I'm sorry. I wanted to see you."

Gertie smiled. "You came all this way to see me."

He nodded. "Can I talk with you? Please?"

She swayed gently against the door for a moment or two longer, then she said, finally, "Okay. Let's go for a walk."

He followed her out of the apartment and past the elevators to the stairs, which surprised him. Her parents lived on the twelfth floor and it was such a humid day, he didn't relish the thought of walking down all those flights. Instead, Gertie led him up two flights, and though he was sweating by the time she opened the door to the roof, he was happy they'd arrived so quickly at a place they could talk.

"This is some view." He whistled. From here he could see the Statue of Liberty all the way across the harbor, all of lower Manhattan, even into the cars streaming over the Brooklyn Bridge. The lights on the tips of the ripples caused by crisscrossing wakes of watercraft big and small blinked in and out of existence like generations of stars born, then burning out in a cosmic instant.

"I never brought you up here?" she asked, twirling a lock of hair around her finger.

"No."

"Mm," she said quietly, as if to herself. "Must have been someone else."

"Is it beautiful at night?"

"It is. It's wonderful. On some nights I could come up here and read by the light of the city. Didn't even need a candle. On the Fourth of July, you can see fireworks going off all up and down the river and across Brooklyn. One day, it was in springtime, my daddy brought us up here and we stood and watched the *Hindenburg* come in from uptown there, circle around the Empire State Building, then drift slowly away over there," she pointed to the far shores of New Jersey. "I remember thinking that the swastika on its fin was so big and scary, and I couldn't believe they let someone fly that here. But Daddy said it was a free country and we weren't at war with them, yet, so they could come and go as they pleased, as long as they paid their landing fees. It was only a little while later that same day that way down there and faraway we could see the smoke from the fire where it crashed. It was like a little black smudge on the horizon. I asked Daddy if that meant we were at war with them now. He said, 'Soon.' I didn't know what it would mean. I didn't know that it would mean that Johnny would go away and I would have to move, and everything would change."

"I wish you'd brought me up here before. I would have liked to have known about this."

"Well, everything was going so fast. I mean, we met and then we were married six months later, and then we had to move. We barely knew each other, Isaac. We still barely know each other. And my poor parents! Both their children gone practically overnight."

"We're not that far away. And as soon as the war is over, we'll come back here. Across the river, like we used to talk about, or here in Brooklyn if you want. We can live in this building if you want."

"I don't know what I want right now, Isaac. Why don't you tell me what you want? Because I'm not sure I know. I know you wanted to marry me, and that's sweet. But what do you want out of our marriage?"

"Me?" His voice cracked a little. "I don't know. I never really thought about it."

"That's a problem, isn't it?"

He thought about it for a moment while he watched the wind gently rearrange the hair around her face. "I guess I just want you to be there, is all."

"I've been there the whole time, Isaac. And you never seem to notice. It's like I'm a ghost."

"There's no scientific evidence for ghosts."

"Restrain your brain, will you? At least for the purposes of this discussion. Even if you don't like to use them, every so often I find a metaphor useful."

"Sorry. A writer should be able to accurately describe something, not lean on the crutch of likening it to something else."

"Isaac."

"Sorry." He focused on the Staten Island Ferry making its slow passage across the harbor for a quick ten count as Sprague had suggested. When he looked back at her, he found he was able to concentrate completely on her. "Go on."

"I'm waiting for you."

"Oh. What do I want for our marriage? I want to be able to do things together like other couples do, like have dinner and go to movies."

"And do those other couples have magical elves that come and handle all the shopping and the cleaning and the laundry so that they can have dinner and go to movies? And don't say there are no such things as magic or elves."

"I recognize your hypothesis," he replied. Sprague would be pleased with him—he was listening. "I know that you do all those things."

"But do you appreciate it? Because Lord knows you never say anything about it to me. Maybe your mother never expected a thank-you, but I am not your mother. Before we got married I helped my mother and father do everything, but no one just expected me to, like I was an employee or something."

"But I have to go to work and write."

"So it sounds like you need a maid."

"That's not what I meant to say."

"Oh really?"

"No. What I meant to say is that while I'm working so hard, I'm happy to know that you're taking care of me."

"Well, that's nice for you, isn't it?"

"Yes. I mean no." He struggled to count to ten again, forgetting what came after seven. "I don't know. Remember how scared you were of that swastika on the *Hindenburg*?"

"Yes?"

He pointed east, toward Long Island. "Imagine a hundred swastikas like that buzzing toward us. Only instead of being on harmless, floating zeppelins, they're on the wings of the largest bomber plane you've ever seen. A plane so large that it's been able to fly from Berlin to America. Imagine that the bombs begin to fall, out there, in Astoria, then move closer and closer, then sweep across the river and over Manhattan."

"Oh my God, Isaac."

"It's called the super-bomber, and it's very real, and it's a huge secret. You tell me I don't talk enough about what I do? There, I've told you a big one. It's one of the things we're trying to stop."

"I have to tell Mom and Dad. They'll have to come with us to Philadelphia."

Isaac kept a firm grip on her arm as she tried to pull away. "No! You can't say a word to anyone, not even them. They're perfectly safe for the time being. If I heard one word that they were in immediate danger, don't you think I'd get them, and my own parents, out of it?"

"Are you sure my parents are safe?"

"Absolutely. Heinlein and de Camp and I, that's what we're going to make sure of."

She seemed to relax. "Thank you for telling me that. I know it was hard for you to talk about it. I have something to tell you, too. Something that's been hard for me to talk about."

"What?"

"You know what it is."

"I do?"

Gertie's cheeks pinkened, but it was more a flush of passion than a blush of awkwardness. "Yes," she dropped her voice to a whisper, "you know what I mean."

"Aw, Jeez! I don't want to talk about this! Not here in the open."

"It's the quietest place I know." She took several steps toward him. "No one in the world can hear us up here."

He made it to two this time, but then she kissed him.

"I want it to be like it is in the movies," she said, unbuttoning her blouse. "I want it to be like it is in the pulps."

Her bra was black and trimmed with lace. She'd never worn anything like it before. Gertie leaned against his chest, pressing her breasts against him—the lingerie kept them firm and high. "Rip my dress," she whispered hoarsely. "Rip it!"

He reached down urgently and grabbed the hem of her skirt, lifting it and twisting it—the fabric parting with unexpected ease. He was strong, a hero, a monster. The stockings were glossy and black, the garters tight against her hot skin, the panties satin. Her fingers fumbled clumsily with his zipper until he grabbed her wrist. She gasped as he pulled her hand away. "I'll do it," he told her, his voice hoarse.

She lifted one of her legs and wrapped it around his hip. "Pull my hair."

His hands worked their way into the tangle and pulled back, exposing her neck, for his hungry mouth.

"You've wanted me this way," she moaned.

"Yes!" he grunted, sliding into her.

He was on top of the world. Invincible. Gertie was making sounds he'd never heard her make before. It only made him more excited. As his climax came, her body shuddered with a spasm as well, and a whimper of utter animal happiness escaped her throat. Their trembling knees unable to support them, they collapsed in each other's arms to the tar-paper surface, already turning from warm to hot beneath the summer sun.

After some time, he caught his breath again. "I want you to come home."

"I will."

"Things will be different."

"I know."

"Are you checking your watch again? Yes."

"Your mission?"

"That's right." He tucked himself away and zipped up, then stood. Gertie looked appealingly disheveled, curled up in the shadow of the stairway access. She gazed at him through heavily lidded eyes. He offered her a hand.

"Come back for me."

"I'll be back by thirteen hundred hours."

"Twelve hundred." She smoothed out her clothes, swept dirt out of her hair, hid the tear. Then she pressed her mouth against his again, hard, her tongue seeking out his. "I'll come home," she said. "Now go save the world."

He ran down a flight of stairs to the nearest floor where he could catch an elevator. As he waited for it, he listened for the door to the roof to slam shut again, but the elevator arrived, he got on, and he never heard her leave.

Outside, he walked swiftly uphill, knowing that even if he was unsure about his direction, up and away from the water was the right way to go. As he ran out of breath, a cab appeared out of nowhere like an answer to a prayer. Isaac jumped into the street to hail it, waving both arms furiously until it stopped.

"Brooklyn Navy Yard," he gasped, before the driver could even ask.

"Honestly, pal, that's only a few blocks from here. I could get a better fare if you'd walk!"

"Just drive." Isaac slammed the door and sank into the backseat.

His pass was at the ready as he entered the compound, a site so small when compared to Philadelphia's that he hesitated to call it a Navy Yard. "I'm looking for Warehouse Seven?" he asked the sentry, who, in a display of helpfulness rare in his kind, pointed out the direction. The heat was turning the pavement into a grill as he walked past the buildings. Of course the warehouse he was looking for was at the far end of the row.

Arriving, he began to show successive guards, each more fearsome and more important-looking than the last, the papers that Heinlein had shoved upon him. Finally, he was ushered into the central room where a large wooden box, about three feet wide and high but as long as a small car, sat all by itself in the middle of the empty space.

"There it is," said the final guard. "It's all yours."

"Wait a minute." Isaac rushed to stop the man before he could leave the room. "I'm supposed to be meeting people here. Robert Heinlein."

"You could be meeting Bob Hope for all I care," the guard said. "All I know is you got the papers that say I gotta let you take it, which means my work here is done."

In spite of further entreaties, the man refused to stop until he had collected all the other members of his unit and reached the outside of the building. And there they left Isaac, without so much as a goodbye.

Where was Heinlein?

Isaac spun around several times. There was no one he recognized, nothing this far down from the rest of the yard but one ship that looked like every other ship to him, at dock. Isaac looked up and down the street, then at his watch, wondering if he had misread the time somehow. He thought about his orders. Bob said Isaac was to examine some mysterious cargo before he arrived. But he hadn't exactly said how he was getting here. Realization came at him like the inspiration for a story, beginning with a tingle, then a rush of electricity through his body. He took several compulsive steps forward, then began to run along the dock, from ship to ship. At last, he saw what he was looking for.

"Hey! Hey there!" he cried. "Is this the *DE-173*?"

"Nah," he heard a loud voice reply, and his heart sank. "This here's the USS *Eldridge*."

Isaac squinted at the head that poked itself over the railing.

"That's what they'll call it once she gets her commission," Olson said with a sardonic grin. Other faces of sailors that Isaac recognized appeared at his side.

"Oh, thank God!" Isaac said. "Hey! Where's Bob? Where's Bob Heinlein?"

"Don't know." Olson shrugged. "He never showed up this morning. But we had our orders from him, so here we are. So now what?"

Isaac scratched his head and looked past the Navy Yard. Bob was supposed to be here, in charge, and he was only supposed to provide assistance if needed. Backup. That's what he was now, he guessed. He wondered if Gertie was still on the roof and if she could see him from there.

"What are we doing, kid?" Olson asked.

He turned his back on the Brooklyn skyline. "What else did his orders say?"

"We're picking up a package here and delivering it to the Naval Station in Newport News, Virginia. Then we pick up another package there and bring it back to Philadelphia."

"How long from here to Virginia?"

"About six hours if we really turn on the rockets and haul ass."

"Then let's turn on the rockets and haul ass."

"Aye-aye," the petty officer responded, with a salute that surprised Isaac as much as himself.

EPISODE 34

"WHAT TIME IS it?" Heinlein asked. "I'm guessing it's about noon?"

"It's just past ten." Killough sighed, pressing the palms of his hands hard into his eyes. Riley had slipped out some time ago to go find a diner. The blackjack lay upon the desk, untouched since it had been placed there hours ago.

"Let me get this straight. You went to Lyman Binch to investigate whether or not it was possible that the old nutjob, Tesla, might actually have created a free energy source that the Nazis are interested in. And Albert Einstein is helping you out. So that's what you're working on?"

"Well, Einstein wasn't exactly on board. But in general you've got it. You want me to go through it again?"

"No. No. There's no need for that. I think I've got it. I don't need to hear it again."

"Then I don't see what the problem is. Why don't you let me go?"

"Oh, there are so many problems with this that I don't know where to start. The first one being, what does this have to do with Cleve Cartmill?"

"Nothing. Like I've said, repeatedly."

"And when you were 'exploring' the secret tunnel under the Empire State Building, was Isaac Asimov carrying secret information passed along to him by either his Communist friends in the Futurians organization or sympathizers within Columbia University? Secret information about a super-bomb?"

"That's a lot of secrets."

Killough picked up the blackjack. "God, I really want to use this."

"Won't change the facts."

"Might make me feel a whole lot better." He rapped it against the desk. "Why was Lafayette Hubbard visiting Cleve Cartmill in California?"

"I wish I knew." He really wished he did. Even he had to wonder if there was something to Killough and Dugan's questions. If it turned out that Hubbard had passed along real Wardenclyffe information to Cartmill for another story, the stuff that he was risking torture to keep from these guys, Heinlein would strap him into the electric chair himself and throw the switch. And if it turned up in next month's *Amazing Stories*, he'd burn down Street & Smith while he was at it. With Campbell inside. He'd spent the night telling these guys just enough to blur the line between what they knew and what they didn't. But the Tesla journal, and Hubbard's real mission, and Menlo Park? That was his. He'd earned it. And he was going to protect it.

"Is John Campbell a Communist?"

"No. John Campbell is a catalyst."

"A what?"

"A catalyst. He provides a spark of creativity, that special idea, that makes a story good enough to publish. All he cares about is the story. Science fiction is it. Politics, religion? Forget about him giving a damn unless they're set in the future or on an alien world. He's not trying to change the world in any way that you can understand. But he is trying to change it."

"What do you mean?"

"He wants the future to come true. Rockets to the stars, the evolution of man toward higher states, opening of other dimensions, the whole cheesesteak of tomorrow. But I promise you, he would be happiest if there were American flags on those rocket ships and if English were spoken by our evolved selves in other planes. So there's no way in hell he'd be printing any kind of stolen information, let alone buying it, or heading up some kind of network of science fiction spies. That's what I've been trying to tell you all night. Now I wish to God you'd let me go."

"Not a chance."

The door behind him opened and he twisted around in his chair. Dugan was carefully balancing cups of coffee and a sack of doughnuts.

"I like jelly," Heinlein said, as the phone began to ring.

"Now we'll see if they'll let me beat you," Killough said, picking up the receiver. "Hello?"

"Ask them if we have to let him live at all?" Dugan placed the grease-stained sack on the desk. The agent looked up at his partner to see if his joke could get an acknowledgment. As he did, Killough jerked ramrod straight, as if the voice on the phone were Franklin Roosevelt's. "Who is it?" Dugan asked with concern.

Killough didn't respond, his face frozen in an expression of shock. The phone was clenched in his fist, stuck to the right side of his head. As Heinlein watched, a wispy curl of smoke, almost imperceptible, twirled up away from his head.

"Don't touch him!" Heinlein shouted, but Dugan was already leaping across the desk to get to Killough. He grabbed the man's hand, and his body went instantly rigid, a grunt escaping him as if great pressure had suddenly been exerted on his diaphragm.

Helpless, Heinlein called for help, but the walls were thick, the building nearly deserted, and no one answered. He tried rising in his chair and moving forward to dislodge Dugan from Killough with a kick, but although he could crabwalk close, he couldn't quite make contact.

Killough's fingers suddenly flew open and the receiver fell to the floor with a thud, emitting nothing more than a steady busy signal. Like a pair of balloons losing air, the two men sagged limply, one in his chair, the other sprawled across the desk. The aroma of charred flesh, like acrid pork, hung in the air. The two men were dead. As if to put a period on the point, Dugan slid free of Killough, dropped off the desk, and crumpled to the ground at Heinlein's feet.

The phone went silent. Without hesitating, Heinlein reached into Dugan's vest pocket and dug out the handcuff keys. In a moment, he was up and rubbing his freed wrist. He looked down at the two men. The room was painfully silent, like a funeral parlor after the mourners have left for the grave site to await the coffin. So when he heard a voice, he jumped.

"Are you there?" the strange voice asked again.

Heinlein realized it was coming from the telephone.

"Are you still there?"

He knelt down in front of the phone, afraid to touch it. "Yes," he whispered.

"You should leave right away." The voice sounded like hundreds of bees buzzing together in a single wave. It was barely distinguishable as human.

"But what about the police? I have to call them."

"Don't worry about the police. You should leave. Now."

Heinlein let the door close behind him and walked as casually as he could down the hall, bursting into a sprint only once he reached the staircase. He continued his run for many blocks, turning randomly every few intersections in order to throw off any followers.

He was in a working-class section of the city just to the east of the river. Fishtown, he guessed. It took him a while but he finally managed to flag down a cab and before long he was pulling up at the gate to the Navy Yard, though at this point, so late in the game, he wondered if it was even worth it. He walked slowly through the facility, disappointed in himself for having been responsible for letting everything fall apart. Not only would Norvell Page not get his package delivered, but Asimov wouldn't get his tiles, and the point of all Heinlein's machinations and bluffs, to find out if he could recreate Tesla's Wardenclyffe, had led to nothing. And Hubbard? Who gave a damn?

Heinlein entered the lab. The sight of all the people he had working for him in good faith almost made him sick to his stomach. He felt like he had let them all down. With a conscious effort, he tried to muster a confident stroll to his office, pausing to inquire after the work and welfare of the men he passed on the way. In his office he flopped down on the sofa, feeling the exhaustion flow through his body.

"Hey, sailor. Why so glum?"

He smiled as he looked up to find Ginny leaning against the doorjamb.

"Long night."

"Wish I'd been there."

"Trust me. You don't."

She shrugged. "I brought you some coffee."

He took the cup from her. It was hot, the milk and sugar just the way he liked it. The brown liquid swirled around, and he stared at its motion as if there was some great meaning to be pulled from it. Then he smiled as if he finally understood something simple. He turned gratefully to her. "Thanks."

"Sure." She tousled his hair. "You look a sight. Maybe you ought to go home and get a shower and some sleep."

"I don't really have a home anymore."

"Really?"

"Yeah. I got the boot. I'm at the Franklin."

"Oh." Ginny pursed her lips thoughtfully and crossed her arms.

"It's not your fault," he said with a sigh.

She sat down next to him. "I've been reading some of your stories." She slipped her hand into his and he gave it a squeeze.

"You have? And you're still here?"

"I think you're amazing. I want to read more. I want to read everything you've ever written. And everything you're ever going to write. I want to be the first one to read everything new."

"I take it you liked it?"

"I did. I loved every word. And you can't stop. You have to write again. Please, tell me you'll write again."

"Well, after today I should have a lot more time to."

"Why?"

"I'm about to be fired."

"Mr. Heinlein?" One of the lab's secretaries entered the office staring at her notepad. Ginny stood up very quickly.

"Yes?"

"I have several messages for you from Mr. Page in Washington. And Dr. Reinhart would like to see you as soon as you're ready."

"Ugh. Thank you." Page would be wondering what had gone wrong. He decided to put that one off for a while. "Would you see if Colonel Slick and General Scoles are on the base today, and if they are, could you schedule a meeting with them, please?"

"Of course."

"What's going on?" Ginny asked.

"My plans have kind of fallen apart," he told her as she straightened his tie. "I've gotta come clean about it."

She followed him out of his office but hung back as he knocked on Reinhart's door.

"Ah, Heinlein." Reinhart folded his arms behind his head as he entered. The room smelled of deviled ham.

"You wanted to see me?"

"I did. But I didn't really expect to."

"Why's that?"

"Well, I'd heard some rumors that you might have been commandeering your research vessel for a trip beyond the river in clear violation of just about every rule, regulation, article, and law from the Constitution on down to your little War Games Club's rules of order."

"Yes, well, I . . ."

"And I was so happy about that because I was kind of hoping that not only would I get to fire you today, but you were going to wind up in jail."

"I get that."

"You've been nothing but rude and insubordinate since I arrived here. And all I ever wanted was to help you facilitate your work. But you didn't want my expertise."

"I'm not arguing with you."

"So, imagine my disappointment when I arrived this morning to find your ship right where it should be."

"Huh?"

Reinhart continued as if Heinlein hadn't spoken. "Running degaussing experiments right in plain view."

He hadn't given so much as a glance to the waterfront today. Now he looked out the window facing the pier and felt a surge of excitement pulse through his chest. The day was cloudy, overcast, gray, but in spite of the gloom, the DE-173 was clearly visible through the glass, up the great river, several thousand feet away. Every now and then sparks would burst from its antennas, seeming to cause a ripple or shudder in the ship.

"Why wouldn't it be where it was supposed to be?" he asked, as a feeling of well-being flowed through him. The sudden euphoria threatened to blur his wits. There it was. As plain as day. His ship.

Even the knock on the door didn't distract him. He kept grinning at the sight out the window. Only when he heard his name called a second time could he bring himself to look away. Then he leaped to his feet. "De Camp!" he cried. "You're here."

"Of course I'm here, Bob," de Camp said with a slight nod of the head and a twinge of a grin. "I'm running the experiments. Like you wanted." Reinhart seemed delighted that his team was working so well.

"I'm so glad you were able to get started without me. I got held up. Asimov?"

"He's, uh, monitoring conditions on the boat."

"Well, let's get him on the horn," Reinhart ordered. "I'd love to hear how it's going out there."

"Well, that's not going to be possible because of the electrical fields the ship is generating right now," de Camp said, without batting an eyelid. "No communication in or out is possible."

"And how realistic do you think it is that this process will make the ship invisible to radar?"

Heinlein looked back from de Camp. "Well, the first phase is to help make the ship invisible to magnetic mines and torpedoes. After that, we'll see what we can do about radar."

Reinhart shrugged. "Fair enough. I'll be watching with great interest. I want the report as soon as she docks."

"Should be a few hours yet," de Camp said, showing the first sign of unease.

"Well, let's go monitor her progress," Heinlein said, practically pushing de Camp out of the office. "Can't waste any more time here." With the door shut behind him, he breathed a huge sigh of relief, then clapped de Camp on the shoulder. "Brother, am I glad to see you."

"Where were you this morning?" De Camp dropped his calm facade as Heinlein navigated him away from possible earshot of the office.

"I'll explain later. I guess our little fight worked."

"I needed every minute to get things set up."

"It all seems to be going well."

"So far. Keep your fingers crossed."

"Believe me. They are."

The phone in his office was ringing as they entered. Heinlein paused for a moment.

"You gonna pick that up?" de Camp asked.

Heinlein took a deep breath and picked it up. His hand was trembling as he brought the receiver to within an inch of his ear. He closed his eyes, took a deep breath, and said, "Hello?"

The scratchy voice was chilling, as always. "Hello, Robert."

He opened his eyes. "Page. Listen, things are a little behind schedule . . ."

"It's my understanding that everything is working out."

"Is it? I mean, it is. Of course, it is."

"Yes."

"I'm glad to hear that."

"Of course, I'm sorry that you weren't able to make the journey yourself. Try and stay out of trouble from here on in, Robert. I don't know how much more cover I can provide."

"I'll do my best."

"Your couriers are on their way from Missouri, by the way. Quite an interesting pair."

Heinlein grinned. "Please give them my regards."

"I'll do that."

"See you in the pulps, Norvell."

"Farewell, Robert."

Heinlein hung up. "The ship's nearly in Norfolk."

"Thank God for the Intracoastal Waterway. That means we've only got to keep this up for the rest of the day."

Heinlein looked out the window at the ship floating in the distance. "Absolutely amazing."

"What is?" Slick and Scoles were entering the office. "You wanted to see us?"

Heinlein clapped his hands together. "Gentlemen. So glad to see you. I thought I was going to have some bad news for you but instead I have some good."

Reinhart rushed up behind the two officers. "My degaussing experiments seem to be going quite well."

"Really?" Slick asked. "That ship is putting out an awful lot of smoke. Is that part of the experiment?"

"I . . . I'm not sure," Reinhart stammered, looking helplessly at Heinlein.

"Congratulations, Reinhart," Scoles scoffed. "You've invented green smoke."

Heinlein shot a glance at de Camp, who responded with a minimalist shrug—he didn't know what was going on. On the river, the *DE-173* was slowly being surrounded by a thick emerald mist, lit from inside by electrical flashes that seemed to emanate from the ship.

Reinhart pointed out the window. "Oh my God!"

"What?" Heinlein grabbed the binoculars. In the brief time it took to raise them to his eyes, Reinhart was already stating the obvious.

"The ship! It's gone!"

EPISODE 35

ISAAC WAS PRETTY sure that the skeleton crew had discovered the stash of liquor Bob was going to reward them with a little early. To begin with, in the absence of a commanding officer or even Bob, and eager to shake out the vessel they had spent all summer outfitting, they had opened up all four engines and poured on the diesel. This had allowed the destroyer escort to roar through the Intracoastal Waterway from New York to Newport News in just five hours. For further evidence, he need look no further than the fact that they were being downright jovial with him, slapping him on the back whenever he passed, calling him Ike, which he let them do, or Lucky Charm.

He found himself by the mysterious box, fastened to the deck, and he wondered what trouble he could get into if he snuck a look. Bob had wanted him to investigate it, after all. With trembling fingers, he slipped back the latches and flipped open the lid. Inside, a heavy sheet of muslin was draped over the contents. Isaac pulled the thick cover back, then gasped.

Resting in a bed of dried hay were ten tubes, each about the size of a lunchbox thermos. They gleamed yellow and he only had to pick one up, feel its heft, to confirm that each was made of gold. He rotated it between his palms, feeling it grow warmer. The thermos analogy wasn't far off. Each canister was fitted with a tightly screwed on lid. When Isaac gave it a shake, he could feel powder move—like a can of Gold Bond. Curious, he began to unscrew the top when the fingers of his other hand felt some engraving. He turned the canister around again and read the writing: UO_2—*Uranium Dioxide.*

In a panic, he threw the canister back into the crate and scrambled away. His hands felt like they were tingling, but he knew it was just his imagination. One couldn't feel radioactivity, only its later effects. He looked at the tube, askew amongst the others, now understanding why the powder had been shipped in canisters of gold. Shielding.

With his toe, he nudged the tube back into place amongst the others. Carefully, he pulled the muslin over the cargo, then slammed the lid down. He threw open the door to the nearby head, put his hands under the sink taps, and scrubbed as hard as he could for five minutes, until they were raw. Then, giving the case a wide berth, he slipped out of the small room and headed forward.

"Ain't this the greatest?" Olson shouted at him from the ship's bow as they came up quickly on the port at Newport News, the wind plastering his muttonchops against his jaw, giving him the look of a rugged, mad prophet. "Twenty-five knots!"

"Is that good?" he hollered back.

The sailor spat, perfectly timing it so a stiff breeze carried the globule away from his lips and over Isaac's head. "Hell, yeah!" He wiped his chin. "It's good. How you like it, Lucky? Having fun?"

A civilian seaplane swung low over them, then shot away toward a landing. Dolphins raced along in the frothy bow wake. Isaac nodded. "This is the farthest away from home I've ever been."

"Yeah?" the petty officer replied. "I am home."

He kept his hand in his pocket, fingers coiled around the metal flask he had meant to give to Bob for good luck. The ship that the sailors told him was to be named for a pilot who had been killed leading an attack on the Solomons began to slow down. A shudder ran through the vessel, the sudden change in inertia causing Isaac's knees to buckle. He clawed at the railing for support while the destroyer escort angled toward a long, empty pier where a canvas-topped Army truck sat idling, several bored soldiers leaning against the hood. Somewhat apart from them stood another figure.

"Is that man wearing a cape?" Olson asked.

Sure enough, a small man stood halfway between the truck and the end of the dock. He wore a three-piece suit and was cloaked in a red-satin-lined cape that fluttered dramatically in the wind.

The *Eldridge* cruised to a gentle rest against the dock, the soldiers rousing themselves to take the lines tossed to them by the sailors, who then leaped ashore like monkeys to complete the tying-up procedure and lower the gangplank. Isaac descended the ramp to the dock, not sure what was supposed to happen next. Fortunately, the little man in the cape seemed to be approaching quickly. With his plastered hair, beaked nose, and stout formality, he reminded Isaac of a penguin from the Bronx Zoo. He scrutinized him in a way that was all too familiar to Isaac: it was the dubious look his new professors had always given him upon discovering his age. "You're Asimov," he stated finally.

"Do I know you?"

"Probably not. But that's not your fault. You're young." He looked at the ship. "You've brought a package for me. And in return, I have a package for you."

"Well, there's a box strapped to the deck up there. But it's a little big for me to haul down by myself."

The little man beckoned to his soldiers. "Follow Mr. Asimov on board and put the box he's got for us on the back of the truck."

The soldiers cast an expectant eye on Isaac. He shrugged and turned, aware of the strange feeling of having armed men following him. The men he had come to think of as his sailors were waiting at the top of the gangplank, arms folded, faces glowering obdurately. "No Army," Olson snarled. Now Isaac was certain the men had been drinking.

"But they need the box."

"No Army on this ship."

"Fine with me," the soldier closest to Isaac said. "I got better things to do than play rowboat anyway."

"Like eat my fist?" the petty officer retorted.

The soldier snorted and motioned to his comrades to turn around and head back down the gangplank.

"Hey!" Isaac felt the situation slipping out of his control. He looked down the dock, but the odd little man was returning to the safety of the truck's cab as if it made no difference to him whether or not the box was actually delivered or if a fistfight broke out on the dock.

"Okay, look!" Isaac dashed up the ramp, stopping at a position where all the sailors could look down upon him with arrogant indifference. "Look. No soldiers on board. You bring the box to me here. All right?"

Olson looked at his mates. "Get it."

As the sailors headed back to get the box, Isaac dashed down the gangplank and ran after the soldiers, shouting, "Hey! Hey!" until at last they stopped. "Look," he explained, "you can't go on the ship, but I'm bringing the box down to you."

"Forget it. We're not even supposed to be here."

"Look. Don't leave. If you just come back, it'll be ready in a minute. Come on, you're already here."

The corporal scratched his head and then shrugged. "What the hell."

Isaac ran back up the gangplank to find the sailors had carried the crate to the ship's edge. There it sat, half hanging over the lip of the gangplank.

"That's as far as we go," the petty officer said.

"And this is it for us," the corporal said from the base of the ramp, lighting a cigarette and passing the pack to his squad.

"Inertia on an incline," Isaac muttered, running back up the gangplank and sliding past the heavy crate. "It's all about friction. Galileo proved that." He grabbed a heavy rope and handed it to Olson. "Tie it to the crate," he commanded.

The big man grinned, shrugged, and handed the line to one of his crew. "Why not?" He tied a loop in it and encircled the end of the huge crate, finishing with some kind of incredible knot that only sailors ever seemed to know. Then he tossed the bitter end to Isaac.

"Okay," Isaac said, as soldiers and sailors eyed him expectantly. "Okay." He wound the rope once around the post at the top of the gangplank, then carried the coils down to the soldiers. "Here you go," he said to the corporal.

The man looked from the limp rope in his hands to the crate, then to Isaac. "So?"

"So? Lower it down."

"But it's still up there."

"Are you kidding me?"

"No."

"Fine." He ran back up the ramp. "Mr. Olson, would you please give it a push."

"This is as far as I go."

"Terrific," Isaac said. There were several piles of rebar tied to the deck, construction remains. Isaac slid one of the heavy bars from its slot and carried it to the crate. "It's all about leverage," he said to himself, slipping it under the box. He crouched down, letting the bar rest on his shoulder. Then, he began to rise, slowly, exerting as much force as he could. The iron bit into his shoulder; his back shook. The cruel chuckles of the sailors filled him with rage, and he threw himself against the bar. The crate shifted, rocking up on its pivot point, but wouldn't tip.

"I knew it was coming to this," he groaned. He climbed on top of the crate and crawled forward to the far end, aware that as he did, it tipped down ever so slightly. He swung his legs over the edge into a sitting position and kicked them back and forth. The box tilted down with a tremendous jolt; even though he had expected it to move, he was still unprepared for the impact. For a moment he was staring down the ramp at the surprised soldiers. Then he was accelerating toward them. The rope ripped easily from the corporal's limp fingers and shot past Isaac.

The crate hit the dock with a thud and stopped abruptly, hurling him off his perch and into the chest of the corporal. Isaac picked himself off the ground while the soldier recovered his breath. The other men shifted nervously. "It's all yours," Isaac told him, then began to walk toward the truck. "You shouldn't have let go of the rope."

The strange little man sat in the front of the truck, a small grin playing across his face. "Nice bit of improvising," he said.

"You have something for me," Isaac replied. "Where is it?"

"Been here all along."

He walked around to the back of the truck and lifted the canvas flap, but the cargo bed was empty. Confused, Isaac looked around, but other than the soldiers struggling to carry the crate, the dock was deserted. He yelled at the cab, "Where?" But he couldn't be heard over the roar of a seaplane pulling alongside. With a shake of his head he started walking back to have another frustrating conversation with the little man, when silence finally fell across the water.

"Excuse me?"

He turned toward the seaplane, several yards away. One of the most beautiful women he'd ever seen was standing on the pontoon, wearing a light tan suit. He felt his knees weaken. The wind whipped her thick blond hair wildly about her face. She held on to the wing strut with one hand while in her other she held a coil of rope.

"If I toss this to you, can you tie us off?"

Isaac had a hard time responding. Her blue eyes were mesmerizing.

"I'd ask the Army to do it, but they don't seem to have much luck with ropes. And the Navy didn't look like they were any help." She gestured with the rope again.

He nodded.

She swayed, using the strut as a fulcrum to build momentum, and then flung the rope toward him. It unspooled perfectly and landed right in front of him. As it began to slide back into the water, he lunged for it, plucking it from the ground. In another moment he had it wound around the iron dock cleat. Then the woman pulled the seaplane against the dock and made it fast. "Give me your hand," she said to him.

"What?"

"Your hand."

Dumbly, he stuck his hand out, and before he realized why, she had taken it and used it to pull herself onto the dock. Still holding it, she smiled at him. "Hello."

"Hi."

"Are you with Bob?"

"Uh . . . Yes, I am. I mean, he's not here. But I'm with him."

"Wonderful!" She smiled brightly and he felt for a moment as if he had forgotten how to breathe. "What's your name?"

Another thing that slipped his mind. Then it came back to him. "Isaac. Isaac Asimov."

"Well, hello, Isaac." Her accent was somewhat flat, a cross between Southern and Midwestern, but the tone was pure music. "My name's Norma."

Behind her, a tall man was unfolding himself out of the small seaplane passenger door.

"And this is my copilot, Lester."

"Hello," the man said, shutting the door; simple stenciled lettering read DENT AERIAL SURVEY, LA PLATA, MISSOURI. He stepped ashore and shook Isaac's hand. "I'm Lester."

Isaac skipped a breath again. "Lester Dent? The *Doc Savage* Lester Dent? I love *Doc Savage*!"

"You look a little old for Doc."

"I've been reading *Doc Savage* since I was eleven years old. I have the first issue safe at home. Oh, I wish I had it with me. I could get you to sign it."

"Wow. We don't even have a copy of the first issue anymore, do we, honey?"

"I can give you mine."

"No, really. That's okay, son. I don't even know you."

"Honey, this is Isaac. He's a friend of Bob's." She gave her husband a nudge in his ribs.

"You don't say. Where is Bob?"

"I don't know," Isaac said with a nervous shrug. "He missed the boat."

"Oh. Well, is he coming? I'm supposed to give him some stuff."

"That's for me, actually."

"Really?" Lester Dent looked down at Isaac from what seemed to be a great height, both of stature and legend. He rubbed his thin mustache thoughtfully, then pulled a pipe from his lightweight coat, tamped some tobacco in, and lit it. After puffing thoughtfully, he asked: "What is it?"

"Several boxes of dielectric barium titanate ceramic tiles comprised of a final mixture of 98 to 99.95 percentage weight having a composition equivalent to a formula I like to call $BaTiO_3$, then kiln-fired at a temperature of 1,260 degrees to 1,400 degrees Centigrade for five hours," Isaac blurted out, unable to stop himself in the face of her stunning beauty and Dent's reputation. He realized by their expressions that he hadn't impressed them at all, only confused them. It was a look he often saw on his parents' faces. "A bunch of green tiles," he muttered, ashamed.

"Prettiest green tiles you ever saw," Norma said with a cheerful lilt to her voice, patting him thoughtfully on the shoulder. The warm sensation lingered long after her hand was withdrawn. "I asked the man at the facility if he would make me some earrings out of them and he said he'd see what he could do. Wasn't that sweet of him?"

"Uh-huh." Isaac nodded, feeling his confidence somewhat restored. If she liked his tiles so much, she must not have thought he'd just made a fool of himself.

"Fine by me," Lester said. He stepped back onto the pontoon and opened a cargo hatch. "Make yourself useful, Isaac," he said, his pipe clenched between his teeth.

Isaac stepped to the edge of the pier and received the first of several cardboard boxes.

"If I'd known that Bob wasn't going to be here, I would have told him to have someone else bring this up for him," Lester muttered, handing Isaac another box. "It's not like I'm not busy or anything."

"Honey, it's not Isaac's fault that Bob's not here, now is it?"

Lester grunted something unintelligible and passed Isaac a box that was bigger than the rest.

"Those aren't tiles," Norma said.

"No?"

Lester pulled himself back onto the dock. "We didn't know this until we got to the mine, but barium is used to make green fireworks. Did you know that?"

"No." Isaac shook his head. "You have to use that in a story sometime. Sounds like a great clue for Doc Savage to come across on his way to defeating the Barium Baron." They had that look on their faces again, and he stopped himself. "Or something like that."

"Anyway," Lester continued, "he doesn't make fireworks there, but he provides the barium to a friend of his who's in the business. I don't know what you paid him for these tiles, but the order must have made him very happy. Because he insisted that we take a couple of cases of fireworks back with us. He says they're the best and greenest green in the business."

"We're saving ours for Christmas," Norma said. "A bonfire and green fireworks."

Isaac looked into the box. Fat rockets and long Roman candles were nestled inside.

"Those were for Bob," Lester said, "but since he didn't have the courtesy to show up . . ."

"Lester."

"Anyway," he drawled again. "You can have these."

"Thanks! I'm a chemist. I love blowing stuff up."

"Oh." Norma sounded surprised. "I thought that if you were a friend of Bob's you were probably a writer."

"I am." Isaac nodded. "I've published over twenty stories."

"Twenty." Lester studied his pipe. "Not bad."

"You're in the pulps?"

"Hmm. *Amazing,* mostly. Some *Astounding.* I'm hoping for something in *Unknown* soon."

"So you're one of Campbell's gang."

He nodded.

"Well, that's a good pack to run with. Campbell's on a tear."

"Mr. Gibson said the same thing."

"Walter?" Norma seemed excited and pleased to hear the name. "Is he working with you?"

"Well, he was. We did a little exploring."

"How is he?"

"Interesting. I don't know how he is usually."

"Interesting about describes him," Lester said.

"I heard something about a car accident," she said. "Did he talk about it at all?"

Isaac shook his head. "Not really."

She turned to her husband. "How nice it would be to see him again."

"We'll have to plan a trip to New York one of these days."

"That'd be nice. It's been too long. Years now since we were last there. Time flies."

"Speaking of flying, I guess we should get airborne while there's still daylight." As Lester spoke, the Army truck chugged to life and backed slowly down the pier. The sun bounced off the windshield, making it hard to discern the figures inside. "Is that your ride?"

"No." Isaac threw a thumb toward the ship. "That is."

"Ah. Well, you better hurry. Looks like they're fixing to leave without you."

"Yeah, they're a real bunch of clowns."

"No, I'm serious. They're getting ready to cast off."

Isaac turned and saw that Lester was right. The gangplank was lifting. "Oh no!"

Lester helped him scoop up the three boxes, which Isaac could barely see over. "Goodbye," he said. "Nice to meet you."

"Okay." Isaac began a shuffling run down the pier, the boxes teetering precariously. "Wait!" he shouted. "Don't go! Don't leave me!"

The smokestack uttered a great belch of smoke.

"Hold up!" Isaac reached the spot where the gangplank had touched the deck. "Come on!"

They were laughing at him. The sailors had lined up at the railing and were laughing at him.

"Come on!" he shouted, barely able to muster the breath to do it after his dash. Slowly, the gangplank came down, then rose, then lowered again, then jumped back up. Each time, the sailors laughed harder. Finally, when it appeared obvious that they weren't going to be able to provoke much of a reaction from Isaac anymore, they lowered it all the way and he made his way up.

Olson shouted at him, "We didn't know you were coming back."

"Well, I was."

Just before he reached the end, the sailor manning the gangplank lever threw it one more time, raising it quickly enough that it propelled Isaac stumbling forward. With a gasp he lost control of the boxes for a moment and watched in horror as the top one fell to the deck. If the tiles were smashed after all this work . . . he couldn't finish the thought. Instead, the fireworks spilled out, rolling to the sailors' feet.

There was a moment of silence, quickly followed by whoops of happiness. The fireworks were scooped up. The gangplank remained up and the ship began to move rapidly away from the dock. Isaac carefully stashed the two boxes of tiles in an equipment locker near the bridge. From outside he heard the sounds of explosions followed by cheers. As he made his way back down to the deck, the smell of cordite tickled his nose. Stepping through the hatch near the half-raised gangplank, it appeared as if the ship were shrouded in green-tinted smoke. Isaac watched the emerald stars bursting off the bow of the ship, the sailors making a point of holding on to the rockets until the last possible moment so they exploded close by. He had to admit that the fireworks were the greenest ones he'd ever seen.

In the distance he could see another ship making its way into port. He wondered how their smoke-bound ship must look to those sailors.

A sense of relief washed over him. He had the tiles and he was heading back to Philadelphia. He had stepped up to the plate and done what Bob hadn't been able to. Plus, he had met Lester Dent, one of the greatest pulp writers of all time, and made a good impression on Norma Dent. As soon as he was back ashore, he would call Gertrude and explain everything. If he had to go to New York again, tonight even, then so be it. Even if Bob had other plans. He wanted to see his wife. He sighed and leaned against the railing.

The ship was new, and it would take many more months of full occupancy and heavy duty before every last bolt and screw was where it ought to be. That was not the first thought that ran through his head as the railing gave way behind him and he toppled backwards; that thought would come later. The thought that ran through his mind just before he fell off the ship and into the Atlantic Ocean was that Einstein would never create a Unified Field Theory because his equations would never account for randomness. And then he lost the ability to think.

EPISODE 36

"RONALD."

"Sara?"

The paddler's oars dug grooves into the blue ocean, driving the *popao* forward with a rhythmic rush.

"Have you discovered yourself?"

"Out here, I am a speck of dirt on the most unimaginably vast plain of nothingness. I am drained. Haunted. I'm afraid, Sara. And I'm alone."

"You're not alone. I'm with you."

"No, you're not. You're in the part of my mind that's slowly growing crazier, creeping up on me like a cancer."

"I want to prove you wrong."

"By keeping you alive."

"What are you laughing at?" Mr. Faaitu'a asked.

"Nothing," he replied. "Absolutely nothing." A canteen sat between his feet on the floor of the traditional canoe Mr. Faaitu'a had insisted on using to transport Hubbard to Niuafo'ou. He picked it up and drained it, licking the last of the drops from his sun-chapped lips. From under the brim of his hat he squinted at the island as they approached it, visible over the broad-shouldered Tongan in front of him, one of two students the librarian had pressed into service to complete Hubbard's journey.

"They call it Tin Can Island because it has no harbor," said Mr. Faaitu'a, seated behind him, "so the mail ships pack everything up in tin cans and throw it overboard to swimmers, who carry it back to the island."

"Fascinating." He had refused Cave's offer to travel along with him; now he found himself missing the chatty journalist's company. Among the foreigners, he felt alone, really wishing he could share the experience with someone like Cave. An American.

In an otherwise cloudless sky, a thick gray mist clung to the summit of the island. Mixed with the tropical scent of rich, decomposing vegetation that drifted to their nostrils, growing stronger with each stroke of the paddles was a stranger, darker smell that seemed so out of place to Hubbard that, even though he recognized it, it took him almost until they had reached the rocky beach for him to name it. Sulphur.

"About thirty families make their home here," his guide continued, with a teacher's pride.

"On an active volcano?"

"They consider it their sacred duty. They are the protectors of the island and the spirits who dwell within the volcano."

"Spirits?"

"The souls of our spirits enter the land of Pulotu through the mouth of the volcano, where they dwell in the eternal glory of Havea Hikule'o, the great ruler of the underworld."

The young man in the front of the canoe turned and gave Hubbard a smirk and a wink. "These are the myths of the old men."

"Yes, you young men are all so civilized and Westernized now. But there are still things about your home you should never forget. Because of their brave proximity to a death that can destroy them at a moment's notice, in addition to their reputation as the guardians of our souls, the families of this island are most highly regarded among all the Tongan clans. In other periods of our history, they were the most feared, too.

Warriors who lived with death and brought death with them into battle. Ask your ancestors when you meet them, Oko," he taunted his pupil. "Ask them how they trembled in fear when the war canoes of Niuafo'ou were sighted. Ask how they hid their women in caves like rodents and pissed themselves like children as those canoes landed upon their beaches."

"If my ancestors had not been able to best their warriors I would not be here, eh?"

"Perhaps only your great-great-great-great-grandfather was beaten," the lad from the back of the canoe said with a laugh. "Maybe they find your great-great-great-great-grandmother in her cave. Or maybe she whored herself to them to save Grandfather's life!"

"Enough of that!" Mr. Faaitu'a said sharply, as Oko used his paddle to splash water back at his taunter, catching Hubbard instead. "Paddle!"

The irregular cliffs of the small island churned the waters that swirled around them into an angry chop of cross-currents. It seemed there was no clear crest to slide into: knifing into one wave seemed to slam them instantly into another coming from a different direction. Great glittering monoliths of oily obsidian rose from the treacherous shallows, like black, jagged teeth waiting to snag the tiny vessel and deliver it into the maw of the ocean.

Hubbard clutched the sides of the canoe, bracing himself against the force, which tossed him from port to starboard and back again with no rhythm or warning. "Jesus Christ," he uttered, as he suddenly found warm water sloshing around his feet. With one hand he grabbed his canteen and began to bail. As they threaded through the jutting rocks that guarded the low cliff, the island itself seemed to grow no closer, as if an undertow were thwarting their progress.

Drowning—it was the death he was most afraid of. Always had been. All his bravado in living his life on or close to the ocean hadn't quite overcome it. It seemed a horrible way to die, the struggle to breathe. He often dreamed of other terrifying ways to go, but some of those, like being drawn and quartered by angry British aristocrats, shot by a Nazi on a battlefield, or ripped to pieces by chemical gas–transformed human monsters, seemed relatively unlikely to happen. Drowning, however, his greatest fear, had never been far and was now closer than ever.

He put out a hand to fend off the slick black boulder that suddenly reared up to port. He pulled it back and stared dumbly at the blood suddenly dripping from the wound in his palm.

"Edges as sharp as a surgeon's blade," Mr. Faaitu'a grunted through gritted teeth. He had an oar and was digging in against the surf now, too.

"It doesn't even hurt," he replied.

"It will."

Hubbard thrust his hand into the warm water.

"Sharks," Mr. Faaitu'a grunted again.

He pulled his hand quickly from the ocean, dripping with blood and foam. Grabbing his handkerchief, he wrapped it around tightly and bound a knot over the back of his hand. Once they got ashore he'd find the island's doctor to take a look at it.

"There's where we will land," he heard Oko call out as he finished tying off the makeshift bandage.

"Thank Christ!" Momentarily heartened, he followed Oko's pointing finger. There was no beach to speak of, just a narrow shelf created by a river of lava that had cut its way through the cliffs before being frozen forever at the water's edge. How long ago? Hubbard couldn't tell. There was no vegetation to be seen upon its surface, whereas higher up the cone he could see the usual palm trees and sawgrass. Several canoes of the style he was riding in rested on the ledge, along with a few more modern deep rowboats and even several aluminum ones. The lip of the slope where the other boats sat was fully fifteen or twenty feet above the waves, which broke heavily against it. "How do we get up there?"

"Climb."

"We should wait for high tide!"

"It doesn't get any higher."

Before he knew it, the two younger men had positioned the boat before the wall, deftly working back and forth to stay on top of the swells and away from the breakers. His hand was beginning to throb and the full backpack was cutting into his shoulders. At least the lava pile wasn't as vertically forbidding as the other cliffs that ringed the island; it could actually, somewhat charitably, be described as a very steep slope.

"Ready?" Mr. Faaitu'a asked. Without waiting for Hubbard's answer, he clambered out of the canoe, timing it so that he had his purchase on the rocky shore even as the boat dropped out from under him.

"Here we go," Oko said a moment later, as they washed back. He repeated himself again on their next approach as Hubbard hadn't moved on their first. Then he had to say it a third time.

"Okay. Okay. Okay," Hubbard yelled, and launched himself over the side. Even as his fingers scratched for a grip, he knew his timing was off; the current swept the boat away from him before he could get his feet under him properly. He began to slide, the salty, porous, shellfish-encrusted surface ripping the handkerchief from his hand, bolts of pain shooting up his arm as he clutched at anything that would slow him down. His heavy boots pedaled desperately, controlled by some unknown animal part of his brain.

A wave fell across his back, pinning him to the rocks and knocking the wind out of him. Fluid filled his mouth and nostrils as his feet found protuberances that stopped his slide. He clung to the spot he had claimed, catching his breath, feeling rivulets running down his face. Already throwing his balance off, his backpack now had filled with water and was dragging on him like an anchor. With some gentle wiggling he managed to release the buckles, letting it fall into the ocean. The lava flow against his cheek held a warmth that felt nearly alive. He thought he heard laughter, but a quick glance back at the men in the canoe showed only grave concern on their faces, no trace of amusement.

Slowly, cautiously, he began to inch upwards. Ignoring the stinging ache in his hand, he palmed the rockface and used his legs to heave himself forward. Several more times the water swirled around his body, but after what seemed like an eternity, he had moved up beyond the sucking reach of the waves. The grade of the slope shifted gradually and soon he was crawling on his hands and knees. Finally, he rose to a crouch and was able to accept Mr. Faaitu'a offered hand. Once he reached the man's side on the flatter land with the boats nearby, his knees gave way and he collapsed.

His body ached; but in particular, his hand felt as if it were on fire. He held it before his face, the edges of the cut straight and clean even as blood continued to well up through it.

"I need a doctor," he wheezed.

"No doctor here," Mr. Faaitu'a replied. He helped Hubbard to his feet and indicated that he should tuck his injured hand under his armpit for the time being, which didn't help at all.

The lava flow had formed a frozen path through the jungle which clung to the crest of the cliffs that protected this side of the island. Hubbard stumbled up it after the spry old man, wet socks squeezing water between his toes with each step. The black lava was remarkably smooth, folded in gentle layers like a thick cream ladled over a dish. He crossed the treeline and stepped into the shade. Within minutes he could no longer hear the ocean.

"What about our ride?"

"They will come back tomorrow."

"So we're spending the night?"

"Yes."

"Damn." Hubbard thought longingly of his backpack. Socks, toilet paper, a K ration. His stomach growled. Funny, he hadn't been hungry until the moment he found himself without food. He began to look at trees for fruit, but there were no bananas to be seen and with his injured hand there was no way he could climb up after a coconut. Scrutinizing his guide, he doubted he could coax him to go up a tree.

At a clearing in the path he looked down on the ocean and realized how far up the cone they had traveled. From here he could see other islands in the chain. He sipped some water from a clear spring, finally washing the salt taste out of his mouth. With shock he noticed that blood had soaked the whole left side of his shirt. "This is bad," he said, but Mr. Faaitu'a was moving on again, stoic and unforgiving. Hubbard took his shirt off; his undershirt showed less of the stains, though it was drenched with sweat. He clenched his fist around the shirt, then started hiking again.

"Do you smell that?" he called out. An aromatic fragrance wafted from the trees. "Barbecue!" A thought struck Hubbard even as he began to salivate. "Hey! Are these guys cannibals?"

"Not anymore."

"Oh, so that's . . . ?"

"Pig."

"My favorite." He stepped into a clearing. "Hello?"

Mr. Faaitu'a followed him and pointed to a lava tube opening as high as a cathedral. "In there."

"Really?"

A light haze drifted from the opening as they entered it, carrying the scent of grilling meat. Torches were set into the walls, leading the way as they followed the smooth tunnel deep into the mountainside. The air was much cooler than outside. At last they found themselves in a large chamber, lit from above by a huge hole in the ceiling. The lava had bored through other holes like the one they had just entered; he could see the openings leading off in every direction. The cavern itself was big enough to house more than a dozen huts: not the thatchwork structures Hubbard expected from Tarzan movies, but solid buildings made of thick wood. In the center of the floor, the glistening carcass of a great pig roasted over an open firepit.

"Hello? Anyone here?"

The door to one of the larger huts opened, and a small, shirtless man, his massively muscled arms and torso covered in fierce tattoos that crept up onto his cheeks, stepped into the daylight.

"Hi," Hubbard began.

The man ignored him completely and took several more steps forward. Meanwhile, other doors in the village began to open. He barked some words in a deep voice, the syllables hard and accented.

Mr. Faaitu'a held out his hands in a gesture of peace and replied in the same tongue. The exchange lasted for several minutes while the villagers gathered behind the man who was the chief, at least as far as Hubbard was concerned. Both men sounded angry, but Hubbard couldn't tell if it was real emotion or just the effect on his ears of the language.

"What's going on?" he asked. "What are you guys saying?"

"I'm explaining that we're here because you are seeking knowledge about the white explorers who came here long ago."

"That's good."

"You should give them the gifts now."

"Gifts?"

"Your Swiss Army knife, flashlight, and compass. I bound them up before we left and put them in your pack. Fresh coffee beans, too."

"I lost my pack."

"What?"

"It almost drowned me. I had to get it off."

"Oh my."

The chief stepped forward and folded his arms across his chest. "Go you away."

He recalled Cave's instructions that the islanders respected formality. "Look, Mr. Cakobau, I've come so far to talk to you and I have so little time left. Does he understand me? Do you understand me?"

"I understand. But go you."

"Please, I understand that it is your custom for a stranger to bring a gift to visit your home, it's my custom, too."

Mr. Cakobau asked for Mr. Faaitu'a to clarify a few words, then nodded at Hubbard to continue.

"I am deeply apologetic that the ocean took away my offering, and I promise that I will deliver great gifts to you and your village, if you will only help me.

"I don't know if you are aware of the great war that rages between a great many people, but very evil men threaten to turn good men like me, and Mr. Faaitu'a here, and even your people, into their slaves. They call this war the world war because there is no corner of this world that is not involved and is not in danger, and that even includes you here, on your great volcano. These evil men will even find you here one day."

"Fight we will," the chief said as a simple statement of fact.

"And I'm sure you will fight bravely, you are all great warriors," Hubbard continued. "But the evil men who will come, they are in number like the sand on a beach, they are so many more than you."

Uncertainty had crept into the man's eyes. He turned to Hubbard's companion and asked several questions that were answered in a humble but affirmative tone.

"Now, thirty-five years ago some men like me came to your island and I believe they may have left something behind here. Something that will let you help us defeat the evil men before they can come here."

"Just past boy then I was," the man said, the odd structure of his sentences sounding less so each time he spoke. Evidently the next part was too difficult for him to articulate, so he spoke to Mr. Faaitu'a while gesturing toward the peak, visible through the crack above, shrouded though it was in volcanic smoke.

"He says they selected his island from all others because they could speak best with the sun and the moon from here. Mau'i was sleeping in the mountain at the time so the skies were clear."

"Mau'i?"

"The volcano god, the essence of the fire."

"They showed him how the moon would cross in front of the sun, but not to be afraid, that it was as natural as a whale which swims past a school of fish. So we weren't afraid when the eclipse happened."

Hubbard distinctly heard the word "eclipse" in the midst of all the Polynesian words.

"They stayed on here for many weeks with us after the eclipse, waiting for the tides to change, and waiting, they said, for some kind of sign from the earth. But it never came."

"A sign?" Hubbard asked, excited. "What kind of sign?"

The chief beckoned Hubbard to follow him and soon they were trekking down one of the smaller tubes. The chief had plucked up a torch on his way in, and at the cramped end of the tunnel, he lit two other torches which leaped instantly to life, so dry that Hubbard couldn't imagine they'd awaited fire. In the flickering light, the chief proudly displayed an object covered by the American flag. Even before he gave Hubbard permission to see for himself what it was, he had recognized it from its shape and its heft.

"That's it," he said, his voice hoarse, no need for translation now. "It's a box with hinges of brass in the back. When it opens, there are dials and gauges like you might have seen on a ship at one time or another." He couldn't be sure how much of this Mr. Faaitu'a could translate, but he had to get it all out. "Also when you open it there is a long golden spear, attached to the box by a length of golden rope.

"Am I right?"

The chief grabbed a corner of the cloth and gently, almost reverentially, pulled it back. "See it you," he said proudly.

"Thank you," Hubbard said. "Thank you." He stepped forward and ran his hands over the familiar brown leather, gently unbuckling the straps and cautiously opening it to see that all was intact and as it should be. The golden spike itself was planted firmly in the stone, patiently awaiting a signal. In spite of himself, he felt tears well up in his eyes. He didn't even care if it worked, he was just so happy that it existed. "The key to the midway," he whispered.

"That will defeat the evil warriors?" Mr. Faaitu'a wasn't translating, he was asking.

Hubbard's whole body seemed to be shaking as he slid one of the pale green slides from its slot, then smiled as he slid it back in. Then he withdrew the golden spike from the spot it had rested in for years and held it up to the light of the torch, watching it glow. The room around him began to spin.

"Hell," he said. "It will." Then he felt his knees give way and a blackness swept over him like the waves against the rocks.

EPISODE 37

ONE MINUTE THE ship had been there, and the next, it was gone. What the hell happened? He looked at de Camp, who gave him a hapless, bewildered shrug.

"Where's my ship?" Reinhart demanded, running after the two of them as they dashed to the brink of the breakwater. To the south, near the tiny island beyond the border of the Navy Yard, a light mist drifted across the otherwise placid waters.

"I'm not sure. Maybe it's around the other side of that island."

"I was watching it when it happened," the little man said. "And I'm telling you, it just disappeared."

Slick and the general arrived at the edge, both gazing with expressions of grave concern down the river. "What's happening, Heinlein?" Scoles asked, in a tone indicating he wanted immediate answers. "I saw it disappear, too. I think."

Down the waterfront, Heinlein could see small clusters of sailors pointing toward the spot on the river where the destroyer escort had been moments ago. A gust of wind ruffled his hair.

"Is the ship invisible?" Slick asked. "Or has it been destroyed?"

"It's just a degaussing experiment," he stammered. "This is . . . unexpected."

"What was that flash of green light?" Reinhart asked. "Right before it vanished."

"It didn't vanish," Heinlein insisted. "It's just on the other side of the island. You'll see in a minute."

"I saw green lightning!"

"St. Elmo's fire." De Camp avoided eye contact with any of the men by squinting into the distance.

"St. Elmo's fire?" General Scoles arched an eyebrow.

"Sure," de Camp offered, with a shrug that was less than confident.

"Doesn't that only happen on the high seas?"

"St. Elmo's fire is caused when a ship becomes charged with static electricity and begins to discharge it into the moist air surrounding the vessel. Now we're running a lot of current through the hull of the ship and the humidity is pretty high, so there's a good chance that we've created some artificial St. Elmo's fire. First time that I know of."

"Can we use it to knock a super-bomber out of the air?"

"No."

"Then it's of no use to me," Scoles said, in a tone which reminded Heinlein in no uncertain terms that he was a commanding officer and they were here at his indulgence.

The scientists and engineers were slowly stepping out of the lab and discussing their own confusion with each other in quiet voices. Even Ginny emerged, carefully clutching a large jar of clear liquid to her chest. Heinlein supposed that since they were about to be shut down, she at least wanted to take a sample of some of her work along. The group began a stealthy approach toward the water so as not to summon the wrath of the general. But it was obvious they wanted to see for themselves what was going on. And why shouldn't they? After all, they were about to lose their jobs. Some of them were going to be sent into war.

An aide to the general drove up in a jeep, the command flags fluttering over the headlamps. The lieutenant climbed out and approached his commander, snapping to attention until Scoles's salute released him.

"What is it?" The general kept his eyes on the river.

"Sir, there's a request for clarification of information from Newport News, Virginia."

"The vacation spot of the Appalachians," the general snorted. "What about it?"

"They've received a report from an officer aboard the SS *Furuseth*, a merchant vessel."

"Cut to the chase, Lieutenant."

"The officer was convinced, sir, that he'd just seen a Navy vessel, the *DE-173*, disappear from Newport News in a flash of green light. This officer, Captain Allende, wanted to know if anyone could explain what he had seen."

The general turned his gaze from the waters to Heinlein. "St. Elmo's fire?"

Heinlein opened his mouth to say something, anything, when he heard a sound, like a distant crowd cheering a home run. He realized that it was the men down the line pointing toward the water.

"There she is!" Ginny cried.

Cruising proudly around the southern end of the island was the destroyer escort. Lightning still flickered from its antennae and its rigging—causing the ship to glow with a ghostly light.

"St. Elmo's fire," he replied to the general, with complete confidence. "Just an optical illusion. A combination of fog and St. Elmo's fire."

"Is it just me?" Reinhart protested. "That ship was gone! We all saw it."

"You can't just make a twelve-hundred-ton ship disappear," Heinlein said. "Am I right, de Camp?"

"Right," de Camp agreed. "There are laws of physics involved."

"To hell with the laws of physics!" Reinhart shouted. "I want that ship brought in and I want those men interviewed. I want to know what happened."

"They'll be in as soon as they're finished running the tests."

"Get on the radio and have them dock."

"I told you, the radio won't work through the electrical interference," de Camp reminded him.

"If it's so important, how come you aren't on board?"

"I get seasick," he stammered.

"And we have Asimov on board," Heinlein said quickly. "He's really our man when it comes to those precise measurements."

"Exactly."

"I've seen enough." General Scoles put his hands on his hips and surveyed the small cluster of lab rats. "Wrap it up. Bring her in. Clean her up. Get her ready. She's going back to the Navy next week, laws of physics or not."

"But what if we're on to something?" Reinhart protested. "Albert Einstein said . . ."

"I don't care what Einstein said," Scoles snapped. He fixed his stare upon Heinlein; there was little tolerance in his eyes. "Quite frankly, I've been spending more time in this building than I fully expected to. And I'm not seeing a lot for it. Not a force field or rocket pack or laser gun to speak of. If a ship that a magnet won't stick to is all I have to show for it, I might just lose my mind. Do you hear me?"

"Yes, sir," Heinlein replied. "Working on it, sir." He couldn't help but feel somewhat cowed by military authority.

The general stalked to the jeep and climbed in, followed by Slick. "Then I'd make something happen. And fast." The aide released the brake and the three men disappeared in a spray of gravel and exhaust.

"I'm going to get on the radio and get them in here, now!" Reinhart began to stride toward the lab door.

"It won't work," Heinlein called after him.

"Then I'll send up a flare!"

De Camp turned quickly to Heinlein. "Uh-oh."

The lab crew were on their way back into the building as Reinhart began pushing past them to get in. Heinlein heard a woman shriek and the sound of glass breaking. He ran into the small crowd, even as the men staggered away from Ginny's shattered jar, the contents of which puddled at Reinhart's feet.

"You moron!" he shouted at her, though she faced him defiantly.

"Hey!" Heinlein rushed to her defense.

"Stand back, Bob!" She held up a hand. "He just made me drop my jar."

"Made you!" Reinhart sputtered. "You practically threw it at me!"

"You mashed into me. You made me lose my whole supply of highly fortified extract of poison ivy. Look. It's all over you."

Reinhart looked aghast. "I'm terribly allergic to poison ivy." The others drew away from him.

"If I were you, I'd get into a bath of tomato juice immediately," she said.

"I thought that only worked for skunks?"

"It's your skin," Ginny replied.

Reinhart wagged a finger at Heinlein. "Don't let any of those sailors go anywhere. I want to interview them personally." Taking swift yet awkward gingerly steps, he headed toward base housing.

Heinlein took hold of Ginny's elbow and leaned close to her ear. Her hair tickled his nose and smelled of jasmine and vanilla. "Thank you."

"I want to know what's going on."

"Me too." He turned to de Camp. "Now what?"

"We've gotta wait for this ship to come in."

"How much longer?"

"That's what I was wondering."

There was a disturbance at the dock. Walb was navigating one of the gray powerboats alongside so the passenger could clamber out. The white hair was disheveled, and seemed even more distinguished because of the all-black clothes, but Walter Gibson was grinning like an imp.

"You scared the hell out of us, Walt." Heinlein offered the magician a hand up to the breakwater. "I thought the whole show was over when the ship disappeared."

"Well, I'm not working in the most controlled circumstances out on that island. The generator started throwing sparks and I had to shut it down to cool it off."

"I know you're doing the best you can."

The destroyer escort still floated placidly on the river. "I hope it didn't cause any problems?"

"Nothing we couldn't handle."

Gibson nodded to de Camp. "Your reflective haze is remarkable stuff. Holds a mirror image as bright as a movie screen, but you can see right through it."

"It's Miss Gerstenfeld's invention," de Camp said. "I only added the compression power to make the haze flow over the river. And Yani's Claw of Archimedes was the finishing touch. It's just like when Myrddin Wyllt had the pillars of Stonehenge moved across country overnight to confuse and deceive the enemies of the Britons." He looked around at the blank faces. "Right? What? Nobody ever heard of Merlin?"

"Pepper's Ghost." Heinlein cocked an eyebrow at Gibson.

"Not just any Pepper's Ghost." Gibson's small chest was practically bursting with pride. "The most elaborate Pepper's Ghost illusion ever created. And you're sure I can't even tell anyone about it?"

"Nope." Heinlein shook his head. "Absolutely no one."

"Not even Welles?"

"Especially not Welles."

Gibson's chest sank, but only a little. "Welles may have panicked America," he said, a touch of pout in his voice, "but this hoax could defeat the Nazis. The beautiful magic here, what really makes this an illusion for the ages, is that it's outdoors in broad daylight."

"Maybe you can make a Shadow story out of it after the war."

Gibson grinned. "Who's the model maker?"

Brinley raised his hand.

"We'll get it back to you when we're done, but I've got to tell you, it looks great when the mirrors and the lights hit it. Makes it look as big as the real thing."

"It took some serious acting to get de Camp off of Reinhart's project." Heinlein turned to the tall young man. "That was an award-winning performance."

"Thanks. I thought I was hamming it up."

"Reinhart bought it."

"Well, we needed every day on the island," Sprague said, "to set things up."

Gibson said, "It's a brilliant distraction, when you think about it. Elementary psychology. Only the people in the lab have considered that a ship could disappear. Hardly anyone else in the yard will have even noticed that the real ship is gone because, in general, they pay no attention to it. If you ask most people here tomorrow if the ship was out of its dock today, they'll say no."

"Don't pat yourself on the back so hard, Walter," Heinlein retorted. "We're not out of the woods yet. Let's keep this ghost ship afloat until we get our real one back."

"How much longer is that?" Gibson asked.

"Christ, any friggin' minute, I hope."

"What happened to you this morning?" de Camp asked, as he and Heinlein left Walter with his illusion and headed back into the lab. "The ship left without you."

"I know," Heinlein said. "I ran into a couple of problems in cheap suits."

"What?"

"We're being watched, and followed."

"By whom? The Nazis?"

"Our own government, if you can believe it."

"What do they know?"

"Nothing anymore. By the way, I want to ask you. You know how you hear the advice not to use a phone during a lightning storm because you can get electrocuted?"

"Sure."

"Is it true?"

"It's possible. If you're on the phone, a surge of electricity could make the leap from the handset to your head. Why?"

"No reason. Have you heard from the kid?"

"Asimov? I know he was on the train to New York early this morning. He ought to be back by now."

"God, this is all one loose screw from falling completely apart."

"How much trouble do you think we're in?"

A loud whistle split the air. Heinlein closed his eyes and uttered a quick prayer of thanks.

"Guess I'd better head back and help Mr. Yani finish up," Gibson said. Heinlein helped him back into the boat, though his leg didn't seem to be bothering him at all.

"Where's your cane?" he asked.

"Guess I forgot it." Gibson seemed surprised.

Heinlein grasped his hand and gave it a solid squeeze.

Gibson grinned. "You know what the difference is between the old pulp days and your new ones?"

"What?"

"We knew how to have more fun." He laughed as Walb cast off and the boat headed quickly downstream until it vanished behind the island. A few minutes later, the destroyer escort winked out of existence.

"There!" a voice cried out. "It did disappear!" Reinhart, in fresh clothes, ran toward them, pointing at the water. "You did it! What you've done here is historic. If you won't take credit for it, I will."

Heinlein grabbed Reinhart. "Look," he said sternly. "We didn't do anything. You're seeing things."

"You're going to tell me it's on the other side of the island again?"

"Not at all," de Camp said. "We're bringing her in." He gestured grandly toward the windows as the ship made its way past the small island and rapidly approached its mooring, where the shore crew seemed to materialize out of thin air.

Reinhart dashed to the ship, grabbing the lines and trying to moor it a little faster. "I want every man on this ship quarantined until I can interview them personally." There were no MPs around to hear his order, Heinlein noted with relief.

The gangplank hit the pier with a loud clang, then all was quiet for a long moment. Suddenly, in groups of two or three at a time, the skeleton crew of the destroyer escort staggered from the deck to the dock. Some roared with fiery belligerence and pushed their way past Reinhart, while others dropped to their knees and vomited as if there was no other way for the contents of their stomachs to be evacuated so quickly. "They got into the booze," Heinlein whispered to Ginny and de Camp. "They'll spill for sure."

Reinhart turned to face him, an expression of disbelief slowly contorting his face. Heinlein had underestimated his intelligence—he was about to put it all together.

"You've driven them mad!" Reinhart cried in a voice filled with shock and horror. "Look at these poor sons of bitches. The experience of our experiment was more than their minds could handle."

"Um," Heinlein said. Followed quickly by, "Exactly!" He looked from Gibson to Ginny. "That's it. Exactly."

"We're going to have to let them recover," de Camp added swiftly. "It's the humane thing to do."

Something exploded with a small green flash upon the deck of the ship. Reinhart ran up the gangplank.

"Shit." Heinlein and the others dashed up after him. A puff of greenish smoke melted into the wisps of the fog, tinted slightly red by the setting sun. Several sailors lay on deck, in various states of consciousness.

"This is a nightmare," Reinhart whispered.

"I agree," Heinlein said. "We should halt all further experiments until we've had a chance to analyze our data."

"Yes." Reinhart nodded. "Yes. That's what we should do. Analyze the data."

"This experiment is too dangerous," Heinlein continued. "I think it's obvious that our degaussing frequency nearly fried their brains."

"Of course it is," de Camp said.

"Hey, Chief!" Heinlein looked up to the bridge to see Olson emerging through a hatch. The sailor swayed and staggered but managed to keep his feet under him. "She's a hell of a ship, ain't she?"

"She sure is. She sure is. I think even the little guy enjoyed it."

"Little guy? What little guy?"

"Your little guy. Lucky!"

"Lucky!" He stepped forward. "Isaac is on board?"

"Sure." Olson nodded heartily, but then looked around as if confused. "He was here a little while ago."

"Where?"

"By the . . . the . . ." He waved his hand toward a spot behind the gangplank.

"Christ almighty!" Heinlein spun around. De Camp, closer to the railing, bent down and picked up an object.

"Oh my God!" Reinhart said, in a low, horror-struck whisper, as de Camp held up a pair of familiar, thick-rimmed glasses for all to see. "You've vaporized Isaac Asimov!"

EPISODE 38

ALL HE KNEW was that he had to get clear of the propellers.

Isaac had hit the water hard enough to be stunned by the impact and the shocking cold. But at the same time, the ungainly flatness of his landing, with limbs splayed, had kept him from plunging too deeply. Which was fortunate because had he sunk any farther, his lungs would have been completely filled with the Atlantic. Instead, he had kicked and flailed wildly, breaching the frothing surface in a panic. At the same instant as the gray flank of the ship slid impassively past him, an image of the butcher on President Street expertly dissecting a chicken for dinner, drops of blood spattering across the brown paper, pieces being cleaved neatly away, flashed through his mind.

Exactly what the immense screws would do to him.

Never one for exercise, he had nevertheless enjoyed his long summers at Brighton Beach and the new Red Hook pool where he learned how to swim. He would never have won a race in his life, but now he swam as if Buster Crabbe himself were coaching him on.

He could feel the sucking traction of the current and was dimly aware that his stiff shoes were making it difficult to progress, so he slapped his arms through the water with even greater energy. It was panic, pure and simple, his mind and body overwhelmed with one single impulse: to survive. The ship's great engines thundered all around, the roar of Monstro rising from the depths to devour him.

And then a still silence enveloped him with astounding rapidity. The ship was past and he was starting at its receding stern, gently bobbing up and down in the expanding V created by the wake.

"Hey!" he cried out. "Help!"

Pyrotechnics continued to burst above and around the ship, emerald blossoms sparkling through the thick gray haze enveloping the destroyer escort. The soot pouring from the stack and the smoke from the fireworks, combining with the afternoon mist rolling in over the waves, quickly swallowed up the vessel until all he could see were green flashes. Before long he was left with the sound of rockets booming in the distance and the distinct, acrid smell of gunpowder.

Isaac had only been in the water for a few moments. He couldn't believe how quickly events had transpired.

"Hello!" His voice sounded hollow and empty, as if it couldn't possibly travel any distance at all. There had been a ship in the distance. Treading water, he worked himself around into something approximating a full circle. Now he could see nothing. No ship. No shore. Only the encroaching line of fog.

He reached down and brought his legs up at the same time, so he could rip off the shoes and socks that were dragging him down. Then he started to pull off his jacket, slipping off one sleeve, then reaching across his chest to free his other arm, stopping only when he felt something hard in the breast pocket. For a moment he couldn't even recall what it might be, as if his mind couldn't process the possibility of the impossible. Then he remembered.

"Please, please, please," he whimpered. His cold fingers fumbled through the pocket, trying to keep the hard metal object from dropping out. The coat slipped away, he let it go. He had what he needed, clutched tightly in his right hand. He let himself breathe a tiny sigh of extremely limited relief, careful not to swallow any salt water.

Slowly he raised the flask he had meant to give to Bob above the waves. Isaac unscrewed the top and brought the open bottle neck below his nose. A long sniff convinced him that it was still good. In a smooth motion he flipped the flask over and emptied every drop of its clear contents into the waters.

The waters around him fizzed slightly, giving off a sound so familiar to him as the first chemical reaction he had ever attempted and returned to again and again, the comforting sound of $NaHCO_3$ meeting CH_3COOH. Isaac laughed out loud, in spite of his situation, as the ocean's surface turned a bright, nearly fluorescent orange.

"It works!" he crowed at his small triumph, wishing he could share it with anyone on the face of the earth. The slick substance oozed around him, thick and clingy, spreading in an uneven circle with Isaac at the center, radiating out several yards, surrounding him. Holding fast. The fizzing sound was something he'd have to look into if he somehow survived. Oddly comforting at first, it grew into a rather incessant buzzing as the marker dye spread. There was no explanation for that. Of course, he was cold, and that sapped mental acuity. Otherwise, he would have figured it out; he was sure of that. With some time and some warmth, he might be able to work out why his chemical creation sounded a lot like an engine.

Something blotted out the sun for an instant. A cloud or a large bird flashed before his eyes, the sight blurry without his glasses. The buzzing turned into a roar as the Dents' seaplane shot over his head. He began to scream and wave. The plane dipped its wing in response. His shrieking turned to cheers, then laughter as Dent Aerial Survey One circled once and then sluiced over the water. The dye was turning into a thick rubbery sludge that clung to his arms as he tried to crawl across it. He switched to a breaststroke, which meant that he was now trying to drag his head through the muck. With the Dents a hundred yards away, he estimated that he would drown from exhaustion at this pace.

He took a deep breath and let himself sink beneath the waves until he felt the last tug of the solution spring free from his clothes and then kicked for the clear surface beyond its edges. Then he swam as hard as he could, pounding at the water, while the seaplane quickly covered the remaining distance. So electrifying was the sensation of elation that flowed through his weary body as his hands grasped for the slippery pontoon that it wasn't until the door opened and the pipe smoke billowed out, and Lester Dent extended his hand, that Isaac realized he actually had to get on board.

A plane.

"C'mon, son," the big man called. "Grab my hand!"

"Uh."

"Kid!"

"Can you just drive me to shore, Mr. Dent?" He waved in the general direction of America. "No need to get into the air."

"Kid, these waters are lousy with U-boats. Now get in here before some kraut takes a shot at us."

"I can just hang on here."

"Hey there, honey." Norma Dent poked her head out the door. "What's the problem?"

"Fool kid won't get on the plane," he growled at her.

But she wasn't looking at her husband. Her blue eyes, when Isaac could see them through the thick blond hair whipping about her face, were focused on him. "Isaac?"

"Yes, ma'am?"

"Why don't you come on into the plane?"

"Okay."

He took the proffered hand and let Mr. Dent pull him into the tiny cabin. There were two small seats behind the pilot and copilot chairs, and Isaac squeezed into one.

"You're shivering," Mrs. Dent said, her voice full of empathy. As Mr. Dent climbed back into his seat and pulled the door shut, she slipped between Isaac and the other chair; he could smell a hint of some exotic flower he would never know the name of as she brushed past him, and opened a traveling trunk. She withdrew several wool blankets and put them around Isaac. They gave off the faint aroma of campfires and adventure. "It's always good to have blankets around," she said, patting his head, tenderly, he thought. "Never know when you're going to find yourself sleeping outdoors. Or wet."

She gave her husband a quick peck on the cheek and Isaac waited for Mr. Dent to get up and move over to his position in the pilot's chair, but instead Mrs. Dent slid into the seat. He heard a low moan and when they both turned to look at him, he realized he'd made the sound.

"Are you okay, kid?" Mr. Dent asked, squinting at him as if he expected Isaac to bolt for the door or the controls.

"She's the pilot?" Isaac blurted out. He hadn't wanted to say it out loud, but he'd been thinking it, and it had just kind of escaped.

Instead of looking insulted, Mrs. Dent laughed, then put on a pair of chic sunglasses. "Yep. I'm the pilot."

Mr. Dent gave Isaac a broad smile, his mustache turning up at the corners. "You're married, right, kid?"

"Yeah."

Mrs. Dent threw a few switches and pulled out a few stoppers. Then she pressed a button and the plane shuddered to life, the propeller outside the window instantly turning into a blur.

"Well, sometimes you have to just sit back and let your wife drive the plane."

Mrs. Dent's short laugh was positively gleeful as she pushed the throttle forward and the seaplane began to pick up speed.

"Keep your mouth shut and don't throw up in my plane!" Mr. Dent commanded.

He wondered if he would feel anything, then there was a great lurch, the ocean dropped away from the porthole next to him, and his stomach tried to escape in several directions at once. Fortunately, he had taken Mr. Dent's order to heart. His jaw was clamped shut. On the other hand, he had forgotten how to breathe.

"You okay back there?" Mrs. Dent asked.

Mr. Dent looked back. "He has really big eyes, right?"

"Yeah."

"He's okay, then."

She banked the plane to the right and he saw the shoreline already so far below and so impossibly distant. Then she leveled out of the curve but continued to shoot skyward at an angle that seemed impossible. Suddenly, he gasped, overwhelmed with the need to breathe. The dizziness passed.

"Eight thousand feet," Mrs. Dent called out, throttling down and leveling out.

"Where are we going?" It had crossed his mind that they might be taking him back to Missouri.

"Philadelphia," she sang out.

"Thank God," he replied.

"Are your eyes closed?"

"Not anymore."

"Well, since you're already up in the air, why don't you enjoy the view." As she spoke, she held her hand out at an angle to her side and Lester Dent took it. She controlled the plane easily with her other hand.

Gertie. How was he going to make this up to her? He watched the Dents holding hands, so easy and comfortable. Meanwhile, he couldn't remember the last time he'd taken Gertie's hand in his. He'd give anything to be with her right now. But more than that, he wanted he and Gertie to have what Norma and Lester Dent had, complete confidence in each other. Isaac so badly just wanted to hold his wife's hand he could practically feel it.

"Can I ask you something?"

"Sure," Lester shouted.

"How come you never sued the Superman guys for ripping you off? I mean, Superman has a Fortress of Solitude, they call him the man of steel instead of the man of bronze. They even stole the name: Clark!"

Both the Dents burst into laughter. "Life's too short," Dent hollered back.

The clouds rose like towering swirls all around their tiny vessel, tinged with the pinks and grays of the late afternoon. He'd never seen anything so majestic and monumental in all his life. Isaac had imagined cities of the future, alien worlds, the vast emptiness of space, yet here before him was something so new and grand as to defy that imagination, even his ability to describe it. Far away and higher than their elevation, something sparkled and caught his attention. He squinted, unsure of his eyes. It came again, the reflection of sunlight off metal.

"There's another plane out there," he warned.

"Where?" Mr. Dent said. Mrs. Dent deftly slipped her hand back and grabbed the stick.

"Over there," Isaac pointed. "Up there. I think we're on track to run into it."

Mr. Dent pulled a pair of heavy binoculars out of a case beneath his seat and raised them. After a moment he let them drop.

"What is it?" Mrs. Dent asked. "Lester?"

After pressing the palms of his hands into his eyes for a few seconds, he brought the glasses up again.

"Honey?"

"I'm not sure. It's up about nineteen thousand feet. We got the fuel for that?"

"Just barely. Extra weight and all." She nodded toward Isaac. "No offense."

Before Isaac could begin to point out that the boxes of ceramic tiles and fireworks had probably weighed more than he did, the plane banked sharply again, pressing him back in his chair.

"Isaac," Mr. Dent shouted. "There's a camera in the case back there. Get it."

"Uh."

"Hurry."

He twisted and could see the camera case, just beyond the reach of his fingertips. God, he'd have to stand up. His fingers trembling, he undid the latches and stood, his knees weak. With an effort, he snatched at the case. At the same time, the plane lurched like a cab hitting a pothole. He stumbled, finding his face pressed up right against the cool glass of the window.

"Sorry," he heard Mrs. Dent call. "Turbulence!" Her voice sounded a million miles away. A thin panel of glass and metal was all that stood between him and a long fall into the ocean. He couldn't move. Couldn't breathe. And then, just as his eyes began to roll up in his head, he saw the plane, and his entire being, mind and body and senses, snapped into focus.

"It's immense," he whispered.

The highly polished aluminum of its hull shimmered in the direct sunlight. Its wing span alone was nearly as big as the *Eldridge* was long.

Six huge engines, three on each wing, kept the giant aloft. Stenciled on the side of the plane was a black, outlined plus sign: the familiar, simplified version of the Iron Cross, the symbol of the *Wehrmacht*.

"*Wunderwaffe*," he whispered.

"I'm going to buzz it," Norma called out.

"No!" he shouted, but the small plane was already banking toward the bigger one. "They're Germans! It's an invasion!"

"It can't be an invasion if there's only one," Mr. Dent shouted back. "Look at those patches around the rivets. That's a prototype. It's a test flight."

The angle of the seaplane was so sharp that Isaac couldn't pull himself back to his seat. The super-bomber grew larger with stunning speed and they shot past it so close that he could see the pilot, a woman, a Valkyrie, with pulled-back curly hair and a grimace on her face. Then the image was gone and Isaac could feel a vibration through the hatch, as if someone were drawing a bow across a bass.

"Are they shooting at us?" Mrs. Dent cried out.

"Dive," Mr. Dent said calmly, and she responded by forcing the stick forward. Isaac stumbled into his seat and strapped on the belt.

"It's turning!" Mr. Dent called out. "I think we've scared it off."

Whether or not that part of what he'd just said was true, what was true was that the great behemoth of the air had begun to make a long, banking turn toward the northeast. Across one of the vertical tail wings, Isaac read the single word: JUNKERS.

"I'm going to chase it," Mrs. Dent said.

"Please God, no," Isaac moaned.

She drove the throttle forward, and banked up again. But no matter how hard she drove their little plane, the massive vehicle soon vanished into the clouds. Gone, as if it had never existed.

Isaac relaxed back in his seat. "Can I go home now?"

"Yes," Mrs. Dent replied.

"Those pictures are gonna be on the front page of every newspaper," Mr. Dent said, turning to look at Isaac. His eyes dropped down to the unopened case still gripped tightly in Isaac's hand. "Oh. No pictures?"

"I forgot."

"Oh."

"Lester," Mrs. Dent chided. "Don't take that tone with the boy. I didn't see you reaching for the radio."

Lester picked up the handset, then paused. "No one's going to believe us, are they?"

"I know people who will," Isaac said meekly. "In Philadelphia."

"That's where we're headed," Mrs. Dent said.

"Finally."

"If there's enough fuel."

"Aw, God!"

Mrs. Dent set her jaw firmly, teeth clenched, as if the exertion of answering any of her husband's questions might add to the consumption of gas. Eventually he grew quiet for the duration of the trip.

As they finally descended toward the river, Isaac saw a landmark he recognized, Independence Hall, standing proudly in the gathering dusk. At the same moment, the engine began to sputter.

"Honey?"

"Shh." Her hands were flying over the controls, tweaking this switch, tapping that gauge, pushing in those stoppers. Still, the droning grew sporadic, intermittent. Then it stopped altogether. The propeller came to a halt, twirling gently like a pinwheel in the wind.

"I love you, Mr. Dent," she said.

"I love you, too, Mrs. Dent," he replied.

Isaac was astounded. Husband and wife were grinning at each other as if falling out of the sky was just another night out on the town for the two of them. All he could do was grip his hands tightly together and think of Gertie.

With the water rushing below and the Navy Yard approaching on the right, Mrs. Dent suddenly reached out and threw a switch. The engine roared to life again and the plane instantly responded to her control. Deftly, she moved the stick and the seaplane dropped heavily onto the Delaware River. She throttled the engine way down, giving it just enough to move the vehicle forward.

"Always keep a little in the tank," she said, motoring toward the familiar shape of the *Eldridge* at the dock.

At the edge of the dock, Mr. Dent threw open the door. Isaac waited for Mrs. Dent to climb out onto the pontoon, then hurried after her. He looked up to see the barrel of a rifle pointed right between his eyes. Both Dents had their hands raised.

"I work here," Isaac shouted. "I work here."

"You're under arrest for the unauthorized landing of a plane in a military installation," the MP holding the rifle shouted.

"But it was an emergency!" he protested.

There were shouts in the distance and sounds of people running. He heard someone shouting his name.

"I'm here," he shouted. "Down here," he added, afraid that the people seeking him couldn't see him below the level of the dock.

To his great relief, Robert and Sprague and a few other people that he couldn't quite make out in the evening gloom appeared at the river's edge. He heard Slick's voice order the Military Police to stand down, then hands were pulling him and the Dents ashore, pounding him on the back, touching him as if they needed physical proof of his existence. He saw Mrs. Dent throw a hearty embrace around Bob. Walter Gibson limped out of the darkness, his cane tapping on the concrete, and eagerly took the hand that Lester Dent offered.

"We saw it." Isaac turned to Sprague and Slick.

"Saw what?" Sprague asked.

"The super-bomber. We saw it."

Slick pursed his lips thoughtfully for a minute. "You'll need to tell us all about it."

Isaac turned to look at the Dents. "Ask them," he said, then he began to walk. Sprague called after him, but he ignored his friend, heading away from the gathering, the seaplane, the destroyer escort, and the lab. He heard footsteps running up behind him but kept his feet moving forward.

"Hey," Bob called. "Hey, Isaac. Wait up."

But he didn't stop.

Bob ran around in front of him and gave him a friendly smile. "Hey, Isaac."

Now Isaac stopped. "Where were you?"

"I got held up." He raised his arms out at his sides. "C'mon, right?"

"You nearly got me killed, Bob. I ended up in the water! And on a plane!"

"You're here now." Bob smiled.

"Not for long." He pushed past Bob and started walking.

"Isaac. Wait. Where are they?"

He paused. "What?"

"The tiles. Did you get them?"

For a moment he felt like telling Bob that he had thrown them overboard. "Is it that important, Bob? Really?" He turned around.

Bob stood, alone and apart, arms hanging down limply. "Yes."

Isaac nodded to himself. A vision of the huge plane appeared in his mind's eye. "Yeah. They're here, Bob. I stowed them in the captain's quarters." He turned his back on the man.

"Where are you going?" Bob called after him.

"To see my wife."

EPISODE 39

LOST IN THE darkness, trees snatching at the car, he realized how tired he was. He should have gone home and slept. Why couldn't he have waited another day? Isaac had asked him if this was really that important.

Yes.

It was the single-word answer that Isaac hadn't wanted to hear. Yes, it was that important. And it wasn't about saving the world. He wanted to know if it was possible. That was it. He couldn't wait. And now he was lost, too tired to recall the way, driving through an unlit countryside. He smiled weakly at the irony of trying to find the birthplace of the light bulb in the dark.

In the end it was the beacon atop the Edison Monument, strobing and sparkling through the zoetrope of tree branches, that helped him find his way. With a sigh of relief, Heinlein spun the wheel a few times, keeping the light on his left, finally making the turn onto Christie Street. At the end of the block he recognized the low building and pulled up in front of it. The meadow that surrounded it was alive with fireflies and the merry sound of crickets. It reminded him of the fields of his youth. He gazed skyward, the full moon mirroring the glowing globe atop the monument. After trying the wooden door and finding it locked, he climbed back into the front seat. The hot air was thick, heavy; his head rested against the back of his seat.

Someone was banging on the hood of his car.

Heinlein opened his eyes, disoriented. For a moment he didn't know where he was or what he was doing there. He held up one hand to block the light flooding his car. Squinting, he could see that it was still dark.

A man stood in front of his car, backlit in the glare, his features indistinguishable. "Are you sleeping?"

"Just resting my eyes," Heinlein replied thickly, running his tongue over his dry teeth and rubbing the grit out of his eyes with the palms of his hands. He climbed out of the car, his knees popping, steadying himself on the door.

"I came down right after you called," the man said. He shifted nervously in the light thrown by the headlamps of the car. "Is it true? Have you and your team really figured out how to make it work?"

Heinlein ran his fingers through his hair. "I hope so." He pointed to the shining light on top of the column. "You had the power turned on."

"The tiles? Where are they?"

"In the trunk."

"May I see them?" The man took several eager steps forward, out of the light, and Heinlein could finally see the pinched, hungry face of Lyman Binch.

"Sure," he said, and led Binch around to the trunk. He opened one of the crates, flipping back the canvas.

"May I?" Binch's eyes were bright, as if it were Christmas morning and he was a seven-year-old kid.

"Be my guest." Heinlein did feel a bit like a proud pop.

With trembling fingers, Binch withdrew a paper-wrapped square and carefully peeled back the folds to reveal a milky jade green square. Even in the distant light from the headlamps, the tile seemed to glow with an inner luster. "It's not radioactive, is it?" Lyman asked, with fascination.

"Not as far as I know," Heinlein replied, hoping that Isaac would have shared that information.

"I've had the best minds in America trying to figure this out for years. How did you do it?"

"I've got a team with good imaginations."

"But you must have found a clue, somehow. Somewhere." Binch's voice took on an almost petulant tone. "You must have found something we overlooked, or discovered some kind of insight. Please, you have to tell me what I overlooked."

"All I can tell you is that the answer was closer than you thought. You were right on top of it. Sometimes you just need to get out of the ivory tower and get your feet wet."

"I thought the expression was 'get your hands dirty.'"

"That works, too."

There was a crack of gray on the bottom edge of the black sky. Heinlein let Binch hold on to the tile he was caressing, and closed the lid on the rest. Now he was the one who sounded eager. "Want to see if it works?"

Binch looked at him, his old eyes brimming with tears that glittered in the car's headlamps. "Yes."

Heinlein offered to carry each crate but Binch insisted on bringing one. The man had surprising strength for his age, easily hoisting up his box. If his own pulse was any indication, then Binch was similarly flooded with adrenaline.

At the door, Binch paused and watched a lightning bug cross his path. "Tom used to envy fireflies," he mused. "They could do so easily what he could not. I wish he were here now."

"What about Nikola?"

"I don't know how he felt about fireflies. But he loved his pigeons." Binch unlocked the door and the two men entered, carefully placing the boxes on the low wooden table just inside. Then Binch found the light switch and banished the gloom. While he trotted back to his car to turn off the headlamps, Heinlein opened the hatch to the lower level.

"How will we know if it works?" Up above, Binch had returned. "Didn't Tesla have someone out there with a receiver? Admiral Peary?"

A twinge of guilt stabbed at Heinlein. "The receiver never mattered."

Binch hadn't heard him. "What?"

"Forget about the damn receiver! If this thing works, we'll know it, with or without a receiver."

"Really? How?" Binch walked slowly down the steps.

"The amount of electricity we bounce off the ionosphere should re-create the aurora borealis overhead. Any lovers at the top of the Empire State Building might see quite a show in the skies over New Jersey."

"And then we'll know?"

"And then we'll know."

"Goddamn!" Binch brought his fist down on the table with enough force to make the tiles jump. "If this works. If this works, we can change the world!"

"We might even be able to save it."

Binch rubbed his hands together, massaging the arthritic knuckles. "Imagine the money we could make. No more damming up rivers for hydroelectricity or building coal plants. We'll build thousands of these towers. We won't have to string any more electrical wires—no more poles. Every building in America will lease our receivers, paying us a yearly dues for our energy."

"Tesla wanted the energy to be free. For the betterment of mankind."

"Tesla was a holy fool! Inspired, yes. But sensible? Not in the least. He never understood the monetary potential in this—his greatest invention. Even Tom came to understand it too late. They're going to make me the Emperor of General Electric for this."

"Be that as it may, your highness, we still need to see if it works. Then we need to figure out how to adjust it so the energy doesn't flow through the earth, but can bounce off the outer edge of the atmosphere and rain hell down on any Nazi super-bomber invasion."

Binch composed himself, closing his eyes for a moment as if he needed to consciously push away all the dollar signs floating through his brain. "Of course," he said at length. "That's what we're here for. And there's a lot of work to do. I got ahead of myself. Forgive me."

As they pulled the lattices that were designed to hold the tiles from their secure nesting places in the great iron capacitors, Heinlein wished he had at least invited Sprague to come with him. The procedure was painstaking and tedious, and the extra set of hands would have been welcome, as would the man's incessant good cheer and encouragement. He felt like he was cheating on him. They brought the tiles down, carefully, a few at a time. Each one had to be wiped with thick cotton cloths to remove any dust or residue, then put into a receptacle and screwed into place. Care had to be taken to apply enough pressure so that the mount would hold the tile in place tight enough to not move at all but not so much as to crack it, which had happened with the first couple they tried. Heinlein finally figured out exactly how many turns of the screw were required to accomplish that task: seventeen. With hundreds of tiles to put into position, even when he took a break, he found himself counting to seventeen in rote fashion.

It was mind-numbing, tedious, and he was exhausted.

"You know, Tom was a big believer in the catnap," Binch said, as Heinlein slumped over the table. "There's a cot in the office upstairs if you want to catch forty winks."

He staggered wearily up the steps to the cot and lay down. He didn't want to stop the work, but his body left him no choice. The morning sun had already filled the building with a hot, sticky haze, and he dropped down heavily, ignoring the sweat gathering under his collar. The last thought he had before he fell asleep was to wonder why Binch was so curious about how they'd figured out the tiles.

He awoke to find Binch sitting in a chair across the room, his head in his hands. The setting sun told him he'd been sleeping for a while. Heinlein cleared his throat and Binch looked up at him; the weariness in his eyes was startling.

"I've been waiting for this moment for forty-five years," Binch said. "I've grown old thinking this day would never come. But I've never given up."

Heinlein sat up on the edge of his cot.

"I've spent my life around genius, but never was one. Can you imagine what that's like?"

Heinlein, still groggy, shrugged slightly.

"I was never smart enough. Nikola always said I lacked that crucial, intangible, elusive spark—the ability to make connections between thoughts and concepts that leads to real intelligence. Tom said that I was skilled and clever, just not brilliant. I can't tell you how many years it took me to come to terms with what they thought about me. To realize, even accept, my own shortcomings.

"I'm not a stupid man. In fact, I see opportunities where others don't. Maybe that's my genius. Or maybe determination is. I'm not sure. I don't even care anymore. It used to matter to me that the world recognize my genius alongside Tom's and Nikola's. Of course, they're both dead, and I'm still here. The only man to ever work with them both. I know what genius is. But I've persisted throughout all these years while others have failed and forgotten. I guess you could say I have a genius for tenacity." He cleared his throat and looked out the window. "What about you, Heinlein? Are you some kind of a genius?"

"I'm no genius. I've only ever met one, and I think even he might have been wrong about a few things."

"Then what's in it for you? I've done my research on you. I know you don't write anymore, even though lots of people think you're the best one out there. Why would you walk away from it and get involved in something like this?"

"I want to serve my country."

"Bullshit." Binch's eyes flashed momentarily, but otherwise his expression remained flat and burdened.

"Since I had to leave the Navy I've led a rather frivolous life. I've done nothing of consequence. Nothing that will be remembered."

"You wanted to do something grand?"

"I want to see the future come true. I want to see men walking on the moon and the planets. I want rocket ships plying our skies like the clipper ships that used to cross our oceans. I didn't want to write about it anymore because that's just this side of pathological. Imagine just sitting around dreaming of traveling to the stars. The only thing that separates me from a nut job is that someone pays me every now and then to put those musings down on paper. But nevertheless, writing puts me just on this side of certifiable. And what happens when they stop paying me and I am still doing it? I've got enough crazy in my life. I don't want to be crazy. I want to do things.

"I want to ride in one of those rocket ships and watch the sun rise over a Martian desert. I want to experience the weightlessness of being freed from gravity. I want to live for hundreds of years and see all these things come true, see if humanity can take the better path. I want to make the future come true. I want us to survive. I want to knock enemy aircraft out of the sky with a death shield that will protect my country. But most of all I want to end this war so we can get on with it. So I can get on with it."

"The future?"

"Yes. The future."

Binch stood. "Then let's finish it up and see if tomorrow brings that future."

They worked through the night, spelling each other for the infrequent breaks, not talking except when assistance was needed, eating from old boxes of crackers and drinking from the tap. The work became an endless, repetitive blur of one damn tile after another. Heinlein's hands ached from the constant torque of the screwdriver, hurt far worse than they had even after marathon writing sessions. The old screws and sharp-edged tiles wore grooves into his fingertips that soon grew bloody.

At midmorning of the following day, the task was completed; the last lattice slid gently into its place. "And that, as they say, is that," Heinlein muttered, as he stood with his hands on his hips gazing at the array of great metal cases before him. "I can't believe it."

"I know what you mean."

"So, where's the start button? Let's fire this sonofabitch up!"

Binch grinned, the first expression of satisfaction Heinlein had seen on the man's usually stoic face. "Not exactly how Nikola or Tom would have put it, but I agree."

They walked together to the office at the far end of the room, past the entrance to the darkened tunnels through which great insulated cables flowed toward the tower. Heinlein helped Binch remove the heavy tarps which had covered the banks of buttons and gauges for years, throwing up great clouds of choking dust that settled to the floor even as Binch set about flipping switches and tapping dials. A hum of energy began to fill the room, and with each snap of a switch flipping into place, the lights in the office would dim momentarily before recovering.

"We're going to put some drain on the local power," Binch said. "You remember those coal generators at Wardenclyffe? Tesla had to create his own electricity, but by the time we started construction here, I decided that we'd just pipe it in. That's one of my improvements."

Heinlein nodded, so eager to see what new thing happened with each move Binch made that he ignored the sense of unease that had begun to gnaw at the furthest edges of his consciousness. "Such as?"

"Well, Tesla needed a full day to charge his capacitors. My solution is more refined. It should only take a matter of hours." He rubbed his hand over the brass instrument with a glass front that reminded Heinlein of a barometer. "This is the one to watch," Binch said. "Once I throw this switch"—he indicated a large, throttlelike lever below—"it'll tell us that the capacitors are charging. If the needle starts to move, and it crosses the green line here, we are ready to transmit."

"Great."

"In the meantime, you'll need to use those dials over there to define the frequency spectrum and range of our test. That will determine whether we broadcast up or down. You'll find some schematics upstairs in the office which define the settings."

Heinlein began to walk when Binch suddenly reached out and stopped him. "Look!"

The red needle on the big gauge was trembling. As Heinlein watched, it ticked ever so slightly to the right. "It moved!"

"It did."

As he passed the capacitors, the waves of humming energy made Heinlein's hair stand on end. He took the stairs two at a time and quickly found the books that Binch had set out him for. They were old, the paper crackled between his fingers. He recognized the Cyrillic writing and smiled to himself at how once, what seemed like a long time ago, they had thought the symbols a code.

He tucked a piece of paper between the pages to bookmark it and then closed it. The cover caught his attention; in his eagerness he hadn't really examined it before. The thick leather was engraved with an image of the huge mushroom-capped tower he had grown used to seeing in his dreams, and just below it was the single word: *Wardenclyffe.*

As the word played through his mind, the nagging concern that had begun in the office below gnawed with growing consistency. Distracted, he nearly hit his head on the beam walking back down the stairs.

"Find the numbers?" Binch asked.

"Yes."

"Look, it's still climbing. Almost green."

"That's terrific."

Binch put his hand on the cherrywood handle of a heavy lever. "This is the transmit switch. Once we throw it up, all we have to do is sit back and wait."

Heinlein twiddled the dials, watching the numbers printed on the ring of each one click through a little viewing pane, until he had all set to the proper sequence. He closed the book and traced the title word again with his fingertip.

He heard a distant sound, almost as if there was something pounding in the distance. Heinlein looked to Binch, but he was too distracted by the crackle and snap coming from the gauges before him.

"I'm going to put this back," Heinlein said, quietly walking past the man to the stairs. The book felt heavy in his hands.

Wardenclyffe.

How had Binch known that he had seen the coal generators at Wardenclyffe?

He sidled up to the front door, gratified to see that the heavy bolt had been lowered. "Who's there?"

"Bob? Is that you?"

"John?" He threw back the bolt and opened the door. The sun had set and it took a moment for his eyes to adjust.

Campbell stood in the doorway, shoulders hunched, cigarette holder hanging limply from his clenched teeth. "Bob!"

"It took you long enough. I called you Sunday night."

Campbell pushed his way in, as if he was afraid someone was watching him, then shut the door and blockaded it with his own large body. "It's over, Bob," he whispered.

"It's not over, John. We're just about to test the tower. It's going to work! We've done it."

"No, you don't understand. They've shut us down. The Kamikaze Group. It's all over."

"What happened?"

"The police found the two agents who were leading the Cartmill investigation. They were dead, Bob. In Philadelphia! They think they were murdered because of us. Maybe by us. The Army invaded my office today, at Street & Smith. They confiscated everything and anything having to do with Kamikaze. I called the Navy Yard and de Camp said the same thing was happening there. The Army was sealing off the lab, kicked everyone out. De Camp said he hadn't seen you in a couple of days but that you might be here."

"John! Stop talking for a moment and listen to me. We're about to do something incredible here."

"Bob, it's over!"

"It's not! We've still got time."

"No, you don't. You don't understand! De Camp and Asimov, I told the boys to cooperate with the Army. Completely."

"They told them about this?"

"By now they must have. It's only a matter of time until the Army arrives. Bob, you're in trouble. I want to get you out of here. We can clean up the mess later. But if they get here and find you there's a good chance they'll shoot first and ask questions later."

"I can't leave, John. I've risked everything to make this work. And it's about to. You won't believe it. You have to see what we've done. Once they see what we're doing, they'll have to let us continue."

"They don't care, Bob. You have to see the bigger picture here. The Kamikaze Group was a decoy."

Heinlein felt dizzy, as if Campbell had punched him. "What do you mean?"

"There is secret scientific work going on, but we're not it. It's a project of such infinite complexity that it encompasses thousands of people and millions of dollars, in facilities all across the country. The Kamikaze Group was a high-profile distraction for that. That was Scoles's plan for us since the beginning. Come on, Bob, think it through. A group of crazy writers toiling trying to come up with invisibility and death rays? If there's a spy looking for secrets, they're going to head in your direction, directly away from the brains working on the bomb."

"What bomb?"

"Christ! Haven't you put it together yet? Why do you think there was so much interest in that damn Cartmill story? Because it's real. The atom bomb. It's real and it's American."

"John," Heinlein said, as calmly as he could, "we're on the verge of a breakthrough here. Right now."

"Bob," Campbell replied, "there are two dead Feds to account for. Your name is being tossed around."

"I didn't kill anyone, John. I was there, but I didn't kill them."

"Oh God," Campbell groaned. "This is getting worse and worse. What do you mean, you were there?"

"I mean, they were in the middle of interviewing me and then they were both dead. I'm telling you, I barely escaped with my life."

"How'd they die?"

"I don't know."

"I can answer your question, Mr. Campbell." Binch slowly emerged from the lower level. "I killed them. In the same way I killed Nikola Tesla. With electricity." He held a pistol that drifted back and forth between its two targets.

"You followed us to Wardenclyffe, didn't you?" Heinlein asked.

"I didn't follow you. I waited for you to show up. I did follow you to the Empire State Building. I really didn't expect you to escape. After finding out you were gone, I was pretty sure the only place you'd go next, if you'd found any clues in the vault, was Wardenclyffe. And soon enough, you showed up."

"You didn't try to kill us again there?"

"At that point it seemed like you were on to something. It was easier to work with you at that point than against you."

"So you just used us."

"No. Really, just you. Because you're the one who really wanted it to work. I don't know why, but you did. Now, why don't we go downstairs and see if it does."

Heinlein led Campbell below. They walked past the iron capacitors; the power flowing off them made Heinlein's fillings ache. In the control office he noticed right away that the needle on the capacitor gauge was pinned all the way to the right. "It's already charged?"

Binch followed them in, still pointing the gun at them. "I told you it would charge quickly. Would you do me a favor and throw the switch?"

"Under the circumstances, I'd rather not."

"I think, given the circumstances, as you say, that you've earned the right to throw the switch and see what happens. None of this would have happened without you. Please, Mr. Heinlein. Robert. I'm offering you the chance to be a part of history. Throw the switch."

Heinlein placed his hand on the wood of the lever. It was cool and smooth and pulsed with life.

"Bob?" Grave apprehension was written on Campbell's face.

"It's okay, John. This is what we set out to do. I want to know as badly as he does. As much as Tesla wanted to know."

The lever provided surprising resistance. Heinlein threw his shoulder into it, and with a shriek of metal grating on metal, the switch snapped up and into place.

"Now"—Lyman Binch waved them away from the panel—"here we go."

EPISODE 40

THE INFECTION HAD begun in his lacerated hand, and the fever it caused was high. How high he couldn't exactly tell, but it was enough so he alternated between shivering uncontrollably under scratchy mats made of woven leaves and being completely out of his head. He could only recall the spells of madness when he awoke in cold sweats, his body aching.

He was dying.

He was going to die in the bowels of a godforsaken volcano and no one would ever find him.

Witch doctors appeared in the firelight cast by the two torches that illuminated the case he now felt he was guarding with his life—fearsome fellows with skulls painted across their grinning faces, dancing and warbling and plying him with foul-smelling brews to the accompaniment of booming, beating drums from somewhere far deeper in the caverns.

From time to time the face of Mr. Faaitu'a would drift in and out of his consciousness. His expression was grim. The sounds flowed around Hubbard without making an impression. The only one who could reach him was his angel. His flame-haired goddess.

"How do I know you're real?" he'd ask.

"Can you feel my desire? Your passion makes me real."

Other times he shook and knew that there was no angel, only that he was infected and dying. Hell, he must be moving toward some kind of enlightenment—he wasn't even angry at Heinlein anymore.

The case was the great center of his universe; Yggdrasil, the world tree, which bore the fruit of all trees. The lotus in the navel of Vishnu. He was its protector.

In lucid moments he could feel the earth tremble around him, vibrations that shook the floor, drowning out the drums altogether. At these times, others would come and argue with him, beg him to leave his post. But he wouldn't. Couldn't. Meanwhile, an alien force crawled through his body, riding through his bloodstream, targeting his organs, attacking him. He had to banish the invasion force. He could use his mind to do it. His will was stronger than any alien invading him. He had to keep them out of his brain. He would survive. Systematically, methodically, he would fight them off. That's why he refused to leave, the growing heat in the cavern would help him burn the aliens out. He could do it.

With no sunlight or moonlight to mark the passage of days, coupled with the intermittent, complete abandonment of reason, Hubbard had no way of knowing how long he'd been living underneath the volcano. It felt like an age. He didn't care. This was the destiny he'd been looking for. To guard the case, the tree, the lotus. To wait for the signal.

"Lafayette."

The angel had returned, terrible this time in her fiery wrath. He could feel the heat in the thick air around him.

"Lafayette."

"Go away."

"Mistakes have been made. The Goddess has not yet been properly released. This age is not ready for her. Your lusts have led you to the verge of death."

"I want to leave."

"It's forbidden."

"What can I do?"

"Take the box. Concentrate upon its stillness for an hour. Gaze into it, until you see my signal. Look for my pattern. Then take the box and send me a signal."

He rolled over on his side, trying to block her from his sight. "I want to leave."

She stroked his hair, and in spite of the heat she radiated, her fingertips were chilling. "You are my Scribe. My muse. You're the one who will reshape everything—the signs, the symbols, everything."

"I can't." He was sobbing, helpless to stop the infantlike tears rolling down his face. "I'm dying."

"Think about me," she said, suddenly not so angry. "Think about touching me. Think about how much you want to be with me."

"I do," he said.

"Then answer my signal."

"The box?"

"Yes. Three days have passed since you've arrived. The end of everything is here."

"Will you help me?" he asked.

"Yes," Mr. Faaitu'a replied. "I want to help you."

"That's good," Hubbard said. "I'm important."

The librarian helped him to sit up; the effort was agony, the aliens in his body screamed in outrage. Several moments passed before the white light of pain faded from his brain and he could bring himself to speak.

"Lieutenant Hubbard, the islanders feel that the volcano is awakening again. They want us to leave for the safety of a neighboring island."

He caressed the case, letting his fingers feel the warm metal and cool glass embedded in the smooth wood. "I can't go yet."

"Why not?"

"I once thought I could be as successful as Edgar Rice Burroughs. I've failed at that. When the war came, I thought, this is my chance, you know? Maybe I could be a hero. Save lives. Kill Hitler. Do something amazing. I didn't want to die, but if I had to die, perhaps I would go out in a legendary blaze of glory so that people would always remember me. Maybe they'd name an aircraft carrier after me. Other soldiers would say, 'Let's do this for old LRH!' and then they'd storm the beach. But no one's ever going to storm a beachhead because of a detective story they once read."

He shook his head. "I'm stuck in a hole in the bottom of the world waiting for a message that will never come. I may as well die here. How many fellows can at least have it said of them they died at the hands of a volcano? Maybe someday an explorer, an archaeologist perhaps, will discover the fossilized remains of my body, like the corpses at Vesuvius. They'll say, 'Here was a good soldier who refused to leave his post.' Like a Kipling hero. Wouldn't that give a little meaning to my life?"

Mr. Faaitu'a remained quiet, thoughtful, for a long while. A rumble echoed through the cave and Hubbard felt the floor shudder as something roiled deep below him.

"On the other hand," Mr. Faaitu'a said, "perhaps all trace of you might be obliterated and no one would ever know of your death here. Except for me. And I am an old man toiling on a quiet island. I cannot even properly pronounce your first name: would you leave it to me to tell the story of Layetteffe Hubbard, who didn't leave his post because he decided to die? That is how I might tell your story."

"It's a cautionary tale."

Another temblor shook the walls, dust and grit fell from the curved ceiling.

"I don't think I can walk on my own yet. And I think I'm a little big for you."

"I'll go get help." Mr. Faaitu'a rose from his crouch with a sprightly leap, and began to head up the tube. He paused for a moment at the bend that would take him from Hubbard's site and looked back. "I think you've made the smart choice."

Hubbard was alone in the cave again. He shook, unsure whether it was another quake or the onset of a new bout of fever. When it happened again an instant later, he knew for certain the aliens were mounting another attack. How much time he had left until he lost his wits he wasn't sure, but he had work to do in the meantime. The case had to come with him.

He wrapped his hands around the gold spike, then ripped them off quickly. A straight white streak crossed both his palms, flesh that would soon blister.

"I don't know if I'll be able to write again even if I wanted to," he muttered. "If I get out of this alive."

The aliens were attacking his brain. He could feel them gathering, planning the final invasion. His hands hurt. Coughing suddenly, he fell over on his side. Why were the aliens trying to kill him? Wasn't it better for them to live with him, symbiotically? They could survive together. They didn't have to kill him.

Dust was falling on his face and someone was shaking him. No, there was nobody there. The earth itself was rocking him back and forth. There was a gold piece of metal right before his eyes, glowing, turning red. His eyes followed the coils of wiring up into a strange box that he knew he had seen before. It had come to life.

He could hear something new, above the rumble of the angry earth. A single tone, pure and crisp, growing in intensity, swelled through the cave. With suspicion he cast his eyes around the smooth walls before discerning the source. The tone flowed from the strange box and then vanished completely. A strange silence descended upon the caverns, as if the volcano had inhaled, then held its breath. In the pause, a voice, loud, clear, as if it had come from someone standing next to him, filled the void.

"Now," he heard the strange voice say. "Here we go."

Then he recognized the next voice. "Binch! Put the damn gun down! No one needs to get hurt here."

Heinlein.

EPISODE 41

ISAAC HADN'T RETURNED for her, but she had somehow known he wouldn't. It wasn't that he didn't want to; she knew he did. There had been something pressing on him, something he had needed to attend to that was more serious than anything he'd ever handled before. Isaac was involved in something important. He needed her support. By nightfall, in spite of her mother's protests, she had decided to return to Philadelphia.

The next morning, she sat quietly by herself, ignoring the entreaties of the rude young sailors and soldiers who saw chatting up a woman alone, even one wearing a wedding ring, as a mission-critical objective. At the 30th Street Station, she caught a cab, crossed the brownish Schuylkill River, passed Rittenhouse Square, then entered the lobby of her building; the place she lived with her husband. Her home.

Gertie had her words prepared. She had pictured him looking up at her from his work at the kitchen table, shocked, startled. Of course, he would appear exhausted, disheveled, surrounded by squalor, and, without her cooking for him, on the verge of starvation. And before he could speak, the carefully prepared words would flow out of her. "We're in this together," she would begin, then the rest would follow. So carefully had she set the stage in her head and rehearsed the action that when the elevator doors opened to reveal Isaac and Mr. de Camp, every single chosen word of reconciliation abandoned her.

"Gertie!" His hug squeezed the breath out of her. "You came home!"

"You don't . . ." she began, but he had her by the hand and was hurrying her out to the street where Mr. de Camp was opening the back door of his sedan for her.

Isaac clambered into the front seat, and in a few moments, Mr. de Camp was motoring through the streets of Philadelphia toward the river. "You'll never believe what happened." Isaac twisted in his seat to see her. "The Army shut us down," he said, quite excited and impressed with himself. "There were soldiers everywhere."

"What?"

Mr. de Camp picked up the narrative. "They stormed the lab a little while ago and drove us all out."

"Isaac! What did you do?"

"Nothing." Isaac shrugged innocently. "Really."

"Are you out of a job?"

He looked at Mr. de Camp, who shrugged in response. "I guess so." The thought obviously had not crossed his mind; his shoulders sagged.

"Are you going to be drafted?"

The remaining flush of rebelliousness drained from his face.

Gertie reached out and straightened a few of the wild hairs, then stroked a reassuring hand down his face. "What are we doing now?"

"We've got to let Bob know. He wasn't at the lab and he's not answering his phone," Isaac said.

As Mr. de Camp pulled the car to the curb, she recognized the house that the Heinleins had rented in Lansdowne, not far from the de Camps'. She followed the men up the stairs to the front door. Mr. de Camp was already knocking hard as she reached the porch. When Mrs. de Camp answered the door, he took several surprised steps back, looking all around the house as if to confirm that he was where he was supposed to be. "Catherine? What are you doing here?"

"Helping." Her pretty eyes were red-lined as if she had been crying.

"What's going on?" her husband asked. "Where's Bob? We need to talk to him."

"He's gone," she replied, holding the door open for them.

"Where's Mrs. Heinlein?" Gertie asked, even though she felt she knew the answer. "She isn't here, is she?"

"No." Mrs. de Camp folded her arms; she was finding it hard to speak without crying. "I spent the night helping her pack. I called her a cab. She left just a little while ago. She says she's going back to California and get a job in the movies. I was just straightening up a little. I didn't know what else to do."

Mr. de Camp put his arms around her and she rested her face against his chest.

"He never even called her," she said sadly.

Gertie hadn't realized how hard she'd been clutching Isaac's hand until he gave hers a gentle, reassuring squeeze. The thought occurred to her that she might have walked right past Mrs. Heinlein in the train station.

"Did she happen to say where Bob's staying?" Mr. de Camp asked.

"I think she mentioned something about the Franklin Hotel. But it was hard to tell for sure. She seemed a little confused."

Gertie looked around the empty room. It seemed dark even though the blinds were open. There were bottles of booze and empty tumblers on every surface. Ashtrays were filled to overflowing with hundreds of cigarette butts. The house reeked of stale smoke.

Mrs. de Camp picked up the phone and asked the operator to connect her to the front desk of the hotel. After a quick conversation, she hung up with a shrug. "He hasn't been there in a few days."

"I know another place he could be," Isaac said. "It's not too far from here."

"Catherine, do you want to come with us?"

"Oh, I don't think so." She shook her head, sadly. "I think I'll just finish straightening up a bit. I'd hate for anyone to see this and think poorly of her."

"Do you need any help?" Gertie asked.

"That's all right." Mrs. de Camp smiled. Her husband gave her a sweet kiss and a tender embrace, stroking her cheek as they parted. Then they were back in the car and Isaac was directing them toward Germantown.

After several, in fact numerous, wrong turns and double-backs, Isaac cried out in triumph and Mr. de Camp stopped the car in front of an honest-to-God mansion.

"Really?" Gertie asked.

"Yep! This is it." Isaac leaped out of the car, charged up the walk, and pounded on the front door. By the time she caught up to him, a small man wearing owlish glasses just below a thick shock of white hair had opened it and was squinting into the sunlight. He appeared to recognize at least Isaac and Mr. de Camp, for without further hesitation he opened the door wide and invited them into the foyer. She was amazed. The foyer was bigger than her living room. The house reminded her of a trip her parents had taken her on once to see the Pierpont Morgan Library. Her mother wanted her to see the collection. Her father wanted to show her what it meant to be truly wealthy.

"Mr. Gibson," Isaac was practically hopping up and down with excitement, "is Mr. Heinlein here?"

"No, he's not."

Isaac smacked his fist into his hand.

With unexpected politeness, the man extended a hand to her. "My name is Walter Gibson," he said.

"I'm Gertrude Asimov," she blurted. "And I love your house."

"Thank you. It would be perfect if it were anywhere but Philadelphia."

"Where the hell could he be?" Isaac moaned.

"Come with me." Mr. Gibson beckoned them on deeper into his home. They followed him through a long, cherry-paneled corridor into a well-appointed chamber. "Come on into the sitting room." His good nature was infectious, as if he didn't care a whit for all the house's splendid furnishings, but like a little kid, was only too happy to have more and more people in his home. For when they entered the room, she saw that there was a beautiful blond woman draped elegantly across a plush recombier while a large man wearing jodhpurs, smoking a pipe, rested at her feet. Both held large cocktail glasses in their hands, and seemed out of breath, as if they had just finished dancing to the Duke Ellington music on the RCA-Victor phonograph.

"These are the Dents, Norma and Lester, from Missouri," Mr. Gibson said. "And this is Isaac's lovely wife, Gertrude."

"Gertie, please." She felt so humbled by the surroundings and the introduction that she had to fight to resist the urge to curtsy.

"Oh, you're as pretty as your husband is brave." Mrs. Dent put down the antique atlas she was flipping through and extended a friendly hand.

"Nice to meet you," Mr. Dent said in an accent so thick, so Southern, she almost didn't understand his words at first.

"Can I pour anyone a drink?" Mr. Gibson was standing ready at the bar.

"A Tom Collins?" Mr. de Camp asked instantly.

Gertie and Isaac politely refused anything, and while Mr. Gibson went to work, merrily clinking bottles, Isaac spoke rapidly, finishing his recap with, "We can't find Bob anywhere."

Mrs. Dent sat up from her languid pose with some urgency. "What?"

"Who was the last person to see him alive?" Mr. Dent asked.

Mrs. Dent gave him a hard poke.

"I just mean, who saw him last?"

"It must have been me," Mr. de Camp said. "You were all gone. I helped him bring a couple of boxes off the ship, where Isaac had put them in Virginia, and stow them in his car."

Gertie turned to Isaac. "You were on a ship? In Virginia?"

"And a plane, too." With a proud nod, he directed her attention back to Mr. de Camp.

"He was very worried. Bob told me he had been interrogated by a couple of federal agents."

She remembered the fear that had gripped her that day inside the department store. "I was too!"

Now it was Isaac's turn to look at her quizzically, and for her to dismiss it with a shrug.

"He said the agents were murdered. He said that the telephone electrocuted them."

"Is that possible?" Mrs. Dent asked, looking from face to face as a hush fell over the room. "Come on. You're all smart people. Use your big brains. Isn't that what the government wants from you?"

"Well," said Mr. Dent, chewing on his pipe stem, "let's start with the phone. After all, it appears to be the murder weapon."

"Everyone has a phone in their home," Mr. Gibson said. "People don't die when they pick up the phone."

"That's right," Mr. de Camp said, "but people can be electrocuted if they're on the phone and lightning strikes the line."

"We haven't had a storm in two weeks," Isaac said. "But someone could have introduced a comparable amount of electricity into the system."

"How?" Mr. Dent asked. "Direct current power for telephone circuits comes from the common battery systems at the central office."

"That could be it," Mr. de Camp said thoughtfully.

"I see where you're going." Isaac nodded.

"The rest of us don't," Gertie said. Mrs. Dent gave her a sympathetic wink.

"Well," Isaac said, "everyone assumes that Tesla and Westinghouse won the power wars because homes are wired for alternating current. Meanwhile, Edison's direct current snuck in through the back door. Through the telephone system."

"DC is far more dangerous than AC," Mr. de Camp continued. "The pulse, the alternating currents, means you've at least got a chance between bursts to pull your hand away from the conductor. Direct current has no breaks. It's steady. And far more lethal. They'll both kill you. But direct will do it more quickly and smoothly."

"That's a comfort," Mrs. Dent said, rubbing her hands up and down her upper arms as if she had caught a chill in spite of the late summer heat.

"Here's a thought," Mr. Gibson said. "When we visited that fella at the RCA Building, he talked about how those rival companies had finally made peace with each other. RCA, AT&T, Westinghouse."

"And General Electric," Mr. de Camp added. "The AT&T phone system was licensed from General Electric's work."

Mr. Gibson nodded. "Think of these big corporations as nation-states connected to each other by a web of treaties. A threat against one is a threat against all. Let's also say that they hear that the military is investigating a previously discredited power and communication technology from the turn of the century. A tale told by a mad scientist. A tale with potential. Whether it works or not, this vast treaty organization has to view the threat as real."

"But those agents, they were asking about Isaac, and Mr. Heinlein, and Communists," Gertie said. "Not mad scientists."

"Obviously the government has an interest in this technology, as well. An interest that differs from that of the corporations. Maybe government was pulling on the other end of the same yarn," Mr. Gibson replied. "And those agents were in the middle when it snapped."

"If you ask me," Mr. Dent said, "someone in the company-state sees profit if what the government is doing succeeds. Countries only value treaties so long as they are relatively equal in strength. When one country becomes so much stronger than its neighbor, then to hell with the treaty, and the weaker country is gobbled up."

"Language, Lester," Mrs. Dent primly corrected her husband.

"So the agents themselves were being watched." Mr. Gibson picked up the thread. "Hassling Bob was a disruption to somebody's plan. When the Feds picked up the phone, the open circuit was closed. A light goes on at the local exchange but somewhere else, as well, while the call is being routed to Washington. Some person, in that somewhere-else place, picks up another phone and calls his counterpart in another company-state, reminds him of their treaty. This second person presses a button and a deadly surge of current, like a lightning bolt, is sent down the line. It probably only takes seconds to do it. And the man in that somewhere-else place sits back and continues to plot the devouring of the other, unsuspecting company-states."

"Binch," Mr. de Camp said. "Lyman Binch."

"It fits." Mr. Gibson nodded.

"If a man killed two federal agents to get at Tesla's secret," Gertie said, trying to understand everything she'd just heard, "what will he do to Mr. Heinlein if he thinks he's actually solved it?"

Looks passed from one to another before Isaac said what everyone feared. "He'll kill him. And then he'll kill us."

"Those boxes that you went to Virginia to get for Bob? Where would he take those?" Mr. Dent asked.

"Menlo Park."

"Where is that?" Mrs. Dent asked.

"It's a little over an hour from here."

"I think that's our next stop," Mr. Gibson said.

"You don't have to come," Mr. de Camp said.

Mrs. Dent rose. Gertie was impressed by the woman's stature, graceful and dynamic. "Bob's a friend of ours. If he's in trouble, we're going to help."

"My car's outside," Mr. de Camp said.

"Mine too," Mr. Gibson added.

"Perhaps the women ought to stay here," Isaac suggested.

"Like hell." Gertie stamped her foot.

Isaac opened his mouth and then closed it, swallowing his words.

"Like hell," she reiterated, before returning Mrs. Dent's wink.

They sped toward New Jersey. She and Isaac rode with Mr. de Camp while the Dents followed in Gibson's sleek roadster. "What were you doing on an airplane?"

"It was the only way to get back after I fell overboard."

"What?"

"I told you it was a hell of a story."

"In Virginia?"

"Yes."

The sun was setting as they pulled into a forlorn little park that had been abandoned by the neighborhood. A tower stood in the center of the park; a crystal globe of the earth perched on top glowed with internal light that pulsed and waned from an intense brightness to a dim glow. As Gertie got out of the car she could feel tremors running through the earth and hear a hum in the air.

There were three cars parked in front of the small building at the other end of the park. One of them was a fancy car, nicer even than Mr. Gibson's. They were empty, but the headlamps were glowing, pulsating.

"Look," Mr. de Camp cried, pointing to his sedan. The engine was off but his headlamps were doing the same thing, as were Mr. Gibson's. "Isaac! I think it's working." His eyes were bright, gleaming in the reflection of the silver pouring from the globe above.

Isaac turned to Gertie. "Would you please just wait here for a few moments?"

"No."

"Why not?"

"Because," she began her prepared words, "as your wife, I need to be a part of your life, the best part, not just a little . . ."

"Okay. Just stay behind me." He kissed her; his lips were dry, so were hers. They were both scared.

"Okay."

The ground shook again. "Come on." Isaac led the way across the meadow, past the tower. She felt the hairs on the back of her neck rise and her skin began to tingle. A jagged streak of white electricity flashed around them. The lightning burst from the ground toward the sky in a sight her mind could barely comprehend.

Gertie shrieked. "The lightning! How is that even possible?"

He grabbed her by her hands. "Listen to me. We're going to be okay. But I want you to know I love you."

"I love you."

"Come on, we've got to run!"

Filled with terror as all around them streaks of light burst skyward, they broke and ran for the building as thunderclaps filled the air and pounded at their heads. Once inside she caught her breath, the protection of shelter instantly helping to calm her. Isaac had to pull her away from the door, mesmerized as she was by the sight of the lightning.

Mr. de Camp, the last one through, shut the door behind him. "To be on the safe side," he said.

Gertie joined the others as they gathered around the top of a staircase that led down into a gloom from which the hum originated, so loud that she had to put her hands over her ears. The scent of ozone stung her nose and throat.

"Bob!" Isaac shouted. The others joined in as well, calling down the stairs.

A shadow coalesced at the foot of the stairs below, long and faint at first, growing thin and gaining definition. An old man she'd never seen before stood below them, looking up.

"Mr. Binch," Mr. Gibson shouted. "Is everything okay? Is Bob Heinlein with you?"

"Yes, Mr. Gibson. He and Mr. Campbell are fine. As you can see, things are working."

"Can we come down?"

"You may as well; it's better than me having to carry all your bodies down."

Mr. Binch raised his arm. Gertie gasped as the light glinted off the gun in his hand.

"Welcome to Wardenclyffe West," he said.

EPISODE 42

HANDS CLUTCHED AT him and Hubbard screamed in terror. He could hear voices, calling to one another, trying to comfort him, asking him to be calm. The box had fallen silent after Heinlein's broadcast. Pieces of rock began to fall from the ceiling. There was something he had to do. He had to respond.

"The signal," he cried out to the men pulling at him. "It's the signal."

Strong forces were carrying him away from the box. His arms and legs were restrained. They shouted to each other. Why were they doing that? Didn't they know he had to find a way to respond? He struggled as he never had before against his captors, immense pillars of meat and gristle and bone that refused to let him go.

Kicking and flailing, he suddenly fell to the floor, which was in a continuous state of motion. Voices cried out at him as he crawled on burning hands toward the case. The torches which guarded the case suddenly toppled over in front of it, spilling blazing oil. Drawing himself to his feet, he prepared to run through the flames. Beyond the fire he could see a variety of gauges under glass bubbles. The needles in each gauge swung back and forth like insects' antennae. Around the edges of a small panel on the right, just below the point where the cable entered the interior of the box, he could see a green glow. A clarity gripped his mind such as he hadn't felt in weeks. "Heinlein!" he gasped.

The button. He could send the signal back. He reached toward the flames, forcing the sensation of the tremendous heat away. If he did it quickly, he could reach it. He threw his hand into the flame, felt a heat which almost seemed cold, before suddenly he was gripped and dragged back over the coarse rock, away from the case.

"Stop!" he screamed at the islanders. "God, stop! I have to press the button!"

They paused and he broke free again. He took a step forward, but before he could take another the cave shook with such force that he was thrown to the ground. He heard the bodies of the others dropping to the cavern floor. A great roar and rush of wind flowed around them. Hubbard lifted his head to see a crack opening up beneath the case, as if the golden spike had broken open the earth. A hellish red light emerged from the widening gap and a great sucking downdraft of wind rushed through the tube, instantly extinguishing the oil fire. As he staggered toward the box, the ground shook violently again and the box rocked on the lip of the crack for a moment before slowly tumbling into the glowing abyss below.

Hubbard heard himself scream.

He was outside now, blinded by the bright sunlight streaming through the thick palm trees. The air was cool but thicker with sulphurous smoke. Hands bore him along like a pig on its way to a roast. As his head lolled back he could see the ground flowing by below him in a smooth motion, a river of dirt flowing in reverse. There were voices in the air, women and children calling, but no shrieks. Except for his. He was certain he had gone mad. The world was turned upside down and something had gone terribly wrong.

He recognized the black rocky shelf where the outriggers waited. There he was dropped roughly to the ground, which still trembled and was hot to the touch. Hubbard rolled over on his back and sighted the island's cone. Great billows of gray smoke poured from it, as if this were the source of all the world's clouds. Showers of sparks belched into the sky, accompanied by a great rocking of the earth. As he watched in horror, rivulets of red began to pour from the mountaintop as it began to bleed.

With practiced precision, the islanders were launching craft after craft into the waters below the shelf. Men carried stashes of fruit, and water in leather sacks, to the edge and dropped them into the boats. Women and children clambered down thick vines into the outriggers, then pushed away as other canoes were dropped in immediately to replace them.

Hubbard had lost sight of Mr. Faaitu'a. He was surrounded only by the native Polynesians, toiling grimly at the task of saving their people. Slowly, the ranks of the islanders on the shelf were thinning. Someone hoisted him into the air; he landed heavily on a broad shoulder. The man carrying him bore him swiftly to the edge of the rock and slid down the vine, Hubbard's cheek only an inch or so from the craggy face of the cliff at any given moment.

He landed in the bottom of an outrigger like one of the sacks of water. He rolled over and looked into the gentle face of a young island girl. Her expression was excited and accepting. He looked up to see other men and women descending the vines like brown spiders, and in a matter of moments, the boat was filled. Someone shouted out an order and all aboard pushed away from the wall. Paddles were quickly in hand and the boat surged away on the next receding breaker. Hubbard hung his head over the side and vomited.

With amazing speed and skill, the tiny fleet navigated through the glittering obsidian monoliths in spite of the heavy surf. They seemed to have a coordinated understanding of how to move together as an organic group. The mountain rumbled and spewed behind them and began to throw great flaming rocks, which hurtled through the air and splashed into the water, shattering the jagged spires and scattering deadly shards. A boatload of men was obliterated in an instant by the impact of one of these projectiles. The others paddled furiously, finally reaching the open sea where they could put all their energy into setting as much distance as possible between themselves and their home.

Hubbard raised himself to a seated position in the bottom of the boat, facing the stern. The mountain roared and spewed fire. Lava streamed down its face; he could see palm trees falling like leaves, bursting into flames as they were devoured by the red river. It rushed over the lip of the shelf that only recently had been teeming with members of the tribe and hit the water, throwing up great plumes of steam as thick as the smoke pouring from the summit. The wrath of the alien king was terrifying to witness.

He slipped into a faint again, awakening to find himself in darkness, still in the boat, as the rowers struggled to put more space between them and the island. In the distance he could see the sky ablaze, hear the thundering as the mountain tried to rip the heavens apart and tear the stars down. And still the incessant repetition of the paddles digging into the water, accompanied by a song of lament in an island tongue so foreign to him he could not distinguish a single word, the syllables flowing one into another with a grace and power so moving that he was brought to tears.

Dawn found them still upon the waters, Tin Can Island still glowing in the distance. Hubbard drew himself up wearily. He could hear the sound of crashing and was surprised that the force of the volcano could reach this distance. In a few moments, he realized that this sound was different than the angry roars that had accompanied the fleet throughout the night.

Breakers.

With an effort, he turned his head. Waves were crashing onto the shore of an island. No daggerlike rocks surrounded its shore. In fact, it looked much as he had pictured a tropical island to look when he was younger and read his Defoe and Stevenson on the cold winter nights in Montana. He could see the other outriggers making their way into the shelter of a perfect lagoon.

He crawled out of the craft onto a pleasant, white sand beach. The islanders stood in clusters, greeting each other as other boats came aboard, and appearing to be congratulating one another on their survival. Hubbard felt a hand upon his shoulder. He smiled with gratitude and placed his hand over Mr. Faaitu'a's.

"I'm very glad to see you alive," the old man said, his face weary but his eyes twinkling.

"I'm happy to see you, too."

The tribe gathered in a cluster on the shoreline, growing silent as the mountain floating on the ocean, the home of their ancestors, blazed like a morning star on the horizon.

"Did we do that?" Hubbard wondered aloud to himself. "Bob. What did you do?"

"This is beyond the power of man," Mr. Faaitu'a said quietly.

There was a flash on the summit and the great gray clouds dispersed as if a hand had waved some cigarette smoke away. Then there was another burst of orange light that painted the sky with great brilliance. Long minutes later, the sound of the great explosion rolled over the waves and reached them with enough force to knock people down. By the time that happened, though, the mountain had ceased to exist.

"Don't be so sure," he heard himself whisper in reply.

"We should head for higher ground," Mr. Faaitu'a said.

"It's not over yet?"

"There may be a tidal wave."

Hubbard saw that the Tongans were already streaming up the beach toward wide paths cut through the palm groves. Other folks were emerging from their jungle to offer assistance, carrying the injured and children and supplies from the outriggers. It was one of the most unexpectedly neighborly sights Hubbard had ever seen. The people were eager to greet and help those who had lost everything. He smiled and turned his eyes inland to where the island swept up gently to a high hill.

"Can you make it or should I call some help over?"

"I couldn't imagine asking for their help at a time like this."

"They're happy to do it."

"I can make it."

Hubbard could make it. Of course he could. He'd beaten the alien invasion force inside his own body. The sand felt warm and comfortable under his bare feet. He joined the line of others heading into the jungle. Out here he knew he would heal and grow stronger again. A new destiny was waiting for him. Something great.

With renewed spirit, Hubbard headed toward the top of the hill. It would take him a long time to get there but he knew it was the place to go, the site where he might spot a ship to bring him back to civilization. He was eager to get to the top. There was nothing to fear from some rising water. The ocean could not claim him now. He felt like laughing.

After all, when he'd raised his eyes to the high ground, hadn't he seen his flame-haired protector, a goddess no longer, no icon of an ancient past but a herald of the future, glowing in alien light, draped in formfitting silver, arms outstretched, surrounded by the planets and stars? Galaxies swirled around her, spiral nebulae burst below her, light vanished into black holes under her feet; the universe was expanding and contracting, waiting to receive him into tomorrow.

And she smiled.

EPISODE 43

HEINLEIN'S HEART SANK as one by one his friends came through the door, hands on top of their heads.

"Getting crowded in here," Campbell said to him.

"Christ," Heinlein replied at the same volume. "If Binch kills us all, then Ron Hubbard will be the most important person in pulps."

"Hi, John," Asimov said, as he reached the floor. "Did you get that robot story I sent you?"

"Not now, Ike." Campbell was the only one who ever got away with calling him that.

Last to enter the room was Lyman Binch, holding the gun with the confidence of a Bogart or a Cagney, and nothing like an engineer. He leaned over to study the gauges, tapping on them the way sailors rap on a barometer, as if the needles needed dislodging. His lips pursed in frustration. "Is it working?" he asked Heinlein.

"I don't know, Lyman. You're the only one who was there. What happened last time?"

"I don't know."

"What do you mean, you don't know? You blew up Siberia, didn't you! How can you not know what happened?"

Binch slammed a fist down on the console. "Nikola never allowed me to enter his precious control room!"

"He had his suspicions of you all along, didn't he? He thought you were spying for Tom Edison, right?" Heinlein asked.

"I knew I was meant for great things even then. Greater than he would let me be."

"You stole secrets from Tesla and went to Edison with them. But that meant Tom couldn't completely trust you, either."

The overhead lights in the room began to flicker and grow dim.

"You're pulling too much power," de Camp said. "The electric company can't keep up with the demand. You should shut it down."

"No!" Binch whirled on de Camp, holding the gun straight out at him. It trembled in his hand.

A shudder ran through the basement and a shower of sparks erupted out of one of the great iron capacitors, the glowing embers skittering across the floor as they burned out.

"What's going on?" Binch cried.

"I think the conductors are buckling under the stress," Isaac said. "I never did get a chance to test them."

"Goddammit!" Binch threw a switch and the capacitor instantly stopped throwing off its electrical discharge. He twisted several dials and the great hum in the air began to diminish.

As the sound of surging electricity faded, Heinlein could hear a new sound over it, diesel engines, gravel crunching, and the shouts of men. "What's that?" he asked.

"Sounds like the cavalry," Campbell replied. "I think the Army's put it all together."

"Lyman." Heinlein took a step toward the man, whose eyes were riveted on the gauges and dials. "It's over."

"The hell it is." Grim-faced, Binch twisted every dial in rapid succession, each to its limit. The hall filled again with the roar of immense energy and the overhead lights faded to dimness while the floor itself shuddered and dust fell from the rafters.

Heinlein took another step forward. "The first thing I ever saw of all of this was an image of the ground swallowing up Wardenclyffe. What if that wasn't a metaphorical image? What if it was a possibility? Maybe it was a fault Tesla recognized in his design." The floor roiled and cracks appeared. "Binch. You could split the surface of the earth, crack New Jersey in two."

"It can't happen."

"Look around you! It's happening now! We have to shut it all down. We know it works now. Let's shut it down and learn some more."

"You want to see what happens as much as I do."

One more step. "I've seen enough. I've seen enough to know we were right." Binch was sweating, his gun trembling. "We'll shut it down. You've waited so long for this. It doesn't have to end here."

Distracted by Heinlein, Binch never saw Dent lunging. With a twist of the man's arm, Dent wrested the gun from his hand. The impact swung Binch around, sending him crashing into the console.

Instantly, Heinlein grabbed the big lever and yanked as hard as he could. "Stuck!" he grunted. De Camp gave him a hand, but even together, they couldn't get it to budge. Smoke rose from the console.

"Where's the off switch?" Dent asked.

"You're looking at it," de Camp replied, trying to force a switch to move. He pulled his fingers away and shook them. "Hot."

"The circuits are fusing," Asimov pointed out. "Too much current. The copper wire is burning right through the insulation."

"Well, that should shut everything down," Campbell said. "Right?"

"The capacitors are fully charged. They'll crank out power until they're drawn or the connection to the tower is broken."

All heads turned to Binch. The old man had slunk into a corner of the room, nursing his hand.

"You can still help us," Mrs. Dent said to him.

Binch bit his upper lip for a long moment. There was a loud pounding on the locked door upstairs. Shouted commands. Finally, the old man nodded. "The tunnels," he said.

"What?" Heinlein asked. "We've never been in the tunnels."

"Each of the capacitors sends power down one of the four cables through the main tunnel where they enter another tunnel that rings around the base of the tower. There are four tunnels off of the ring that feed power into the final transformer before it enters the tower. Each of the transformers has a coupling with a safety cutoff switch on it. It's heavily insulated so it can't melt or fuse. If we cut the flow to the tower, we can shut the signal off. After that we'll be able to cut the power to the capacitors."

"Lead the way," Heinlein said.

"Hurry," Gibson added.

They followed Binch out of the office and into the main section of the basement. Smoke poured from between the seams of the capacitor, oily and foul-smelling, drifting fluidly down its great iron sides. Binch turned to the right, picking up a flashlight from the workbench. "It's dark down there. The lights burned out long ago. Never took the time to replace them. Didn't think I'd ever have reason to go down there again."

Heinlein turned to the others. "Listen, you don't have to come with us."

"Yeah, we do," de Camp insisted.

"We are," Asimov added.

Binch turned on the lamp and opened the heavy door. A damp, moldy breeze brushed past Heinlein. He headed in after Binch, followed by Asimov and his wife, de Camp and Gibson, and the Dents.

"Shut the door," Binch ordered. When Lester Dent began to protest, he snapped, "If the soldiers get down in here they might stop us before we can turn it off. Then what? Think they'll listen to reason?"

The door closed and the bolt thrown, the little group moved forward, first down a small flight of concrete steps, and then through corridors lined from floor to arched ceiling with bricks. The thick cables snaked like pythons along the floor. Heavy cobwebs snagged at their hair and clothes. "Don't step in any puddles," Binch cautioned.

"Great," Campbell muttered. "Says the only one who can see them."

Heinlein could feel the near-continuous vibration beneath his feet with every step now. The intensity had only grown stronger as they moved closer to beneath the tower, he noted. Finally, they reached an intersection in a tunnel; they could follow curving paths to the left and to the right.

"Two down that way and two down this way," Binch said.

"Let's split up," Heinlein suggested. "We can get to them faster that way."

"Okay," Norma said. "Lester and I will go to the left."

"We'll go with you," Gertie added.

"Looks like Gibson and I are staying with you."

"Okay, let's go."

As Campbell, de Camp, and Gibson followed Binch, Dent pulled Heinlein aside, discreetly pressed something into his hand, and whispered in his ear, "Take this just in case."

He took the gun and slipped it into his pocket, then watched as Dent pulled out his Zippo, struck it, and held it aloft, the little flame flickering pathetically in the darkness, finally disappearing as the curve of the corridor took them from sight.

"Come on," Binch snapped. "Hurry." With his flashlight, they were able to make quick progress, and before too long they had come to an arch in the left-hand side of the wall. "This is the first one," he said.

"We'll take it," de Camp said.

"You know what to do?"

"Find the big switch and pull it."

"Right."

"I wish I had a light for you."

"Abracadabra," Walter said, with a touch of nonchalance. A flame appeared, dancing on the tip of his thumb. "Follow me, boys," he said to de Camp and Campbell.

"Magician," de Camp offered Binch, by way of explanation. Clapping Campbell on the back, they plunged into the gloom after Gibson.

"Come on," Binch said, and Heinlein followed him, or at least the cone of light through the tunnel until the final arch appeared. The vibrations were nearly continuous now, surging so often that Heinlein had to place a hand on the cool bricks to keep himself standing. He crept forward. The tunnel continued on at a greater length than he expected, until he reminded himself just how far the tower was across the meadow from the building.

Ahead, Binch stood silhouetted by a faint glow in another arch. Heinlein reached his side and the old man held out an arm to keep him from going any farther.

"That's the tower." He shone the light upward and Heinlein saw a great open pillar, formed by section after cross section of iron bars, soaring upward to vanish into the dome high above. Binch directed the light down and now Heinlein could see why he had stopped him. "And that's the pit."

They stood on the brink of a gaping hole through which the iron pillar plunged into darkness. Wooden struts held it in place in the center of the pit. A thick cable swung, like a black spiderweb, from his side to a connection socket on the side of the pillar. He could see three other cables slung the same way, swinging off into the darkness at quarter increments from the cable nearest to him.

"Two hundred feet to the bottom. Deeper than at Wardenclyffe. It needed to be since the tower was smaller," Binch said, with a quiet pride in his voice. "Then the device extends another hundred feet through the rock, radiating its power through the earth."

Far across the gap, Heinlein could see two of the other archways were already dimly lit by the flames Dent and Gibson carried. The third, barely visible in the shadows, was still dark. If Asimov and his wife had ventured down that one, they had no light to guide them. The tunnels shook with a strong tremor. Something crashed to the floor in the distant reaches of the maze. The wood and iron joints of the pillar groaned in unison; an orchestra tuning up for a symphony of impending collapse.

"Where's the switch?" Heinlein yelled over the quaking.

"On the wall," Binch shouted back. "Follow the cable!"

Heinlein tracked the thick black cord back from the tunnel's edge. It was anchored to the wall just beyond the mouth of the arch, then tacked up in several places until it terminated in a thick iron box. A slender iron lever stuck out from the top, just above the point where the cable plugged into the box. "Here it is!" He reached for the lever, his finger less than an inch away when a spark suddenly appeared, leaping across the gap from the metal to his hand. The shock was so painful that his whole arm twitched involuntarily, snapping back from the lever and driving him to his knees.

"Thought that might happen," he heard Binch muse behind him. "It's not the real electrical current. Had that been the case, you would have been dead in an instant. That's static electricity created by the friction of the current through the cable. Should be safely discharged now, thanks to you."

Binch reached out and clutched the handle, suffering no noticeable effect. In a smooth, simple motion, he slid the switch from the left until it clicked into its new position on the right. The humming in the air instantly dwindled away, diminishing, somewhat, the overall din.

Cradling his injured arm, Heinlein looked up with relief. "That's just . . ."

An arc of light, like a scythe, curved down toward his head as Binch brought the flashlight down. Fireworks exploded in front of his eyes and he felt his skull bounce off the floor of the tunnel, quickly followed by the rest of his body. Something clamped itself around his ankle, he was being dragged backwards, his cheek scraping across the floor, pulling his lip up, teeth meeting the bricks. He tried to move his arms, but only the fingers seemed to twitch in response. "Wait," he murmured. "Wait." It sounded a little louder the second time.

"Can't wait. Sorry. My time is money. In this case millions, if not potentially billions."

"You can't kill us all."

"Yes, I can."

His ankle released, his leg fell to the floor. Heinlein was now able to crack his eyes, or rather one eye, open. He was on the brink of the pit.

"One by one I'll send you all into the abyss. No one will ever even know you're down there. There's a hatch at the base of the tower. I'll escape through that and disappear. By the time anyone even figures out how to get in touch with me, I'll be back in New York, safely defended by the greatest army the world has ever seen—the lawyers of General Electric.

"I'll tell them all about how curious you were to use my research facility here and suggest that you must have had an accident. Oh, and by the way, did you search the bottom of the pit? No? Maybe you should. Maybe Robert Heinlein, the crazy science fiction writer, went insane and killed a bunch of people and then killed himself. You never know about those creative types."

"Stop." Heinlein groped in his pocket and withdrew the gun. His hand was so numb he could barely feel it. He felt Binch plant his foot squarely on his hip, grinding it in. He struggled to raise the gun.

Binch leaned down. "I will never stop," he hissed. "Which is why I win." And he kicked.

Heinlein flailed as he rolled over the edge, letting go of the gun, clutching for anything even as the bottom fell out from under him.

There was something there and he grabbed at it as hard as he could. As he went over the edge he heard a scream, realized it wasn't him, and threw his other hand around Binch's leg as well. The man fell and scrabbled at the ground while Heinlein hung on as tightly as he possibly could. He swung into the pit wall while Binch, still struggling to free himself, to stay out of the pit, stopped Heinlein's fall. Binch's flashlight swung back and forth as he tried to club at Heinlein's head.

"Let go! You'll kill us both!"

Heinlein looked down, ducking his head as the flashlight grazed his hair. Still hanging from Binch's legs, he kicked off the wall as hard as he could, yanking the man over the edge. As Binch tumbled into the void, Heinlein let go of his legs and reached for the wood strut he'd seen as the flashlight fell from Binch's hand. With a shriek, Binch plummeted past him into the darkness, as he found a purchase on the wood.

He hung there for a moment, breathless, drained. The beam quivered under his grip, as the pillar seemed to struggle to shake itself free of its bindings. Far below him he could see a tiny, still point of light. Binch's flashlight had found the bottom of the pit. The distance was almost unfathomable.

"Bob!"

He looked up. Dent was crouched in the arch, hand extended. It was so close.

"Can you reach me?"

"I don't know, Lester."

"Do I need to come down there?"

"I'll see what I can do." He pulled himself up until he was able to wrap his elbow around the beam. As he caught his breath he suddenly realized the beam was no longer shaking, the air no longer filled with noise. "We shut it off?"

"Yeah. At least I think so. Why don't you get up here and make sure?"

"If you insist." He swung his right arm up as hard as he could and grabbed Dent's hand. The man's grip was strong and confident and Heinlein knew he was going to be okay. Dent pulled him up toward the edge. Heinlein managed to get his feet upon the beam and stood up, bringing his eyes almost level with his friend's. Standing behind Dent he could see Asimov and all the others. Dent helped him back into the tunnel, patting him heartily on the back.

"We just saved New Jersey," Campbell said, joining the others as they gathered around Heinlein.

"Thank goodness for that," Norma replied.

"We should get a permanent turnpike pass for this," de Camp added.

"I'd be happy with free passes to the Palisades Amusement Park." In the dim light of Dent's Zippo, Asimov was grinning.

Heinlein was about to say something overly sentimental that expressed his gratitude in sappy terms when something loud, like wood breaking, snapped behind him and he saw sparks burst off the wall near his face. Bewildered, he turned back toward the pit.

Lyman Binch was perched in the iron lattice of the great pillar. His face was covered in blood, which poured from a gash on his nearly bald head. He fired another shot at Heinlein's head.

The others scattered and Heinlein pressed himself into the wall behind the junction box. Binch must have grabbed the gun Heinlein had dropped as he fell over the edge. Lester and Gibson doused their lights.

"Don't look so stupid," Binch snarled. "If you can catch on to a piece of wood, so can I."

Asimov shouted, "Gertie!" His wife stood, dumbfounded, feet rooted to the spot in the center of the tunnel. She was the easiest target, dimly outlined. Another shot rang out, the burst of light dazzling in the darkness.

"Ike!" Heinlein shouted. "Over here."

Asimov rushed for his wife and Heinlein grabbed them both, swinging them to the wall of the tunnel.

Binch fired again and Heinlein, disoriented, tripped and fell into de Camp. Together, they stumbled backwards. Heinlein stuck out his hands to soften the impact he knew was coming, as his momentum drove him forward. Instead of a brick wall, he struck metal, felt something shift.

The air in the corridor was once again rent with the great hum of energy. Binch uttered a gasp that cut off abruptly and suddenly Heinlein realized he could see. He turned toward the pit and the source of the light.

His mouth open in a rictus of agony, his body frozen and curved as taut as a drawn bow, Binch was glowing from within as an incredible amount of current surged through him. The soft tissue of his eyes burst. The skull under his skin became visible as his skin became as translucent as a frosted light bulb, then the brain inside the skull was visible. His clothes burst into flames.

"Shut it off!" Norma cried. "For God's sake, turn it off!"

Heinlein reached for the switch he had stumbled into and slammed it back into place. Instantly, the hum vanished. Released from the current, Binch's body sagged, then pitched forward, falling like a shooting star into the darkness of the great pit.

"Gertrude?" he called. "Are you all right?"

"Yes, Mr. Heinlein," she responded. "We're both fine."

"Anyone else shot?"

The replies were negative. He heaved a sigh of relief.

"Can you believe that?" de Camp asked.

"Pretty disturbing."

"Not that. Didn't you notice that he didn't jerk? Who would have thought that Tesla powered Wardenclyffe with direct current."

They made their way back to the main tunnel and suddenly Asimov cried out. "Damn!"

"What?"

"The roof's collapsed."

Heinlein pushed forward to join Asimov, standing in the light of Gibson's magic thumb candle. Bricks, beams, and dirt had closed off their exit. "I felt this happen." He rubbed his head. "Right before Binch shut off our circuit. I heard it, but I didn't know what it was."

"Now what?" Campbell asked.

"We find the escape hatch."

"Okay. Sounds good. Where is it?"

"Binch said it was in the base of the monument."

"We have to go back?"

"Yes."

He smelled the smoke before they reached the edge of the pit. Looking down, a red glare filled the pit floor. "Binch's body started a fire."

"That's not encouraging," Gibson muttered.

"At least we can see now." Dent closed his lighter.

"We're going to have to each climb down to the beam that saved my life. Then we're going to have to move to the pillar and climb to the top. That's where we'll find the exit.

"I'll go first, and get to the pillar. Dent, why don't you help everyone onto the beam? I'll wait for them on the other side and send them up."

"Right."

Dent clung on to Heinlein as he dropped onto the beam. He crossed his ankles over the beam and crawled until he was within inches of the iron. As he reached out, he heard de Camp's voice; the acoustics were such that his whisper carried across the void as if he had been standing right next to Heinlein.

"Sure hope the power's off."

"Only one way to find out," he told himself, and as the sweat began to pour off him, he grabbed the iron. It was warm to the touch, but other than that, he was alive. "Okay," he shouted. "Let's get this parade started."

Dent dropped down to the beam and helped de Camp down, too, so he could assist Heinlein on the pillar. The flames were growing below, the old wood of the support struts readily catching fire. Next Gertie and Norma came across, slowly. He and de Camp guided them onto the pillar, then de Camp began to ascend with them while Dent worked on ferrying Gibson, Asimov, and Campbell over. Next, he crept across, too, and Heinlein got him started on his way up.

The sounds of the fire from below reached his ears as he climbed. He quickly caught up with Gertie, the slowest of all them, as she took the rungs one thoughtful move at a time. Her husband waited just above her and touchingly encouraged her every step. She stopped, out of breath, clinging to the lattice.

The pillar shuddered and he realized that as the bottom of the wood struts burned away, the pillar would collapse against the side of the pit. He held his hand out to the brave but frightened girl. "Gertie?"

"I can't do it, Mr. Heinlein. I can't make it."

"Sure you can. You're almost there. The others are just about there. Everyone's waiting for you."

"I'm sorry, Mr. Heinlein."

"Gertie, will you do me one favor?"

"What?"

"Please stop calling me Mr. Heinlein. Just call me Bob."

"I'll stop calling you Mr. Heinlein when you make sure everyone stops calling my husband Ike."

"I wish he'd told me that."

"I'm sure he has. He's not shy like that."

"No. He's not." He chuckled. "You ready to move along?"

She nodded. "I guess so."

"I'll stay by you and show you where to put your hands and feet."

"Okay."

Together, they began making progress. He heard a shout from above and looked up to see something he was beginning to think he'd never see again: the beacon at the top of the Edison Monument glowing against a dark summer sky, framed in the square of an open hatch.

"Look, honey!" Isaac called down to her. "Sprague's found the way out."

"Thank God," she exclaimed, and picked up her pace.

Heinlein looked down and saw the flames writhing around and rising up the sides of the pillar as if this were some massive jet-propelled rocket straining to burst its bonds and escape gravity.

The iron, designed to transmit electricity, was now conducting the fire's heat. Each bar he touched seemed to be hotter than the last. Isaac reached the top, vanished out of the hatch for only a moment before he was hanging back down into it, offering his wife a hand up and out. She took it. Heinlein watched with relief as the bottoms of her shoes slipped from his sight.

He looked down one last time. The bottom part of the pillar was beginning to sway and buckle. Heinlein climbed as fast as he could. Fresh air, cool, caressed his face. His hands reached through the hatch and found concrete. He was being helped out. As his feet left the shivering pillar, he heard one last, massive groan and it began to collapse onto itself like an accordion.

Heinlein rolled onto the steps of the monument, looking up gratefully at the glimmering beacon for one instant, for in the next it flickered and blinked out. He was about to burst forth with the speech of gratitude he'd been denied earlier when he heard the sounds of gun chambers being loaded. His head cleared quickly as he sat up. His friends kneeled all around him, hands on their heads. Encircling them all was a heavily armed squad of very angry Marines training their rifles at the captives who had just emerged from the ground.

"The next person who moves gets his head blown off! Or hers!"

ABSOLUTE HORIZON

"A SECRET MISSION in the South Pacific," Campbell said to the man sitting next to him at the bar before raising his pint glass and draining it in huge gulps, as he'd done all afternoon.

"That's right."

"And that's how you wound up in Australia?"

"Yep," Hubbard said. "An Australian troop transport on its way to Sydney was provisioning on Tonga and they offered me a way off. I took it. Spent two months there before I figured out how to get back."

"I'd always heard you were bouncing around posts here stateside."

"That's the official story. That's what the military wants everyone to believe. But there's a secret history to every war, Campbell. And I'm part of that."

The bartender refilled their empty glasses. Campbell fastened another cigarette into its holder. "How come you never told me about your mission before?"

Hubbard shrugged. "Something about being here in the old White Horse Tavern brings out the storyteller in me, I guess." He glanced around the old room, full of smoke and mysteries. Other than a young man reading a pulp near the fan at the end, the bar itself was empty; the few other customers drinking at round tables. "Plus I haven't been back in New York since."

"Well, it's a hell of a story. Hell of a story. You should write it down, I'll run it in *Unknown*."

Hubbard shrugged. "Finish telling me what happened to you after Scoles called off the Marines."

"Not much to tell, really. The lab was shut down. I spent some time in hot water, but at least I didn't go to jail. Isaac was drafted."

"Really?"

"Tested highest in his company in intelligence and lowest in physical condition."

"No surprise there, right?"

"No fighting for him, though. They sent him to Hawaii until the war ended."

"Hawaii. Not bad."

"Except you know how he is about ships and the sun. He and Gertie are back in Brooklyn now. He'll earn his PhD any day now and I suppose he'll lord it over us all. You want to know something crazy? Turns out he actually did see a super-bomber."

"Yeah?"

"The Junkers Ju-390. It was the only one ever built. The pilot, Anna Kreisling, was smuggled stateside after the war. Colonel Slick told me about it before he headed off to the Himalayas to search for the yeti."

Hubbard smiled. "How about the skinny guy?"

"De Camp? Yeah, he survived the Navy in one piece. Writing a lot of fantasy these days. Heinlein is . . ."

Hubbard held up his hand. "I don't really care."

Campbell didn't seem surprised. After a moment, he said, "Did you hear the Supreme Court decided in Tesla's favor? They've assigned all of Marconi's radio patents back to Tesla. Of course, it turns out that Tesla had sold his designs to another company years ago. And that company was bought by . . ."

"RCA."

"You guessed it."

"What do you think happened at Menlo Park?" Hubbard asked, after several silent moments of drinking. "Do you think it worked? Or was it all just a big light show?"

Campbell tamped out the finished cigarette. "I think we were victims of our own desire for it to work. I read a report last year which indicates that what happened in Siberia—the explosion that Tesla thought he had caused—was probably the result of a comet exploding in the atmosphere above. Tesla was seeking a result and I think he latched on to one. Coincidence is the gremlin of science. We let our imaginations get the better of us."

Hubbard stared at his reflection in the mirror behind the rows of bottles. "The mind's a funny place, isn't it?"

"You can say that again, brother. Ackerman's brother bought it in Europe."

"I heard about that. I wonder . . ."

"What?"

"Ever find out what happened to the crate Asimov delivered? The one he said was full of uranium?"

"I forgot all about it until I told you tonight. So, no."

The door opened, Hubbard looked up. Then he stood.

"Hi, Ron."

"Bob."

Heinlein was in the doorway, his hat in his hand. His head was nearly bald. Nevertheless, he looked healthier, more tan, than the last time Hubbard had seen him.

"I wished you'd a told me, John," he said.

"I'm as surprised as you are," Heinlein said.

"You were both in town for the convention," Campbell said. "As I'm guest of honor, I insist you consider burying the hatchet."

Hubbard shrugged. "There's no hatchet to bury."

"Come on, you guys haven't spoken to each other in four years."

"We have nothing to say to each other," Hubbard replied.

"I hear you got married," Heinlein said. "Congratulations."

"Thanks. I hear you're getting married again, too."

"True. Are you still staying up at Jack Parsons's in Pasadena?"

"No. Parsons is an idiot fool who's going to blow himself up one of these days."

"Can I buy you fellas a round?" Campbell sounded a hopeful note.

"I don't think so." Hubbard began pulling his stuff together.

"Don't leave on my account," Heinlein said. "Are Ginny and I still on for meeting you and Dona for dinner?"

"Yes, we should probably go get them. Ron, do you want to come?"

"No, thanks. I'm going to finish up here."

Campbell clapped his hands together. "All right! I'm just going to go to the bathroom."

Heinlein leaned against the bar. Hubbard tapped the elephant-shaped pin the man wore on his lapel. "You're a Dewey man these days?"

"I like what he says about the future." He declined the bartender's drink offer. "You know, I tried to reach you for weeks. No one knew where you were. It's like you disappeared out there."

"I did."

Heinlein leaned forward conspiratorially. "Did you find the case there?"

Hubbard stared at Heinlein through the mirror. "It's been eating at you for four years?" he asked.

"Yes." In the reflection, Heinlein's eyes seemed dark, haunted.

He smiled slightly at the image of Heinlein. "No," he said. "There was nothing there." He broke into a grin.

"Really?"

"Really."

"We got the machine turned on at Menlo Park. It really worked. For a few moments, at least. I really hoped . . ."

"Nothing. I sat on the beach, getting a tan and drinking beers."

"Oh."

"Yeah. Big disappointment, right?"

Heinlein sighed. Hubbard could tell he really wanted a drink now. "You writing again?" he asked.

"Actually, I cracked the slicks with 'The Green Hills of Earth' in the *Saturday Evening Post*. I even finished a novel."

"Looks like married life agrees with you. What's the novel?"

"*Space Cadet*. It's for Scribner's juvenile line, but it's a real hardcover. There's some interest in turning it into a television series."

"Really. Is there any money in that?"

Heinlein shrugged. "Who goes into writing to make money?"

Campbell returned and settled up the tab. "Are you sure you won't come to the restaurant?"

"I'm sure, John. Thanks for the drinks. Please, give my best to Dona."

"Okay. I'll see you next year in Toronto, if not before then." Campbell shook his hand. "I'm looking forward to meeting Sara one of these days."

"Sure."

"And get back to writing again, would you? Remember the FANS."

"I'm working on something big," he replied. "For the FANS."

Campbell headed toward the door, and the hot Greenwich Village night beyond.

Heinlein hung back for a moment. "So nothing happened out there, huh?" he asked at last. "Nothing at all?"

"All was quiet on the southern Pacific front."

"Yeah. Well. Okay. You take care, Ron."

"You, too, Bob."

Soon, the two men were gone. Hubbard slipped a few bucks from Campbell's tip pile while the bartender's attention was diverted and ordered a glass of White Horse whiskey.

"Excuse me."

Hubbard looked up.

The young man who had been reading the mag was looking at him.

"What is it?"

"I know who Jack Parsons is. From the Jet Propulsion Lab."

"Isn't that good for you." Hubbard was in no mood to talk to a fan of sci-fi, the occult, or anything else, for that matter. "Buddy, I've got my wife waiting for me at the Edison Hotel."

The man slid down the bar, bringing his drink. "I overheard some of your friend's story. You want to know what happened to the uranium?"

This was not what Hubbard had expected. "I guess so."

"We were running out of time," the young man said, holding up his hand to stop Hubbard's questions. "We were coming up short with our enriched uranium. Turns out the Nazis and the Japanese were working on a super-bomb of their own. We were having a hard time creating enough fissionable material. When that crate was delivered to the Oak Ridge National Laboratory in Tennessee, it was like, well, Christmas had come in June. July, actually, that's when we had our first test."

"Trinity?"

The young man nodded. "Codename Trinity at White Sands."

"The Manhattan Project."

He nodded again. "Richard Feynman." He extended his hand.

"Lafayette Ron Hubbard," Hubbard said, shaking it. "What can I do for you?"

"Jack Parsons is kind of a legend in my field. I'd like to hear a good Jack Parsons story."

"Dick," he said, "you want a story about Jack Parsons? It starts in Pasadena."

"If this is a long story, I'll order another round of drinks."

"Let me tell you what I did in the war. Let me tell you about Jack Parsons. Let me tell you about the volcano."

"You sure this is a Parsons story?"

"Parsons is yesterday's news." He caught one last glimpse of himself in the mirror, surrounded, as always, by stars. "I'm going to tell you about the future."

ACKNOWLEDGMENTS

Thanks to all these people who took the time to write these books: *I. Asimov* and *In Memory Yet Green*, by Isaac Asimov; *The Futurians*, by Damon Knight; *The John W. Campbell Letters*, edited by Perry A. Chapdelaine, Sr., Tony Chapdelaine, and George Hay; *The Philadelphia Experiment: Project Invisibility*, by William L. Moore in consultation with Charles Berlitz; *The War Magician*, by David Fisher; *Tesla: Man Out of Time*, by Margaret Cheney; *Sex and Rockets: The Occult World of Jack Parsons*, by John Carter; *Better to Have Loved: The Life of Judith Merril*, by Judith Merril and Emily Pohl-Weary; *1939: The Lost World of the Fair*, by David Gelernter; *The Way the Future Was*, by Frederik Pohl; *Saboteurs: The Nazi Raid on America*, by Michael Dobbs; *Rocket to the Morgue*, by Anthony Boucher; *The Empire State Building*, by John Tauranac; *Time and Chance*, by L. Sprague de Camp; *Doc Savage: His Apocalyptic Life*, by Philip José Farmer; *The Duende History of The Shadow Magazine*, by Will Murray; and *The Shadow Scrapbook*, by Walter B. Gibson himself. Spider Robinson's introduction to *For Us, The Living*, by Robert A. Heinlein; *The Immortal Storm*, by Sam Moskowitz; *Man of Magic and Mystery: A Guide to the Work of Walter B. Gibson*, by J. Randolph Cox; *Walter B. Gibson and The Shadow*, by Thomas J. Shimeld; *Lester Dent: The Man, His Craft and His Market*, by M. Martin McCarey-Laird; *L. Ron Hubbard, Messiah or Madman?*, by Bent Corydon and L. Ron Hubbard, Jr.; *Bigger Than Life*, by Marilyn Cannaday; *Shudder Pulps: A History of the Weird Menace Magazines of the 1930s*, by Robert Kenneth Jones; *The Great Pulp Heroes*, by Don Hutchinson; *The Encyclopedia of Science Fiction*, by John Clute and Peter Nicholls; *Bare-Faced Messiah*, by Russell Miller.

Anton Salaks and Tracy Fullerton helped me find my way through an early draft and I'm forever thankful for their time, effort, and insight.

Special thanks to pulp historians Geoffrey Wynkoop, Will Murray, and Anthony Tollin for their particular knowledge. Also to Mark Seltzer for hooking me up at the Philadelphia Navy Yard, and Laura Spagnoli for guiding my family and me around her City of Brotherly Love. As always, I appreciate my friends and coworkers at R/GA for their support and patience: Ray Fallon, Chapin Clark, Steve Caputo, Dan Harvey, Kara Benton, Scott Goodwin, John Antinori, Andy Clark, and, of course, Bob Greenberg.

Thanks to Michele Bové at Simon & Schuster for bravely stepping up to edit and for doing such a great job. I'm grateful for the support and encouragement of my editor, Jofie Ferrari-Adler, and publisher, Jonathan Karp. As anyone who was unfortunate enough to read my early drafts knows, I really depend on my copy editors, so I'm indebted to Loretta Denner and her team for their efforts. I always appreciate Jackie Seow and her department for tolerating and accommodating all my jacket design requests. And thanks to Emer Flounders and Nina Pajak for their heroic efforts.

Thanks again, as always, to my agent, Susan Golomb, and her crack team of Eliza Rothstein and Terra Chalberg, for that magic that they do. And many thanks to Matthew Snyder at CAA. Adrienne Marcino, thanks for all the help while I wrote. And, finally, thank you to my wife and boys for their astounding and amazing love.

ABOUT THE AUTHOR

Paul Malmont works as an advertising copywriter in New York City. He attended the Interlochen Arts Academy and New York University. He lives in New Jersey with his family.